MASTERS'
CHOICE

*The Best Science-Fiction Stories
of All Time
Chosen by the
Masters of Science Fiction*

Edited by Laurence M. Janifer

SIMON AND SCHUSTER NEW YORK

The author and publisher gratefully acknowledge permission from the following to reprint:

LIAR!, by Isaac Asimov, copyright 1941 by Street & Smith Publications, Inc. First appeared in *Astounding Science Fiction*, May 1941. Reprinted by permission of the author.

IT'S A *Good* LIFE, by Jerome Bixby, copyright 1953 by Ballantine Books, Inc. Reprinted by permission of the author.

THE VELDT, by Ray Bradbury, copyright 1950 by the Curtis Publishing Company, Inc. Reprinted by permission of the Harold Matson Co., Inc.

THE GOLEM, by Avram Davidson, copyright 1955 by Fantasy House, Inc.; reprinted by permission of the author and the author's agents, Scott Meredith Literary Agency, Inc.

HELEN O'LOY, by Lester del Rey, copyright 1938 by Street & Smith Publications, Inc.; reprinted by permission of the author and the author's agents, Scott Meredith Literary Agency, Inc.

THE COLD EQUATIONS, by Tom Godwin, copyright 1954 by Street & Smith Publications, Inc. Reprinted by permission of the author's agent, Theron Raines.

THE DWINDLING SPHERE, by Willard Hawkins, copyright 1940 by Street & Smith Publications, Inc. Reprinted by permission of the author.

REQUIEM, by Robert A. Heinlein, copyright 1939 by Street & Smith Publications, Inc., originally published in *Astounding Science Fiction*. Reprinted by permission of the author.

THEORY OF ROCKETRY, by C. M. Kornbluth, copyright 1958 by Fantasy House, Inc. Reprinted by permission of the Estate of C. M. Kornbluth.

DON'T LOOK NOW, by Henry Kuttner, copyright 1948 by Better Publications, Inc. Reprinted by permission of the Harold Matson Co., Inc.

SEVEN-DAY TERROR, by R. A. Lafferty, copyright 1962 by Galaxy Publishing Corp. Reprinted by permission of the author.

COMING ATTRACTION, by Fritz Leiber, copyright 1950 by World Editions, Inc. Reprinted by permission of the author.

POLITICS, by Murray Leinster, copyright *Astounding Stories*, 1932. Reprinted by permission of the author.

MEMENTO HOMO, by Walter M. Miller, Jr., copyright 1954 by Ziff Davis Publishing Co. Reprinted by permission of the Harold Matson Co., Inc.

THE BRIGHT ILLUSION, by C. L. Moore, copyright 1934 by Street & Smith Publications, Inc. Reprinted by permission of the Harold Matson Co., Inc.

AND NOW THE NEWS, by Theodore Sturgeon, copyright 1956 by Fantasy House, Inc. Reprinted by permission of the author.

THE CUSTODIAN, by William Tenn, copyright 1953 by Quinn Publishing Company, Inc. Originally appeared in *If*. Reprinted by permission of Philip Klass.

CONTENTS

PREFACE

The basic form of science fiction, for a great many years, was the short story. There are a variety of reasons for this. One of them, at least, is that only in magazines, which could be satisfied with a smaller percentage of sales, was science fiction at all acceptable. Very few book publishers in the 1930s and 1940s were experimenting with this sort of stuff, and those few were mostly small houses which could not pay the writer enough to keep him even slightly solvent. The writer of science fiction, typically, was then a man who wrote for the magazines. The days of André Norton, Edgar Pangborn and others whose main reputations came from the hard-cover or the paperback novel were yet to come, and the days of the great originals—Wells, Verne, Stapledon—were gone. During what is now called the Golden Age of science fiction, the magazine reigned supreme, and the short story was its backbone.

The natural result of this parade of extremely perishable pulp paper has been the appearance of the anthology. I have no idea how many anthologies have been published in this country alone within our field. Walter Cole's *Checklist of Science-Fiction Anthologies* is an enormous volume filled with nothing but the contents pages of various such works, each displaying what the individual editor thinks science fiction is, or thinks it ought to be —or, in the simplest possible terms of the problem, what the editor thinks he can sell as science fiction to a reasonably numerous reading public.

This anthology (not as an excuse, but in the way of explanation) is a little different. The stories contained herein, and the Honor Roll at the back of the book, do not concern themselves with what I think science fiction is; they concern themselves with what science fiction thinks science fiction is. Twenty-three major authors and editors in the field were asked to provide a list of five stories which they felt worthy of inclusion in this Honor Roll as among the best of all time. (Three of these refused, on the perfectly reasonable ground that it required altogether too much work.) To the twenty whose lists I've got I can only try to convey my amazement at their willingness to do the work, and my heartfelt gratitude.

The voting lists ranged in length from two stories to thirty-two, and, although there was some attempt on my part to keep the stories nominated as short as possible, individual pieces as long as 35,000 words were listed. This made for problems, and I've been forced to leave out a great number of very popular stories, which is more regrettable than I can say. Unfortunately, there is a limit to the amount of words that can be packed into one volume.

This anthology, then, consists of stories which were selected from the Honor Roll on various bases: the number of votes received for each story, the comparative availability of a story (where possible, I've tried to pick less familiar works), and the total number of votes for a given author. Personal choice (which is to say mine) played a small but definitive part for which I offer no excuse whatever.

To print the entire Honor Roll would have required a small five-foot shelf. To print only those stories which were currently unavailable, or, again, only those which received the most votes, would have been a disservice to any picture of the field as a whole —which picture I hope this anthology can begin to provide. Where several of an author's stories were nominated, but no single story seemed to bulk especially large in the nominators' minds to the exclusion of others, I've made, simply, what choice I could, and tried to explain that choice in the introduction to the story.

It ought to go without saying that any opinions expressed here, or in the introductions to the various stories, are mine; the authors whose stories were chosen, or the authors and editors who did the choosing, are not responsible; the publishers are not responsible; the printers (except by inadvertence) are not responsible; and I don't feel so well myself.

However . . .

The question, after all these years, remains: what is science fiction? Every writer and every editor in the field seems to have his own definition, and most of them appear to cherish a desire to get rid of the term entirely. I don't have any particular animus against the words "science fiction," either separately or together, and I think we might as well stick to the phrase as a label—since, eventually, it will mean what you put into it, and nothing else.

But what have we put into it? Well, more and more, science fiction seems to me to separate itself into three distinct forms, and three distinct kinds of literature. The first sort, of which "The Dwindling Sphere," "Politics" and "Don't Look Now" can serve as handy examples, is what the fan or regular reader usually means when he uses the term. These are stories dealing with ourselves and with the societies we variously live in, looking, in that set of frameworks, at a new invention, a new concept, a strange society or a strange being. The viewpoint, however odd the material, remains the normal viewpoint of the author's society at the time of writing: he may approve or disapprove the novelty at which he's looking—he may, for that matter, approve or disapprove the society through which he's looking at it—but he takes his stand for reasons normally available and in currency within the society by which he's surrounded. Quite a lot of this type is being written, most of it for science-fiction magazines and a very little of it for the major mass-circulation-magazine markets. Most new science-fiction novels are of this type. It does not, however, seem to be increasing in quantity; it remains the standard form, and has become a form whose sales are small, steady and predictable, like the standard detective story.

The second type is here, too, in such different stories as "The Golem," "And Now the News" and "The Veldt." These stories take as their model something which was not originally a part of the field: the quality story, the little-magazine story, and the story or novel for which critical acclaim is seen as a more urgent factor than high sales. This type of story is not on the increase, either: it can't increase. Such stories rapidly become indistinguishable from the field in which they reside, the little-magazine field, and glad cries go up from here and there to the effect that science fiction is being accepted. It isn't: it's being diluted in the mainstream, as our critics are fond of calling it—as, in quite a different way, the picaresque novel was lost in the novel proper.

The third type, though, is quite independent. Such stories as "Coming Attraction," "Theory of Rocketry" and, in its own strange way, "The Bright Illusion" take their initial stand in an alien environment and judge both their own environment and ours by standards which may not meet either present or popular approval—standards which may not be visible at all within any actual society. In such stories as these (and a few novels of the same sort), the—overly familiar—"sense of wonder" is given free play and, since it is the living basis of all fiction, illuminates the work. The reader is given the opportunity of truly new experience, in an alien mode, and, therefore, the chance to widen his own background and his own equipment for judgment and for appreciation. It seems to me that there are more stories and novels of this sort around now than there used to be, and that, if science fiction is experiencing a real growth in any direction, this is it. It appears to require a stronger mind, and a less limited one, than most writers in the field have to succeed with a story of this type—just as the growth of a certain amount of literacy in the field forced its own higher standards.

So much for argument.

Even more than the usual literary work, an anthology is, in however unrecognized a manner, a collaborative effort. Without a great many different jobs done by a great many different people, this book would not have been possible. I want to thank a few of them here, with deep appreciation: Miss Barbara Norville and Mr. Clayton Rawson of Simon and Schuster, both very present helps in time of trouble; Mr. Philip Klass, the Gadfly of the Western World, for encouragement, argument and faith; Mr. Walter Cole, whose *Checklist* was a constant aid, and whose assistance far overstepped its bounds; Mr. Jim Sanders, science-fiction fan and collector of index cards; and, most particularly, Miss Greer Aladàr Russell, without whom neither the anthology nor the anthologist might have survived.

LAURENCE M. JANIFER

MASTERS'
CHOICE

LIAR!

ISAAC ASIMOV

I sometimes have the feeling that a twenty-first-century school child, when asked who invented the robot which will be a common feature of his daily life, is going to answer, "Dr. Isaac Asimov of the Boston University School of Medicine." Actually, Dr. Asimov didn't even invent the robot in science fiction; the credit apparently ought to go to Eando Binder, or possibly to Karel Capek. But Dr. Asimov, creator of the Three Laws of Robotics, has certainly done more about the idea of the robot than anyone else in the field.

"Liar!" is an unusual story even for Dr. Asimov. It is difficult to imagine a crossbreeding between his robots and the tragic heroes of Graham Greene, but here it is: a retelling of "The Heart of the Matter," if slightly revised.

Alfred Lanning lit his cigar carefully, but the tips of his fingers were trembling slightly. His gray eyebrows hunched low as he spoke between puffs.

"It reads minds all right—damn little doubt about that! But why?" He looked at mathematician Peter Bogert. "Well?"

Bogert flattened his black hair down with both hands. "That was the thirty-fourth RB model we've turned out, Lanning. All the others were strictly orthodox."

The third man at the table frowned. Milton Ashe was the youngest officer of U. S. Robot and Mechanical Men, Inc., and proud of his post.

"Listen, Bogert. There wasn't a hitch in the assembly from start to finish. I guarantee that."

Bogert's thick lips spread in a patronizing smile. "Do you? If you can answer for the entire assembly line, I recommend your promotion. By exact count, there are seventy-five thousand, two hundred and thirty-four operations necessary for the manufacture of a single positronic brain, each separate operation depending for successful completion upon any number of factors, from five to a hundred and five. If any one of them goes seriously wrong, the 'brain' is ruined. I quote our own information folder, Ashe."

Milton Ashe flushed, but a fourth voice cut off his reply.

"If we're going to start by trying to fix the blame on one another, I'm leaving." Susan Calvin's hands were folded tightly in her lap, and the little lines about her thin, pale lips deepened. "We've got a mind-reading robot on our hands and it strikes me as rather important that we find out just why it reads minds. We're not going to do that by saying, 'Your fault! My fault!' "

Her cold gray eyes fastened upon Ashe and he grinned.

Lanning grinned too, and, as always at such times, his long white hair and shrewd little eyes made him the picture of a Biblical patriarch. "True for you, Dr. Calvin." His voice became suddenly crisp. "Here's everything in pill-concentrate form. We've produced a positronic brain of supposedly ordinary vintage that's got a remarkable property of being able to tune in on thought waves. It would mark the most important advance in robotics in decades if we knew how it happened. We don't, and we have to find out. Is that clear?"

"May I make a suggestion?" asked Bogert.

"Go ahead!"

"I'd say that until we do figure out the mess—and as a mathematician I expect it to be a very devil of a mess—we keep the existence of RB-34 a secret. I mean even from the other members of the staff. As heads of the departments, we ought not to find it an insoluble problem, and the fewer know about it . . ."

"Bogert is right," said Dr. Calvin. "Every since the Interplanetary Code was modified to allow robot models to be tested in the plants before being shipped out to space, antirobot propaganda has increased. If any word leaks out about a robot being able to read minds before we can announce complete control of the phenomenon, pretty effective capital could be made out of it."

Lanning sucked at his cigar and nodded gravely. He turned to

Ashe. "I think you said you were alone when you first stumbled on this thought-reading business."

"I'll say I was alone—I got the scare of my life. RB-34 had just been taken off the assembly table and they sent him down to me. Obermann was off somewheres, so I took him down to the testing rooms myself—at least I started to take him down." Ashe paused, and a tiny smile tugged at his lips. "Say, did any of you ever carry on a thought conversation without knowing it?"

No one bothered to answer, and he continued. "You don't realize it at first, you know. He just spoke to me—as logically and sensibly as you can imagine—and it was only when I was most of the way down to the testing rooms that I realized that I hadn't said anything. Sure, I thought lots, but that isn't the same thing, is it? I locked that thing up and ran for Lanning. Having it walking beside me, calmly peering into my thoughts and picking and choosing among them, gave me the willies."

"I imagine it would," said Susan Calvin thoughtfully. Her eyes fixed themselves upon Ashe in an oddly intent manner. "We are so accustomed to considering our own thoughts private."

Lanning broke in impatiently. "Then only the four of us know. All right! We've got to go about this systematically. Ashe, I want you to check over the assembly line from beginning to end— everything. You're to eliminate all operations in which there was no possible chance of an error, and list all those where there were, together with its nature and possible magnitude."

"Tall order," grunted Ashe.

"Naturally! Of course you're to put the men under you to work on this—every single one if you have to, and I don't care if we go behind schedule, either. But they're not to know why, you understand."

"Hm-m-m, yes!" The young technician grinned wryly. "It's still a lulu of a job."

Lanning swiveled about in his chair and faced Calvin. "You'll have to tackle the job from the other direction. You're the robo-psychologist of the plant, so you're to study the robot itself and work backward. Try to find out how he ticks. See what else is tied up with his telepathic powers, how far they extend, how they warp his outlook, and just exactly what harm it has done to his ordinary RB properties. You've got that?"

Lanning didn't wait for Dr. Calvin to answer. "I'll co-ordinate the work and interpret the findings mathematically." He puffed violently at his cigar and mumbled the rest through the smoke. "Bogert will help me there, of course."

Bogert polished the nails of one pudgy hand with the other and said blandly, "I daresay. I know a little in the line."

"Well! I'll get started." Ashe shoved his chair back and rose. His pleasantly youthful face crinkled in a grin. "I've got the darnedest job of any of us, so I'm getting out of here and to work." He left with a slurred "B' seein' ye!"

Susan Calvin answered with a barely perceptible nod, but her eyes followed him out of sight and she did not answer when Lanning grunted and said, "Do you want to go up and see RB-34 now, Dr. Calvin?"

RB-34's photoelectric eyes lifted from the book at the muffled sound of hinges turning, and he was upon his feet when Susan Calvin entered.

She paused to readjust the huge "No Entrance" sign upon the door and then approached the robot.

"I've brought you the texts upon hyperatomic motors, Herbie—a few, anyway. Would you care to look at them?"

RB-34—otherwise known as Herbie—lifted the three heavy books from her arms and opened to the title page of one.

"Hm-m-m! 'Theory of Hyperatomics.'" He mumbled inarticulately to himself as he flipped the pages, and then spoke with an abstracted air. "Sit down, Dr. Calvin! This will take me a few minutes."

The psychologist seated herself and watched Herbie narrowly as he took a chair at the other side of the table and went through the three books systematically.

At the end of half an hour he put them down. "Of course, I know why you brought these."

The corner of Dr. Calvin's lip twitched. "I was afraid you would. It's difficult to work with you, Herbie. You're always a step ahead of me."

"It's the same with these books, you know, as with the others.

They just don't interest me. There's nothing to your textbooks. Your science is just a mass of collected data plastered together by makeshift theory—and all so incredibly simple that it's scarcely worth bothering about. It's your fiction that interests me. Your studies of the interplay of human motives and emotions . . ." His mighty hand gestured vaguely as he sought the proper words.

Dr. Calvin whispered, "I think I understand."

"I see into minds, you see," the robot continued, "and you have no idea how complicated they are. I can't begin to understand everything, because my own mind has so little in common with them—but I try, and your novels help."

"Yes, but I'm afraid that after going through some of the harrowing emotional experiences of our present-day sentimental novel"—there was a tinge of bitterness in her voice—"you find real minds like ours dull and colorless."

"But I don't!"

The sudden energy in the response brought the other to her feet. She felt herself reddening, and thought wildly, He must know!

Herbie subsided suddenly and muttered in a low voice from which the metallic timbre departed almost entirely, "But of course I know about it, Dr. Calvin. You think of it always, so how can I help but know?"

Her face was hard. "Have you—told anyone?"

"Of course not!" This with genuine surprise. "No one has asked me."

"Well, then," she flung out, "I suppose you think I am a fool."

"No! It is a normal emotion."

"Perhaps that is why it is so foolish." The wistfulness in her voice drowned out everything else. Some of the woman peered through the layer of doctorhood. "I am not what you would call—attractive."

"If you are referring to mere physical attraction, I couldn't judge. But I know, in any case, that there are other types of attraction."

"Nor young." Dr. Calvin had scarcely heard the robot.

"You are not yet forty." An anxious insistence had crept into Herbie's voice.

"Thirty-eight as you count the years; a shriveled sixty as far as my emotional outlook on life is concerned. Am I a psychologist for nothing?" She drove on with bitter breathlessness. "And he's barely thirty-five and looks and acts younger. Do you suppose he ever sees me as anything but . . . but what I am?"

"You are wrong!" Herbie's steel fist struck the plastic-topped table with a strident clang. "Listen to me—"

But Susan Calvin whirled on him now, and the hunted pain in her eyes became a blaze. "Why should I? What do you know about it all, anyway, you . . . you machine. I'm just a specimen to you; an interesting bug with a peculiar mind spread-eagled for inspection. It's a wonderful example of frustration, isn't it? Almost as good as your books." Her voice, emerging in dry sobs, choked into silence.

The robot cowered at the outburst. He shook his head pleadingly. "Won't you listen to me, please? I could help you if you would let me."

"How?" Her lips curled. "By giving me good advice?"

"No, not that. It's just that I know what other people think—Milton Ashe, for instance."

There was a long silence, and Susan Calvin's eyes dropped. "I don't want to know what he thinks," she gasped. "Keep quiet."

"I think you would want to know what he thinks."

Her head remained bent, but her breath came more quickly. "You are talking nonsense," she whispered.

"Why should I? I am trying to help. Milton Ashe's thought of you—" he paused.

And then the psychologist raised her head. "Well?"

The robot said quietly, "He loves you."

For a full minute Dr. Calvin did not speak. She merely stared. Then: "You are mistaken! You must be. Why should he?"

"But he does. A thing like that cannot be hidden, not from me."

"But I am so . . . so—" she stammered to a halt.

"He looks deeper than the skin, and admires intellect in others. Milton Ashe is not the type to marry a head of hair and a pair of eyes."

Susan Calvin found herself blinking rapidly and waited before speaking. Even then her voice trembled. "Yet he certainly never in any way indicated—"

"Have you ever given him a chance?"

"How could I? I never thought that—"

"Exactly!"

The psychologist paused in thought and then looked up suddenly. "A girl visited him here at the plant half a year ago. She was pretty, I suppose—blond and slim. And, of course, could scarcely add two and two. He spent all day puffing out his chest, trying to explain how a robot was put together." The hardness had returned. "Not that she understood! Who was she?"

Herbie answered without hesitation, "I know the person you are referring to. She is his first cousin, and there is no romantic interest there, I assure you."

Susan Calvin rose to her feet with a vivacity almost girlish. "Now, isn't that strange? That's exactly what I used to pretend to myself sometimes, though I never really thought so. Then it all must be true."

She ran to Herbie and seized his cold, heavy hand in both hers. "Thank you, Herbie." Her voice was an urgent, husky whisper. "Don't tell anyone about this. Let it be our secret—and thank you again." With that, and a convulsive squeeze of Herbie's unresponsive metal fingers, she left.

Herbie turned slowly to his neglected novel, but there was no one to read *his* thoughts.

Milton Ashe stretched slowly and magnificently, to the tune of cracking joints and a chorus of grunts, and then glared at Peter Bogert, Ph.D.

"Say," he said, "I've been at this for a week now with just about no sleep. How long do I have to keep it up? I thought you said the positronic bombardment in Vac Chamber D was the solution."

Bogert yawned delicately and regarded his white hands with interest. "It is. I'm on the track."

"I know what *that* means when a mathematician says it. How near the end are you?"

"It all depends."

"On what?" Ashe dropped into a chair and stretched his long legs out before him.

"On Lanning. The old fellow disagrees with me." He sighed. "A bit behind the times, that's the trouble with him. He clings to matrix mechanics as the all in all, and this problem calls for more powerful mathematical tools. He's so stubborn."

Ashe muttered sleepily, "Why not ask Herbie and settle the whole affair?"

"Ask the robot?" Bogert's eyebrows climbed.

"Why not? Didn't the old girl tell you?"

"You mean Calvin?"

"Yeah! Susie herself. That robot's a mathematical wiz. He knows all about everything plus a bit on the side. He does triple integrals in his head and eats up tensor analysis for dessert."

The mathematician stared skeptically, "Are you serious?"

"So help me! The catch is that the dope doesn't like math. He would rather read slushy novels. Honest! You should see the tripe Susie keeps feeding him: *Purple Passion* and *Love in Space*."

"Dr. Calvin hasn't said a word of this to us."

"Well, she hasn't finished studying him. You know how she is. She likes to have everything just so before letting out the big secret."

"She's told *you*."

"We sort of got to talking. I have been seeing a lot of her lately." He opened his eyes wide and frowned. "Say, Bogie, have you been noticing anything queer about the lady lately?"

Bogert relaxed into an undignified grin. "She's using lipstick, if that's what you mean."

"Hell, I know that. Rouge, powder and eye shadow too. She's a sight. But it's not that. I can't put my finger on it. It's the way she talks—as if she were happy about something." He thought a little and then shrugged.

The other allowed himself a leer, which, for a scientist past fifty, was not a bad job. "Maybe she's in love."

Ashe allowed his eyes to close again. "You're nuts, Bogie. You go speak to Herbie; I want to stay here and go to sleep."

"Right! Not that I particularly like having a robot tell me my job, nor that I think he can do it!"

A soft snore was his only answer.

Herbie listened carefully as Peter Bogert, hands in pockets, spoke with elaborate indifference.

"So there you are. I've been told you understand these things, and I am asking you more in curiosity than anything else. My line of reasoning, as I have outlined it, involves a few doubtful steps, I admit, which Dr. Lanning refuses to accept, and the picture is still rather incomplete."

The robot didn't answer, and Bogert said, "Well?"

"I see no mistake," Herbie studied the scribbled figures.

"I don't suppose you can go any further than that?"

"I daren't try. You are a better mathematician than I, and—well, I'd hate to commit myself."

There was a shade of complacency in Bogert's smile. "I rather thought that would be the case. It is deep. We'll forget it." He crumpled the sheets, tossed them down the waste shaft, turned to leave, and then thought better of it. "By the way . . ."

The robot waited.

Bogert seemed to have difficulty. "There is something—that is, perhaps you can—" He stopped.

Herbie spoke quietly. "Your thoughts are confused, but there is no doubt at all that they concern Dr. Lanning. It is silly to hesitate, for as soon as you compose yourself I'll know what it is you want to ask."

The mathematician's hand went to his sleek hair in the familiar smoothing gesture. "Lanning is nudging seventy," he said, as if that explained everything.

"I know that."

"And he's been director of the plant for almost thirty years."

Herbie nodded.

"Well, now—" Bogert's voice became ingratiating—"you would know whether . . . whether he's thinking of resigning. Health, perhaps, or some other—"

"Quite," said Herbie, and that was all.

"Well, do you know?"

"Certainly."

"Then—uh—could you tell me?"

"Since you ask, yes." The robot was quite matter-of-fact about it. "He has already resigned!"

"What!" The exclamation was an explosive, almost inarticulate sound. The scientist's large head hunched forward. "Say that again!"

"He has already resigned," came the quiet repetition, "but it has not yet taken effect. He is waiting, you see, to solve the problem of—er—myself. That finished, he is quite ready to turn the office of director over to his successor."

Bogert expelled his breath sharply. "And this successor? Who is he?" He was quite close to Herbie now, eyes fixed fascinatedly on those unreadable dull-red photoelectric cells that were the robot's eyes.

Words came slowly. "You are the next director."

And Bogert relaxed into a tight smile. "This is good to know. I've been hoping and waiting for this. Thanks, Herbie."

Peter Bogert was at his desk until five that morning, and he was back at nine. The shelf just over the desk emptied of its row of reference books and tables as he referred to one after the other. The pages of calculations before him increased microscopically, and the crumpled sheets at his feet mounted into a hill of scribbled paper.

At precisely noon he stared at the final page, rubbed a blood-shot eye, yawned and shrugged. "This is getting worse each minute. Damn!"

He turned at the sound of the opening door and nodded at Lanning, who entered, cracking the knuckles of one gnarled hand with the other.

The director took in the disorder of the room, and his eyebrows furrowed together.

"New lead?" he asked.

"No," came the defiant answer. "What's wrong with the old one?"

Lanning did not trouble to answer, nor to do more than bestow a single cursory glance at the top sheet upon Bogert's desk. He spoke through the flare of a match as he lit a cigar. "Has Calvin told you about the robot? It's a mathematical genius. Really remarkable."

The other snorted loudly. "So I've heard. But Calvin had better stick to robopsychology. I've checked Herbie on math, and he can scarcely struggle through calculus."

"Calvin didn't find it so."

"She's crazy."

"And I don't find it so." The director's eyes narrowed dangerously.

"You!" Bogert's voice hardened. "What are you talking about?"

"I've been putting Herbie through his paces all morning, and he can do tricks you never heard of."

"Is that so?"

"You sound skeptical!" Lanning flipped a sheet of paper out of his vest pocket and unfolded it. "That's not my handwriting, is it?"

Bogert studied the large angular notation covering the sheet. "Herbie did this?"

"Right! And if you'll notice, he's been working on your time integration of Equation 22. It comes"—Lanning tapped a yellow fingernail upon the last step—"to the identical conclusion I did, and in a quarter the time. You had no right to neglect the Linger Effect in positronic bombardment."

"I didn't neglect it. For heaven's sake, Lanning, get it through your head that it would cancel out—"

"Oh, sure, you explained that. You used the Mitchell Translation Equation, didn't you? Well—it doesn't apply."

"Why not?"

"Because you've been using hyperimaginaries, for one thing."

"What's that to do with?"

"Mitchell's equation won't hold when—"

"Are you crazy? If you'll reread Mitchell's original paper in the *Transactions of the Far*—"

"I don't have to. I told you in the beginning that I didn't like his reasoning, and Herbie backs me in that."

"Well, then," Bogert shouted, "let that clockwork contraption solve the entire problem for you. Why bother with nonessentials?"

"That's exactly the point. Herbie can't solve the problem. And if he can't, we can't—alone. I'm submitting the entire question to the National Board. It's gotten beyond us."

Bogert's chair went over backward as he jumped up asnarl, face crimson. "You're doing nothing of the sort."

Lanning flushed in his turn. "Are you telling me what I can't do?"

"Exactly," was the gritted response. "I've got the problem

beaten and you're not to take it out of my hands, understand? Don't think I don't see through you, you desiccated fossil. You'd cut your own nose off before you'd let me get the credit for solving robotic telepathy."

"You're a damned idiot, Bogert, and in one second I'll have you suspended for insubordination." Lanning's lower lip trembled with passion.

"Which is one thing you won't do, Lanning. You haven't any secrets with a mind-reading robot around so don't forget that I know all about your resignation."

The ash on Lanning's cigar trembled and fell, and the cigar itself followed, "What . . . what—"

Bogert chuckled nastily. "And I'm the new director, be it understood. I'm very aware of that; don't think I'm not. Damn your eyes, Lanning, I'm going to give the orders about here or there will be the sweetest mess that you've ever been in."

Lanning found his voice and let it out with a roar. "You're suspended, d'ye hear? You're relieved of all duties. You're broken, do you understand?"

The smile on the other's face broadened. "Now, what's the use of that? You're getting nowhere. I'm holding the trumps. I know you've resigned. Herbie told me, and he got it straight from you."

Lanning forced himself to speak quietly. He looked an old, old man, with tired eyes peering from a face in which the red had disappeared, leaving the pasty yellow of age behind, "I want to speak to Herbie. He can't have told you anything of the sort. You're playing a deep game, Bogert, but I'm calling your bluff. Come with me."

Bogert shrugged. "To see Herbie? Good! Damned good!"

It was also precisely at noon that Milton Ashe looked up from his clumsy sketch and said, "You get the idea? I'm not too good at getting this down, but that's about how it looks. It's a honey of a house, and I can get it for next to nothing."

Susan Calvin gazed across at him with melting eyes. "It's really beautiful," she sighed. "I've often thought that I'd like to—" Her voice trailed away.

"Of course," Ashe continued briskly, putting away his pencil, "I've got to wait for my vacation. It's only two weeks off, but this Herbie business has everything up in the air." His eyes dropped to his fingernails. "Besides, there's another point—but it's a secret."

"Then don't tell me."

"Oh, I'd just as soon, I'm just busting to tell someone, and you're just about the best—er—confidante I could find here." He grinned sheepishly.

Susan Calvin's heart bounded, but she did not trust herself to speak.

"Frankly"—Ashe scraped his chair closer and lowered his voice into a confidential whisper—"the house isn't to be only for myself. I'm getting married!" And then he jumped out of his seat. "What's the matter?"

"Nothing!" The horrible spinning sensation had vanished, but it was hard to get words out. "Married? You mean—"

"Why, sure! About time, isn't it? You remember that girl who was here last summer. That's she! But you *are* sick. You—"

"Headache!" Susan Calvin motioned him away weakly. "I've . . . I've been subject to them lately. I want to . . . to congratulate you, of course. I'm very glad—" The inexpertly applied rouge made a pair of nasty splotches upon her chalk-white face. Things had begun spinning again. "Pardon me—please—"

The words were a mumble, as she stumbled blindly out the door. It had happened with the sudden catastrophe of a dream—and with all the unreal horror of a dream.

But how could it be? Herbie had said—

And Herbie knew! He could see into minds!

She found herself leaning breathlessly against the door jamb, staring into Herbie's metal face. She must have climbed the two flights of stairs, but she had no memory of it. The distance had been covered in an instant, as in a dream.

As in a dream!

And still Herbie's unblinking eyes stared into hers, and their dull red seemed to expand into dimly shining nightmarish globes.

He was speaking, and she felt the cold glass pressing against her lips. She swallowed and shuddered into a certain awareness of her surroundings.

Still Herbie spoke, and there was agitation in his voice—as if he were hurt and frightened and pleading.

The words were beginning to make sense. "This is a dream," he was saying, "and you mustn't believe in it. You'll wake into the real world soon and laugh at yourself. He loves you, I tell you. He does, he does! But not here! Not now! This is an illusion."

Susan Calvin nodded, her voice a whisper. "Yes! Yes!" She was clutching Herbie's arm, clinging to it, repeating over and over, "It isn't true, is it? It isn't, is it?"

Just how she came to her senses, she never knew—but it was like passing from a world of misty unreality to one of harsh sunlight. She pushed him away from her, pushed hard against that steely arm, and her eyes were wide.

"What are you trying to do?" Her voice rose to a harsh scream. "What are you trying to do?"

Herbie backed away. "I want to help."

The psychologist stared. "Help? By telling me this is a dream? By trying to push me into schizophrenia?" A hysterical tenseness seized her. "This is no dream! I wish it were!" She drew her breath sharply. "Wait! Why . . . why, I understand. Merciful heavens, it's so obvious."

There was horror in the robot's voice. " I had to!"

"And I believed you! I never thought—"

Loud voices outside the door brought her to a halt. She turned away, fists clenching spasmodically, and when Bogert and Lanning entered she was at the far window. Neither of the men paid her the slightest attention.

They approached Herbie simultaneously, Lanning angry and impatient, Bogert coolly sardonic. The director spoke first.

"Here, now, Herbie. Listen to me!"

The robot brought his eyes sharply down upon the aged director. "Yes, Dr. Lanning."

"Have you discussed me with Dr. Bogert?"

"No, sir." The answer came slowly, and the smile on Bogert's face flashed off.

"What's that?" Bogert shoved in ahead of his superior and straddled the ground before the robot. "Repeat what you told me yesterday."

"I said that—" Herbie fell silent. Deep within him his metallic diaphragm vibrated in soft discords.

"Didn't you say he had resigned?" roared Bogert. "Answer me!"

Bogert raised his arm frantically, but Lanning pushed him aside. "Are you trying to bully him into lying?"

"You heard him, Lanning. He began to say 'Yes' and stopped. Get out of my way! I want the truth out of him, understand!"

"I'll ask him!" Lanning turned to the robot. "All right, Herbie, take it easy. Have I resigned?"

Herbie stared, and Lanning repeated anxiously, "Have I resigned?" There was the faintest trace of a negative shake of the robot's head. A long wait produced nothing further.

The two men looked at each other, and the hostility in their eyes was all but tangible.

"What the devil," blurted Bogert, "has the robot gone mute? Can't you speak, you monstrosity?"

"I can speak," came the ready answer.

"Then answer the question. Didn't you tell me Lanning had resigned? Hasn't he resigned?"

And again there was nothing but dull silence, until from the end of the room, Susan Calvin's laugh rang out suddenly, high-pitched and semihysterical.

The two mathematicians jumped, and Bogert's eyes narrowed. "You here? What's so funny?"

"Nothing's funny." Her voice was not quite natural. "It's just that I'm not the only one that's been caught. There's irony in three of the greatest experts in robotics in the world falling into the same elementary trap, isn't there?" Her voice faded, and she put a pale hand to her forehead, "But it isn't funny!"

This time the look that passed between the two men was one of raised eyebrows. "What trap are you talking about?" asked Lanning stiffly. "Is something wrong with Herbie?"

"No." She approached them slowly. "Nothing is wrong with him—only with us." She whirled suddenly and shrieked at the robot, "Get away from me! Go to the other end of the room and don't let me look at you."

Herbie cringed before the fury of her eyes and stumbled away in a clattering trot.

Lanning's voice was hostile. "What is all this, Dr. Calvin?"

She faced them and spoke sarcastically. "Surely you know the fundamental First Law of Robotics."

The other two nodded together. "Certainly," said Bogert irritably. "A robot may not injure a human being or, through inaction, allow him to come to harm."

"How nicely put," sneered Calvin. "But what kind of harm?"

"Why—any kind."

"Exactly! Any kind! But what about hurt feelings? What about deflation of one's ego? What about the blasting of one's hopes? Is that injury?"

Lanning frowned. "What would a robot know about—" And then he caught himself with a gasp.

"You've caught on, have you? *This* robot reads minds. Do you suppose it doesn't know everything about mental injury? Do you suppose that if asked a question it wouldn't give exactly that answer that one wants to hear? Wouldn't any other answer hurt us, and wouldn't Herbie know that?"

"Good heavens!" muttered Bogert.

The psychologist cast a sardonic glance at him. "I take it you asked him whether Lanning had resigned. You wanted to hear that he had resigned and so that's what Herbie told you."

"And I suppose that is why," said Lanning tonelessly, "it would not answer a little while ago. It couldn't answer either way without hurting one of us."

There was a short pause in which the men looked thoughtfully across the room at the robot, crouching in the chair by the bookcase, head resting in one hand.

Susan Calvin stared steadfastly at the floor. "He knew of all this. That . . . that devil knows everything—including what went wrong in his assembly." Her eyes were dark and brooding.

Lanning looked up. "You're wrong there, Dr. Calvin. He doesn't know what went wrong. I asked him."

"What does that mean?" cried Calvin. "Only that you didn't want him to give you the solution. It would puncture your ego to have a machine do what you couldn't. Did you ask him?" she shot at Bogert.

"In a way." Bogert coughed and reddened. "He told me he knew very little about mathematics."

Lanning laughed, not very loudly and the psychologist smiled caustically. She said, "I'll ask him! A solution by him won't hurt my ego." She raised her voice into a cold, imperative "Come here!"

Herbie rose and approached with hesitant steps.

"You know, I suppose," she continued, "just exactly at what point in the assembly an extraneous factor was introduced or an essential one left out."

"Yes," said Herbie, in tones barely heard.

"Hold on," broke in Bogert angrily. "That's not necessarily true. You want to hear that, that's all."

"Don't be a fool," replied Calvin. "He certainly knows as much math as you and Lanning together, since he can read minds. Give him his chance."

The mathematician subsided, and Calvin continued, "All right, then, Herbie, give! We're waiting." And in an aside, "Get pencils and paper, gentlemen."

But Herbie remained silent, and there was triumph in the psychologist's voice. "Why don't you answer, Herbie?"

The robot blurted out suddenly, "I cannot. You know I cannot! Dr. Bogert and Dr. Lanning don't want me to."

"They want the solution."

"But not from me."

Lanning broke in, speaking slowly and distinctly. "Don't be foolish, Herbie. We do want you to tell us."

Bogert nodded curtly.

Herbie's voice rose to wild heights. "What's the use of saying that? Don't you suppose that I can see past the superficial skin of your mind? Down below, you don't want me to. I'm a machine, given the imitation of life only by virtue of the positronic interplay in my brain—which is man's device. You can't lose face to me without being hurt. That is deep in your mind and won't be erased. I can't give the solution."

"We'll leave," said Dr. Lanning. "Tell Calvin."

"That would make no difference," cried Herbie, "since you would know anyway that it was I that was supplying the answer."

Calvin resumed, "But you understand, Herbie, that despite that, Doctors Lanning and Bogert want that solution."

"By their own efforts!" insisted Herbie.

"But they want it, and the fact that you have it and won't give it hurts them. You see that, don't you?"

"Yes! Yes!"

"And if you tell them that will hurt them, too."

"Yes! Yes!" Herbie was retreating slowly, and step by step Susan Calvin advanced. The two men watched in frozen bewilderment.

"You can't tell them," droned the psychologist slowly, "because that would hurt and you mustn't hurt. But if you don't tell them, you hurt, so you must tell them. And if you do, you will hurt and you mustn't, so you can't tell them; but if you don't you hurt, so you must; but if you do, you hurt, so you mustn't; but if you don't, you hurt, so you must; but if you do, you—"

Herbie was up against the wall, and here he dropped to his knees. "Stop!" he shrieked. "Close your mind! It is full of pain and frustration and hate! I didn't mean it, I tell you! I tried to help! I told you what you wanted to hear. I had to!"

The psychologist paid no attention. "You must tell them, but if you do, you hurt, so you mustn't; but if you don't, you hurt, so you must; but—"

And Herbie screamed!

It was like the whistling of a piccolo many times magnified—shrill and shriller till it keened with the terror of a lost soul and filled the room with the piercingness of itself.

And when it died into nothingness, Herbie collapsed into a huddled heap of motionless metal.

Bogert's face was bloodless. "He's dead!"

"No!" Susan Calvin burst into body-racking gusts of wild laughter. "Not dead—merely insane. I confronted him with the insoluble dilemma, and he broke down. You can scrap him now—because he'll never speak again."

Lanning was on his knees beside the thing that had been Herbie. His fingers touched the cold, unresponsive metal face and he shuddered. "You did that on purpose." He rose and faced her, face contorted.

"What if I did? You can't help it now." And in a sudden access of bitterness: "He deserved it."

The director seized the paralyzed, motionless Bogert by the wrist. "What's the difference. Come, Peter." He sighed. "A thinking robot of this type is worthless, anyway." His eyes were old and tired, and he repeated, "Come, Peter!"

It was minutes after the two scientists left that Dr. Susan Calvin regained part of her mental equilibrium. Slowly her eyes turned to the living-dead Herbie, and the tightness returned to her face. Long she stared while the triumph faded and the helpless frustration returned—and of all her turbulent thoughts only one infinitely bitter word passed her lips:

"*Liar!*"

IT'S A *GOOD* LIFE

JEROME BIXBY

> *This is one of the most frightening stories I've ever*
> *read. Jerry Bixby, enthusiastic piano-pounder, former*
> *editor, West Coast denizen, and all-round good fellow,*
> *has never written anything else quite like it. I went*
> *around wondering for days after I read it, and I*
> *shouldn't be at all surprised if you did. But, after all, it's*
> *only a story.*
> *I hope.*

Aunt Amy was out on the front porch, rocking back and forth
in the high-backed chair and fanning herself, when Bill Soames
rode his bicycle up the road and stopped in front of the house.

Perspiring under the afternoon "sun," Bill lifted the box of
groceries out of the big basket over the front wheel of the bike
and came up the front walk.

Little Anthony was sitting on the lawn, playing with a rat. He
had caught the rat down in the basement—he had made it think
that it smelled cheese, the most rich-smelling and crumbly-deli-
cious cheese a rat had ever thought it smelled, and it had come out
of its hole, and now Anthony had hold of it with his mind and
was making it do tricks.

When the rat saw Bill Soames coming, it tried to run, but Anthony thought at it, and it turned a flip-flop on the grass and lay
trembling, its eyes gleaming in small black terror.

Bill Soames hurried past Anthony and reached the front steps,
mumbling. He always mumbled when he came to the Fremont
house, or passed by it, or even thought of it. Everybody did.
They thought about silly things, things that didn't mean very
much, like two-and-two-is-four-and-twice-is-eight and so on; they

tried to jumble up their thoughts and keep them skipping back and forth, so Anthony couldn't read their minds. The mumbling helped. Because if Anthony got anything strong out of your thoughts, he might take a notion to do something about it—like curing your wife's sick headaches or your kid's mumps, or getting your old milk cow back on schedule, or fixing the privy. And while Anthony mightn't actually mean any harm, he couldn't be expected to have much notion of what was the right thing to do in such cases.

That was if he liked you. He might try to help you, in his way. And that could be pretty horrible.

If he didn't like you—well, that could be worse.

Bill Soames set the box of groceries on the porch railing and stopped his mumbling long enough to say, "Everythin' you wanted, Miss Amy."

"Oh, fine, William," Amy Fremont said lightly. "My, ain't it terrible hot today?"

Bill Soames almost cringed. His eyes pleaded with her. He shook his head violently *no*, and then interrupted his mumbling again, though obviously he didn't want to. "Oh, don't say that, Miss Amy. It's fine, just fine. A real *good* day!"

Amy Fremont got up from the rocking chair and came across the porch. She was a tall woman, thin, a smiling vacancy in her eyes. About a year ago Anthony had got mad at her, because she'd told him he shouldn't have turned the cat into a cat rug, and although he had always obeyed her more than anyone else, which was hardly at all, this time he'd snapped at her. With his mind. And that had been the end of Amy Fremont's bright eyes, and the end of Amy Fremont as everyone had known her. And that was when word got around in Peaksville (population forty-six) that even the members of Anthony's own family weren't safe. After that, everyone was twice as careful.

Someday Anthony might undo what he'd done to Aunt Amy. Anthony's Mom and Pop hoped he would. When he was older, and maybe sorry. If it was possible, that is. Because Aunt Amy had changed a lot, and besides, now Anthony wouldn't obey anyone.

"Land alive, William," Aunt Amy said, "you don't have to mumble like that. Anthony wouldn't hurt you. My goodness,

Anthony likes you!" She raised her voice and called to Anthony, who had tired of the rat and was making it eat itself, "Don't you, dear? Don't you like Mr. Soames?"

Anthony looked across the lawn at the grocery man—a bright, wet, purple gaze. He didn't say anything. Bill Soames tried to smile at him. After a second Anthony returned his attention to the rat. It had already devoured its tail, or at least chewed it off—for Anthony had made it bite faster than it could swallow, and little pink and red furry pieces lay around it on the green grass. Now the rat was having trouble reaching its hindquarters.

Mumbling silently, thinking of nothing in particular as hard as he could, Bill Soames went stiff-legged down the walk, mounted his bicycle and pedaled off.

"We'll see you tonight, William," Aunt Amy called after him.

As Bill Soames pumped the pedals, he was wishing deep down that he could pump twice as fast, to get away from Anthony all the faster, and away from Aunt Amy, who sometimes just forgot how *careful* you had to be. And he shouldn't have thought that. Because Anthony caught it. He caught the desire to get away from the Fremont house as if it was something *bad*, and his purple gaze blinked, and he snapped a small, sulky thought after Bill Soames—just a small one, because he was in a good mood today, and besides, he liked Bill Soames, or at least didn't dislike him, at least today. Bill Soames wanted to go away—so, petulantly, Anthony helped him.

Pedaling with superhuman speed—or, rather, appearing to, because in reality the bicycle was pedaling *him*—Bill Soames vanished down the road in a cloud of dust, his thin, terrified wail drifting back across the summerlike heat.

Anthony looked at the rat. It had devoured half its belly, and had died from pain. He thought it into a grave out deep in the cornfield—his father had once said, smiling, that he might as well do that with the things he killed—and went around the house, casting his odd shadow in the hot, brassy light from above.

In the kitchen, Aunt Amy was unpacking the groceries. She put the Mason-jarred goods on the shelves, and the meat and milk in the icebox, and the beet sugar and coarse flour in big cans under the sink. She put the cardboard box in the corner, by the door, for Mr. Soames to pick up next time he came. It was stained and battered and torn and worn fuzzy, but it was one of the few left in Peaksville. In faded red letters it said "Campbell's Soup." The last cans of soup, or of anything else, had been eaten long ago, except for a small communal hoard which the villagers dipped into for special occasions—but the box lingered on, like a coffin, and when it and the other boxes were gone the men would have to make some out of wood.

Aunt Amy went out in back, where Anthony's Mom—Aunt Amy's sister—sat in the shade of the house, shelling peas. The peas, every time Mom ran a finger along a pod, went *lollop-lollop-lollop* into the pan on her lap.

"William brought the groceries," Aunt Amy said. She sat down wearily in the straight-backed chair beside Mom and began fanning herself again. She wasn't really old; but ever since Anthony had snapped at her with his mind, something had seemed to be wrong with her body as well as her mind, and she was tired all the time.

"Oh, good," said Mom. *Lollop* went the fat peas into the pan.

Everybody in Peaksville always said, "Oh, fine," or "Good," or "Say, that's swell!" when almost anything happened or was mentioned—even unhappy things like accidents or even deaths. They'd always say "Good" because if they didn't try to cover up how they really felt Anthony might overhear with his mind, and then nobody knew what might happen. Like the time Mrs. Kent's husband, Sam, had come walking back from the graveyard because Anthony liked Mrs. Kent and had heard her mourning.

Lollop.

"Tonight's television night," said Aunt Amy. "I'm glad. I look forward to it so much every week. I wonder what we'll see tonight."

"Did Bill bring the meat?" asked Mom.

"Yes." Aunt Amy fanned herself, looking up at the featureless brassy glare of the sky. "Goodness, it's so hot! I wish Anthony would make it just a little cooler—"

"*Amy!*"

"Oh!" Mom's sharp tone had penetrated where Bill Soames's agonized expression had failed. Aunt Amy put one thin hand to her mouth in exaggerated alarm. "Oh . . . I'm sorry, dear." Her pale-blue eyes shuttled around, right and left, to see if Anthony was in sight. Not that it would make any difference if he was or wasn't—he didn't have to be near you to know what you were thinking. Usually, though, unless he had his attention on somebody, he would be occupied with thoughts of his own.

But some things attracted his attention—you could never be sure just what.

"This weather's just *fine*," Mom said.

Lollop.

"Oh, yes," Aunt Amy said. "It's a wonderful day. I wouldn't want it changed for the world!"

Lollop.

Lollop.

"What time is it?" Mom asked.

Aunt Amy was sitting where she could see through the kitchen window to the alarm clock on the shelf above the stove. "Four-thirty," she said.

Lollop.

"I want tonight to be something special," Mom said. "Did Bill bring a good lean roast?"

"Good and lean, dear. They butchered just today, you know, and sent us over the best piece."

"Dan Hollis will be *so* surprised when he finds out that tonight's television party is a birthday party for him, too!"

"Oh *I* think he will! Are you sure nobody's told him?"

"Everybody swore they wouldn't."

"That'll be real nice." Aunt Amy nodded, looking off across the cornfield. "A birthday party."

"Well—" Mom put the pan of peas down beside her, stood up and brushed her apron—"I'd better get the roast on. Then we can set the table." She picked up the peas.

Anthony came around the corner of the house. He didn't look at them, but continued on down through the carefully kept garden—*all* the gardens in Peaksville were carefully kept, very carefully kept—and went past the rustling, useless hulk that had been the Fremont family car, and went smoothly over the fence and out into the cornfield.

"Isn't this a lovely day!" said Mom, a little loudly, as they went toward the back door.

Aunt Amy fanned herself. "A beautiful day, dear. Just *fine!*"

Out in the cornfield, Anthony walked between the tall, rustling rows of green stalks. He liked to smell the corn. The alive corn overhead, and the old dead corn underfoot. Rich Ohio earth, thick with weeds and brown, dry-rotting ears of corn, pressed between his bare toes with every step—he had made it rain last night so everything would smell and feel nice today.

He walked clear to the edge of the cornfield, and over to where a grove of shadowy green trees covered cool, moist, dark ground and lots of leafy undergrowth and jumbled moss-covered rocks and a small spring that made a clear, clean pool. Here Anthony liked to rest and watch the birds and insects and small animals that rustled and scampered and chirped about. He liked to lie on the cool ground and look up through the moving greenness overhead and watch the insects flit in the hazy soft sunbeams that stood like slanting, glowing bars between ground and treetops. Somehow, he liked the thoughts of the little creatures in this place better than the thoughts outside; and while the thoughts he picked up here weren't very strong or very clear, he could get enough out of them to know what the little creatures liked and wanted, and he spent a lot of time making the grove more like what they wanted it to be. The spring hadn't always been here; but one time he had found thirst in one small furry mind, and had brought subterranean water to the surface in a clear cold flow and had watched, blinking, as the creature drank, feeling its pleasure. Later he had made the pool, when he found a small urge to swim.

He had made rocks and trees and bushes and caves, and sunlight here and shadows there, because he had felt in all the tiny minds around him the desire—or the instinctive want—for this kind of resting place, and that kind of mating place, and this kind of place to play, and that kind of home. And somehow the creatures from all the fields and pastures around the grove had seemed to know that this was a good place, for there were always more of them coming in. Every time Anthony came out here there were more creatures than the last time, and more desires and needs to be tended to. Every time there would be some kind of creature he had never seen before, and he would find its mind, and see what it wanted, and then give it to it. He liked to help them. He liked to feel their simple gratification.

Today he rested beneath a thick elm and lifted his purple gaze to a red-and-black bird that had just come to the grove. It twittered on a branch over his head, and hopped back and forth, and thought its tiny thoughts, and Anthony made a big, soft nest for it, and pretty soon it hopped in.

A long brown, sleek-furred animal was drinking at the pool. Anthony found its mind next. The animal was thinking about a smaller creature that was scurrying along the ground on the other side of the pool, grubbing for insects. The little creature didn't know that it was in danger. The long brown animal finished drinking and tensed its legs to leap, and Anthony thought it into a grave in the cornfield.

He didn't like those kinds of thoughts. They reminded him of the thoughts outside the grove. A long time ago some of the people outside had thought that way about *him,* and one night they'd hidden and waited for him to come back from the grove—and he'd just thought them all into the cornfield. Since then the rest of the people hadn't thought that way—at least, very clearly. Now their thoughts were all mixed up and confusing whenever they thought about him or near him, so he didn't pay much attention.

He liked to help them too, sometimes—but it wasn't simple, or very gratifying either. They never thought happy thoughts when he did—just the jumble. So he spent more time out here.

He watched all the birds and insects and furry creatures for a while, and played with a bird, making it soar and dip and streak madly around tree trunks until, accidentally, when another bird caught his attention for a moment, he ran it into a rock. Petulantly, he thought the rock into a grave in the cornfield; but he couldn't do anything more with the bird. Not because it was dead, though it was; but because it had a broken wing. So he went back to the house. He didn't feel like walking back through the cornfield, so he just *went* to the house, right down into the basement.

It was nice down here. Nice and dark and damp and sort of fragrant, because once Mom had been making preserves in a rack along the far wall and then she'd stopped coming down ever since Anthony had started spending time here, and the preserves had spoiled and leaked down and spread over the dirt floor and Anthony liked the smell.

He caught another rat, making it smell cheese, and after he played with it he thought it into a grave right beside the long animal he'd killed in the grove. Aunt Amy hated rats, and so he killed a lot of them, because he liked Aunt Amy most of all and sometimes did things Aunt Amy wanted. Her mind was more like the little furry minds out in the grove. She hadn't thought anything bad at all about him for a long time.

After the rat, he played with a big black spider in the corner under the stairs, making it run back and forth until its web shook and shimmered in the light from the cellar window like a reflection in silvery water. Then he drove fruit flies into the web until the spider was frantic trying to wind them all up. The spider liked flies, and its thoughts were stronger than theirs, so he did it. There was something bad in the way it liked flies, but it wasn't clear— and besides, Aunt Amy hated flies too.

He heard footsteps overhead—Mom moving around in the kitchen. He blinked his purple gaze and almost decided to make her hold still—but instead he went up to the attic, and, after looking out the circular window for a while at the front lawn and the dusty road and Henderson's tip-waving wheatfield beyond, he curled into an unlikely shape and went partly to sleep.

Soon people would be coming for television, he heard Mom think.

He went more to sleep. He liked television night. Aunt Amy had always liked television a lot, so one time he had thought some for her, and a few other people had been there at the time, and Aunt Amy had felt disappointed when they wanted to leave. He'd done something to them for that—and now everybody came to television.

He liked all the attention he got when they did.

Anthony's father came home around six-thirty, looking tired and dirty and bloody. He'd been over in Dunn's pasture with the other men, helping pick out the cow to be slaughtered this month, and doing the job, and then butchering the meat and salting it away in Soames's icehouse. Not a job he cared for, but every man had his turn. Yesterday he had helped scythe down old McIntyre's wheat. Tomorrow they would start threshing. By hand. Everything in Peaksville had to be done by hand.

He kissed his wife on the cheek and sat down at the kitchen table. He smiled and said, "Where's Anthony?"

"Around someplace," Mom said.

Aunt Amy was over at the wood-burning stove, stirring the big pot of peas. Mom went back to the oven and opened it and basted the roast.

"Well, it's been a *good* day," Dad said. By rote. Then he looked at the mixing bowl and breadboard on the table. He sniffed at the dough. "M'm," he said. "I could eat a loaf all by myself, I'm so hungry."

"No one told Dan Hollis about its being a birthday party, did they?" his wife asked.

"Nope. We kept as quiet as mummies."

"We've fixed up such a lovely surprise!"

"Um? What?"

"Well . . . you know how much Dan likes music. Well, last week Thelma Dunn found a *record* in her attic!"

"No!"

"Yes! And we had Ethel sort of ask—you know, without really *asking*—if he had that one. And he said no. Isn't that a wonderful surprise?"

"Well, now, it sure is. A record, imagine! That's a real nice thing to find! What record is it?"

"Perry Como, singing 'You Are My Sunshine.' "

"Well, I'll be darned. I always liked that tune." Some raw carrots were lying on the table. Dad picked up a small one, scrubbed it on his chest, and took a bite. "How did Thelma happen to find it?"

"Oh, you know—just looking around for new things."

"M'm." Dad chewed the carrot. "Say, who has that picture we found a while back? I kind of liked it—that old clipper sailing along . . ."

"The Smiths. Next week the Sipiches get it, and they give the Smiths old McIntyre's music-box, and we give the Sipiches . . ." And she went down the tentative order of things that would exchange hands among the women at church this Sunday.

He nodded. "Looks like we can't have the picture for a while, I guess. Look, honey, you might try to get that detective book back from the Reillys. I was so busy the week we had it, I never got to finish all the stories."

"I'll try," his wife said doubtfully. "But I hear the Van Husens have a stereoscope they found in the cellar." Her voice was just a little accusing. "They had it two whole months before they told anybody about it."

"Say," Dad said, looking interested, "that'd be nice, too. Lots of pictures?"

"I suppose so. I'll see on Sunday. I'd like to have it—but we still owe the Van Husens for their canary. I don't know why that bird had to pick *our* house to die—it must have been sick when we got it. Now there's just no satisfying Betty Van Husen. She even hinted she'd like our *piano* for a while!"

"Well, honey, you try for the stereoscope—or just anything you think we'll like." At last he swallowed the carrot. It had been a little young and tough. Anthony's whims about the weather made it so that people never knew what crops would come up, or what shape they'd be in if they did. All they could do was plant a lot; and always enough of something came up any one season to live on. Just once there had been a grain surplus; tons of it had been hauled to the edge of Peaksville and dumped off into the nothingness. Otherwise, nobody could have breathed when it started to spoil.

"You know," Dad went on, "it's nice to have the new things around. It's nice to think that there's probably still a lot of stuff nobody's found yet, in cellars and attics and barns and down behind things. They help, somehow. As much as anything can help—"

"Sh-h!" Mom glanced nervously around.

"Oh," Dad said, smiling hastily, "it's all right! The new things are *good!* It's *nice* to be able to have something around you've never seen before, and know that something you've given somebody else is making them happy. That's a real *good* thing."

"A good thing," his wife echoed.

"Pretty soon," Aunt Amy said, from the stove, "there won't be any more new things. We'll have found everything there is to find. Goodness, that'll be too bad."

"*Amy!*"

"Well . . ." Her pale eyes were shallow and fixed, a sign of her recurrent vagueness. "It will be kind of a shame—no new things—"

"Don't *talk* like that," Mom said, trembling. "Amy, be *quiet!*"

"It's *good*," said Dad, in the loud, familiar, wanting-to-be-overheard tone of voice. "Such talk is *good.* It's okay, honey—don't you see? It's good for Amy to talk any way she wants. It's good for her to feel bad. Everything's good. Everything *has* to be good."

Anthony's mother was pale. And so was Aunt Amy—the peril of the moment had suddenly penetrated the clouds surrounding her mind. Sometimes it was difficult to handle words so that they might not prove disastrous. You just never *knew*. There were so many things it was wise not to say, or even think—but remonstration for saying or thinking them might be just as bad, if Anthony heard and decided to do anything about it. You could just never tell what Anthony was liable to do.

Everything had to be good. Had to be fine just as it was, even if it wasn't. Always. Because any change might be worse. So terribly much worse.

"Oh, my goodness, yes, of course it's good," Mom said. "You talk any way you want to, Amy, and it's just fine. Of course, you want to remember that some ways are *better* than others."

Aunt Amy stirred the peas, fright in her pale eyes.

"Oh, yes," she said. "But I don't feel like talking right now. It . . . it's *good* that I don't feel like talking."

Dad said tiredly, smiling, "I'm going out and wash up."

They started arriving around eight o'clock. By that time Mom and Aunt Amy had the big table in the dining room set, and two more tables off to the side. The candles were burning, and the chairs situated, and Dad had a big fire going in the fireplace.

The first to arrive were the Sipiches, John and Mary. John wore his best suit, and was well scrubbed and pink-faced after his day in McIntyre's pasture. The suit was neatly pressed but getting threadbare at elbows and cuffs. Old McIntyre was working on a loom, designing it out of schoolbooks, but so far it was slow going. McIntyre was a capable man with wood and tools, but a loom was a big order when you couldn't get metal parts. McIntyre had been one of the ones who, at first, had wanted to try to get Anthony to make things the villagers needed, like clothes and canned goods and medical supplies and gasoline. Since then he felt that what had happened to the whole Terrance family and Joe Kinney was his fault, and he worked hard trying to make it up to the rest of them. And since then no one had tried to get Anthony to do anything.

Mary Sipich was a small, cheerful woman in a simple dress. She immediately set about helping Mom and Aunt Amy put the finishing touches on the dinner.

The next arrivals were the Smiths and the Dunns, who lived right next to each other down the road, only a few yards from the nothingness. They drove up in the Smiths' wagon, drawn by their old horse.

Then the Reillys showed up, from across the darkened wheatfield, and the evening really began. Pat Reilly sat down at the big upright in the front room and began to play from the popular sheet music on the rack. He played softly, as expressively as he could—and nobody sang. Anthony liked piano playing a whole lot, but not singing; often he would come up from the basement, or down from the attic, or just *come,* and sit on top of the piano, nodding his head as Pat played "Lover" or "Boulevard of Broken Dreams" or "Night and Day." He seemed to prefer ballads, sweet-sounding songs—but the one time somebody had started to sing, Anthony had looked over from the top of the piano and done something that made everybody afraid of singing from then on. Later they'd decided that the piano was what Anthony had heard first, before anybody had ever tried to sing, and now anything else added to it didn't sound right and distracted him from his pleasure.

So every television night Pat would play the piano, and that was the beginning of the evening. Wherever Anthony was, the music would make him happy and put him in a good mood, and he would know that they were gathering for television and waiting for him.

By eight-thirty everybody had shown up, except for the seventeen children and Mrs. Soames, who was off watching them in the schoolhouse at the far end of town. The children of Peaksville were never, never allowed near the Fremont house—not since little Fred Smith had tried to play with Anthony on a dare. The younger children weren't even told about Anthony. The others had mostly forgotten about him, or were told that he was a nice, nice goblin but they must never go near him.

Dan and Ethel Hollis came late, and Dan walked in not suspecting a thing. Pat Reilly had played the piano until his hands ached —he'd worked pretty hard with them today—and now he got up, and everybody gathered around to wish Dan Hollis a happy birthday.

"Well, I'll be darned," Dan grinned. "This is swell. I wasn't expecting this at all . . . gosh, this is *swell!*"

They gave him his presents—mostly things they had made by hand, though some were things that people had possessed as their own and now gave him as his. John Sipich gave him a watch charm, hand-carved out of a piece of hickory wood. Dan's watch had broken down a year or so ago, and there was nobody in the village who knew how to fix it, but he still carried it around because it had been his grandfather's and was a fine old heavy thing of gold and silver. He attached the charm to the chain while everybody laughed and said John had done a nice job of carving. Then Mary Sipich gave him a knitted necktie, which he put on, removing the one he'd worn.

The Reillys gave him a little box they had made, to keep things in. They didn't say what things, but Dan said he'd keep his personal jewelry in it. The Reillys had made it out of a cigar box, carefully peeled of its paper and lined on the inside with velvet. The outside had been polished, and carefully if not expertly carved by Pat—but his carving got complimented, too. Dan Hollis received many other gifts—a pipe, a pair of shoelaces, a tiepin, a knit pair of socks, some fudge, a pair of garters made from old suspenders.

He unwrapped each gift with vast pleasure and wore as many of them as he could right there, even the garters. He lit up the pipe and said he'd never had a better smoke. Which wasn't quite true, because the pipe wasn't broken in yet; Pete Manners had had it lying around ever since he'd received it as a gift four years ago from an out-of-town relative who hadn't known he'd stopped smoking.

Dan put the tobacco into the bowl very carefully. Tobacco was precious. It was only pure luck that Pat Reilly had decided to try to grow some in his back yard just before what had happened to Peaksville had happened. It didn't grow very well, and then they had to cure it and shred it and all, and it was just precious stuff. Everybody in town used wooden holders old McIntyre had made, to save on butts.

Last of all, Thelma Dunn gave Dan Hollis the record she had found.

Dan's eyes misted even before he opened the package. He knew it was a record.

"Gosh," he said softly. "What one is it? I'm almost afraid to look . . ."

"You haven't got it, darling," Ethel Hollis smiled. "Don't you remember, I asked about 'You Are My Sunshine'?"

"Oh, gosh," Dan said again. Carefully he removed the wrapping and stood there fondling the record, running his big hands over the worn grooves with their tiny, dulling crosswise scratches. He looked around the room, eyes shining, and they all smiled back, knowing how delighted he was.

"Happy birthday, darling!" Ethel said, throwing her arms around him and kissing him.

He clutched the record in both hands, holding it off to one side as she pressed against him. "Hey," he laughed, pulling back his head. "Be careful—I'm holding a priceless object!" He looked around again, over his wife's arms, which were still around his neck. His eyes were hungry. "Look . . . do you think we could play it? Lord, what I'd give to hear some new music. Just the first part, the orchestra part, before Como sings?"

Faces sobered. After a minute, John Sipich said, "I don't think we'd better, Dan. After all, we don't know just where the singer comes in—it'd be taking too much of a chance. Better wait till you get home."

Dan Hollis reluctantly put the record on the buffet with all his other presents. "It's *good*," he said automatically, but disappointedly, "that I can't play it here."

"Oh, yes," said Sipich. "It's good." To compensate for Dan's disappointed tone, he repeated, "It's *good*."

They ate dinner, the candles lighting their smiling faces, and ate it all right down to the last delicious drop of gravy. They complimented Mom and Aunt Amy on the roast beef, and the peas and carrots, and the tender corn on the cob. The corn hadn't come from the Fremonts' cornfield, naturally—everybody knew what was out there, and the field was going to weeds. Then they polished off the dessert—homemade ice cream and cookies. And then they sat back, in the flickering light of the candles, and chatted, waiting for television.

There never was a lot of mumbling on television night—everybody came and had a good dinner at the Fremonts', and that was nice, and afterward there was television, and nobody really thought much about that—it just had to be put up with. So it was a pleasant enough get-together, aside from your having to watch what you said just as carefully as you always did everyplace. If a dangerous thought came into your mind, you just started mumbling, even right in the middle of a sentence. When you did that, the others just ignored you until you felt happier again and stopped.

Anthony liked television night. He had done only two or three awful things on television night in the whole past year.

Mom had put a bottle of brandy on the table, and they each had a tiny glass of it. Liquor was even more precious than tobacco. The villagers could make wine, but the grapes weren't right, and certainly the techniques weren't, and it wasn't very good wine. There were only a few bottles of real liquor left in the village—four rye, three Scotch, three brandy, nine real wine and half a bottle of Drambuie belonging to old McIntyre (only for marriages)—and when those were gone, that was it.

Afterward everybody wished that the brandy hadn't been brought out. Because Dan Hollis drank more of it than he should have, and mixed it with a lot of the homemade wine. Nobody thought anything about it at first, because he didn't show it much outside, and it was his birthday party and a happy party, and Anthony liked these get-togethers and shouldn't see any reason to do anything even if he was listening. But Dan Hollis got high, and did a fool thing. If they'd seen it coming, they'd have taken him outside and walked him around.

The first thing they knew, Dan stopped laughing right in the middle of the story about how Thelma Dunn had found the Perry Como record and dropped it and it hadn't broken because she'd moved faster than she ever had before in her life and caught it. He was fondling the record again, and looking longingly at the Fremonts' gramophone over in the corner, and suddenly he stopped laughing and his face got slack, and then it got ugly, and he said, "Oh, *Christ!*"

Immediately the room was still. So still they could hear the whirring movement of the grandfather's clock out in the hall. Pat Reilly had been playing the piano, softly. He stopped, his hands poised over the yellowed keys.

The candles on the dining-room table flickered in a cool breeze that blew through the lace curtains over the bay window.

"Keep playing, Pat," Anthony's father said softly.

Pat started again. He played "Night and Day," but his eyes were sidewise on Dan Hollis, and he missed notes.

Dan stood in the middle of the room, holding the record. In his other hand he held a glass of brandy so hard his hand shook.

They were all looking at him.

"*Christ*," he said again, and he made it sound like a dirty word.

Reverend Younger, who had been talking with Mom and Aunt Amy by the dining-room door, said "Christ," too—but he was using it in a prayer. His hands were clasped, and his eyes were closed.

John Sipich moved forward. "Now, Dan. It's *good* for you to talk that way, but you don't want to talk too much, you know."

Dan shook off the hand Sipich put on his arm.

"Can't even play my record," he said loudly. He looked down at the record, and then around at their faces. "Oh, my *God*—" He threw the glassful of brandy against the wall. It splattered and ran down the wallpaper in streaks.

Some of the women gasped.

"Dan," Sipich said in a whisper. "Dan, cut it out."

Pat Reilly was playing "Night and Day" louder, to cover up the sounds of the talk. It wouldn't do any good, though, if Anthony was listening. Dan Hollis went over to the piano and stood by Pat's shoulder, swaying a little. "Pat," he said, "don't play *that*. Play *this*." And he began to sing, softly, hoarsely, miserably, "Happy birthday to me, happy birthday to me . . ."

"*Dan!*" Ethel Hollis screamed. She tried to run across the room to him. Mary Sipich grabbed her arm and held her back. "Dan," Ethel screamed again, "stop—"

"My God, be quiet!" hissed Mary Sipich, and pushed her toward one of the men, who put his hand over her mouth and held her still.

". . . happy birthday, dear Danny," Dan sang, "happy birthday to me!" He stopped and looked down at Pat Reilly. "Play it, Pat. Play it, so I can sing right. You know I can't carry a tune unless somebody plays it!"

Pat Reilly put his hands on the keys and began "Lover"—in a slow waltz tempo, the way Anthony liked it. Pat's face was white. His hands fumbled.

Dan Hollis stared over at the dining-room door. At Anthony's mother, and at Anthony's father, who had gone to join her. "*You* had him," he said. Tears gleamed on his cheeks as the candlelight caught them. "*You* had to go and *have* him . . ." He closed his eyes, and the tears squeezed out. He sang loudly, "You are my sunshine . . . my only sunshine . . . you make me happy . . . when I am blue . . ."

Anthony came into the room.

Pat stopped playing. He froze. Everybody froze. The breeze rippled the curtains. Ethel Hollis couldn't even try to scream—she had fainted.

". . . please don't take my sunshine . . . away . . ." Dan's voice faltered into silence. His eyes widened. He put both hands out in front of him, the empty glass in one, the record in the other. He hiccuped and said, "*No—*"

"Bad man," Anthony said, and thought Dan Hollis into something like nothing anyone would have believed possible, and then he thought the thing into a grave deep, deep in the cornfield.

The glass and the record thumped on the rug. Neither broke.

Anthony's purple gaze went around the room.

Some of the people began mumbling. They all tried to smile. The sound of mumbling filled the room like a far-off approval. Out of the murmuring came one or two clear voices:

"Oh, it's a very *good* thing," said John Sipich.

"A good thing," said Anthony's father, smiling. He'd had more practice in smiling than most of them. "A wonderful thing."

"It's swell . . . just swell," said Pat Reilly, tears leaking from eyes and nose, and he began to play the piano again, softly, his trembling hands feeling for "Night and Day."

Anthony climbed up on top of the piano, and Pat played for two hours.

Afterward, they watched television. They all went into the front room, and lit just a few candles, and pulled up chairs around the set. It was a small-screen set, and they couldn't all sit close enough to it to see, but that didn't matter. They didn't even turn the set on. It wouldn't have worked anyway, there being no electricity in Peaksville.

They just sat silently, and watched the twisting, writhing shapes on the screen, and listened to the sounds that came out of the speaker, and none of them had any idea of what it was all about. They never did. It was always the same.

"It's real nice," Aunt Amy said once, her pale eyes on the meaningless flickers and shadows. "But I liked it a little better when there were cities outside and we could get real—"

"Why, Amy!" said Mom. "It's good for you to say such a thing. Very good. But how can you mean it? Why, this television is *much* better than anything we ever used to get!"

"Yes," chimed in John Sipich. "It's fine. It's the best show we've ever seen!"

He sat on the couch with two other men, holding Ethel Hollis flat against the cushions, holding her arms and legs and putting their hands over her mouth so she couldn't start screaming again.

"It's really *good!*" he said again.

Mom looked out of the front window, across the darkened road, across Henderson's darkened wheat field to the vast, endless, gray nothingness in which the little village of Peaksville floated like a soul—the huge nothingness that was most evident at night, when Anthony's brassy day had gone.

It did no good to wonder where they were—no good at all. Peaksville was just someplace. Someplace away from the world. It was wherever it had been since that day three years ago when Anthony had crept from her womb and old Doc Bates—God rest him—had screamed and dropped him and tried to kill him, and Anthony had whined and done the thing. Had taken the village someplace. Or had destroyed the world and left only the village, nobody knew which.

It did no good to wonder about it. Nothing at all did any good—except to live as they must live. Must always, always live, if Anthony would let them.

These thoughts were dangerous, she thought.

She began to mumble. The others started mumbling, too. They had all been thinking, evidently.

The men on the couch whispered and whispered to Ethel Hollis, and when they took their hands away she mumbled, too.

While Anthony sat on top of the set and made television, they sat around and mumbled and watched the meaningless, flickering shapes far into the night.

Next day it snowed, and killed off half the crops—but it was a *good* day.

THE VELDT

RAY BRADBURY

*It is very clear that if this anthology had been begun
ten years ago Ray Bradbury would have received a
great many more than four votes. The fashion began to
change, as nearly as I can see, when it was discovered
that Mr. Bradbury either could not write like or had no
interest in writing like Heinlein, Campbell, Wells or,
for that matter, John O'Hara. This, for some reason,
seemed to irritate people.*

*Mr. Bradbury, meanwhile, has simply continued to
write like Bradbury, an enviable thing to be able to do.
I don't think we have the right to ask for more than this,
and I, for one, really don't want to. While such a mythi-
cal reshifting took place, we might miss another story as
good as this one.*

The original appearance of "The Veldt" in The Saturday Evening Post *must have turned a number of normally cheerful suburbanites the color of their own
lawns. Don't say you weren't warned.*

"George, I wish you'd look at the nursery."

"What's wrong with it?"

"I don't know."

"Well, then."

"I just want you to look at it, is all, or call a psychologist in to
look at it."

"What would a psychologist want with a nursery?"

"You know very well what he'd want." His wife paused in the
middle of the kitchen and watched the stove busy humming to
itself, making supper for four. "It's just that the nursery is different now than it was."

"All right, let's have a look."

They walked down the hall of their soundproofed Happy-Life Home, which had cost them thirty thousand dollars installed, this house which clothed and fed them and rocked them to sleep and played and sang and was good to them. Their approach sensitized a switch somewhere and the nursery light flicked on when they came within ten feet of it. Similarly, behind them, in the halls, lights went on and off as they left them behind, with a soft automaticity.

"Well," said George Hadley.

They stood on the thatched floor of the nursery. It was forty feet across by forty feet long and thirty feet high; it had cost half again as much as the rest of the house. "But nothing's too good for our children," George had said.

The nursery was silent. It was empty as a jungle glade at hot high noon. The walls were blank and two-dimensional. Now, as George and Lydia Hadley stood in the center of the room, the walls began to purr and recede into crystalline distance, it seemed, and presently an African veldt appeared, in three dimensions; on all sides, in colors reproduced to the final pebble and bit of straw. The ceiling above them became a deep sky with a hot yellow sun.

George Hadley felt the perspiration start on his brow.

"Let's get out of the sun," he said. "This is a little too real. But I don't see anything wrong."

"Wait a moment, you'll see," said his wife.

Now the hidden odorophonics were beginning to blow a wind of odor at the two people in the middle of the baked veldtland. The hot straw smell of lion grass, the cool green smell of the hidden water hole, the great rusty smell of animals, the smell of dust like a red paprika in the hot air. And now the sounds: the thump of distant antelope feet on grassy sod, the papery rustling of vultures. A shadow passed through the sky. The shadow flickered on George Hadley's upturned, sweating face.

"Filthy creatures," he heard his wife say.

"The vultures."

"You see, there are the lions, far over, that way. Now they're on their way to the water hole. They've just been eating," said Lydia. "I don't know what."

"Some animal." George Hadley put his hand up to shield off the burning light from his squinted eyes. "A zebra or a baby giraffe, maybe."

"Are you sure?" His wife sounded peculiarly tense.

"No, it's a little late to be sure," he said, amused. "Nothing over there I can see but cleaned bone, and the vultures dropping for what's left."

"Did you hear that scream?" she asked.

"No."

"About a minute ago?"

"Sorry, no."

The lions were coming. And again George Hadley was filled with admiration for the mechanical genius who had conceived this room. A miracle of efficiency selling for an absurdly low price. Every home should have one. Oh, occasionally they frightened you with their clinical accuracy, they startled you, gave you a twinge, but most of the time what fun for everyone—not only for your own son and daughter, but for yourself when you felt like a quick jaunt to a foreign land, a quick change of scenery. Well, here it was!

And here were the lions now, fifteen feet away, so real, so feverishly and startlingly real that you could feel the prickling fur on your hand, and your mouth was stuffed with the dusty upholstery smell of their heated pelts, and the yellow of them was in your eyes like the yellow of an exquisite French tapestry, the yellows of lions and summer grass, and the sound of the matted lion lungs exhaling on the silent noontide, and the smell of meat from the panting, dripping mouths.

The lions stood looking at George and Lydia Hadley with terrible green-yellow eyes.

"Watch out!" screamed Lydia.

The lions came running at them.

Lydia bolted and ran. Instinctively, George sprang after her. Outside, in the hall, with the door slammed, he was laughing and she was crying, and they both stood appalled at the other's reaction.

"George!"

"Lydia! Oh, my dear poor sweet Lydia!"

"They almost got us!"

"Walls, Lydia, remember; crystal walls, that's all they are. Oh, they look real, I must admit—Africa in your parlor—but it's all dimensional superreactionary, supersensitive color film and mental tape film behind glass screens. It's all odorophonics and sonics, Lydia. Here's my handkerchief."

"I'm afraid." She came to him and put her body against him and cried steadily. "Did you see? Did you *feel?* It's too real."

"Now Lydia . . ."

"You've got to tell Wendy and Peter not to read any more on Africa.

"Of course—of course." He patted her.

"Promise?"

"Sure."

"And lock the nursery for a few days until I get my nerves settled."

"You know how difficult Peter is about that. When I punished him a month ago by locking the nursery for even a few hours, the tantrum he threw! And Wendy too. They *live* for the nursery."

"It's got to be locked, that's all there is to it."

"All right." Reluctantly he locked the huge door. "You've been working too hard. You need a rest."

"I don't know—I don't know," she said, blowing her nose, sitting down in a chair that immediately began to rock and comfort her. "Maybe I don't have enough to do. Maybe I have time to think too much. Why don't we shut the whole house off for a few days and take a vacation?"

"You mean you want to fry my eggs for me?"

"Yes." She nodded.

"And darn my socks?"

"Yes." A frantic, watery-eyed nodding.

"And sweep the house?"

"Yes, yes—oh, yes!"

"But I thought that's why we bought this house, so we wouldn't have to do anything?"

"That's just it. I feel like I don't belong here. The house is wife and mother now, and nursemaid. Can I compete with an African veldt? Can I give a bath and scrub the children as efficiently or quickly as the automatic scrub bath can? I cannot. And it isn't just me. It's you. You've been awfully nervous lately."

"I suppose I have been smoking too much."

"You look as if you didn't know what to do with yourself in this house, either. You smoke a little more every morning and drink a little more every afternoon and need a little more sedative every night. You're beginning to feel unnecessary, too."

"Am I?" He paused and tried to feel into himself to see what was really there.

"Oh, George!" She looked beyond him, at the nursery door. "Those lions can't get out of there, can they?"

He looked at the door and saw it tremble as if something had jumped against it from the other side.

"Of course not," he said.

At dinner they ate alone, for Wendy and Peter were at a special plastic carnival across town and had televised home to say they'd be late, to go ahead eating. So George Hadley, bemused, sat watching the dining-room table produce warm dishes of food from its mechanical interior.

"We forgot the ketchup," he said.

"Sorry," said a small voice within the table, and ketchup appeared.

As for the nursery, thought George Hadley, it won't hurt for the children to be locked out of it a while. Too much of anything isn't good for anyone. And it was clearly indicated that the children had been spending a little too much time on Africa. That *sun*. He could feel it on his neck, still, like a hot paw. And the *lions*. And the smell of blood. Remarkable how the nursery caught the telepathic emanations of the children's minds and created life to fill their every desire. The children thought lions, and there were lions. The children thought zebras, and there were zebras. Sun—sun. Giraffes—giraffes. Death and death.

That *last*. He chewed tastelessly on the meat that the table had cut for him. Death thoughts. They were awfully young, Wendy and Peter, for death thoughts. Or, no, you were never too young, really. Long before you knew what death was you were wishing it on someone else. When you were two years old you were shooting people with cap pistols.

But this—the long, hot African veldt, the awful death in the jaws of a lion. And repeated again and again.

"Where are you going?"

He didn't answer Lydia. Preoccupied, he let the lights glow softly on ahead of him, extinguish behind him as he padded to the nursery door. He listened against it. Far away, a lion roared.

He unlocked the door and opened it. Just before he stepped inside, he heard a faraway scream. And then another roar from the lions, which subsided quickly.

He stepped into Africa. How many times in the last year had he opened this door and found Wonderland, Alice, the Mock Turtle, or Aladdin and his magical lamp, or Jack Pumpkinhead of Oz, or Dr. Doolittle, or the cow jumping over a very real-appearing moon—all the delightful contraptions of a make-believe world. How often had he seen Pegasus flying in the sky ceiling, or seen fountains of red fireworks, or heard angel voices singing. But now, this yellow hot Africa, this bake oven with murder in the heat . . . Perhaps Lydia was right. Perhaps they needed a little vacation from the fantasy which was growing a bit too real for ten-year-old children. It was all right to exercise one's mind with gymnastic fantasies, but when the lively child mind settled on *one* pattern . . . ? It seemed that at a distance for the past month he had heard lions roaring and smelled their strong odor seeping as far away as his study door. But, being busy, he had paid it no attention.

George Hadley stood on the African grassland alone. The lions looked up from their feeding, watching him. The only flaw to the illusion was the open door through which he could see his wife, far down the dark hall, like a framed picture, eating her dinner abstractedly.

"Go away," he said to the lions.

They did not go.

He knew the principle of the room exactly. You sent out your thoughts. Whatever you thought would appear.

"Let's have Aladdin and his lamp," he snapped.

The veldtland remained; the lions remained.

"Come on, room! I demand Aladdin!" he said.

Nothing happened. The lions mumbled in their baked pelts.

"Aladdin!"

He went back to dinner. "The fool room's out of order," he said. "It won't respond."

"Or . . ."

"Or what?"

"Or it *can't* respond," said Lydia, "because the children have thought about Africa and lions and killing so many days that the room's in a rut."

"Could be."

"Or Peter's set it to remain that way."

"*Set* it?"

"He may have got into the machinery and fixed something."

"Peter doesn't know machinery."

"He's a wise one for ten. That I.Q. of his . . ."

"Nevertheless—"

"Hello, Mom. Hello, Dad."

The Hadleys turned. Wendy and Peter were coming in the front door, cheeks like peppermint candy, eyes like bright-blue agate marbles, a smell of ozone on their jumpers from their trip in the helicopter.

"You're just in time for supper," said both parents.

"We're full of strawberry ice cream and hot dogs," said the children, holding hands. "But we'll sit and watch."

"Yes, come tell us about the nursery," said George Hadley.

The brother and sister blinked at him and then at each other. "Nursery?"

"All about Africa and everything," said the father, with false joviality.

"I don't understand," said Peter.

"Your mother and I were just traveling through Africa with rod and reel; Tom Swift and his electric lion," said George Hadley.

"There's no Africa in the nursery," said Peter simply.

"Oh, come now, Peter. We know better."

"I don't remember any Africa," said Peter to Wendy. "Do you?"

"No."

"Run see and come tell."

She obeyed.

"Wendy, come back here!" said George Hadley, but she was gone. The house lights followed her like a flock of fireflies. Too late, he realized he had forgotten to lock the nursery door after his last inspection.

"Wendy'll look and come tell us," said Peter.

"She doesn't have to tell *me*. I've seen it."

"I'm sure you're mistaken, Father."

"I'm not, Peter. Come along, now."

But Wendy was back. "It's not Africa," she said breathlessly.

"We'll see about this," said George Hadley, and they all walked down the hall together and opened the nursery door.

There was a green, lovely forest, a lovely river, a purple mountain, high voices singing, and Rima, lovely and mysterious, lurking in the trees with colorful flights of butterflies, like animated bouquets, lingering in her long hair. The African veldtland was gone. The lions were gone. Only Rima was here now, singing a song so beautiful that it brought tears to your eyes.

George Hadley looked in at the changed scene. "Go to bed," he said to the children.

They opened their mouths.

"You heard me," he said.

They went off to the air closet, where a wind sucked them like brown leaves up the flue to their slumber rooms.

George Hadley walked through the singing glade and picked up something that lay in the corner near where the lions had been. He walked slowly back to his wife.

"What is that?" she asked.

"An old wallet of mine," he said.

He showed it to her. The smell of hot grass was on it, and the smell of a lion. There were drops of saliva on it, it had been chewed, and there were blood smears on both sides.

He closed the nursery door and locked it, tight.

In the middle of the night he was still awake and he knew his wife was awake. "Do you think Wendy changed it?" she said at last, in the dark room.

"Of course."

"Made it from a veldt into a forest and put Rima there instead of lions?"

"Yes."

"Why?"

"I don't know. But it's staying locked until I find out."

"How did your wallet get there?"

"I don't know anything," he said, "except that I'm beginning to be sorry we bought that room for the children. If children are neurotic at all, a room like that . . ."

"It's supposed to help them work off their neuroses in a healthful way."

"I'm starting to wonder." He stared at the ceiling.

"We've given the children everything they ever wanted. Is this our reward—secrecy, disobedience?"

"Who was it said, 'Children are carpets, they should be stepped on occasionally'? We've never lifted a hand. They're insufferable —let's admit it. They come and go when they like; they treat us as if we were offspring. They're spoiled and we're spoiled."

"They've been acting funny ever since you forbade them to take the rocket to New York a few months ago."

"They're not old enough to do that alone, I explained."

"Nevertheless, I've noticed they've been decidedly cool toward us since."

"I think I'll have David McClean come tomorrow morning to have a look at Africa."

"But it's not Africa now, it's Green Mansions country and Rima."

"I have a feeling it'll be Africa again before then."

A moment later they heard the screams.

Two screams. Two people screaming from downstairs. And then a roar of lions.

"Wendy and Peter aren't in their rooms," said his wife.

He lay in his bed with his beating heart. "No," he said. "They've broken into the nursery."

"Those screams—they sound familiar."

"Do they?"

"Yes, awfully."

And although their beds tried very hard, the two adults couldn't be rocked to sleep for another hour. A smell of cats was in the night air.

"Father?" said Peter.

"Yes."

Peter looked at his shoes. He never looked at his father any more, nor at his mother. "You aren't going to lock up the nursery for good, are you?"

"That all depends."

"On what?" snapped Peter.

"On you and your sister. If you intersperse this Africa with a little variety—oh, Sweden perhaps, or Denmark or China—"

"I thought we were free to play as we wished."

"You are, within reasonable bounds."

"What's wrong with Africa, Father?"

"Oh, so now you admit you have been conjuring up Africa, do you?"

"I wouldn't want the nursery locked up," said Peter coldly. "Ever."

"Matter of fact, we're thinking of turning the whole house off for about a month. Live sort of a carefree one-for-all existence."

"That sounds dreadful! Would I have to tie my own shoes instead of letting the shoe tier do it? And brush my own teeth and comb my hair and give myself a bath?"

"It would be fun for a change, don't you think?"

"No, it would be horrid. I didn't like it when you took out the picture painter last month."

"That's because I wanted you to learn to paint all by yourself, son."

"I don't want to do anything but look and listen and smell; what else is there to do?"

"All right, go play in Africa."

"Will you shut off the house sometime soon?"

"We're considering it."

"I don't think you'd better consider it any more, Father."

"I won't have any threats from my son!"

"Very well." And Peter strolled off to the nursery.

"Am I on time?" said David McClean.

"Breakfast?" asked George Hadley.

"Thanks, had some. What's the trouble?"

"David, you're a psychologist."

"I should hope so."

"Well, then, have a look at our nursery. You saw it a year ago when you dropped by; did you notice anything peculiar about it then?"

"Can't say I did; the usual violences, a tendency toward a slight paranoia here or there, usual in children because they feel persecuted by parents constantly, but, oh, really nothing."

They walked down the hall. "I locked the nursery up," explained the father, "and the children broke back into it during the night. I let them stay so they could form the patterns for you to see."

There was a terrible screaming from the nursery.

"There it is," said George Hadley. "See what you make of it."

They walked in on the children without rapping.

The screams had faded. The lions were feeding.

"Run outside a moment, children," said George Hadley. "No, don't change the mental combination. Leave the walls as they are. Get!"

With the children gone, the two men stood studying the lions clustered at a distance, eating with great relish whatever it was they had caught.

"I wish I knew what it was," said George Hadley. "Sometimes I can almost see. Do you think if I brought high-powered binoculars here and—"

David McClean laughed dryly. "Hardly." He turned to study all four walls. "How long has this been going on?"

"A little over a month."

"It certainly doesn't *feel* good."

"I want facts, not feelings."

"My dear George, a psychologist never saw a fact in his life. He only hears about feelings; vague things. This doesn't feel good, I tell you. Trust my hunches and my instincts. I have a nose for something bad. This is very bad. My advice to you is to have the whole damn room torn down and your children brought to me every day during the next year for treatment."

"Is it that bad?"

"I'm afraid so. One of the original uses of these nurseries was so that we could study the patterns left on the walls by the child's mind, study at our leisure, and help the child. In this case, however, the room has become a channel toward—destructive thoughts, instead of a release away from them."

"Didn't you sense this before?"

"I sensed only that you had spoiled your children more than

most. And now you're letting them down in some way. What way?"

"I wouldn't let them go to New York."

"What else?"

"I've taken a few machines from the house and threatened them, a month ago, with closing up the nursery unless they did their homework. I did close it for a few days to show I meant business."

"Ah, ha!"

"Does that mean anything?"

"Everything. Where before they had a Santa Claus now they have a Scrooge. Children prefer Santas. You've let this room and this house replace you and your wife in your children's affections. This room is their mother and father, far more important in their lives than their real parents. And now you come along and want to shut it off. No wonder there's hatred here. You can feel it coming out of the sky. Feel that sun. George, you'll have to change your life. Like too many others, you've built it around creature comforts. Why, you'd starve tomorrow if something went wrong in your kitchen. You wouldn't know how to tap an egg. Nevertheless, turn everything off. Start new. It'll take time. But we'll make good children out of bad in a year, wait and see."

"But won't the shock be too much for the children, shutting the room up abruptly, for good?"

"I don't want them going any deeper into this, that's all."

The lions were finished with their red feast.

The lions were standing on the edge of the clearing watching the two men.

"Now *I'm* feeling persecuted," said McClean. "Let's get out of here. I never have cared for these damned rooms. Make me nervous."

"The lions look real, don't they?" said George Hadley. "I don't suppose there's any way . . ."

"What?"

". . . that they could *become* real?"

"Not that I know."

"Some flaw in the machinery, a tampering or something?"

"No."

They went to the door.

"I don't imagine the room will like being turned off," said the father.

"Nothing ever likes to die—even a room."

"I wonder if it hates me for wanting to switch it off?"

"Paranoia is thick around here today," said David McClean. "You can follow it like a spoor. Hello." He bent and picked up a bloody scarf. "This yours?"

"No." George Hadley's face was rigid. "It belongs to Lydia."

They went to the fuse box together and threw the switch that killed the nursery.

The two children were in hysterics. They screamed and pranced and threw things. They yelled and sobbed and swore and jumped at the furniture.

"You can't do that to the nursery, you can't!"

"Now, children."

The children flung themselves onto a couch, weeping.

"George," said Lydia Hadley, "turn on the nursery, just for a few moments. You can't be so abrupt."

"No."

"You can't be so cruel."

"Lydia, it's off, and it stays off. And the whole damn house dies as of here and now. The more I see of the mess we've put ourselves in, the more it sickens me. We've been contemplating our mechanical, electronic navels for too long. My God, how we need a breath of honest air!"

And he marched about the house turning off the voice clocks, the stoves, the heaters, the shoe shiners, the shoe lacers, the body scrubbers and swabbers and massagers, and every other machine he could put his hand to.

The house was full of dead bodies, it seemed. It felt like a mechanical cemetery. So silent. None of the humming hidden energy of machines waiting to function at the tap of a button.

"Don't let them do it!" wailed Peter at the ceiling, as if he was talking to the house, the nursery. "Don't let Father kill everything." He turned to his father. "Oh, I hate you!"

"Insults won't get you anywhere."

"I wish you were dead!"

"We were, for a long while. Now we're going to really start

living. Instead of being handled and massaged, we're going to *live*."

Wendy was still crying, and Peter joined her again. "Just a moment, just one moment, just another moment of nursery," they wailed.

"Oh, George," said the wife, "it can't hurt."

"All right—all right, if they'll only just shut up. One minute, mind you, and then off forever."

"Daddy, Daddy, Daddy!" sang the children, smiling with wet faces.

"And then we're going on a vacation. David McClean is coming back in half an hour to help us move out and get to the airport. I'm going to dress. You turn the nursery on for a minute, Lydia, just a minute, mind you."

And the three of them went babbling off while he let himself be vacuumed upstairs through the air flue and set about dressing himself. A minute later Lydia appeared.

"I'll be glad when we get away," she sighed.

"Did you leave them in the nursery?"

"I wanted to dress, too. Oh, that horrid Africa. What can they see in it?"

"Well, in five minutes we'll be on our way to Iowa. Lord, how did we ever get in this house? What prompted us to buy a nightmare?"

"Pride, money, foolishness."

"I think we'd better get downstairs before those kids get engrossed with those damned beasts again."

Just then they heard the children calling, "Daddy, Mommy, come quick—quick!"

They went downstairs in the air flue and ran down the hall. The children were nowhere in sight. "Wendy? Peter!"

They ran into the nursery. The veldtland was empty save for the lions waiting, looking at them. "Peter, Wendy?"

The door slammed.

"Wendy, Peter!"

George Hadley and his wife whirled and ran back to the door.

"Open the door!" cried George Hadley, trying the knob. "Why, they've locked it from the outside! Peter!" He beat at the door. "Open up!"

He heard Peter's voice outside, against the door.

"Don't let them switch off the nursery and the house," he was saying.

Mr. and Mrs. George Hadley beat at the door. "Now, don't be ridiculous, children. It's time to go. Mr. McClean'll be here in a minute and . . ."

And then they heard the sounds.

The lions on three sides of them, in the yellow veldt grass, padding through the dry straw, rumbling and roaring in their throats.

The lions.

Mr. Hadley looked at his wife and they turned and looked back at the beasts edging slowly forward, crouching, tails stiff.

Mr. and Mrs. Hadley screamed.

And suddenly they realized why those other screams had sounded familiar.

"Well, here I am," said David McClean in the nursery doorway. "Oh, hello." He stared at the two children seated in the center of the open glade eating a little picnic lunch. Beyond them was the water hole and the yellow veldtland; above was the hot sun. He began to perspire. "Where are your father and mother?"

The children looked up and smiled. "Oh, they'll be here directly."

"Good, we must get going." At a distance Mr. McClean saw the lions fighting and clawing and then quieting down to feed in silence under the shady trees.

He squinted at the lions with his hand up to his eyes.

Now the lions were done feeding. They moved to the water hole to drink.

A shadow flickered over Mr. McClean's hot face. Many shadows flickered. The vultures were dropping down the blazing sky.

"A cup of tea?" asked Wendy in the silence.

THE GOLEM

AVRAM DAVIDSON

Eventually, every Jewish writer takes a crack at telling his own version of this Yiddish myth. Mr. Davidson, I think, is the first to transport it to Southern California. He also appears to be the first to realize that the golem is not only horrible but funny too.

The gray-faced person came along the street where old Mr. and Mrs. Gumbeiner lived. It was afternoon, it was autumn, the sun was warm and soothing to their ancient bones. Anyone who attended the movies in the twenties or the early thirties has seen that street a thousand times. Past these bungalows with their half-double roofs Edmund Lowe walked arm in arm with Leatrice Joy, and Harold Lloyd was chased by Chinamen waving hatchets. Under these squamous palm trees Laurel kicked Hardy and Woolsey beat Wheeler upon the head with codfish. Across these pocket-handkerchief-sized lawns the juveniles of the Our Gang Comedies pursued one another and were pursued by angry fat men in golf knickers. On this same street—or perhaps on some other one of five hundred streets exactly like it.

Mrs. Gumbeiner indicated the gray-faced person to her husband.

"You think maybe he's got something the matter?" she asked. "He walks kind of funny, to me."

"Walks like a golem," Mr. Gumbeiner said indifferently.

The old woman was nettled.

"Oh, I don't know," she said. "*I* think he walks like your cousin Mendel."

The old man pursed his mouth angrily and chewed on his pipe-stem. The gray-faced person turned up the concrete path, walked up the steps to the porch, sat down in a chair. Old Mr. Gumbeiner ignored him. His wife stared at the stranger.

"Man comes in without a hello, goodbye or howareyou, sits himself down and right away he's at home. The chair is comfortable?" she asked. "Would you like maybe a glass tea?" She turned to her husband. "Say something, Gumbeiner!" she demanded. "What are you, made of wood?"

The old man smiled a slow, wicked, triumphant smile. "Why should *I* say anything?" he asked the air. "Who am I? Nothing, that's who."

The stranger spoke. His voice was harsh and monotonous. "When you learn who—or, rather, what—I am, the flesh will melt from your bones in terror." He bared porcelain teeth.

"Never mind about my bones!" the old woman cried. "You've got a lot of nerve talking about my bones!"

"You will quake with fear," said the stranger.

Old Mrs. Gumbeiner said that she hoped he would live so long. She turned to her husband once again. "Gumbeiner, when are you going to mow the lawn?"

"All mankind—" the stranger began.

"*Shah!* I'm talking to my husband. He talks *eppis* kind of funny, Gumbeiner, no?"

"Probably a foreigner," Mr. Gumbeiner said complacently.

"You think so?" Mrs. Gumbeiner glanced fleetingly at the stranger. "He's got a very bad color in his face, *nebbich*. I suppose he came to California for his health."

"Disease, pain, sorrow, love, grief—all are nought to—"

Mr. Gumbeiner cut in on the stranger's statement. "Gall bladder," the old man said. "Guinzburg down at the shul looked exactly the same before his operation. Two professors they had in for him, and a private nurse day and night."

"I am not a human being!" the stranger said loudly.

"Three thousand seven hundred fifty dollars it cost his son, Guinzburg told me. 'For you, Poppa, nothing is too expensive—only get well,' the son told him."

"*I am not a human being!*"

"Ai, is that a son for you!" the old woman said, rocking her head. "A heart of gold, pure gold." She looked at the stranger. "All right, all right, I heard you the first time. Gumbeiner! I asked you a question. When are you going to cut the lawn?"

"On Wednesday, *odder* maybe Thursday, comes the Japaneser

to the neighborhood. To cut lawns is *his* profession. *My* profession is to be a glazier—retired."

"Between me and all mankind is an inevitable hatred," the stranger said. "When I tell you what I am, the flesh will melt—"

"You said, you said already," Mr. Gumbeiner interrupted.

"In Chicago where the winters were as cold and bitter as the Czar of Russia's heart," the old woman intoned, "you had strength to carry the frames with the glass together day in and day out. But in California with the golden sun, to mow the lawn when your wife asks, for this you have no strength. Do I call in the Japaneser to cook for you supper?"

"Thirty years Professor Allardyce spent perfecting his theories. Electronics, neuronics—"

"Listen how educated he talks," Mr. Gumbeiner said admiringly. "Maybe he goes to the university here?"

"If he goes to the university, maybe he knows Bud?" his wife suggested.

"Probably they're in the same class and he came to see him about the homework, no?"

"Certainly he must be in the same class. How many classes are there? Five *in ganzen:* Bud showed me on his program card." She counted off on her fingers. "Television Appreciation and Criticism, Small-Boat Building, Social Adjustment, The American Dance . . . The American Dance—*nu*, Gumbeiner—"

"Contemporary Ceramics," her husband said, relishing the syllables. "A fine boy, Bud. A pleasure to have him for a boardner."

"After thirty years spent in these studies," the stranger, who had continued to speak unnoticed, went on, "he turned from the theoretical to the pragmatic. In ten years' time he had made the most titanic discovery in history: he made mankind, *all* mankind, superfluous: he made *me*."

"What did Tillie write in her last letter?" asked the old man.

The old woman shrugged. "What should she write? The same thing. Sidney was home from the Army, Naomi has a new boy friend—"

"*He made* ME!"

"Listen, Mr. Whatever-your-name-is," the old woman said, "maybe where you came from is different, but in *this* country you don't interrupt people the while they're talking— Hey. Listen, what do you mean, he *made* you? What kind of talk is that?"

The stranger bared all his teeth again, exposing the too-pink gums.

"In his library, to which I had a more complete access after his sudden and as yet undiscovered death from entirely natural causes, I found a complete collection of stories about androids, from Shelley's *Frankenstein* through Capek's *R.U.R.* to Asimov's—"

"Frankenstein?" said the old man, with interest. "There used to be Frankenstein who had the soda-*wasser* place on Halstead Street: a Litvack, *nebbich*."

"What are you talking?" Mrs. Gumbeiner demanded. "His name was Frankenthal, and it wasn't on Halstead, it was on Roosevelt."

"—clearly shown that all mankind has an instinctive antipathy toward androids and there will be an inevitable struggle between them—"

"Of course, of course!" Old Mr. Gumbeiner clicked his teeth against his pipe. "I am always wrong, you are always right. How could you stand to be married to such a stupid person all this time?"

"I don't know," the old woman said. "Sometimes I wonder myself. I think it must be his good looks." She began to laugh. Old Mr. Gumbeiner blinked, then began to smile, then took his wife's hand.

"Foolish old woman," the stranger said, "why do you laugh? Do you not know I have come to destroy you?"

"What!" old Mr. Gumbeiner shouted. "Close your mouth, you!" He darted from his chair and struck the stranger with the flat of his hand. The stranger's head struck against the porch pillar and bounced back.

"When you talk to my wife, talk respectable, you hear?"

Old Mrs. Gumbeiner, cheeks very pink, pushed her husband back in his chair. Then she leaned forward and examined the stranger's head. She clicked her tongue as she pulled aside the flap of gray skinlike material.

"Gumbeiner, look! He's all springs and wires inside!"

"I *told* you he was a golem, but no, you wouldn't listen," the old man said.

"You said he *walked* like a golem."

"How could he walk like a golem unless he *was* one?"

"All right, all right. You broke him, so now fix him."

"My grandfather, his light shines from Paradise, told me that when MoHaRaL—Moreynu Ha-Rav Löw—his memory for a blessing, made the golem in Prague, three hundred? four hundred years ago? he wrote on his forehead the Holy Name."

Smiling reminiscently, the old woman continued, "And the golem cut the rabbi's wood and brought his water and guarded the ghetto."

"And one time only he disobeyed the Rabbi Löw, and Rabbi Löw erased the *Shem Ha-Mephorash* from the golem's forehead and the golem fell down like a dead one. And they put him up in the attic of the shul and he's still there today if the Communisten haven't sent him to Moscow. This is not just a story," he said.

"*Avadda* not!" said the old woman.

"I myself have seen both the shul *and* the rabbi's grave," her husband said conclusively.

"But I think this must be a different kind golem, Gumbeiner. See, on his forehead: nothing written."

"What's the matter, there's a law I can't write something there? Where is that lump clay Bud brought us from his class?"

The old man washed his hands, adjusted his little black skullcap, and slowly and carefully wrote four Hebrew letters on the gray forehead.

"Ezra the Scribe himself couldn't do better," the old woman said admiringly. "Nothing happens," she observed, looking at the lifeless figure sprawled in the chair.

"Well, after all, am I Rabbi Löw?" her husband asked deprecatingly. "No," he answered. He leaned over and examined the exposed mechanism. "This spring goes here . . . this wire comes with this one . . ." The figure moved. "But this one goes where? And this one?"

"Let be," said his wife. The figure sat up slowly and rolled its eyes loosely.

"Listen, Reb Golem," the old man said, wagging his finger. "Pay attention to what I say—you understand?"

"Understand . . ."

"If you want to stay here, you got to do like Mr. Gumbeiner says."

"Do-like-Mr.-Gumbeiner-says . . ."

"*That's* the way I like to hear a golem talk. Malka, give here the mirror from the pocketbook. Look, you see your face? You see on the forehead, what's written? If you don't do like Mr. Gumbeiner says, he'll wipe out what's written and you'll be no more alive."

"No-more-alive . . ."

"*That's* right. Now, listen. Under the porch you'll find a lawnmower. Take it. And cut the lawn. Then come back. Go."

"Go . . ." The figure shambled down the steps. Presently the sound of the lawnmower whirred through the quiet air in the street just like the street where Jackie Cooper shed huge tears on Wallace Beery's shirt and Chester Conklin rolled his eyes at Marie Dressler.

"So what will you write to Tillie?" old Mr. Gumbeiner asked.

"What should I write?" Old Mrs. Gumbeiner shrugged. "I'll write that the weather is lovely out here and that we are both, blessed be the Name, in good health."

The old man nodded his head slowly, and they sat together on the front porch in the warm afternoon sun.

HELEN O'LOY

LESTER DEL REY

There are a few stories which come up regularly in misty-eyed discussions of the real classics of sf. Lester del Rey has written two: Nerves (*too long for inclusion here in its magazine version, and much more satisfactory as a novel anyhow*), *and this one.*

I am an old man now, but I can still see Helen as Dave unpacked her, and still hear him gasp as he looked her over.

"Man, isn't she a beauty?"

She was beautiful, a dream in spun plastics and metals, something Keats might have seen dimly when he wrote his sonnet. If Helen of Troy had looked like that the Greeks must have been pikers when they launched only a thousand ships; at least, that's what I told Dave.

"Helen of Troy, eh?" He looked at her tag. "At least it beats this thing—K$_2$W88. Helen . . . Mmmm . . . Helen of Alloy."

"Not much swing to that, Dave. Too many unstressed syllables in the middle. How about Helen O'Loy?"

"Helen O'Loy she is, Phil." And that's how it began—one part beauty, one part dream, one part science; add a stereo broadcast, stir mechanically, and the result is chaos.

Dave and I hadn't gone to college together, but when I came to Messina to practice medicine I found him downstairs in a little robot repair shop. After that we began to pal around, and when I started going with one twin he found the other equally attractive, so we made it a foursome.

When our business grew better, we rented a house near the rocket field—noisy but cheap, and the rockets discouraged apartment building. We liked room enough to stretch ourselves. I suppose if we hadn't quarreled with them we'd have married the twins in time. But Dave wanted to look over the latest Venus-rocket attempt when his twin wanted to see a display stereo starring Larry Ainslee, and they were both stubborn. From then on we forgot the girls and spent our evenings at home.

But it wasn't until "Lena" put vanilla on our steak instead of salt that we got off on the subject of emotions and robots. While Dave was dissecting Lena to find the trouble, we naturally mulled over the future of the mechs. He was sure that the robots would beat men someday, and I couldn't see it.

"Look here, Dave," I argued. "You know Lena doesn't think—not really. When those wires crossed, she could have corrected herself. But she didn't bother; she followed the mechanical impulse. A man might have reached for the vanilla, but when he saw it in his hand, he'd have stopped. Lena has sense enough, but she has no emotions, no consciousness of self."

"All right, that's the big trouble with the mechs now. But we'll get around it, put in some mechanical emotions or something." He screwed Lena's head back on, turned on her juice. "Go back to work, Lena, it's nineteen o'clock."

Now, I specialized in endocrinology and related subjects. I wasn't exactly a psychologist, but I did understand the glands, secretions, hormones, and miscellanies that are the physical causes of emotions. It took medical science three hundred years to find out how and why they worked, and I couldn't see men duplicating them mechanically in much less time.

I brought home books and papers to prove it, and Dave quoted the invention of memory coils and veritoid eyes. During that year we swapped knowledge until Dave knew the whole theory of endocrinology and I could have made Lena from memory. The more we talked, the less sure I grew about the impossibility of *homo mechanensis* as the perfect type.

Poor Lena. Her cuproberyl body spent half its time in scattered pieces. Our first attempts were successful only in getting her to serve fried brushes for breakfast and wash the dishes in oleo oil. Then one day she cooked a perfect dinner with six wires crossed, and Dave was in ecstasy.

He worked all night on her wiring, put in a new coil, and taught her a fresh set of words. And the next day she flew into a tantrum and swore vigorously at us when we told her she wasn't doing her work right.

"It's a lie," she yelled, shaking a suction brush. "You're all liars. If you so-and-so's would leave me whole long enough, I might get something done around the place."

When we had calmed her temper and got her back to work, Dave ushered me into the study. "Not taking any chances with Lena," he explained. "We'll have to cut out that adrenal pack and restore her to normalcy. But we've got to get a better robot. A housemaid mech isn't complex enough."

"How about Dillard's new utility models? They seem to combine everything in one."

"Exactly. Even so, we'll need a special one built to order, with a full range of memory coils. And out of respect to old Lena, let's get a female case for its works."

The result, of course, was Helen. The Dillard people had performed a miracle and put all the works in a girl-modeled case. Even the plastic-and-rubberite face was designed for flexibility to express emotions, and she was complete with tear glands and taste buds, ready to simulate every human action, from breathing to pulling hair. The bill they sent with her was another miracle, but Dave and I scraped it together; we had to turn Lena over to an exchange to complete it, though, and thereafter we ate out.

I'd performed plenty of delicate operations on living tissues, and some of them had been tricky, but I still felt like a pre-med student as we opened the front plate of her torso and began to sever the leads of her "nerves." Dave's mechanical glands were all prepared, complex little bundles of radio tubes and wires that heterodyned on the electrical thought impulses and distorted them as adrenalin distorts the reaction of human minds.

Instead of sleeping that night, we pored over the schematic diagrams of her structures, tracing the thought mazes of her wiring, severing the leaders, implanting the heterones, as Dave called them. And while we worked, a mechanical tape fed carefully prepared thoughts of consciousness and awareness of life and feeling into an auxiliary memory coil. Dave believed in leaving nothing to chance.

It was growing light as we finished, exhausted and exultant. All that remained was the starting of her electrical power; like all the

Dillard mechs, she was equipped with a tiny atomotor instead of batteries, and once started she would need no further attention.

Dave refused to turn her on. "Wait until we've slept and rested," he advised. "I'm as eager to try her as you are, but we can't do much studying with our minds half dead. Turn in, and we'll leave Helen until later."

Even though we were both reluctant to follow it, we knew the idea was sound. We turned in, and sleep hit us before the air conditioner could cut down to sleeping temperature. And then Dave was pounding on my shoulder.

"Phil! Hey, snap out of it!"

I groaned, turned over, and faced him. "Well? . . . Uh! What is it? Did Helen—"

"No, it's old Mrs. Van Styler. She 'visored to say her son has an infatuation for a servant girl, and she wants you to come out and give counterhormones. They're at the summer camp in Maine."

Rich Mrs. Van Styler! I couldn't afford to let that account down, now that Helen had used up the last of my funds. But it wasn't a job I cared for.

"Counterhormones! That'll take two weeks' full time. Anyway, I'm no society doctor, messing with glands to keep fools happy. My job's taking care of serious trouble."

"And you want to watch Helen." Dave was grinning, but he was serious too. "I told her it'd cost her fifty thousand!"

"*Huh?*"

"And she said okay, if you hurried."

Of course, there was only one thing to do, though I could have wrung fat Mrs. Van Styler's neck cheerfully. It wouldn't have happened if she'd used robots like everyone else—but she had to be different.

Consequently, while Dave was back home puttering with Helen, I was racking my brain to trick Archy Van Styler into getting the counterhormones, and giving the servant girl the same. Oh, I wasn't supposed to, but the poor kid was crazy about Archy. Dave might have written, I thought, but never a word did I get.

It was three weeks later instead of two when I reported that Archy was "cured," and collected on the line. With that money in my pocket, I hired a personal rocket and was back in Messina in half an hour. I didn't waste time in reaching the house.

As I stepped into the alcove, I heard a light patter of feet, and an eager voice called out, "Dave, dear?" For a minute I couldn't answer, and the voice came again, pleading, "Dave?"

I don't know what I expected, but I didn't expect Helen to meet me that way, stopping and staring at me, obvious disappointment on her face, little hands fluttering up against her breast.

"Oh," she cried. "I thought it was Dave. He hardly comes home to eat now, but I've had supper waiting hours." She dropped her hands and managed a smile. "You're Phil, aren't you? Dave told me about you when . . . at first. I'm so glad to see you home, Phil."

"Glad to see you doing so well, Helen." Now, what does one say for light conversation with a robot? "You said something about supper?"

"Oh, yes. I guess Dave ate downtown again, so we might as well go in. It'll be nice having someone to talk to around the house, Phil. You don't mind if I call you Phil, do you? You know, you're sort of a godfather to me."

We ate. I hadn't counted on such behavior, but apparently she considered eating as normal as walking. She didn't do much eating, at that; most of the time she spent staring at the front door.

Dave came in as we were finishing, a frown a yard wide on his face. Helen started to rise, but he ducked toward the stairs, throwing words over his shoulder.

"Hi, Phil. See you up here later."

There was something radically wrong with him. For a moment I'd thought his eyes were haunted, and as I turned to Helen hers were filling with tears. She gulped, choked them back, and fell to viciously on her food.

"What's the matter with him . . . and you?" I asked.

"He's sick of me." She pushed her plate away and got up hastily. "You'd better see him while I clean up. And there's nothing wrong with me. And it's not my fault, anyway." She grabbed the dishes and ducked into the kitchen; I could have sworn she was crying.

Maybe all thought is a series of conditioned reflexes—but she certainly had picked up a lot of conditioning while I was gone. Lena in her heyday had been nothing like this. I went up to see if Dave could make any sense out of the hodgepodge.

He was squirting soda into a large glass of apple brandy, and I saw that the bottle was nearly empty. "Join me?" he asked.

It seemed like a good idea. The roaring blast of an ion rocket overhead was the only familiar thing left in the house. From the look around Dave's eyes, it wasn't the first bottle he'd emptied while I was gone, and there were more left. He dug out a new bottle for his own drink.

"Of course, it's none of my business, Dave, but that stuff won't steady your nerves any. What's gotten into you and Helen? Been seeing ghosts?"

Helen was wrong; he hadn't been eating downtown—nor anywhere else. His muscles collapsed into a chain in a way that spoke of fatigue and nerves, but mostly of hunger. "You noticed it, eh?"

"Noticed it? The two of you jammed it down my throat."

'Uhmmm." He swatted at a nonexistent fly and slumped farther down in the pneumatic. "Guess maybe I should have waited with Helen until you got back. But if that stereo cast hadn't changed . . . Anyway, it did. And those mushy books of yours finished the job."

"Thanks. That makes it all clear."

"You know, Phil, I've got a place up in the country—fruit ranch. My dad left it to me. Think I'll look it over."

And that's the way it went. But finally, by much liquor and more perspiration, I got some of the story out of him before I gave him an amytal and put him to bed. Then I hunted up Helen and dug the rest of the story from her, until it made sense.

Apparently as soon as I was gone Dave had turned her on and made preliminary tests, which were entirely satisfactory. She had reacted beautifully—so well that he decided to leave her and go down to work as usual.

Naturally, with all her untried emotions, she was filled with curiosity and wanted him to stay. Then he had an inspiration. After showing her what her duties about the house would be, he set her down in front of the stereovisor, tuned in a travelogue, and left her to occupy her time with that.

The travelogue held her attention until it was finished, and the station switched over to a current serial with Larry Ainslee, the same cute emoter who'd given us all the trouble with the twins. Incidentally, he looked something like Dave.

Helen took to the serial like a seal to water. This play-acting was a perfect outlet for her newly excited emotions. When that particular episode finished, she found a love story on another station and added still more to her education. The afternoon programs were mostly news and music, but by then she'd found my books; and I do have rather adolescent taste in literature.

Dave came home in the best of spirits. The front alcove was neatly swept, and there was the odor of food in the air that he'd missed around the house for weeks. He had visions of Helen as the superefficient housekeeper.

So it was a shock to him to feel two strong arms around his neck from behind and hear a voice all aquiver coo into his ears, "Oh, Dave, darling, I've missed you so, and I'm so *thrilled* that you're back." Helen's technique may have lacked polish, but it had enthusiasm, as he found when he tried to stop her from kissing him. She had learned fast and furiously—also, Helen was powered by an atomotor.

Dave wasn't a prude, but he remembered that she was only a robot, after all. The fact that she felt, acted, and looked like a young goddess in his arms didn't mean much. With some effort, he untangled her and dragged her off to supper, where he made her eat with him to divert her attention.

After her evening work, he called her into the study and gave her a thorough lecture on the folly of her ways. It must have been good, for it lasted three solid hours and covered her station in life, the idiocy of stereos, and various other miscellanies. When he had finished, Helen looked up with dewy eyes and said wistfully, "I know, Dave, but I still love you."

That's when Dave started drinking.

It grew worse each day. If he stayed downtown, she was crying when he came home. If he returned on time, she fussed over him and threw herself at him. In his room, with door locked, he could hear her downstairs pacing up and down and muttering; and when he went down, she stared at him reproachfully until he had to go back up.

I sent Helen out on a fake errand in the morning and got Dave up. With her gone, I made him eat a decent breakfast and gave him a tonic for his nerves. He was still listless and moody.

"Look here, Dave," I broke in on his brooding. "Helen isn't

human, after all. Why not cut off her power and change a few memory coils? Then we can convince her that she never was in love and couldn't get that way."

"You try it. I had that idea, but she put up a wail that would wake Homer. She says it would be murder—and the hell of it is that I can't help feeling the same about it. Maybe she isn't human, but you wouldn't guess it when she puts on that martyred look and tells you to go ahead and kill her."

"We never put in substitutes for some of the secretions present in man during the love period."

"I don't know what we put in. Maybe the heterones backfired or something. Anyway, she's made this idea so much a part of her thoughts that we'd have to put in a whole new set of coils."

"Well, why not?"

"Go ahead. You're the surgeon of this family. I'm not used to fussing with emotions. Matter of fact, since she's been acting this way I'm beginning to hate work on any robot. My business is going to blazes."

He saw Helen coming up the walk and ducked out the back door for the monorail express. I'd intended to put him back in bed, but let him go. Maybe he'd be better off at his shop than at home.

"Dave's gone?" Helen did have that martyred look now.

"Yeah. I got him to eat, and he's gone to work."

"I'm glad he ate." She slumped down in a chair as if she were worn out, though how a mech could be tired beat me. "Phil?"

"Well, what is it?"

"Do you think I'm bad for him? I mean, do you think he'd be happier if I weren't here?"

"He'll go crazy if you keep acting this way around him."

She winced. Those little hands were twisting about pleadingly, and I felt like an inhuman brute. But I'd started, and I went ahead. "Even if I cut out your power and changed your coils, he'd probably still be haunted by you."

"I know. But I can't help it. And I'd make him a good wife, really I would, Phil."

I gulped; this was going a little too far. "And give him strapping sons to boot, I suppose. A man wants flesh and blood, not rubber and metal."

"Don't, please! I can't think of myself that way; to me, I'm a woman. And you know how perfectly I'm made to imitate a real woman—in all ways. I couldn't give him sons, but in every other way I'd try so hard, I know I'd make him a good wife."

I gave up.

Dave didn't come home that night, nor the next day. Helen was fussing and fuming, wanting me to call the hospitals and the police, but I knew nothing had happened to him. He always carried identification. Still, when he didn't come on the third day, I began to worry. And when Helen started out for his shop, I agreed to go with her.

Dave was there, with another man I didn't know. I parked Helen where he couldn't see her, but where she could hear, and went in as soon as the other fellow left.

Dave looked a little better and seemed glad to see me. "Hi, Phil—just closing up. Let's go eat."

Helen couldn't hold back any longer, but came trooping in. "Come on home, Dave. I've got roast duck with spice stuffing, and you know you love that."

"Scat!" said Dave. She shrank back, turned to go. "Oh, all right, stay. You might as well hear it, too. I've sold the shop. The fellow you saw just bought it, and I'm going up to the old fruit ranch I told you about, Phil. I can't stand the mechs any more."

"You'll starve to death at that," I told him.

"No, there's a growing demand for old-fashioned fruit, raised out of doors. People are tired of this water-culture stuff. Dad always made a living out of it. I'm leaving as soon as I can get home and pack."

Helen clung to her idea. "I'll pack, Dave, while you eat. I've got apple cobbler for dessert." The world was toppling under her feet, but she still remembered how crazy he was for apple cobbler.

Helen was a good cook; in fact she was a genius, with all the good points of a woman and a mech combined. Dave ate well enough, after he got started. By the time supper was over, he'd thawed out enough to admit he liked the duck and the cobbler, and to thank her for packing. In fact, he even let her kiss him goodbye, though he firmly refused to let her go to the rocket field with him.

Helen was trying to be brave when I got back, and we carried on a stumbling conversation about Mrs. Van Styler's servants for a while. But the talk began to lull, and she sat staring out of the window at nothing most of the time. Even the stereo comedy lacked interest for her, and I was glad enough to have her go off to her room. She could cut her power down to simulate sleep when she chose.

As the days slipped by, I began to realize why she couldn't believe herself a robot. I got to thinking of her as a girl and companion myself. Except for odd intervals when she went off by herself to brood, or when she kept going to the telescript for a letter that never came, she was as good a companion as a man could ask. There was something homey about the place that Lena had never put there.

I took Helen on a shopping trip to Hudson, and she giggled and purred over the wisps of silk and glassheen that were the fashion, tried on endless hats, and conducted herself as any normal girl might. We went trout fishing for a day, where she proved to be as good a sport and as sensibly silent as a man. I thoroughly enjoyed myself and thought she was forgetting Dave. That was before I came home unexpectedly and found her doubled up on the couch, threshing her legs up and down and crying to the high heavens.

It was then I called Dave. They seemed to have trouble in reaching him, and Helen came over beside me while I waited. She was tense and fidgety as an old maid trying to propose. But finally they located Dave.

"What's up, Phil?" he asked as his face came on the viewplate. "I was just getting my things together to—"

I broke him off. "Things can't go on the way they are, Dave. I've made up my mind. I'm yanking Helen's coils tonight. It won't be worse than what she's going through now."

Helen reached up and touched my shoulder. "Maybe that's best, Phil. I don't blame you."

Dave's voice cut in. "Phil, you don't know what you're doing!"

"Of course I do. It'll all be over by the time you can get here. As you heard, she's agreeing."

There was a black cloud sweeping over Dave's face. "I won't have it, Phil. She's half mine and I forbid it!"

"Of all the—"

"Go ahead, call me anything you want. I've changed my mind. I was packing to come home when you called."

Helen jerked around me, her eyes glued to the panel. "Dave, do you . . . are you . . ."

"I'm just waking up to what a fool I've been, Helen. Phil, I'll be home in a couple of hours, so if there's anything . . ."

He didn't have to chase me out. But I heard Helen cooing something about loving to be a rancher's wife before I could shut the door.

Well, I wasn't as surprised as they thought. I think I knew when I called Dave what would happen. No man acts the way Dave had been acting because he hates a girl; only because he thinks he does —and thinks wrong.

No woman ever made a lovelier bride or a sweeter wife. Helen never lost her flare for cooking and making a home. With her gone, the old house seemed empty, and I began to drop out to the ranch once or twice a week. I suppose they had trouble at times, but I never saw it, and I know the neighbors never suspected they were anything but normal man and wife.

Dave grew older, and Helen didn't, of course. But between us we put lines in her face and grayed her hair without letting Dave know that she wasn't growing old with him; he'd forgotten that she wasn't human, I guess.

I practically forgot, myself. It wasn't until a letter came from Helen this morning that I woke up to reality. There, in her beautiful script, just a trifle shaky in places, was the inevitable that neither Dave nor I had seen.

Dear Phil,

As you know, Dave has had heart trouble for several years now. We expected him to live on just the same, but it seems that wasn't to be. He died in my arms just before sunrise. He sent you his greetings and farewell.

I've one last favor to ask of you, Phil. There is only one thing for me to do when this is finished. Acid will burn out metal as well as flesh, and I'll be dead with Dave. Please see that we are buried together, and that the morticians do not find my secret. Dave wanted it that way, too.

Poor, dear Phil. I know you loved Dave as a brother, and how you felt about me. Please don't grieve too much for us, for we have had a happy life together, and both feel that we should cross this last bridge side by side.

With love and thanks from

HELEN

It had to come sooner or later, I suppose, and the first shock has worn off now. I'll be leaving in a few minutes to carry out Helen's last instructions.

Dave was a lucky man, and the best friend I ever had. And Helen—well, as I said, I'm an old man now and can view things more sanely; I should have married and raised a family, I suppose. But . . . there was only one Helen O'Loy.

THE COLD EQUATIONS

TOM GODWIN

I am reliably informed that this story, by a comparative unknown, drew more reader mail than any other story in the history of Astounding Science Fiction. *I am also reliably informed that it is possible to find a way out of the dilemma the story poses. Unfortunately, the first two methods proposed by my informant (who is not a science-fiction writer, but a working physicist) do not work.*

This is not Mr. Godwin's only story; it is, however, his best—and, as the nominations show, one of the best of all time. It requires an unusual writer and an unusual human being to look at the result which a situation demands rather than at one's own hopes (or, for that matter, the downbeat trend being what it is in sf., one's own fears). Mr. Godwin's gaze is steady, his understanding exact. When he or anybody else is going to turn out another story this final and this complete I have no idea. But I buy a good many science-fiction magazines and books each month hoping to find out.

He was not alone.

There was nothing to indicate the fact but the white hand of the tiny gauge on the board before him. The control room was empty but for himself; there was no sound other than the murmur of the drives—but the white hand had moved. It had been on zero when the little ship was launched from the *Stardust;* now, an hour later, it had crept up. There was something in the supplies closet across the room, it was saying, some kind of a body that radiated heat.

It could be but one kind of a body—a living, human body.

He leaned back in the pilot's chair and drew a deep, slow breath, considering what he would have to do. He was an EDS pilot, inured to the sight of death, long since accustomed to it and to viewing the dying of another man with an objective lack of emotion, and he had no choice in what he must do. There could be no alternative—but it required a few moments of conditioning for even an EDS pilot to prepare himself to walk across the room and coldly, deliberately, take the life of a man he had yet to meet.

He would, of course, do it. It was the law, stated very bluntly and definitely in grim Paragraph L, Section 8, of Interstellar Regulations: *"Any stowaway discovered in an EDS shall be jettisoned immediately following discovery."*

It was the law, and there could be no appeal.

It was a law not of men's choosing but made imperative by the circumstances of the space frontier. Galactic expansion had followed the development of the hyperspace drive, and as men scattered wide across the frontier there had come the problem of contact with the isolated first colonies and exploration parties. The huge hyperspace cruisers were the product of the combined genius and effort of Earth and were long and expensive in the building. They were not available in such numbers that small colonies could possess them. The cruisers carried the colonists to their new worlds and made periodic visits, running on tight schedules, but they could not stop and turn aside to visit colonies scheduled to be visited at another time; such a delay would destroy their schedule and produce a confusion and uncertainty that would wreck the complex interdependence between old Earth and the new worlds of the frontier.

Some method of delivering supplies or assistance when an emergency occurred on a world not scheduled for a visit had been needed, and the Emergency Dispatch Ships had been the answer. Small and collapsible, they occupied little room in the hold of the cruiser; made of light metal and plastics, they were driven by a small rocket drive that consumed relatively little fuel. Each cruiser carried four EDS's, and when a call for aid was received the nearest cruiser would drop into normal space long enough to launch an EDS with the needed supplies or personnel, then vanish again as it continued on its course.

The cruisers, powered by nuclear converters, did not use the liquid rocket fuel, but nuclear converters were far too large and complex to permit their installation in the EDS's. The cruisers were forced by necessity to carry a limited amount of the bulky rocket fuel, and the fuel was rationed with care, the cruiser's computers determining the exact amount of fuel each EDS would require for its mission. The computers considered the course coordinates, the mass of the EDS, the mass of pilot and cargo; they were very precise and accurate and omitted nothing from their calculations. They could not, however, foresee and allow for the added mass of a stowaway.

The *Stardust* had received the request from one of the exploration parties stationed on Woden, the six men of the party already being stricken with the fever carried by the green kala midges and their own supply of serum destroyed by the tornado that had torn through their camp. The *Stardust* had gone through the usual procedure, dropping into normal space to launch the EDS with the fever serum, then vanishing again in hyperspace. Now, an hour later, the gauge was saying there was something more than the small carton of serum in the supplies closet.

He let his eyes rest on the narrow white door of the closet. There, just inside, another man lived and breathed and was beginning to feel assured that discovery of his presence would now be too late for the pilot to alter the situation. It *was* too late; for the man behind the door it was far later than he thought and in a way he would find terrible to believe.

There could be no alternative. Additional fuel would be used during the hours of deceleration to compensate for the added mass of the stowaway; infinitesimal increments of fuel that would not be missed until the ship had almost reached its destination. Then, at some distance above the ground that might be as near as a thousand feet or as far as tens of thousands of feet, depending upon the mass of ship and cargo and the preceding period of deceleration, the unmissed increments of fuel would make their absence known; the EDS would expend its last drops of fuel with a sputter and go into whistling free fall. Ship and pilot and stowaway would merge together upon impact as a wreckage of metal and plastic, flesh and blood, driven deep into the soil. The stowaway had signed his own death warrant when he concealed himself on the ship; he could not be permitted to take seven others with him.

He looked again at the telltale white hand, then rose to his feet. What he must do would be unpleasant for both of them; the sooner it was over, the better. He stepped across the control room to stand by the white door.

"Come out!" His command was harsh and abrupt above the murmur of the drive.

It seemed he could hear the whisper of a furtive movement inside the closet, then nothing. He visualized the stowaway cowering closer into one corner, suddenly worried by the possible consequences of his act, his self-assurance evaporating.

"I said *out!*"

He heard the stowaway move to obey, and he waited with his eyes alert on the door and his hand near the blaster at his side.

The door opened and the stowaway stepped through it, smiling. "All right—I give up. Now what?"

It was a girl.

He stared without speaking, his hand dropping away from the blaster and acceptance of what he saw coming like a heavy and unexpected physical blow. The stowaway was not a man—she was a girl in her teens, standing before him in little white gypsy sandals, with the top of her brown, curly head hardly higher than his shoulder, with a faint, sweet scent of perfume coming from her, and her smiling face tilted up so her eyes could look unknowing and unafraid into his as she waited for his answer.

Now what? Had it been asked in the deep, defiant voice of a man he would have answered it with action, quick and efficient. He would have taken the stowaway's identification disk and ordered him into the air lock. Had the stowaway refused to obey, he would have used the blaster. It would not have taken long; within a minute the body would have been ejected into space— had the stowaway been a man.

He returned to the pilot's chair and motioned her to seat herself on the boxlike bulk of the drive-control units that were set against the wall beside him. She obeyed, his silence making the smile fade into the meek and guilty expression of a pup that has been caught in mischief and knows it must be punished.

"You still haven't told me," she said. "I'm guilty, so what happens to me now? Do I pay a fine, or what?"

"What are you doing here?" he asked. "Why did you stow away on this EDS?"

"I wanted to see my brother. He's with the government survey crew on Woden and I haven't seen him for ten years, not since he left Earth to go into government survey work."

"What was your destination on the *Stardust?*"

"Mimir. I have a position waiting for me there. My brother has been sending money home all the time to us—my father and mother and I—and he paid for a special course in linguistics I was taking. I graduated sooner than expected and I was offered this job on Mimir. I knew it would be almost a year before Gerry's job was done on Woden so he could come on to Mimir, and that's why I hid in the closet there. There was plenty of room for me and I was willing to pay the fine. There were only the two of us kids—Gerry and I—and I haven't seen him for so long, and I didn't want to wait another year when I could see him now, even though I knew I would be breaking some kind of a regulation when I did it."

I knew I would be breaking some kind of a regulation. In a way, she could not be blamed for her ignorance of the law; she was of Earth and had not realized that the laws of the space frontier must, of necessity, be as hard and relentless as the environment that gave them birth. Yet, to protect such as her from the results of their own ignorance of the frontier, there had been a sign over the door that led to the section of the *Stardust* that housed the EDS's; a sign that was plain for all to see and heed: UNAUTHORIZED PERSONNEL KEEP OUT!

"Does your brother know that you took passage on the *Stardust* for Mimir?"

"Oh, yes. I sent him a spacegram telling him about my graduation and about going to Mimir on the *Stardust* a month before I left Earth. I already knew Mimir was where he would be stationed in a little over a year. He gets a promotion then, and he'll be based on Mimir and not have to stay out a year at a time on field trips, like he does now."

There were two different survey groups on Woden, and he asked, "What is his name?"

"Cross—Gerry Cross. He's in Group Two—that was the way his address read. Do you know him?"

Group One had requested the serum; Group Two was eight thousand miles away, across the Western Sea.

"No, I've never met him," he said, then turned to the control board and cut the deceleration to a fraction of a gravity, knowing as he did so that it could not avert the ultimate end, yet doing the only thing he could do to prolong that ultimate end. The sensation was like that of the ship suddenly dropping, and the girl's involuntary movement of surprise half lifted her from the seat.

"We're going faster now, aren't we?" she asked. "Why are we doing that?"

He told her the truth. "To save fuel for a little while."

"You mean we don't have very much?"

He delayed the answer he must give her so soon to ask, "How did you manage to stow away?"

"I just sort of walked in when no one was looking my way," she said. "I was practicing my Gelanese on the native girl who does the cleaning in the Ship's Supply office when someone came in with an order for supplies for the survey crew on Woden. I slipped into the closet there after the ship was ready to go and just before you came in. It was an impulse of the moment to stow away, so I could get to see Gerry—and from the way you keep looking at me so grim, I'm not sure it was a very wise impulse. But I'll be a model criminal—or do I mean prisoner?" She smiled at him again. "I intended to pay for my keep on top of paying the fine. I can cook and I can patch clothes for everyone and I know how to do all kinds of useful things, even a little bit about nursing."

There was one more question to ask:

"Did you know what the supplies were that the survey crew ordered?"

"Why, no. Equipment they needed in their work, I supposed."

Why couldn't she have been a man with some ulterior motive? A fugitive from justice, hoping to lose himself on a raw new world; an opportunist, seeking transportation to the new colonies where he might find golden fleece for the taking; a crackpot with a mission. Perhaps once in his lifetime an EDS pilot would find such a stowaway on his ship—warped men, mean and selfish men, brutal and dangerous men—but never before a smiling blue-eyed girl who was willing to pay her fine and work for her keep that she might see her brother.

He turned to the board and turned the switch that would signal the *Stardust*. The call would be futile, but he could not, until he had exhausted that one vain hope, seize her and thrust her into the air lock as he would an animal—or a man. The delay, in the meantime, would not be dangerous with the EDS decelerating at fractional gravity.

A voice spoke from the communicator. "*Stardust*. Identify yourself and proceed."

"Barton, EDS 34G11. Emergency. Give me Commander Delhart."

There was a faint confusion of noises as the request went through the proper channels. The girl was watching him, no longer smiling.

"Are you going to order them to come back after me?" she asked.

The communicator clicked and there was the sound of a distant voice saying, "Commander, the EDS requests . . ."

"Are they coming back after me?" she asked again. "Won't I get to see my brother after all?"

"Barton?" The blunt, gruff voice of Commander Delhart came from the communicator. "What's this about an emergency?"

"A stowaway," he answered.

"A stowaway?" There was a slight surprise to the question. "That's rather unusual—but why the 'emergency' call? You discovered him in time, so there should be no appreciable danger, and I presume you've informed Ship's Records so his nearest relatives can be notified."

"That's why I had to call you, first. The stowaway is still aboard and the circumstances are so different—"

"Different?" the commander interrupted, impatience in his voice. "How can they be different? You know you have a limited supply of fuel; you also know the law as well as I do: 'Any stowaway discovered in an EDS shall be jettisoned immediately following discovery.'"

There was the sound of a sharply indrawn breath from the girl. "*What does he mean?*"

"The stowaway is a girl."

"*What?*"

"She wanted to see her brother. She's only a kid and she didn't know what she was really doing."

"I see." All the curtness was gone from the commander's voice. "So you called me in the hope I could do something?" Without waiting for an answer he went on, "I'm sorry—I can do nothing. This cruiser must maintain its schedule; the life of not one person but the lives of many depend on it. I know how you feel but I'm powerless to help you. You'll have to go through with it. I'll have you connected with Ship's Records."

The communicator faded to a faint rustle of sound, and he turned back to the girl. She was leaning forward on the bench, almost rigid, her eyes fixed wide and frightened.

"What did he mean, to go through with it? To jettison me . . . to go through with it—what did he mean? Not the way it sounded . . . he couldn't have. What did he mean—what did he really mean?"

Her time was too short for the comfort of a lie to be more than a cruelly fleeting delusion.

"He meant it the way it sounded."

"*No!*" She recoiled from him as though he had struck her, one hand half upraised as though to fend him off and stark unwillingness to believe in her eyes.

"It will have to be."

"No! You're joking—you're insane! You can't mean it!"

"I'm sorry." He spoke slowly to her, gently. "I should have told you before—I should have, but I had to do what I could first; I had to call the *Stardust*. You heard what the commander said."

"But you can't—if you make me leave the ship, I'll *die*."

"I know."

She searched his face, and the unwillingness to believe left her eyes, giving way slowly to a look of dazed horror.

"You know?" She spoke the words far apart, numb and wonderingly.

"I know. It has to be like that."

"You mean it—you really mean it." She sagged back against the wall, small and limp like a little rag doll, and all the protesting and disbelief gone. "You're going to do it—you're going to make me die?"

"I'm sorry," he said again. "You'll never know how sorry I am. It has to be that way and no human in the universe can change it."

"You're going to make me die and I didn't do anything to die for—I didn't *do* anything—"

He sighed, deep and weary. "I know you didn't, child. I know you didn't."

"EDS." The communicator rapped brisk and metallic. "This is Ship's Records. Give us all information on subject's identification disk."

He got out of his chair to stand over her. She clutched the edge of the seat, her upturned face white under the brown hair and the lipstick standing out like a blood-red cupid's bow.

"*Now?*"

"I want your identification disk," he said.

She released the edge of the seat and fumbled at the chain that suspended the plastic disk from her neck with fingers that were trembling and awkward. He reached down and unfastened the clasp for her, then returned with the disk to his chair.

"Here's your data, Records: Identification Number T837—"

"One moment," Records interrupted. "This is to be filed on the gray card, of course?"

"Yes."

"And the time of the execution?"

"I'll tell you later."

"Later? This is highly irregular; the time of the subject's death is required before—"

He kept the thickness out of his voice with an effort. "Then we'll do it in a highly irregular manner—you'll hear the disk read first. The subject is a girl and she's listening to everything that's said. Are you capable of understanding that?"

There was a brief, almost shocked silence, then Records said meekly, "Sorry. Go ahead."

He began to read the disk, reading it slowly to delay the inevitable for as long as possible, trying to help her by giving her what little time he could to recover from her first horror and let it resolve into the calm of acceptance and resignation.

"Number T8374 dash Y54. Name, Marilyn Lee Cross. Sex, female. Born July 7, 2160." *She was only eighteen.* "Height, five-three. Weight, a hundred and ten." *Such a slight weight, yet enough to add fatally to the mass of the shell-thin bubble that was an EDS.* "Hair, brown. Eyes, blue. Complexion, light. Blood type,

O." *Irrelevant data.* "Destination, Port City, Mimir." *Invalid data.*

He finished and said, "I'll call you later," then turned once again to the girl. She was huddled back against the wall, watching him with a look of numb and wondering fascination.

"They're waiting for you to kill me, aren't they? They want me dead, don't they? You and everybody on the cruiser want me dead, don't you?" Then the numbness broke and her voice was that of a frightened and bewildered child. "Everybody wants me dead and I didn't *do* anything. I didn't hurt anyone—I only wanted to see my brother."

"It's not the way you think—it isn't that way at all," he said. "Nobody wants it this way; nobody would ever let it be this way if it was humanly possible to change it."

"Then why is it? I don't understand. Why is it?"

"This ship is carrying kala fever serum to Group One on Woden. Their own supply was destroyed by a tornado. Group Two—the crew your brother is in—is eight thousand miles away across the Western Sea, and their helicopters can't cross it to help Group One. The fever is invariably fatal unless the serum can be had in time, and the six men in Group One will die unless this ship reaches them on schedule. These little ships are always given barely enough fuel to reach their destination, and if you stay aboard your added weight will cause it to use up all its fuel before it reaches the ground. It will crash then, and you and I will die and so will the six men waiting for the fever serum."

It was a full minute before she spoke, and as she considered his words the expression of numbness left her eyes.

"Is that it?" she asked at last. "Just that the ship doesn't have enough fuel?"

"Yes."

"I can go alone or I can take seven others with me—is that the way it is?"

"That's the way it is."

"And nobody wants me to have to die?"

"Nobody."

"Then maybe— Are you sure nothing can be done about it? Wouldn't people help me if they could?"

"Everyone would like to help you, but there is nothing anyone can do. I did the only thing I could do when I called the *Stardust*."

"And it won't come back—but there might be other cruisers, mightn't there? Isn't there any hope at all that there might be someone, somewhere, who could do something to help me?"

She was leaning forward a little in her eagerness as she waited for his answer.

"No."

The word was like the drop of a cold stone and she again leaned back against the wall, the hope and eagerness leaving her face. "You're sure—you *know* you're sure?"

"I'm sure. There are no other cruisers within forty light-years; there is nothing and no one to change things."

She dropped her gaze to her lap and began twisting a pleat of her skirt between her fingers, saying no more as her mind began to adapt itself to the grim knowledge.

It was better so; with the going of all hope would go the fear; with the going of all hope would come resignation. She needed time and she could have so little of it. How much?

The EDS's were not equipped with hull-cooling units; their speed had to be reduced to a moderate level before entering the atmosphere. They were decelerating at .10 gravity, approaching their distination at a far higher speed than the computers had calculated on. The *Stardust* had been quite near Woden when she launched the EDS; their present velocity was putting them nearer by the second. There would be a critical point, soon to be reached, when he would have to resume deceleration. When he did so the girl's weight would be multiplied by the gravities of deceleration, would become, suddenly, a factor of paramount importance, the factor the computers had been ignorant of when they determined the amount of fuel the EDS should have. She would have to go when deceleration began; it could be no other way. When would that be—how long could he let her stay?

"How long can I stay?"

He winced involuntarily from the words that were so like an echo of his own thoughts. How long? He didn't know; he would have to ask the ship's computers. Each EDS was given a meager surplus of fuel to compensate for unfavorable conditions within the atmosphere, and relatively little fuel was being consumed for the time being. The memory banks of the computers would still contain all data pertaining to the course set for the EDS; such data would not be erased until the EDS reached its destination. He had only to give the computers the new data—the girl's weight and the exact time at which he had reduced the deceleration to .10.

"Barton." Commander Delhart's voice came abruptly from the communicator as he opened his mouth to call the *Stardust*. "A check with Records shows me you haven't completed your report. Did you reduce the deceleration?"

So the commander knew what he was trying to do.

"I'm decelerating at point ten," he answered. "I cut the deceleration at seventeen fifty and the weight is a hundred and ten. I would like to stay at point ten as long as the computers say I can. Will you give them the question?"

It was contrary to regulations for an EDS pilot to make any changes in the course or degree of deceleration the computers had set for him, but the commander made no mention of the violation. Neither did he ask the reason for it. It was not necessary for him to ask; he had not become commander of an interstellar cruiser without both intelligence and an understanding of human nature. He said only, "I'll have that given the computers."

The communicator fell silent and he and the girl waited, neither of them speaking. They would not have to wait long; the computers would give the answer within moments of the asking. The new factors would be fed into the steel maw of the first bank and the electrical impulses would go through the complex circuits. Here and there a relay might click, a tiny cog turn over, but it would be essentially the electrical impulses that found the answer; formless, mindless, invisible, determining with utter precision how long the pale girl beside him might live. Then five little segments of metal in the second bank would trip in rapid succession against an inked ribbon and a second steel maw would spit out the slip of paper that bore the answer.

The chronometer on the instrument board read 18:10 when the commander spoke again.

"You will resume deceleration at nineteen ten."

She looked toward the chronometer, then quickly away from it. "Is that when . . . when I go?" she asked. He nodded and she dropped her eyes to her lap again.

"I'll have the course correction given you," the commander said. "Ordinarily I would never permit anything like this, but I understand your position. There is nothing I can do, other than what I've just done, and you will not deviate from these new instructions. You will complete your report at nineteen ten. Now—here are the course corrections."

The voice of some unknown technician read them to him, and he wrote them down on the pad clipped to the edge of the control board. There would, he saw, be periods of deceleration when he neared the atmosphere when the deceleration would be five gravities—and at five gravities one hundred ten pounds would become five hundred fifty pounds.

The technician finished and he terminated the contact with a brief acknowledgment. Then, hesitating a moment, he reached out and shut off the communicator. It was 18:13 and he would have nothing to report until 19:10. In the meantime, it somehow seemed indecent to permit others to hear what she might say in her last hour.

He began to check the instrument readings, going over them with unecessary slowness. She would have to accept the circumstances, and there was nothing he could do to help her into acceptance; words of sympathy would only delay it.

It was 18:20 when she stirred from her motionlessness and spoke.

"So that's the way it has to be with me?"

He swung around to face her. "You understand now, don't you? No one would ever let it be like this if it could be changed."

"I understand," she said. Some of the color had returned to her face and the lipstick no longer stood out so vividly red. "There isn't enough fuel for me to stay. When I hid on this ship I got into something I didn't know anything about and now I have to pay for it."

She had violated a man-made law that said KEEP OUT, but the penalty was not for men's making or desire and it was a penalty men could not revoke. A physical law had decreed: *h amount of fuel will power an EDS with a mass of m safely to its destination;* and a second physical law had decreed: *h amount of fuel will not power an EDS with a mass of m plus x safely to its destination.*

EDS's obeyed only physical laws, and no amount of human sympathy for her could alter the second law.

"But I'm afraid. I don't want to die—not now. I want to live, and nobody is doing anything to help me; everybody is letting me go ahead and acting just like nothing was going to happen to me. I'm going to die and nobody *cares*."

"We all do," he said. "I do and the commander does and the clerk in Ship's Records; we all care and each of us did what little he could to help you. It wasn't enough—it was almost nothing—but it was all we could do."

"Not enough fuel—I can understand that," she said, as though she had not heard his own words. "But to have to die for it. *Me* alone . . ."

How hard it must be for her to accept the fact. She had never known danger of death; had never known the environments where the lives of men could be as fragile and fleeting as sea foam tossed against a rocky shore. She belonged on gentle Earth, in that secure and peaceful society where she could be young and gay and laughing with the others of her kind; where life was precious and well guarded and there was always the assurance that tomorrow would come. She belonged in that world of soft winds and a warm sun, music and moonlight and gracious manners, and not on the hard, bleak frontier.

"How did it happen to me so terribly quickly? An hour ago I was on the *Stardust*, going to Mimir. Now the *Stardust* is going on without me and I'm going to die and I'll never see Gerry and Mama and Daddy again—I'll never see anything again."

He hesitated, wondering how he could explain it to her so she would really understand and not feel she had somehow been the victim of a reasonlessly cruel injustice. She did not know what the frontier was like; she thought in terms of safe-secure Earth. Pretty girls were not jettisoned on Earth; there was a law against it. On Earth her plight would have filled the newscasts and a fast black patrol ship would have been racing to her rescue. Everyone, everywhere, would have known of Marilyn Lee Cross, and no effort would have been spared to save her life. But this was not Earth and there were no patrol ships; only the *Stardust*, leaving them behind at many times the speed of light. There was no one to help her, there would be no Marilyn Lee Cross smiling from the newscasts tomorrow. Marilyn Lee Cross would be but a poignant memory for an EDS pilot and a name on a gray card in Ship's Records.

"It's different here; it's not like back on Earth," he said. "It isn't that no one cares; it's that no one can do anything to help. The frontier is big, and here along its rim the colonies and exploration parties are scattered so thin and far between. On Woden, for example, there are only sixteen men—sixteen men on an entire world. The exploration parties, the survey crews, the little first colonies—they're all fighting alien environments, trying to make a way for those who will follow after. The environments fight back, and those who go first usually make mistakes only once. There is no margin of safety along the rim of the frontier; there can't be until the way is made for the others who will come later, until the new worlds are tamed and settled. Until then men will have to pay the penalty for making mistakes, with no one to help them, because there is no one *to* help them."

"I was going to Mimir," she said. "I didn't know about the frontier; I was only going to Mimir and *it's* safe."

"Mimir is safe, but you left the cruiser that was taking you there."

She was silent for a little while. "It was all so wonderful at first; there was plenty of room for me on this ship and I would be seeing Gerry so soon. I didn't know about the fuel, didn't know what would happen to me . . ."

Her words trailed away, and he turned his attention to the viewscreen, not wanting to stare at her as she fought her way through the black horror of fear toward the calm gray of acceptance.

Woden was a ball, enshrouded in the blue haze of its atmosphere, swimming in space against the background of star-sprinkled dead blackness. The great mass of Manning's Continent sprawled like a gigantic hourglass in the Eastern Sea, with the western half of the Eastern Continent still visible. There was a thin line of shadow along the right-hand edge of the globe, and the Eastern Continent was disappearing into it as the planet turned on its axis. An hour before, the entire continent had been in view; now a thousand miles of it had gone into the thin edge of shadow and around to the night that lay on the other side of the world. The dark-blue spot that was Lotus Lake was approaching the shadow. It was somewhere near the southern edge of the lake that Group Two had their camp. It would be night there soon, and quick behind the coming of night the rotation of Woden on its axis would put Group Two beyond the reach of the ship's radio.

He would have to tell her before it was too late for her to talk to her brother. In a way, it would be better for both of them should they not do so, but it was not for him to decide. To each of them the last words would be something to hold and cherish, something that would cut like the blade of a knife yet would be infinitely precious to remember, she for her own brief moments to live and he for the rest of his life.

He held down the button that would flash the grid lines on the viewscreen and used the known diameter of the planet to estimate the distance the southern tip of Lotus Lake had yet to go until it passed beyond radio range. It was approximately five hundred miles. Five hundred miles; thirty minutes—and the chronometer read 18:30. Allowing for error in estimating, it could not be later than 19:05 that the turning of Woden would cut off her brother's voice.

The first border of the Western Continent was already in sight along the left side of the world. Four thousand miles across it lay the shore of the Western Sea and the camp of Group One. It had been in the Western Sea that the tornado had originated, to strike with such fury at the camp and destroy half their prefabricated buildings, including the one that housed the medical supplies. Two days before, the tornado had not existed; it had been no more than great gentle masses of air out over the calm Western Sea. Group One had gone about their routine survey work, unaware of the meeting of air masses out at sea, unaware of the force the union was spawning. It had struck their camp without warning—a thundering, roaring destruction that sought to annihilate all that lay before it. It had passed on, leaving the wreckage in its wake. It had destroyed the labor of months and had doomed six men to die and then, as though its task was accomplished, it once more began to resolve into gentle masses of air. But, for all its deadliness, it had destroyed with neither malice nor intent. It had been a blind and mindless force, obeying the laws of nature, and it would have followed the same course with the same fury had men never existed.

Existence required order, and there was order; the laws of nature, irrevocable and immutable. Men could learn to use them, but men could not change them. The circumference of a circle was always pi times the diameter, and no science of man would ever make it otherwise. The combination of chemical A with chemical B under condition C invariably produced reaction D. The law of gravitation was a rigid equation, and it made no distinction between the fall of a leaf and the ponderous circling of a binary star system. The nuclear conversion process powered the cruisers that carried men to the stars; the same process in the form of a nova would destroy a world with equal efficiency. The laws *were*, and the universe moved in obedience to them. Along the frontier were arrayed all the forces of nature, and sometimes they destroyed those who were fighting their way outward from Earth. The men of the frontier had long ago learned the bitter futility of cursing the forces that would destroy them, for the forces were blind and deaf; the futility of looking to the heavens for mercy, for the stars of the galaxy swung in their long, long sweep of two hundred million years, as inexorably controlled as they by the laws that knew neither hatred nor compassion. The men of the frontier knew—but how was a girl from Earth to fully understand? *H amount of fuel will not power an EDS with a mass of m plus x safely to its destination.* To himself and her brother and parents she was a sweet-faced girl in her teens; to the laws of nature she was *x*, the unwanted factor in a cold equation.

She stirred again on the seat. "Could I write a letter? I want to write to Mama and Daddy. And I'd like to talk to Gerry. Could you let me talk to him over your radio there?"

"I'll try to get him," he said.

He switched on the normal-space transmitter and pressed the signal button. Someone answered the buzzer almost immediately.

"Hello. How's it going with you fellows now—is the EDS on its way?"

"This isn't Group One; this is the EDS," he said. "Is Gerry Cross there?"

"Gerry? He and two others went out in the helicopter this morning and aren't back yet. It's almost sundown, though, and he ought to be back right away—in less than an hour at the most."

"Can you connect me through to the radio in his 'copter?"

"Huh-uh. It's been out of commission for two months—some

printed circuits went haywire and we can't get any more until the next cruiser stops by. Is it something important—bad news for him, or something?"

"Yes—it's very important. When he comes in get him to the transmitter as soon as you possibly can."

"I'll do that; I'll have one of the boys waiting at the field with a truck. Is there anything else I can do?"

"No, I guess that's all. Get him there as soon as you can and signal me."

He turned the volume to an inaudible minimum, an act that would not affect the functioning of the signal buzzer, and unclipped the pad of paper from the control board. He tore off the sheet containing his flight instructions and handed the pad to her, together with pencil.

"I'd better write to Gerry too," she said as she took them. "He might not get back to camp in time."

She began to write, her fingers still clumsy and uncertain in the way they handled the pencil, and the top of it trembling a little as she poised it between words. He turned back to the viewscreen, to stare at it without seeing it.

She was a lonely little child trying to say her last goodbye, and she would lay out her heart to them. She would tell them how much she loved them and she would tell them to not feel badly about it, that it was only something that must happen eventually to everyone and she was not afraid. The last would be a lie and it would be there to read between the sprawling uneven lines: a valiant little lie that would make the hurt all the greater for them.

Her brother was of the frontier and he would understand. He would not hate the EDS pilot for doing nothing to prevent her going; he would know there had been nothing the pilot could do. He would understand, though the understanding would not soften the shock and pain when he learned his sister was gone. But the others, her father and mother—they would not understand. They were of Earth and they would think in the manner of those who had never lived where the safety margin of life was a thin, thin line—and sometimes not at all. What would they think of the faceless, unknown pilot who had sent her to her death?

They would hate him with cold and terrible intensity, but it really didn't matter. He would never see them, never know them.

He would have only the memories to remind him; only the nights to fear, when a blue-eyed girl in gypsy sandals would come in his dreams to die again. . . .

He scowled at the viewscreen and tried to force his thoughts into less emotional channels. There was nothing he could do to help her. She had unknowingly subjected herself to the penalty of a law that recognized neither innocence nor youth nor beauty, that was incapable of sympathy or leniency. Regret was illogical—and yet, could knowing it to be illogical ever keep it away?

She stopped occasionally, as though trying to find the right words to tell them what she wanted them to know, then the pencil would resume its whispering to the paper. It was 18:37 when she folded the letter in a square and wrote a name on it. She began writing another, twice looking up at the chronometer as though she feared the black hand might reach its rendezvous before she had finished. It was 18:45 when she folded it as she had done the first letter and wrote a name and address on it.

She held the letters out to him. "Will you take care of these and see that they're enveloped and mailed?"

"Of course." He took them from her hand and placed them in a pocket of his gray uniform shirt.

"These can't be sent off until the next cruiser stops by, and the *Stardust* will have long since told them about me, won't it?" she asked. He nodded and she went on: "That makes the letters not important in one way, but in another way they're very important —to me, and to them."

"I know. I understand, and I'll take care of them."

She glanced at the chronometer, then back to him. "It seems to move faster all the time, doesn't it?"

He said nothing, unable to think of anything to say, and she asked, "Do you think Gerry will come back to camp in time?"

"I think so. They said he should be in right away."

She began to roll the pencil back and forth between her palms. "I hope he does. I feel sick and scared and I want to hear his voice again and maybe I won't feel so alone. I'm a coward and I can't help it."

"No," he said, "you're not a coward. You're afraid, but you're not a coward."

"Is there a difference?"

He nodded. "A lot of difference."

"I feel so alone. I never did feel like this before; like I was all by myself and there was nobody to care what happened to me. Always, before, there was Mama and Daddy there and my friends around me. I had lots of friends, and they had a going-away party for me the night before I left."

Friends and music and laughter for her to remember—and on the viewscreen Lotus Lake was going into the shadow.

"Is it the same with Gerry?" she asked. "I mean, if he should make a mistake, would he have to die for it, all alone and with no one to help him?"

"It's the same with all, along the frontier; it will always be like that so long as there is a frontier."

"Gerry didn't tell us. He said the pay was good, and he sent money home all the time because Daddy's little shop just brought in a bare living, but he didn't tell us it was like this."

"He didn't tell you his work was dangerous?"

"Well—yes. He mentioned that, but we didn't understand. I always thought danger along the frontier was something that was a lot of fun; an exciting adventure, like in the three-D shows." A wan smile touched her face for a moment. "Only it's not, is it? It's not the same at all, because when it's real you can't go home after the show is over."

"No," he said. "No, you can't."

Her glance flicked from the chronometer to the door of the air lock, then down to the pad and pencil she still held. She shifted her position slightly to lay them on the bench beside her, moving one foot out a little. For the first time he saw that she was not wearing Vegan gypsy sandals, but only cheap imitations; the expensive Vegan leather was some kind of grained plastic, the silver buckle was gilded iron, the jewels were colored glass. *Daddy's little shop just brought in a bare living* . . . She must have left college in her second year, to take the course in linguistics that would enable her to make her own way and help her brother provide for her parents, earning what she could by part-time work after classes were over. Her personal possessions on the *Stardust* would be taken back to her parents—they would neither be of much value nor occupy much storage space on the return voyage.

"Isn't it—" She stopped, and he looked at her questioningly.

"Isn't it cold in here?" she asked, almost apologetically. "Doesn't it seem cold to you?"

"Why, yes," he said. He saw by the main temperature gauge that the room was at precisely normal temperature. "Yes, it's colder than it should be."

"I wish Gerry would get back before it's too late. Do you really think he will, and you didn't just say so to make me feel better?"

"I think he will—they said he would be in pretty soon." On the viewscreen Lotus Lake had gone into the shadow but for the thin blue line of its western edge, and it was apparent he had overestimated the time she would have in which to talk to her brother. Reluctantly, he said to her, "His camp will be out of radio range in a few minutes; he's on that part of Woden that's in the shadow" —he indicated the viewscreen—"and the turning of Woden will put him beyond contact. There may not be much time left when he comes in—not much time to talk to him before he fades out. I wish I could do something about it—I would call him right now if I could."

"Not even as much time as I will have to stay?"

"I'm afraid not."

"Then—" She straightened and looked toward the air lock with pale resolution. "Then I'll go when Gerry passes beyond range. I won't wait any longer after that—I won't have anything to wait for."

Again there was nothing he could say.

"Maybe I shouldn't wait at all. Maybe I'm selfish—maybe it would be better for Gerry if you just told him about it afterward."

There was an unconscious pleading for denial in the way she spoke and he said, "He wouldn't want you to do that, to not wait for him."

"It's already coming dark where he is, isn't it? There will be all the long night before him, and Mama and Daddy don't know yet that I won't ever be coming back like I promised them I would. I've caused everyone I love to be hurt, haven't I? I didn't want to —I didn't intend to."

"It wasn't your fault," he said. "It wasn't your fault at all. They'll know that. They'll understand."

"At first I was so afraid to die that I was a coward and thought only of myself. Now I see how selfish I was. The terrible thing about dying like this is not that I'll be gone but that I'll never see them again; never be able to tell them that I didn't take them for granted; never be able to tell them I knew of the sacrifices they made to make my life happier, that I knew all the things they did for me and that I loved them so much more than I ever told them. I've never told them any of those things. You don't tell them such things when you're young and your life is all before you—you're so very afraid of sounding sentimental and silly. But it's so different when you have to die—you wish you had told them while you could and you wish you could tell them you're sorry for all the little mean things you ever did or said to them. You wish you could tell them that you didn't really mean to ever hurt their feelings and for them to only remember that you always loved them far more than you ever let them know."

"You don't have to tell them that," he said. "They will know—they've always known it."

"Are you sure?" she asked. "How can you be sure? My people are strangers to you."

"Wherever you go, human nature and human hearts are the same."

"And they will know what I want them to know—that I love them?"

"They've always known it, in a way far better than you could ever put in words for them."

"I keep remembering the things they did for me, and it's the little things they did that seem to be the most important to me, now. Like Gerry—he sent me a bracelet of fire-rubies on my sixteenth birthday. It was beautiful—it must have cost him a month's pay. Yet I remember him more for what he did the night my kitten got run over in the street. I was only six years old and he held me in his arms and wiped away my tears and told me not to cry, that Flossy was gone for just a little while, for just long enough to get herself a new fur coat, and she would be on the foot of my bed the very next morning. I believed him and quit crying and went to sleep dreaming about my kitten coming back. When I woke up the next morning, there was Flossy on the foot of my bed in a brand-new white fur coat, just like he had said she would be. It wasn't until a long time later that Mama told me

Gerry had got the pet-shop owner out of bed at four in the morning and, when the man got mad about it, Gerry told him he was either going to go down and sell him the white kitten right then or he'd break his neck."

"It's always the little things you remember people by; all the little things they did because they wanted to do them for you. You've done the same for Gerry and your father and mother; all kinds of things that you've forgotten about but that they will never forget."

"I hope I have. I would like for them to remember me like that."

"They will."

"I wish—" She swallowed. "The way I'll die—I wish they wouldn't ever think of that. I've read how people look who die in space—their insides all ruptured and exploded and their lungs out between their teeth and then, a few seconds later, they're all dry and shapeless and horribly ugly. I don't want them to ever think of me as something dead and horrible like that."

"You're their own, their child and their sister. They could never think of you other than the way you would want them to, the way you looked the last time they saw you."

"I'm still afraid," she said. "I can't help it, but I don't want Gerry to know it. If he gets back in time, I'm going to act like I'm not afraid at all and—"

The signal buzzer interrupted her, quick and imperative.

"Gerry!" She came to her feet. "It's Gerry now!"

He spun the volume control knob and asked, "Gerry Cross?"

"Yes," her brother answered, an undertone of tenseness to his reply. "The bad news—what is it?"

She answered for him, standing close behind him and leaning down a little toward the communicator, her hand resting small and cold on his shoulder.

"Hello, Gerry." There was only a faint quaver to betray the careful casualness of her voice. "I wanted to see you—"

"Marilyn!" There was sudden and terrible apprehension in the way he spoke her name. "What are you doing on that EDS?"

"I wanted to see you," she said again. "I wanted to see you, so I hid on this ship—"

"You *hid* on it?"

"I'm a stowaway . . . I didn't know what it would mean—"

"*Marilyn!*" It was the cry of a man who calls, hopeless and desperate, to someone already and forever gone from him. "What have you done?"

"I . . . it's not—" Then her own composure broke and the cold little hand gripped his shoulder convulsively. "Don't, Gerry—I only wanted to see you; I didn't intend to hurt you. Please, Gerry, don't feel like that—"

Something warm and wet splashed on his wrist and he slid out of the chair, to help her into it and swing the microphone down to her level.

"Don't feel like that. Don't let me go knowing you feel like that—"

The sob she had tried to hold back choked in her throat, and her brother spoke to her. "Don't cry, Marilyn." His voice was suddenly deep and infinitely gentle, with all the pain held out of it. "Don't cry, Sis—you mustn't do that. It's all right, honey—everything is all right."

"I—" Her lower lip quivered and she bit into it. "I didn't want you to feel that way—I just wanted us to say goodbye, because I have to go in a minute."

"Sure—sure. That's the way it'll be, Sis. I didn't mean to sound the way I did." Then his voice changed to a tone of quick and urgent demand. "EDS—have you called the *Stardust?* Did you check with the computers?"

"I called the *Stardust* almost an hour ago. It can't turn back, there are no other cruisers within forty light-years, and there isn't enough fuel."

"Are you sure that the computers had the correct data—sure of everything?"

"Yes—do you think I could ever let it happen if I wasn't sure? I did everything I could do. If there was anything at all I could do now, I would do it."

"He tried to help me, Gerry." Her lower lip was no longer trembling and the short sleeves of her blouse were wet where she had dried her tears. "No one can help me and I'm not going to cry any more and everything will be all right with you and Daddy and Mama, won't it?"

"Sure—sure it will. We'll make out fine."

Her brother's words were beginning to come in more faintly, and he turned the volume control to maximum. "He's going out of range," he said to her. "He'll be gone within another minute."

"You're fading out, Gerry," she said. "You're going out of range. I wanted to tell you—but I can't now. We must say goodbye so soon—but maybe I'll see you again. Maybe I'll come to you in your dreams with my hair in braids and crying because the kitten in my arms is dead; maybe I'll be the touch of a breeze that whispers to you as it goes by; maybe I'll be one of those gold-winged larks you told me about, singing my silly head off to you; maybe, at times, I'll be nothing you can see, but you will know I'm there beside you. Think of me like that, Gerry; always like that and not—the other way."

Dimmed to a whisper by the turning of Woden, the answer came back:

"Always like that, Marilyn—always like that and never any other way."

"Our time is up, Gerry—I have to go now. Good—" Her voice broke in mid-word and her mouth tried to twist into crying. She pressed her hand hard against it and when she spoke again the words came clear and true:

"Goodbye, Gerry."

Faint and ineffably poignant and tender, the last words came from the cold metal of the communicator:

"Goodbye, little sister . . ."

She sat motionless in the hush that followed, as though listening to the shadow-echoes of the words as they died away, then she turned away from the communicator, toward the air lock, and he pulled down the black lever beside him. The inner door of the air lock slid swiftly open, to reveal the bare little cell that was waiting for her, and she walked to it.

She walked with her head up and the brown curls brushing her shoulders, with the white sandals stepping as sure and steady as the fractional gravity would permit and the gilded buckles twinkling with little lights of blue and red and crystal. He let her walk alone and made no move to help her, knowing she would not want it that way. She stepped into the air lock and turned to face him, only the pulse in her throat to betray the wild beating of her heart.

"I'm ready," she said.

He pushed the lever up and the door slid its quick barrier between them, enclosing her in black and utter darkness for her last moments of life. It clicked as it locked in place and he jerked down the red lever. There was a slight waver to the ship as the air gushed from the lock, a vibration to the wall as though something had bumped the outer door in passing, then there was nothing and the ship was dropping true and steady again. He shoved the red lever back to close the door on the empty air lock and turned away, to walk to the pilot's chair with the slow steps of a man old and weary.

Back in the pilot's chair he pressed the signal button of the normal-space transmitter. There was no response; he had expected none. Her brother would have to wait through the night until the turning of Woden permitted contact through Group One.

It was not yet time to resume deceleration, and he waited while the ship dropped endlessly downward with him and the drives purred softly. He saw that the white hand of the supplies-closet temperature gauge was on zero. A cold equation had been balanced and he was alone on the ship. Something shapeless and ugly was hurrying ahead of him, going to Woden where its brother was waiting through the night, but the empty ship still lived for a little while with the presence of the girl who had not known about the forces that killed with neither hatred nor malice. It seemed, almost, that she still sat, small and bewildered and frightened, on the metal box beside him, her words echoing hauntingly clear in the void she had left behind her:

I didn't do anything to die for . . . I didn't do anything . . .

THE DWINDLING SPHERE

WILLARD HAWKINS

*This, fellow readers, is what the Golden Age was like.
The great flowering of* Astounding Science Fiction
*in the 1940s began with stories like Mr. Hawkins' fas-
cinating speculation—which, by the way, has never been
previously reprinted.*

*EXTRACTS FROM THE DIARY OF
FRANK BAXTER, B.S., M.Sc.*

June 23, 1945. I thought today I was on the track of something,
but the results, while remarkable in their way, were disappointing.
The only thing of importance I can be said to have demonstrated
is that, with my new technique of neutron bombardment, it is
unnecessary to confine experiments to the heavier elements. This
broadens the field of investigation enormously. Substituted a lump
of common coal for uranium in today's experiment, and it was reduced to a small cinder. Probably oxidized, owing to a defect in
the apparatus or in my procedure.

However, it seems remarkable that, despite the almost instantaneous nature of the combustion, there was no explosion. Nor,
as far as I could detect, was any heat generated. In fact, I un-
thinkingly picked up the cinder—a small, smooth buttonlike object
—and it was scarcely warm.

June 24, 1945. Repeated yesterday's experiment, carefully checking each step, with results practically identical to yesterday's. Can
it be that I am on the verge of success? But that is absurd. If—as
might be assumed from the evidence—my neutron bombardment
started a self-perpetuating reaction which continued until every

atom in the mass had been subjected to fission, enormous energy would have been generated. In fact, I would no longer be here, all in one piece, to tell about it. Even the combustion of my lump of coal at such a practically instantaneous rate would be equivalent to exploding so much dynamite.

It is very puzzling, for the fact remains that the lump has been reduced to a fraction of its original weight and size. There is, after all, only one possible answer: the greater part of its mass must have been converted into energy. The question, then, is what became of the energy?

June 28, 1945.   Have been continuing my experiments, checking and rechecking. I have evidently hit upon some new principle in the conversion of matter into energy. Here are some of the results thus far:

Tried the same experiment with a chunk of rock—identical result. Tried it with a lump of earth, a piece of wood, a brass doorknob. Only difference in results was the size and consistency of the resulting cinder. Have weighed the substance each time, then the residue after neutron bombardment. The original substance seems to be reduced to approximately one twentieth of its original mass, although this varies somewhat according to the strength of the magnetic field and various adjustments in the apparatus. These factors also seem to affect the composition of the cinder.

The essence of the problem, however, has thus far baffled me. Why is it that I cannot detect the force generated? What is its nature? Unless I can solve this problem, the whole discovery is pointless.

I have written to my old college roommate, Bernard Ogilvie, asking him to come and check my results. He is a capable engineer and I have faith in his honesty and common sense—even though he appears to have been lured away from scientific pursuits by commercialism.

July 15, 1945.   Ogilvie has been here now for three days. He is greatly excited, but I am sorry that I sent for him. He has given me no help at all on my real problem—in fact, he seems more interested in the by-products than in the experiment itself. I had hoped he would help me to solve the mystery of what becomes of the energy generated by my process. Instead, he appears to be fascinated by those little chunks of residue—the cinders.

When I showed that it was possible, by certain adjustments in the apparatus, to control their texture and substance, he was beside himself with excitement. The result is that I have spent all my time since his arrival in making these cinders. We have produced them in consistency ranging all the way from hard little buttons to a mushy substance resembling cheese.

Analysis shows them to be composed of various elements, chiefly carbon and silica. Ogilvie appears to think there has been an actual transmutation of elements into this final result. I question it. The material is simply a form of ash—a residue.

We have enlarged the apparatus and installed a hopper, into which we shovel rock, debris—in fact, anything that comes handy, including garbage and other waste. If my experiment after all proves a failure, I shall at least have the ironic satisfaction of having produced an ideal incinerator. Ogilvie declares there is a fortune in that alone.

July 20, 1945. Bernard Ogilvie has gone. Now I can get down to actual work again. He took with him a quantity of samples and plans for the equipment. Before he left, he revealed what is on his mind. He thinks my process may revolutionize the plastics industry. What a waste of time to have called him in! A fine mind spoiled by commercialism. With an epochal discovery in sight, all he can think of is that here is an opportunity to convert raw material which costs practically nothing into commercial gadgets. He thinks the stuff can be molded and shaped—perhaps through a matrix principle incorporated right in the apparatus.

Partly, I must confess, to get rid of him, I signed the agreement he drew up. It authorizes him to patent the process in my name, and gives me a major interest in all subsidiary devices and patents that may be developed by his engineers. He himself is to have what he calls the promotion rights, but there is some sort of a clause whereby the control reverts wholly to me or to my heirs at his death. Ogilvie says it will mean millions to both of us.

He undoubtedly is carried away by his imagination. What could I do with such an absurd sum of money? However, a few thousand dollars might come in handy for improved equipment. I must find a means of capturing and controlling that energy.

EXTRACTS FROM THE DIARY OF QUENTIN BAXTER, PRESIDENT OF PLASTOSCENE PRODUCTS, INC.

August 3, 2065. I have made a discovery today which moved me profoundly—so profoundly that I have opened this journal so that my own thoughts and reactions may be likewise recorded for posterity. Diary-keeping has heretofore appeared to me as a rather foolish vanity—it now appears in an altogether different light.

The discovery which so altered my viewpoint was of a diary kept by my great-grandfather, Frank Baxter, the actual inventor of plastoscene.

I have often wondered what sort of a man this ancestor of mine could have been. History tells us almost nothing about him. I feel now that I know him as intimately as I know my closest associates. And what a different picture this diary gives from the prevailing concept!

Most of us have no doubt thought of the discoverer of the plastoscene principle as a man who saw the need for a simple method of catering to humanity's needs—one which would supplant the many laborious makeshifts of his day—and painstakingly set out to evolve it.

Actually, the discovery appears to have been an accident. Frank Baxter took no interest in its development—regarded it as of little account. Think of it! An invention more revolutionary than the discovery of fire, yet its inventor failed entirely to grasp its importance! To the end of his days it was to him merely a by-product. He died considering himself a failure, because he was unable to attain the goal he sought—the creation of atomic power.

In a sense, much of the credit apparently belongs to his friend Bernard Ogilvie, who grasped the possibilities inherent in the new principle. Here again, what a different picture the diary gives from that found in our schoolbooks! The historians would have us regard Frank Baxter as a sort of master mind, Bernard Ogilvie as his humble disciple and man Friday.

Actually, Ogilvie was a shrewd promoter who saw the possibilities of the discovery and exploited them—not especially to benefit humanity, but for personal gain. We must give him credit, however, for a scrupulous honesty which was amazing for his time. It would have been easy for him to take advantage of the impractical, dreamy scientist. Instead, he arranged that the inventor of the process should reap its rewards, and it is wholly owing to his insistence that control reverted to our family, where it has remained for more than a century.

All honor to these two exceptional men!

Neither, it is true, probably envisioned the great changes that would be wrought by the discovery. My ancestor remained to the end of his days dreamy and aloof, concerned solely with his futile efforts to trap the energy which he was sure he had released. The wealth which rolled up for him through Plastoscene Products, Inc.—apparently the largest individual fortune of his time—was to him a vague abstraction. I find a few references to it in his diary, but they are written in a spirit of annoyance. He goes so far as to mention once—apparently exasperated because the responsibilities of his position called him away from his experiments for a few hours—that he would like to convert the millions into hard currency and pour them into a conversion hopper, where at least they might be turned into something useful.

It is strange, by the way, that the problem he posed has never been demonstrably solved. Scientists still are divided in their allegiance to two major theories—one, that the force generated by this conversion of elements escapes into the fourth dimension; the other that it is generated in the form of radiations akin to cosmic rays, which are dissipated with a velocity approaching the infinite. These rays do not affect ordinary matter, according to the theory, because they do not impinge upon it, but instead pass through it, as light passes through a transparent substance.

August 5, 2065.   I have read and reread my grandfather's diary, and confess that I more and more find in him a kindred spirit. His way of life seems to me infinitely more appealing than that which inheritance has imposed upon me. The responsibilities resting on my shoulders, as reigning head of the Baxter dynasty, become exceedingly onerous at times. I even find myself wondering whether plastoscene has, after all, proved such an unmixed blessing for mankind.

Perhaps the greatest benefits may lie in the future. Certainly each stage in its development has been marked by economic readjustments—some of them well-nigh world-shattering. I have often been glad that I did not live through those earlier days of stress, when industry after industry was wiped out by the remorseless juggernaut of technological progress. When, for example, hundreds of thousands were thrown out of employment in the metal-mining and -refining and allied industries. It was inevitable that plastoscene substitutes, produced at a fraction of the cost from common dirt of the fields, should wipe out this industry—but the step could have been taken, it seems to me, without subjecting the dispossessed workers and employers to such hardship, thereby precipitating what amounted to a civil war. When we pause to think of it, almost every article in common use today represents one or more of those industries which was similarly wiped out, and on which vast numbers of people depended for their livelihood.

We have, at length, achieved a form of stable society—but I, for one, am not wholly satisfied with it. What do we have? A small owning class—a cluster of corporations grouped around the supercorporation, Plastoscene Products, Inc., of which I am—heaven help me!—the hereditary ruler. Next, a situation-holding class, ranging from scientists, executives and technicians down to the mechanical workers. Here again—because there are so few situations open, compared with the vast reservoir of potential producers—the situation holders have developed what amounts to a system of hereditary succession. I am told that it is almost impossible for one whose father was not a situation holder even to obtain the training necessary to qualify him for any of the jealously guarded positions.

Outside of this group is that great, surging mass, the major part of human society. These millions, I grant, are fed and clothed and housed and provided with a standard of living which their ancestors would have regarded as luxurious. Nevertheless, their lot is pitiful. They have no incentives; their status is that of a subject class. Particularly do I find distasteful the law which makes it a crime for any member of this enforced leisure group to be caught engaging in useful labor. The appalling number of convictions in our courts for this crime shows that there is in mankind an instinct to perform useful service, which cannot be eradicated merely by passing laws.

The situation is unhealthy as well from another standpoint. To me it seems a normal thing that society should progress. Yet we cannot close our eyes to the fact that the most highly skilled scientific minds the world has ever known have failed to produce a worth-while advance in technology for over a quarter of a century. Has science become sterile? No. In fact, every schoolboy knows the answer.

Our scientists do not dare to announce their discoveries. I am supposed to shut my eyes to what I know—that every vital discovery along the lines of technology has been suppressed. The plain, blunt truth is that we dare not introduce any technical advance which would eliminate more situation holders. A major discovery —one that reduced an entire class of situation holders to enforced leisure—would precipitate another revolution.

Is human society, as a result of its greatest discovery, doomed to sterility?

October 17, 2089. It has been nearly a quarter of a century since I first read the diary of my great-grandfather, Frank Baxter. I felt an impulse to get it out to show to my son, and before I realized it I had reread the volume in its entirety. It stirred me even more than it did back in my younger days. I must preserve its crumbling pages in facsimile, on permanent plastoscene parchment, so that later descendants—finding our two journals wrapped together —will thrill as I have thrilled to that early record of achievement.

The reading has crystallized thoughts long dormant in my mind. I am nearing the end of the trail. Soon I will turn over the presidency of Plastoscene Products, Inc., to my son—if he desires it. Perhaps he will have other ideas. He is now a full-fledged Pl. T. D. Doctor of Plastoscene Technology. It may be that power and position will mean as little to him as they have come to mean to me. I shall send for him tomorrow.

October 18, 2089. I have had my discussion with Philip, but I fear I bungled matters. He talked quite freely of his experiments. It seems that he has been working along the line of approach started by Levinson some years ago. As we know, the plastoscene principle in use involves the making of very complex adjustments. That is to say, if we wish to manufacture some new type of object —say a special gyroscope bearing—the engineer in charge first sets the machine to produce material of a certain specific hardness and temper, then he adjusts the controls which govern size and shape, and finally, having roughly achieved the desired result, he refines the product with micrometer adjustments—but largely through the trial-and-error method—until the quality, dimensions and so on meet the tests of his precision instruments. If the object involved is complex—involving two or more compounds, for example—the adjustments are correspondingly more difficult. We have not succeeded in producing palatable foodstuffs, though our engineers have turned out some messes which are claimed to have nourishing qualities. I suspect that the engineers have purposely made them nauseous to the taste.

True, once the necessary adjustments have been made, they are recorded on microfilm. Thereafter, it is only necessary to feed this film into the control box, where the electric eye automatically makes all the adjustments for which the skill of the technician was initially required. Levinson, however, proposed to reproduce natural objects in plastoscene by photographic means.

It is this process which Philip apparently has perfected. His method involves a three-dimensional "scanning" device which records the texture, shape and the exact molecular structure of the object to be reproduced. The record is made on microfilm, which then needs only to be passed through the control box to re-create the object as many times as may be required.

"Think of the saving of effort!" Philip remarked enthusiastically. "Not only can objects of the greatest intricacy be reproduced without necessity of assembling, but even natural foods can be created in all their flavor and nourishing quality. I have eaten synthetic radishes—I have even tasted synthetic chicken—that could not be told from the original which formed its matrix."

"You mean," I demanded in some alarm, "that you can reproduce life?"

His face clouded. "No. That is a quality that seems to elude the scanner. But I can reproduce the animal, identical with its live prototype down to the last nerve tip and hair, except that it is inert—lifeless. The radishes I spoke of will not grow in soil—they cannot reproduce themselves—but chemically and in cell structure they image the originals."

"Philip," I declared, "this is an amazing achievement! It removes the last limitation upon the adaptability of plastoscene. It means that we can produce not merely machine parts but completely assembled machines. It means that foodstuffs can be—"

I stopped, brought to myself by his sudden change in expression.

"True, Father," he observed coldly, "except that it happens to be a pipe dream. I did not expect that you would be taken in by my fairy tale. I have an engagement and must go."

He hurried from the room before I could get my wits about me.

October 23, 2089. Philip has been avoiding me, but I managed at last to corner him.

I began this time by mentioning that it would soon be necessary for me to turn over the burden of Plastoscene Products, Inc., to him as my logical successor.

He hesitated, then blurted, "Father, I know this is going to hurt you, but I don't want to carry on the succession. I prefer to remain just a cog in the engineering department."

"Responsibility," I reminded him, "is something that cannot be honorably evaded."

"Why should it be my responsibility?" he demanded vehemently. "I didn't ask to be your son."

"Nor," I countered, "did I ask to be my father's son, nor the great-grandson of a certain inventor who died in the twentieth century. Philip, I want you to do one thing for me. Take this little book, read it, then bring it back and tell me what you think of it." I handed him Frank Baxter's diary.

October 24, 2089. Philip brought back the diary today. He admitted that he had sat up all night reading it.

"But I'm afraid the effect isn't what you expected," he told me frankly. "Instead of instilling the idea that we Baxters have a divine mission to carry on the dynasty, it makes me feel that our responsibility is rather to undo the damage already caused by our meddling. That old fellow back there—Frank Baxter—didn't intend to produce this hideous stuff."

"Hideous stuff?" I demanded.

"Don't be shocked, Father," he said, a trifle apologetically. "I can't help feeling rather deeply about this. Perhaps you think we're better off than people in your great-grandfather's time. I doubt it. They had work to do. There may have been employment problems, but it wasn't the enforced idleness of our day. Look at Frank Baxter—he could work and invent things with the assurance that he was doing something to advance mankind. He wasn't compelled to cover up his discoveries for fear they'd cause further—"

He stopped suddenly, as if realizing that he had said more than he intended.

"My boy," I told him, speaking slowly, "I know just how you feel—and knowing it gives me more satisfaction than you can realize."

He stared at me, bewildered. "You mean—you don't want me to take on the succession?"

I unfolded my plan.

FROM THE DIARY OF RAN RAXLER, TENTH-RANKING HONOR STUDENT, NORTH-CENTRAL FINALS, CLASS OF 2653

December 28, 2653.   I have had two thrills today—an exciting discovery right on the heels of winning my diploma in the finals. Being one of the high twenty practically assures me of a chance to serve in the production pits this year.

But the discovery—I must record that first of all. It consists of a couple of old diaries. I found them in a chestful of family heirlooms which I rescued as they were about to be tossed into the waste tube. In another minute, they would have been on their way to the community plastoscene converter.

There has been a legend in our family that we are descended from the original discoverer of plastoscene, and this find surely tends to prove it. Even the name is significant. Frank Baxter. Given names as well as surnames are passed down through the generations. My grandfather before me was Ran Raxler. The dropping of a letter here, the corruption of another there, could easily have resulted in the modification of Frank Baxter to Ran Raxler.

What a thrill it will be to present to the world the authentic diary of the man who discovered the plastoscene principle! Not the impossible legendary figure, but the actual, flesh-and-blood man. And what a shock it will be to many! For it appears that Frank Baxter stumbled upon this discovery quite by accident, and regarded it to the end of his days as an unimportant by-product of his experiments.

And this later Baxter—Quentin—who wrote the companion diary and sealed the two together. What a martyr to progress he proved himself—he and his son, Philip. The diary throws an altogether different light on their motives than has been recorded in history. Instead of being selfish oligarchs who were overthrown by a mass uprising, this diary reveals that they themselves engineered the revolution.

The final entry in Quentin Baxter's diary consists of these words: "I unfolded my plan." The context—when taken with the undisputed facts of history—makes it clear what the plan must have been. As I reconstruct it, the Baxters, father and son, determined to abolish the control of plastoscene by a closed corporation of hereditary owners, and to make it the property of the whole people.

The son had perfected the scanning principle which gives plastoscene its present unlimited range. His impulse was to withhold it—in fact, it had become a point of honor among technicians to bury such discoveries, after showing them to a few trusted associates. Incomprehensible? Perhaps so at first, but not when we understand the upheavals such discoveries might cause in the form of society then existing. To make this clear, I should, perhaps, point to the record of history, which proves that up to the time of plastoscene, foodstuffs had been largely produced by growing them in the soil. This was accomplished through a highly technical process, which I cannot explain, but I am told that the University of Antarctica maintains an experimental laboratory in which the method is actually demonstrated to advanced classes. Moreover, we know what these foods were like through the microfilm matrices which still reproduce some of them for us.

The right to produce such foods for humanity's needs was jealously guarded by the great agricultural aristocracy. And, of course, this entire situation-holding class, together with many others, would be abolished by Philip's invention.

We know what happened. Despite the laws prohibiting the operation of plastoscene converters except by licensed technicians and situation holders, contraband machines suddenly began to appear everywhere among the people. Since these machines were equipped with the new scanning principle, it is obvious, in view of the diary, that they must have been deliberately distributed at strategic points by the Baxters.

At first, the contraband machines were confiscated and destroyed—but since they were, of course, capable of reproducing themselves through the matrix library of microfilm which was standard equipment, the effort to keep pace with their spread through the masses was hopeless. The ruling hierarchies appealed to the law, and to the Baxters, whose hereditary control of the plastoscene monopoly had been supposedly a safeguard against its falling into the hands of the people as a whole. The Baxters, father and son, then played their trump card. They issued a proclamation deeding the plastoscene principle in perpetuity to all the people. History implies that they were forced to do this—but fails to explain how or why. There was a great deal of confusion and bloodshed during this period; no wonder that historians jumped at conclusions—even assuming that the Baxters were assassinated by revolutionists, along with others of the small owning group who made a last stand, trying to preserve their monopolies. In light of Quentin Baxter's diary, there is far better ground for believing that they were executed by members of their own class, who regarded them as traitors.

We should be thankful indeed that those ancient days of war and bloodshed are over. Surely such conditions can never reappear on Earth. What possible reason can there be for people to rise up against each other? Just as we can supply all our needs with plastoscene, so can our neighbors on every continent supply theirs.

March 30, 2654. I have completed my service in the production pits, and thrilling weeks they have been. To have a part in the great process which keeps millions of people alive, even for a brief four weeks' period, makes one feel that life has not been lived in vain.

One could hardly realize, without such experience, what enormous quantities of raw material are required for the sustenance and needs of the human race. How fortunate I am to have been one of the few to earn this privilege of what the ancients called "work."

The problem must have been more difficult in the early days. Where we now distribute raw-material concentrates in the form of plastoscene-B, our forefathers had to transport the actual rock as dredged from the gravel pits. Even though the process of distribution was mechanical and largely automatic, still it was cumbersome, since material for conversion is required in a ratio of about twenty to one as compared with the finished product.

Today, of course, we have the intermediate process, by which soil and rock are converted at the pits into blocks of plastoscene-B. This represents, in a sense, the conversion process in an arrested stage. The raw material emerges in these blocks reduced to a tenth of its original weight and an even smaller volume than it will occupy in the finished product—since the mass has been increased by close packing of molecules.

A supply of concentrate sufficient to last the ordinary family for a year can now easily be stored in the standard-sized converter, and even the huge community converters have a capacity sufficient to provide for all the building, paving of roadways, recarpeting of recreation grounds, and like purposes, that are likely to be required in three months' time. I understand that experimental stations in South America are successfully introducing liquid concentrate, which can be piped directly to the consumers from the vast production pits.

I was amused on my last day by a question asked by a ten-year-old boy, the son of one of the supervisors. We stood on a rampart overlooking one of the vast production pits, several hundred feet deep and miles across—the whole space filled with a bewildering network of towers, girders, cranes, spires and cables, across and through which flashed transports of every variety. Far below us, the center of all this activity, could be discerned the huge conversion plant, in which the rock is reduced to plastoscene-B.

The little boy looked with awe at the scene, then turned his face upward, demanding, "What are we going to do when this hole gets so big that it takes up the whole world?"

We laughed, but I could sympathize with the question. Man is such a puny creature that it is difficult for him to realize what an infinitesimal thing on the Earth's surface is a cavity which to him appears enormous. The relationship, I should say, is about the same as a pinprick to a ball which a child can toss in the air.

FROM THE INTRODUCTION TO OUR EIGHTY YEARS' WAR, *SIGNED BY GLUX GLUXTON, CHIEF HISTORIAN, THE NAPHALI INSTITUTE OF SCIENCE (DATED AS OF THE SIXTH DAY, SIXTH LUNAR MONTH, YEAR 10,487)*

The Eighty Years' War is over. It has been concluded by a treaty of eternal amity signed at Latex on the morning of the twenty-ninth day of the fifth month.

By the terms of the treaty, all peoples of the world agree to subject themselves to control by the World Court. The Court, advised through surveys continuously conducted by the International Institute of Science, will have absolute authority over the conversion of basic substance into plastoscene, to the end that further disputes between regions and continents shall be impossible.

To my distinguished associates and to myself was allotted the task of compiling a history of the causes behind this prolonged upheaval and of its course. How well we have succeeded posterity must judge. In a situation so complex, how, indeed, may one declare with assurance which were the essential causes? Though known as *the* Eighty Years' War, a more accurate expression would be "the Eighty Years *of* War," for the period has been one marked by a constant succession of wars—of outbreaks originating spontaneously and from divers causes in various parts of the world.

Chief among the basic causes, of course, were the disputes between adjoining districts over the right to extend their conversion pits beyond certain boundaries. Nor can we overlook the serious situation precipitated when it was realized that the Antarctican sea-water conversion plants were sucking up such great quantities that the level of the oceans was actually being lowered—much as the Great Lakes once found on the North American continent were drained of their water centuries ago. Disputes, alliances and counteralliances, regions arrayed against each other, and finally engines of war raining fearful destruction. What an unprecedented bath of blood the world has endured!

The whole aim, from this time forth, will be to strip off the earth's surface evenly, so that it shall become smooth and even, not rough and unsightly and covered with abandoned pits as now viewed from above. To prevent a too rapid lowering of sea level, it is provided that Antarctica and some other sections which have but a limited amount of land surface shall be supplied with concentrate from the more favored regions.

Under such a treaty, signed with fervent good will by the representatives of a war-weary world population, is it farfetched to assert that permanent peace has been assured? Your historian holds that it is not.

FROM THE REPORT OF RAGNAR DUGH, DELEGATE TO THE WORLD PEACE CONFERENCE, TO THE 117th DISTRICT (CIRCUIT 1092, REV. 148)

Honored confrères: It gives me pleasure to present, on behalf of the district which has honored me as its representative, concurrence in the conditions for peace as proposed in the majority report.

As I view your faces in the televisor, I see in them the same sense of deep elation that I feel in the thought that this exhausting era of bloodshed and carnage has run its course, and that war is to be rendered impossible from this time forth. Is this too strong a statement? I read in your eyes that it is not, for we are at last abolishing the cause of war—namely, the overcrowding of the earth's surface.

The proposed restrictions may seem drastic, but the human race will accustom itself to them. And let us remember that they would be even more drastic if the wars themselves had not resulted in depopulating the world to a great extent. I am glad that it has not been found necessary to impose a ten-year moratorium on all childbearing. As matters stand, by limiting childbirth to a proportion of one child per circuit of the sun for each three deaths within any given district, scientists agree that the population of the earth will be reduced at a sufficient rate to relieve the tension.

The minority report, which favors providing more room for the population by constructing various levels or concentric shells, which would gird the world's surface and to which additional levels would be added as needed, I utterly condemn. It is impractical chiefly for the reason that the conversion of so much material into these various dwelling surfaces would cause a serious shrinkage in the earth's mass.

Let us cast our votes in favor of the majority proposition, thus insuring a long life for the human race and for the sphere on which we dwell, and removing the last cause of war between peoples of the earth.

FROM THE MEMOIRS OF XLAR XVII, PRINCEP OF PLES

Cycle 188, 400-43. What an abomination is this younger generation! I am glad the new rules limit offspring to not more than one in a district per cycle. My nephew, Ryk LVX, has been saturating himself with folklore at the Museum of Antiquity, and had the audacity to assure me that there are records which suggest the existence of mankind before plastoscope. Why will people befog their minds with the supernatural?

"There is a theory," he brazenly declared, "that at one time the world was partly composed of food, which burst up through its crust ready for the eating. It is claimed that even the carpet we now spread over the earth's surface had its correspondence in a substance which appeared there spontaneously."

"In that case," I retorted sarcastically, "what became of this— this exudation of the rocks?"

Of course, he had an answer ready: "Plastoscene was discovered and offered mankind an easier method of supplying its needs, with the result that the surface of the earth, containing the growth principle, was stripped away. I do not say that this is a fact," he hastened to add, "but merely that it may have some basis."

Here is what I told my nephew. I sincerely tried to be patient and to appeal to his common sense. "The basis in fact is this: It is true that the earth's surface has been many times stripped during the long existence of the human race. There is only one reasonable theory of life on this planet. Originally man—or rather his evolutionary predecessor—possessed within himself a digestive apparatus much wider in scope than at present. He consumed the rock, converted it into food, and thence into the elements necessary to feed his tissues, all within his own body. Eventually, as he developed intelligence, man learned how to produce plastoscene by mechanical means. He consumed this product as food, as well as using it for the myriad other purposes of his daily life. As a result, the organs within his own body no longer were needed to produce plastoscene directly from the rock. They gradually atrophied and disappeared, leaving only their vestiges in the present digestive tract."

This silenced the young man for a time, but I have no doubt he will return later with some other fantastic delusion. On one occasion it was the legend that, instead of being twin planets, our earth and Luna were at one time of differing sizes, and that Luna revolved around the earth as some of the distant moons revolve around their primaries. This theory has been thoroughly discredited. It is true that there is a reduction of the earth's mass every time we scrape its surface to produce according to our needs; but it is incredible that the earth could ever have been several times the size of its companion planet, as these imaginative theorists would have us believe. They forget, no doubt, that the volume and mass of a large sphere is greater, in proportion to its area and consequent human population, than that of a smaller sphere. Our planet even now would supply man for an incomprehensible time, yet it represents but a tiny fraction of such a mass as these theorists would have us believe in. They forget that diminution would proceed at an ever-mounting rate as the size decreased; that such a huge sphere as they propose would have lasted forever.

It is impossible. As impossible as to imagine that a time will come when there will be no more Earth for man's conversion—

REQUIEM

ROBERT A. HEINLEIN

Robert A. Heinlein received more nominations for this anthology than any other author, a fact that does not surprise anybody. So many Heinlein stories were listed that picking one becomes a very individual business. My own favorite Heinlein short story is "They," but "They," like most of Mr. Heinlein's work, is readily available elsewhere, as the Honor Roll will tell you. I finally picked, in order to duck out of as many fights as possible, the single Heinlein story which received the most votes. This is it.

Mr. Heinlein was once called by Alfred Bester "the Kipling of science fiction." This seems to me one of the most accurate statements made recently about any writer in or out of sf. I cannot think of anything to add to it, except my own admiration for the man who has, in great part, spent the last twenty-seven years in showing the rest of us what science fiction can be.

On a high hill in Samoa there is a grave. Inscribed on the marker are these words:

> Under the wide and starry sky
> Dig my grave and let me lie.
> Glad did I live and gladly die
> And I lay me down with a will!
>
> This be the verse which you grave for me:
> Here he lies where he longed to be,
> Home is the sailor, home from the sea,
> And the hunter home from the hill.

These lines appear another place—scrawled on a shipping tag torn from a compressed-air container and pinned to the ground with a knife.

It wasn't much of a fair, as fairs go. The trottin' races didn't promise much excitement, even though several entries claimed the blood of the immortal Dan Patch. The tents and concession booths barely covered the circus grounds, and the pitchmen seemed discouraged.

D. D. Harriman's chauffeur could not see any reason for stopping. They were due in Kansas City for a directors' meeting. That is to say, Harriman was. The chauffeur had private reasons for promptness, reasons involving darktown society on Eighteenth Street. But the Boss not only stopped but hung around.

Bunting and a canvas arch made the entrance to a large enclosure beyond the race track. Red and gold letters announced:

This way to the
MOON ROCKET!!!!
See it in actual flight!
Public Demonstration Flights
Twice Daily
This is the ACTUAL TYPE used by the
First Man to Reach the MOON!!!
YOU can ride it!!—$50.00

A boy nine or ten years old hung around the entrance and stared at the posters.

"Want to see the ship, son?"

The kid's eyes shone. "Gee, mister, I sure would."

"So would I. Come on." Harriman paid out fifty dollars for two pink tickets which entitled them to enter the enclosure and examine the rocket ship. The kid took his and ran on ahead with the single-mindedness of youth. Harriman looked over the stubby curved lines of the ovoid body. He noted with a professional eye that she was a single-jet type with fractional controls around her midriff. He squinted through his glasses at the name painted in gold on the carnival red of the body. *Carefree.* He paid another quarter to enter the control cabin.

When his eyes had adjusted to the gloom caused by the strong ray filters of the ports, he let them rest lovingly on the keys of the console and the semicircle of dials above. Each beloved gadget was in its proper place. He knew them—graven in his heart.

While he mused over the instrument board, with the warm liquid of content soaking through his body, the pilot entered and touched his arm.

"Sorry, sir. We've got to cast loose for the flight."

"Eh?" Harriman started, then looked at the speaker. Handsome devil, with a good skull and strong shoulders—reckless eyes and a self-indulgent mouth, but a firm chin. "Oh, excuse me, Captain."

"Quite all right."

"Oh, I say, Captain, er, uh—"

"McIntyre."

"Captain McIntyre, could you take a passenger this trip?" The old man leaned eagerly toward him.

"Why, yes, if you wish. Come along with me." He ushered Harriman into a shed marked "Office" which stood near the gate. "Passenger for a checkover, Doc."

Harriman looked startled, but permitted the medico to run a stethoscope over his thin chest and strap a rubber bandage around his arm. Presently he unstrapped it, glanced at McIntyre, and shook his head.

"No go, Doc?"

"That's right, Captain."

Harriman looked from face to face. "My heart's all right—that's just a flutter."

The physician's brows shot up. "It is? But it's not just your heart; at your age your bones are brittle, too brittle to risk a take-off."

"Sorry, sir," added the pilot, "but the Bates County Fair Association pays the doctor here to see to it that I don't take anyone up who might be hurt by the acceleration."

The old man's shoulders drooped miserably. "I rather expected it."

"Sorry, sir." McIntyre turned to go, but Harriman followed him out.

"Excuse me, Captain—"

"Yes?"

"Could you and your, uh, engineer have dinner with me after your flight?"

The pilot looked at him quizzically. "I don't see why not. Thanks."

"Captain McIntyre, it is difficult for me to see why anyone would quit the Earth–moon run." Fried chicken and hot biscuits in a private dining room of the best hotel the little town of Butler afforded, three-star Hennessey and Corona-Coronas had produced a friendly atmosphere in which three men could talk freely.

"Well, I didn't like it."

"Aw, don't give him that, Mac—you know it was Rule G that got you." McIntyre's mechanic poured himself another brandy as he spoke.

McIntyre looked sullen. "Well, what if I did take a couple o' drinks? Anyhow, I could have squared that—it was the dern persnickety regulations that got me fed up. Who are you to talk? Smuggler!"

"Sure I smuggled! Who wouldn't with all those beautiful rocks just aching to be taken back to Earth? I had a diamond once as big as— But if I hadn't been caught I'd be in Luna City tonight. And so would you, you drunken blaster—with the boys buying us drinks, and the girls smiling . . ." He put his face down and began to weep quietly.

McIntyre shook him. "He's drunk."

"Never mind." Harriman interposed a hand. "Tell me, are you really satisfied not to be on the run any more?"

McIntyre chewed his lip. "No—he's right, of course. This barnstorming isn't what it's all cracked up to be. We've been hopping junk at every pumpkin doin's up and down the Mississippi Valley —sleeping in tourist camps and eating at greaseburners. Half the time the sheriff has an attachment on the ship, the other half the Society for the Prevention of Something or Other gets an injunction to keep us on the ground. It's no sort of a life for a rocket man."

"Would it help any for you to get to the moon?"

"Well . . . yes. I couldn't get back on the earth–moon run, but if I was in Luna City I could get a job hopping ore for the company—they're always short of rocket pilots for that, and they wouldn't mind my record. If I kept my nose clean, they might even put me back on the run, in time."

Harriman fiddled with a spoon, then looked up. "Would you young gentlemen be open to a business proposition?"

"Perhaps. What is it?"

"You own the *Carefree?*"

"Yeah. That is, Charlie and I do—barring a couple of liens against her. What about it?"

"I want to charter her . . . for you and Charlie to take me to the moon!"

Charlie sat up with a jerk. "D'joo hear what he said, Mac? He wants us to fly that old heap to the moon!"

McIntyre shook his head. "Can't do it, Mr. Harriman. The old boat's worn out. You couldn't convert to escape fuel. We don't even use standard juice in her—just gasoline and liquid air. Charlie spends all of his time tinkering with her at that. She's going to blow up someday."

"Say, Mr. Harriman," put in Charlie, "what's the matter with getting an excursion permit and going in a company ship?"

"No, son," the old man replied, "I can't do that. You know the conditions under which the U.N. granted the company a monopoly on lunar exploitation—no one to enter space who was not physically qualified to stand up under it. Company to take full responsibility for the safety and health of all citizens beyond the stratosphere. The official reason for granting the franchise was to avoid unnecessary loss of life during the first few years of space travel."

"And you can't pass the physical exam?"

Harriman shook his head.

"Well—if you can afford to hire us, why don't you just bribe yourself a brace of company docs? It's been done before."

Harriman smiled ruefully. "I know it has, Charlie, but it won't work for me. You see, I'm a little too prominent. My full name is Delos D. Harriman."

"What? *You* are old D. D.? But you own a big slice of the company yourself—you practically *are* the company; you ought to be able to do anything you like, rules or no rules."

"That is a not unusual opinion, son, but it is incorrect. Rich men aren't more free than other men; they are less free, a good deal less free. I tried to do what you suggest, but the other directors would not permit me. They are afraid of losing their franchise. It costs them a good deal in—uh—political-contact expenses to retain it, as it is."

"Well, I'll be a— Can you tie that, Mac? A guy with lots of dough, and he can't spend it the way he wants to."

McIntyre did not answer, but waited for Harriman to continue.

"Captain McIntyre, if you had a ship, would you take me?"

McIntyre rubbed his chin. "It's against the law."

"I'd make it worth your while."

"Sure he would, Mr. Harriman. Of course you would, Mac. Luna City! Oh, baby!"

"Why do you want to go to the moon so badly, Mr. Harriman?"

"Captain, it's the one thing I've really wanted to do all my life —ever since I was a young boy. I don't know whether I can explain it to you or not. You young fellows have grown up to rocket travel the way I grew up to aviation. I'm a great deal older than you are, at least fifty years older. When I was a kid practically nobody believed that men would ever reach the moon. You've seen rockets all your lives, and the first to reach the moon got there before you were a young boy. When I was a boy they laughed at the idea. But I believed—I believed. I read Verne, and Wells, and Smith, and I believed that we could do it—that we *would* do it. I set my heart on being one of the men to walk on the surface of the moon, to see her other side, and to look back on the face of the earth hanging in the sky. I used to go without my lunches to pay my dues in the American Rocket Society, because I wanted to believe that I was helping to bring the day nearer when we would reach the moon. I was already an old man when that day arrived. I've lived longer than I should, but I would not let myself die . . . I will not!—until I have set foot on the moon."

McIntyre stood up and put out his hand. "You find a ship, Mr. Harriman. I'll drive 'er."

"Atta' boy, Mac! I told you he would, Mr. Harriman."

Harriman mused and dozed during the half-hour run to the north into Kansas City, dozed in the light troubled sleep of old age. Incidents out of a long life ran through his mind in vagrant dreams. There was that time . . . oh, yes, 1910 . . . A little boy on a warm spring night: "What's that, Daddy?" "That's Halley's comet, Sonny." "Where did it come from?" "I don't know, son. From way out in the sky somewhere." "It's *beyooootiful*, Daddy. I want to touch it." " 'Fraid not, Son."

"Delos, do you mean to stand there and tell me you put the money we have saved for the house into that crazy rocket company?" "Now, Charlotte, please! It's not crazy; it's a sound business investment. Someday soon rockets will find the sky. Ships and trains will be obsolete. Look what happened to the men that had the foresight to invest in Henry Ford." "We've been all over this before." "Charlotte, the day will come when men will rise up off the earth and visit the moon, even the planets. This is the beginning." "Must you shout?" "I'm sorry, but—" "I feel a headache coming on. Please try to be a little quiet when you come to bed."

He hadn't gone to bed. He had sat out on the veranda all night long, watching the full moon move across the sky. There would be the devil to pay in the morning, the devil and a thin-lipped silence. But he'd stick by his guns. He'd given in on most things, but not on this. But the night was his. Tonight he'd be alone with his old friend. He searched her face. Where was Mare Crisium? Funny, he couldn't make it out. He used to be able to see it plainly when he was a boy. Probably needed new glasses—this constant office work wasn't good for his eyes.

But he didn't need to see, he knew where they all were: Crisium, Mare Fecunditatis, Mare Tranquilitatis—that one had a satisfying roll!—the Apennines, the Carpathians, old Tycho with its mysterious rays. Two hundred and forty thousand miles—ten times around the earth. Surely men could bridge a little gap like that. Why, he could almost reach out and touch it, nodding there behind the elm trees.

Not that he could help. He hadn't the education.

"Son, I want to have a little serious talk with you." "Yes, Mother." "I know you had hoped to go to college next year" (Hoped! He had lived for it. The University of Chicago to study under Moulton, then on to the Yerkes Observatory to work under the eye of Dr. Frost himself), "and I had hoped so, too. But with your father gone and the girls growing up, it's harder to make ends meet. You've been a good boy, and worked hard to help out. I know you'll understand." "Yes, Mother."

"Extra! Extra! Stratosphere Rocket Reaches Paris! Read aaaaa-llllll about 't." The thin little man in the bifocals snatched at the paper and hurried back to the office. "Look at this, George." "Huh? Hmm, interesting, but what of it?" "Can't you see? The next stage is to the moon!" "God, but you're a sucker, Delos. The trouble with you is you read too many of those trashy magazines. Now, I caught my boy reading one of 'em just last week, *Stunning Stories* or some such title, and dressed him down proper. Your folks should have done you the same favor."—Harriman squared his narrow middle-aged shoulders. "They will so reach the moon!"—His partner laughed. "Have it your own way. If baby wants the moon, Papa bring it for him. But you stick to your discounts and commissions; that's where the money is."

The big car droned down the Paseo and turned off on Armour Boulevard. Old Harriman stirred uneasily in his sleep and muttered to himself.

"But, Mr. Harriman—" The young man with the notebook was plainly perturbed.

The old man grunted. "You heard me. Sell 'em. I want every share I own realized in cash as rapidly as possible. Spaceways, Spaceways Provisioning Company, Artemis Mines, Luna City Recreations—the whole lot of them."

"It will depress the market. You won't realize the full value of your holdings."

"Don't you think I know that? I can afford it."

"What about the shares you had earmarked for Richardson Observatory and for the Harriman Scholarships?"

"Oh, yes. Don't sell those. Set up a trust. Should have done it long ago. Tell young Kamens to draw up the papers. He knows what I want."

The interoffice visor flashed into life. "The gentlemen are here, Mr. Harriman."

"Send 'em in. That's all Ashley. Get busy."

Ashley went out as McIntyre and Charlie entered. Harriman got up and trotted forward to greet them.

"Come in, boys, come in. I'm so glad to see you. Sit down. Sit down. Have a cigar."

"Mighty pleased to see you, Mr. Harriman," acknowledged Charlie. "In fact, you might say we need to see you."

"Some trouble, gentlemen?" Harriman glanced from face to face.

McIntyre answered him. "You still mean that about a job for us, Mr. Harriman?"

"Mean it? Certainly I do. You're not backing out on me?"

"Not at all. We need that job now. You see, the *Carefree* is lying in the middle of the Osage River with her jet split clear back to the injector."

"Dear me! You weren't hurt?"

"No, aside from sprains and bruises. We jumped."

Charlie chortled. "I caught a catfish with my bare teeth."

In short order they got down to business. "You two will have to buy a ship for me. I can't do it openly; my colleagues would figure out what I mean to do and stop me. I'll supply you with all the cash you need. You go out and locate some sort of a ship that can be refitted for the trip. Work up some good story about how you are buying it for some playboy as a stratosphere yacht, or that you plan to establish an Arctic–Antarctic tourist route. Anything as long as no one suspects that she is being outfitted for space flight. Then, after the Department of Transport licenses her for strato flight, you move out to a piece of desert out West—I'll find a likely parcel of land and buy it—and then I'll join you. Then we'll install the escape-fuel tanks, change the injectors and timers and so forth, to fit her for the hop. How about it?"

McIntyre looked dubious. "It'll take a lot of doing, Charlie. Do you think you can accomplish that change-over without a dock-yard and shops?"

"Me? Sure I can—with your thick-fingered help. Just give me the tools and materials I want, and don't hurry me too much. Of course, it won't be fancy—"

"Nobody wants it to be fancy. I just want a ship that won't blow when I start slapping the keys. Isotope fuel is no joke."

"It won't blow, Mac."

"That's what you thought about the *Carefree*."

"That ain't fair, Mac. I ask you, Mr. Harriman—that heap was junk, and we knew it. This'll be different. We're going to spend some dough and do it right. Ain't we, Mr. Harriman?"

Harriman patted him on the shoulder. "Certainly we are, Charlie. You can have all the money you want. That's the least of our worries. Now, do the salaries and bonuses I mentioned suit you? I don't want you to be short."

". . . As you know, my clients are his nearest relatives and have his interests at heart. We contend that Mr. Harriman's conduct for the past several weeks, as shown by the evidence here adduced, gives clear indication that a mind once brilliant in the world of finance has become senile. It is therefore with the deepest regret that we pray this honorable court, if it pleases, to declare Mr. Harriman incompetent and to assign a conservator to protect his financial interests and those of his future heirs and assigns." The attorney sat down, pleased with himself.

Mr. Kamens took the floor. "May it please the court, if my esteemed friend is *quite* through, may I suggest that in his last few words he gave away his entire thesis: 'financial interests of future heirs and assigns.' It is evident that the petitioners believe that my client should conduct his affairs in such a fashion as to insure that his nieces and nephews, and their issue, will be supported in unearned luxury for the rest of their lives. My client's wife has passed on, he has no children. It is admitted that he has provided generously for his sisters and their children in times past, and that he has established annuities for such near kin as are without means of support. But now, like vultures—worse than vultures, for they are not content to let him die in peace—they would prevent my client from enjoying his wealth in whatever manner best suits him for the few remaining years of his life. It is true that he has sold his holdings; is it strange that an elderly man should wish to retire? It is true that he suffered some paper losses in liquidation. 'The value of a thing is what that thing will bring.' He was retiring and demanded cash. Is there anything strange about that? It is admitted that he refused to discuss his actions with his so-loving kinfolk. What law or principle requires a man to consult with his nephews on anything? Therefore we pray that this court will confirm my client in his right to do what he likes with his own, deny this petition, and send these meddlers about their business."

The judge took off his spectacles and polished them thoughtfully. "Mr. Kamens, this court has as high a regard for individual liberty as you have, and you may rest assured that any action taken will be solely in the interests of your client. Nevertheless, men do grow old, men do become senile, and in such cases must be protected. I shall take this matter under advisement until tomorrow. Court is adjourned."

From the *Kansas City Star:*

ECCENTRIC MILLIONAIRE DISAPPEARS

. . . failed to appear for the adjourned hearing. The bailiffs returned from a search of places usually frequented by Harriman with the report that he had not been seen since the previous day. A bench warrant under contempt proceedings has been issued and . . .

A desert sunset is a better stimulant for the appetite than a hot dance orchestra. Charlie testified to this by polishing the last of the ham gravy with a piece of bread. Harriman handed each of the younger men cigars and took one himself.

"My doctor claims that these weeds are bad for my heart condition," he remarked as he lighted it, "but I've felt so much better since I joined you boys here on the ranch that I am inclined to doubt him." He exhaled a cloud of blue-gray smoke and resumed. "I don't think a man's health depends so much on what he does as on whether he wants to do it. I'm doing what I want to do."

"That's all a man can ask of life," agreed McIntyre.

"How does the work look now, boys?"

"My end's in pretty good shape," Charlie answered. "We finished the second pressure tests on the new tanks and the fuel lines today. The ground tests are all done, except the calibration runs. Those won't take long—just the four hours to make the runs if I don't run into some bugs. How about you, Mac?"

McIntyre ticked them off on his fingers. "Food supplies and water on board. Three vacuum suits, a spare, and service kits. Medical supplies. The buggy already had all the standard equipment for strato flight. The late lunar ephemerides haven't arrived yet."

"When do you expect them?"

"Any time—they should be here now. Not that it matters. This guff about how hard it is to navigate from here to the moon is hokum to impress the public. After all, you can *see* your destination—it's not like ocean navigation. Gimme a sextant and a good radar and I'll set you down anyplace on the moon you like, without cracking an almanac or a star table, just from a general knowledge of the relative speeds involved."

"Never mind the personal buildup, Columbus," Charlie told him. "We'll admit you can hit the floor with your hat. The general idea is, you're ready to go now. Is that right?"

"That's it."

"That being the case, I *could* run those tests tonight. I'm getting jumpy—things have been going too smoothly. If you'll give me a hand, we ought to be in bed by midnight."

"O.K., when I finish this cigar."

They smoked in silence for a while, each thinking about the coming trip and what it meant to him. Old Harriman tried to repress the excitement that possessed him at the prospect of immediate realization of his lifelong dream.

"Mr. Harriman—"

"Eh? What is it, Charlie?"

"How does a guy go about getting rich, like you did?"

"Getting rich? I can't say; I never tried to get rich. I never wanted to be rich, or well known, or anything like that."

"Huh?"

"No, I just wanted to live a long time and see it all happen. I wasn't unusual; there were lots of boys like me—radio hams, they were, and telescope builders, and airplane amateurs. We had science clubs, and basement laboratories, and science-fiction leagues —the kind of boys who thought there was more romance in one issue of the *Electrical Experimenter* than in all the books Dumas ever wrote. We didn't want to be one of Horatio Alger's get-rich heroes either, we wanted to build spaceships. Well, some of us did."

"Jeez, Pop, you make it sound exciting."

"It was exciting, Charlie. This has been a wonderful, romantic century, for all of its bad points. And it's grown more wonderful and more exciting every year. No, I didn't want to be rich; I just wanted to live long enough to see men rise up to the stars, and, if God was good to me, to go as far as the moon myself." He carefully deposited an inch of white ash in a saucer. "It has been a good life. I haven't any complaints."

McIntyre pushed back his chair. "Come on, Charlie, if you're ready."

"O.K."

They all got up. Harriman started to speak, then grabbed at his chest, his face a dead gray-white.

"Catch him, Mac!"

"Where's his medicine?"

"In his vest pocket."

They eased him over to a couch, broke a small glass capsule into a handkerchief, and held it under his nose. The volatile released by the capsule seemed to bring a little color into his face. They did what little they could for him, then waited for him to regain consciousness.

Charlie broke the uneasy silence. "Mac, we ain't going through with this."

"Why not?"

"It's murder. He'll never stand up under the initial acceleration."

"Maybe not, but it's what he wants to do. You heard him."

"But we oughtn't to let him."

"Why not? It's neither your business nor the business of this blasted paternalistic government to tell a man not to risk his life doing what he really wants to do."

"All the same, I don't feel right about it. He's such a swell old duck."

"Then what d'yuh want to do with him—send him back to Kansas City so those old harpies can shut him up in a laughing academy till he dies of a broken heart?"

"N-no-o-o—not that."

"Get out there and make your setup for those test runs. I'll be along."

A wide-tired desert runabout rolled in the ranch-yard gate the next morning and stopped in front of the house. A heavy-set man with a firm but kindly face climbed out and spoke to McIntyre, who approached to meet him.

"You James McIntyre?"

"What about it?"

"I'm the deputy federal marshal hereabouts. I got a warrant for your arrest."

"What's the charge?"

"Conspiracy to violate the Space Precautionary Act."

Charlie joined the pair. "What's up, Mac?"

The deputy answered. "You'd be Charles Cummings, I guess. Warrant here for you. Got one for a man named Harriman, too, and a court order to put seals on your spaceship."

"We've no spaceship."

"What d'yuh keep in that shed?"

"Strato yacht."

"So? Well, I'll put seals on her until a spaceship comes along. Where's Harriman?"

"Right in there." Charlie obliged by pointing, ignoring McIntyre's scowl.

The deputy turned his head. Charlie couldn't have missed the button by a fraction of an inch, for the deputy collapsed quietly to the ground.

Charlie stood over him, rubbing his knuckles and mourning. "That's the finger I broke playing shortstop. I'm always hurting that finger."

"Get Pop into the cabin," Mac cut him short, "and strap him into his hammock."

"Aye aye, Skipper."

They dragged the ship by tractor out of the hanger, turned, and went out on the desert plain to find elbow room for the take-off. They climbed in. McIntyre saw the deputy from his starboard conning port. He was staring disconsolately after them.

McIntyre fastened his safety belt, settled his corset, and spoke into the engine-room speaking tube. "All set, Charlie?"

"All set, Skipper. But you can't raise ship yet, Mac—*she ain't named!*"

"No time for your superstitions!"

Harriman's thin voice reached them. "Call her the *Lunatic*. It's the only appropriate name!"

McIntyre settled his head into the pads, punched two keys, then three more in rapid succession, and the *Lunatic* raised ground.

"How are you, Pop?" Charlie searched the old man's face anxiously.

Harriman licked his lips and managed to speak. "Doing fine, son. Couldn't be better."

"The acceleration is over; it won't be so bad from here on. I'll unstrap you so you can wiggle around a little. But I think you'd better stay in the hammock." He tugged at buckles.

Harriman partially repressed a groan.

"What is it, Pop?"

"Nothing. Nothing at all. Just go easy on that side."

Charlie ran his fingers over the old man's side with the sure, delicate touch of a mechanic. "You ain't foolin' me none, Pop. But there isn't much I can do until we ground."

"Charlie—"

"Yes, Pop?"

"Can't I move to a port? I want to watch the earth."

"Ain't nothin' to see yet; the ship hides it. As soon as we turn ship, I'll move you. Tell you what: I'll give you a sleepy pill, and then wake you when we do."

"No!"

"Huh?"

"I'll stay awake."

"Just as you say, Pop."

Charlie clambered monkey fashion to the nose of the ship and anchored to the gimbals of the pilot's chair.

McIntyre questioned him with his eyes.

"Yeah, he's alive all right," Charlie told him, "but he's in bad shape."

"How bad?"

"Couple of cracked ribs, anyhow. I don't know what else. I don't know whether he'll last out the trip, Mac. His heart was pounding something awful."

"He'll last, Charlie. He's tough."

"Tough? He's delicate as a canary."

"I don't mean that. He's tough way down inside—where it counts."

"Just the same, you'd better set her down awful easy if you want to ground with a full complement aboard."

"I will. I'll make one full swing around the moon and ease her in on an involute approach curve. We've got enough fuel, I think."

They were now in a free orbit; after McIntyre turned ship, Charlie went back, unslung the hammock, and moved Harriman, hammock and all, to a side port. McIntyre steadied the ship about a transverse axis so that the tail pointed toward the sun, then gave a short blast on two tangential jets opposed in couple to cause the ship to spin slowly about her longitudinal axis, and thereby create a slight artificial gravity. The initial weightlessness when coasting commenced had knotted the old man with the characteristic nausea of free flight, and the pilot wished to save his passenger as much discomfort as possible.

But Harriman was not concerned with the condition of his stomach.

There it was, all as he had imagined it so many times. The moon swung majestically past the view port, wider than he had ever seen it before, all of her familiar features cameo clear. She gave way to the earth as the ship continued its slow swing, the earth itself as he had envisioned her, appearing like a noble moon, many times as wide as the moon appears to the earthbound, and more luscious, more sensuously beautiful than the silver moon could be. It was sunset near the Atlantic seaboard—the line of shadow cut down the coast line of North America, clashed through Cuba, and obscured all but the west coast of South America. He savored the mellow blue of the Pacific Ocean, felt the texture of the soft green and brown of the continents, admired the blue-white cold of the polar caps. Canada and the northern states were obscured by cloud, a vast low-pressure area that spread across the continent. It shone with an even more satisfactory dazzling white than the polar caps.

As the ship swung slowly around, Earth would pass from view, and the stars would march across the port—the same stars he had always known, but steady, brighter, and unwinking against a screen of perfect, live black. Then the moon would swim into view again to claim his thoughts.

He was serenely happy in a fashion not given to most men, even in a long lifetime. He felt as if he were every man who has ever lived, looked up at the stars, and longed.

As the long hours came and went he watched and dozed and dreamed. At least once he must have fallen into deep sleep, or possibly delirium, for he came to with a start, thinking that his wife, Charlotte, was calling to him. "Delos!" the voice had said. "Delos! Come in from there! You'll catch your death of cold in that night air."

Poor Charlotte! She had been a good wife to him, a good wife. He was quite sure that her only regret in dying had been her fear that he could not take proper care of himself. It had not been her fault that she had not shared his dream and his need.

Charlie rigged the hammock in such a fashion that Harriman could watch from the starboard port when they swung around the far face of the moon. He picked out the landmarks made familiar to him by a thousand photographs with nostalgic pleasure, as if he were returning to his own country. McIntyre brought her slowly down as they came back around to the earthward face, and prepared to land east of Mare Fecunditatis, about ten miles from Luna City.

It was not a bad landing, all things considered. He had to land without coaching from the grounds, and he had no second pilot to watch the radar for him. In his anxiety to make it gentle he missed his destination by some thirty miles, but he did his cold-sober best. But at that it was bumpy.

As they grounded and the pumice dust settled around them, Charlie came up to the control station.

"How's our passenger?" Mac demanded.

"I'll see, but I wouldn't make any bets. That landing stunk, Mac."

"Damn it, I did my best."

"I know you did, Skipper. Forget it."

But the passenger was alive and conscious, although bleeding from the nose and with a pink foam on his lips. He was feebly trying to get himself out of his cocoon. They helped him, working together.

"Where are the vacuum suits?" was his first remark.

"Steady, Mr. Harriman. You can't go out there yet. We've got to give you some first aid."

"Get me that suit! First aid can wait."

Silently they did as he ordered. His left leg was practically use-less, and they had to help him through the lock, one on each side. But, with his inconsiderable mass having a lunar weight of only twenty pounds, he was no burden. They found a place some fifty yards from the ship where they could prop him up and let him look, a chunk of scoria supporting his head.

McIntyre put his helmet against the old man's and spoke. "We'll leave you here to enjoy the view while we get ready for the trek into town. It's a forty-miler, pretty near, and we'll have to break out spare air bottles and rations and stuff. We'll be back soon."

Harriman nodded without answering and squeezed their gaunt-lets with a grip that was surprisingly strong.

He sat very quietly, rubbing his hands against the soil of the moon and sensing the curiously light pressure of his body against the ground. At long last there was peace in his heart. His hurts had ceased to pain him. He *was* where he had longed to be—he had followed his need. Over the western horizon hung the earth at last quarter, a green-blue giant moon. Overhead the sun shone down from a black and starry sky. And underneath the moon the soil of the moon itself. He was on the moon!

He lay back, still, while a bath of content flowed over him like a tide at flood and soaked to his very marrow.

His attention strayed momentarily, and he thought once again that his name was called. Silly, he thought, I'm getting old—my mind wanders.

Back in the cabin Charlie and Mac were rigging shoulder yokes on a stretcher. "There. That will do," Mac commented. "We'd better stir Pop out; we ought to be going."

"I'll get him," Charlie replied. "I'll just pick him up and carry him. He don't weigh nothing."

Charlie was gone longer than McIntyre had expected him to be. He returned alone. Mac waited for him to close the lock and swing back his helmet. "Trouble?"

"Never mind the stretcher, Skipper. We won't be needin' it."

"Yeah, I mean it," he continued. "Pop's done for. I did what was necessary."

McIntyre bent down without a word and picked up the wide

skis necessary to negotiate the powdery ash. Charlie followed his example. Then they swung the spare air bottles over their shoulders and passed out through the lock.

They didn't bother to close the outer door of the lock behind them.

THEORY OF ROCKETRY

C. M. KORNBLUTH

*The peculiar reality of Cyril Kornbluth's sf led one edi-
tor to comment that Mr. Kornbluth was writing stories
aimed at the* Saturday Evening Post *of the year 2100. I
don't think he has ever done better than in this bitter,
precise and perfectly real picture of a future very near
and quite entirely possible.*

Mr. Edel taught six English classes that year at Richard M. Nixon
High School, and the classes averaged seventy-five pupils each.
That was four hundred and fifty boys and girls, but Mr. Edel still
tried to have the names down cold by at least the third week of
the semester. As English 308 stormed into his room he was aware
that he was not succeeding, and that next year he would even stop
trying, for in 1978 the classes would average eighty-two pupils
instead of seventy-five.

One seat was empty when the chime sounded; Mr. Edel was
pleased to notice that he remembered whose it was. The absent
pupil was a Miss Kahn, keyed into his memory by "Kahnsti-
pated," which perhaps she was, with her small pinched features
centered in a tallow acre of face. Miss Kahn slipped in some three
seconds late; Edel nodded at his intern, Mrs. Giovino, and Mrs.
Giovino coursed down the aisle to question, berate and possibly
demerit Miss Kahn. Edel stood up, the Modern Revised Old Testament already open before him.

"*You're blessed,*" he read, "*if you're excused for your wrong-
doing and your sin is forgiven. You're blessed if God knows that
you're not evil and sly any more. I, King David, used to hide my
sins from God while I grew old and blustered proudly all day.
But all day and all night too your hand was heavy on me,
God . . .*"

It would be the flat, crystal-clear, crystal-blank M.R.O.T. all this week; next week he'd read (with more pleasure) from the Roman Catholic Knox translation; the week after that, from the American Rabbinical Council's crabbed version heavy with footnotes; and the week after that, back to M.R.O.T. Thrice blessed was he this semester that there were no Moslems, Buddhists, militant atheists or miscellaneous cultists to sit and glower through the reading or exercise their legal right to wait it out in the corridor. This semester the classes were All-American: Protestant, Catholic, Jewish—choice of one.

"Amen," chorused the class, and they sat down; two minutes of his fifty-minute hour were gone forever.

Soft spring was outside the windows, and they were restless. Mr. Edel "projected" a little as he told them, "This is the dreaded three-minute impromptu speech for which English Three Oh Eight is notorious, young ladies and gentlemen. The importance of being able to speak clearly on short notice should be obvious to everybody. You'll get nowhere in your military service if you can't give instructions and verbal orders. You'll get less than nowhere in business if you can't convey your ideas crisply and accurately." A happy thought struck him: great chance to implement the Spiritual-Values Directive. He added, "You may be asked to lead in prayer or say grace on short notice." (He'd add *that* one to his permanent repertoire; it was a natural.) "We are not asking the impossible. Anybody can talk interestingly, easily and naturally for three minutes if they try. Miss Gerber, will you begin with a little talk on your career plans?"

Miss Gerber ("Grapefruit" was the mnemonic) rose coolly and driveled about the joys of motherhood until Mrs. Giovino passed her card to Edel and called time.

"You spoke freely, Miss Gerber, but perhaps not enough to the point," said Edel. "I'm pleased, though, that you weren't bothered by any foolish shyness. I'm sure everybody I call on will be able to talk right up like you did." (He liked that *"like"* the way you like biting on a tooth that aches; *he'd* give them Artificial-Grammar De-emphasis . . .) "Foster, may we hear from you on the subject of your coming summer vacation?" He jotted down a C for the Grapefruit.

Foster ("Fireball") rose and paused an expert moment. Then in a firm and manly voice he started with a little joke ("If I survive English Three Oh Eight . . ."), stated his theme ("A vacation is not a time for idling and wasted opportunity"), developed it ("harvest crew during the day for *physical*—my Science Search Project during the evenings for *mental*"), elevated it ("no excuse for neglecting one's regular attendance at one's place of worship") and concluded with a little joke ("should be darned glad to get back to school!").

The speech clocked 2:59. It was masterly; none of the other impromptus heard that morning came close to it.

"And," said Mr. Edel at lunch to his semi-crony Dr. Fugua, biology, "between classes I riffled through the grade cards again and found I'd marked him F. Of course I changed it to A. The question is, *why?*"

"Because you'd made a mistake," said Fuqua absently. Something was on his mind, thought Edel.

"No, no. Why did I make the mistake?"

"Well, Fured, in *The Psychology of Everyday—*"

"Roland, please, I know all that. Assume I do. Why do I unconsciously dislike Foster? I should get down on my knees and thank God for Foster."

Fugua shook his head and began to pay attention. "Foster?" he said. "You don't know the half of it. I'm his faculty adviser. Quite a boy, Foster."

"To me just a name, a face, a good recitation every time. You know: seventy-five to a class. What's he up to here at dear old Tricky Dicky?"

"Watch the funny jokes, Edel," said Fuqua, alarmed.

"Sorry. It slipped out. But Foster?"

"Well, he's taking an inhuman pre-engineering schedule. Carrying it with ease. Going out for all the extracurricular stuff the law allows. R.O.T.C. Drill Team, Boxing Squad, Math Club, and there I had to draw the line. He wanted on the Debating Team too. I've seen him upset just once. He came to me last year when the school dentist wanted to pull a bad wisdom tooth he had. He made me make the dentist wait until he had a chance to check the dental requirements of the Air Force Academy. They allow four extractions, so he let the dentist yank it. Fly boy. Off we go into the whatsit. He wants it bad."

"I see. Just a boy with motivation. How long since you've seen one, Roland?"

Dr. Fuqua leaned forward, his voice low and urgent. "To hell with Foster, Dave. I'm in trouble. Will you help me?"

"Why, of course, Roland. How much do you need?" Mr. Edel was a bachelor and had found one of the minor joys of that state to be "tiding over" his familied friends.

"Not that kind of trouble, Dave. Not yet. They're sharpening the ax for me. I get a hearing this afternoon."

"Good God! What are you supposed to have done?"

"Everything. Nothing. It's one of those 'best interests' things. Am I taking the Spiritual-Values Directive *seriously* enough? Am I *thinking* about patting any adolescent fannies? Exactly *why* am I in the lowest quarter for my seniority group with respect to voluntary hours of refresher summer courses? Am I *happy* here?"

Edel said, "These things always start somewhere. Who's out to get you?"

Fuqua took a deep breath and said in a surprisingly small voice, "Me, I suppose."

"Oh?"

Then it came out with a rush. "It was the semester psychometrics. I'd been up all night almost, fighting with Beth. She does *not* understand how to handle a fifteen-year-old boy—never mind. I felt sardonic, so I did something sardonic. And stupid. Don't ever get to feeling sardonic, Dave. I took the psychometric and I checked their little boxes and I told the goddamned truth right down the line. I checked them where I felt like checking them and not where a prudent biology teacher *ought* to check them."

"You're dead," Mr. Edel said after a pause.

"I thought I could get a bunch of the teachers to say they lie their way through the psychometrics. Start a real stink."

"I'd make a poor ditch digger, Roland, but—if you can get nine others, I'll speak up. No, make that six others. I don't think they could ignore eight of us."

"You're a good man," Dr. Fuqua said. "I'll let you know. There's old McGivern—near retirement. I want to try him." He gulped his coffee and headed across the cafeteria.

Edel sat there, mildly thunderstruck at Fuqua's folly and his own daring. Fuqua had told them the kind of bird he was by checking "Yes" or "No" on the silly-clever statements. He had told them that he liked a drink, that he thought most people were stupider than he, that he talked without thinking first, that he ate too much, that he was lazy, that he had an eye for a pretty ankle —that he was a human being not much better or worse than any other human being. But that wasn't the way to do it, and damned well Fuqua had known it. You simply told yourself firmly, for the duration of the test, "*I am a yuk. I have never had an independent thought in my life; independent thinking scares me. I am utterly monogamous and heterosexual. I go bowling with the boys. Television is the greatest of the art forms. I believe in installment purchasing. I am a yuk.*"

That these parlor games were taken seriously by some people was an inexplicable but inexorable fact of life in the twentieth century. Edel had yukked his way through scholarships, college admissions, faculty appointment and promotions and had never thought the examination worse than a bad cold. Before maturity set in, in the frat house, they had eased his qualms about psychometric testing with the ancient gag "You ain't a man until you've had it three times."

Brave of him, pretty brave at that, to back up Fuqua—if Roland could find six others.

Roland came to him at four o'clock to say he had not even found one other. "I don't suppose— No. I'm not asking you to, Dave. Two—it wouldn't be any good."

He went into the principal's office.

The next day a bright young substitute was teaching biology in his place and his student advisees had been parceled out among other teachers. Mr. Edel found that young Foster had now become his charge.

The seventy-two pupils in his English 114 class sat fascinated and watched the television screen. Dr. Henley Ragen was teaching them *Macbeth*, was teaching about nine hundred English 114 classes throughout the state *Macbeth*, and making them like it. The classroom rapport was thick enough to cut and spread with a shingle. The man's good, Edel thought, but *that* good? How much is feedback from their knowing he's famous for his rapport, how much is awe of his stupendous salary, still nowhere equal to nine hundred teachers' salaries?

Dr. Henley Ragen, *el magnífico*, portentously turned a page; there was grim poetry in the gesture. He transfixed the classroom (nine hundred classrooms) with Those Eyes. Abruptly he became Macbeth at the Banquet prepar'd. With nervous hilarity he shouted at his guests, *"You know your own degrees; sit down! At first and last, the hearty welcome!"* Stockstill at a lectern he darted around the table, bluffly rallying the company, slipped off to chat, grimly merry, with the First Murtherer at the door, returned to the banquet, stood in chilled horror at the Ghost in the chair, croaked, *"The table's full."*

Mr. Edel studied the faces of his seventy-two English 114ers. They were in hypnotic states of varying depths, except Foster. The Fireball was listening and learning, his good mind giving as well as taking. The intelligent face was alive, the jaw firm, and around him eyes were dull and jaws went slack. Foster could speak and write an English sentence, which perhaps was the great distinguishing mark between him and the rest of English 114. Blurted fragments of thought came from them, and the thoughts were clichés a hundred times out of a hundred.

Dr. Henley Ragen growled at them, *"We are yet but young in deed . . ."* and his eyes said the rest, promising horrors to come. He snapped the book shut like a pistol's bang; the 114ers popped out of their trances into dazed attentiveness. "Notebooks!" said Ragen (*qua* Ragen) and, seventy-two gunfighters quick on the draw, they snapped out books and poised their pens. Ragen spoke for ten minutes about the scene; every so often Those Eyes and an intensification of That Voice cued them to write a word or a phrase, almost without glancing at the paper. (Later each would look at his notes and not be surprised to find them lucid, orderly, even masterful summations of the brief lecture.)

As Dr. Henley Ragen bluffly delivered a sort of benediction from the altar of learning, Mr. Edel thought, Well, they've got the Banquet Scene now; they'll own it forever. The way they own the Prologue to *The Canterbury Tales*, the "Ode to the West Wind," *Arrowsmith*. A good deal better than nothing; *pauca sed matura*. Or so he supposed.

That afternoon from three to five Mr. Edel was available to his advisees. It was a period usually devoted to catching up on his paperwork; beyond making out the students' assignment schedule, a task traditionally considered beyond the capacity of the young, he had done no advising in years. And Foster appeared.

His handshake was manly, his grin was modest but compelling. He got to the point. "Mr. Edel, do you think I could swing an Enrichment Project in English?"

The teacher hardly knew what he meant. "Enrichment? Well, we haven't been doing that lately, Foster. I suppose it's still in the optional curriculum—"

"Yes, sir, Form Sixty-eight, English, Paragraph Forty-five, Section Seven. '*Opportunities shall be afforded to students believed qualified by advisers to undertake projects equivalent to College Freshman English term papers, and the grades therefor shall be entered on the students' records and weighed as evidence in assigning students' positions in the graduating class.*'"

Mr. Edel had found Foster's card by then and was studying it. The boy's schedule was brutal, but his grade average was somewhere between B-plus and A. "Foster," he told him, "there's such a thing as a breaking point. I—I understand you want very much to go to Colorado Springs." (Poor Fuqua! What had become of . . . ?)

"Very much, sir. They expect the best—they have a right to expect the best. I'm not complaining, Mr. Edel, but there are girls with straight-A averages who aren't working as hard as I am. Well, I've just got to beat them at their own game."

Mr. Edel understood. It wasn't just girls, though mostly it was. There was a type of student who was no trouble, who did the work, every smidgen of it, who read every word of every assigned page, who turned in accurate, curiously dead, echoless, unresonant papers which you could not in decency fault though you wanted to tear them up and throw them in their authors' bland faces. You had a curious certainty that the adeptly memorized data they reeled back on demand vanished forever once the need for a grade was gone, that it never by any chance became bone of their bone to strengthen them against future trials. Often enough when you asked them what they hoped to be they smilingly said, "I am going to teach."

Foster, now. A boy who *fought* with the material and whipped it. He said, "Why so strong, Foster? What's it about?"

The boy said, "Space, partly. And my father. Two big challenges, Mr. Edel. I think I'm a very lucky fellow. Here I am with a new frontier opening up, but there are lot's of fellows my age who don't see it. I see it because of my father. It's wonderful to have a challenge like that: Can I be the man he is? Can I learn even more, be a better leader, a better engineer?"

Mr. Edel was moved deeply. "Your father just missed space flight, is that it?"

"By a whisker," Foster said regretfully. "Nothing can be done about it except what I'm doing."

"He's an aeroengineer?"

"He can do *anything*," Foster said positively. "And he has!"

A picture of the elder Foster was forming in Mr. Edel's mind—young Fireball grown taller, solider and grizzled, the jaw firmed and controlled, the voice more powerful and sure. And, unquestionably, leather puttees.

Foster's card said he had no mother, which made it more understandable. This fine boy was hard material honed to an edge, single-purposed. Did he have a young Hap Arnold here in his office? A Curtis LeMay? They had to come from somewhere, those driving, wide-ranging leaders and directors of millions. The slow-rolling conquest of space needed such men, first to navigate and pilot so no navigator or pilot would ever be able to snow them, then to move up step by step through research to command, then to great command.

"I'll bet on you, Foster," he said abruptly. "We can't let the—the future *English* teachers outpoint you with their snap courses. You'll do me a term paper on . . . on *Henry V*. First, read it. Read *hell* out of it and take notes. Get in touch with me when you think you're ready to talk it over. I happen to be a bachelor; I have time in the evenings. And talk it over with your father, if you can persuade him to read along with you."

Foster laughed. "I'm afraid Dad's much too busy for Shakespeare, but I'll try. Thanks, Mr. Edel." He left.

Mr. Edel, with considerable trouble, found a pad of forms in his desk which covered Enrichment Projects, English, Adviser's Permission for. He filled one out for Foster, looked it over and said, surprised, "Again, damn it!" He had checked the box for "Permission denied." He tore up the form—it was discolored anyway from being so long on the top of the pad—and meticulously made out another, checking the various boxes with exquisite care.

That night after dinner he tried to telephone Roland Fuqua, but service to his number had been discontinued. Alarmed, he buzzed over on his scooter to Fuqua's apartment, one of a quarter million in the Dearborn Village Development of Metropolitan Life and Medical. Roland's hulking, spoiled and sullen boy Edward (who had unilaterally changed his name last year to Rocky) was the only person there, and he was on his way out—"to an orgy with some pigs," if you believed him. He said "Little Rollo" was now a night-shift lab assistant in a pet-food company's quality-control department and this was his mother's Bingo night. "You want I should give a message?" he asked satirically, overplaying the role of intolerably burdened youth.

"If it won't break your back," Mr. Edel said, "please ask your father to give me a ring sometime."

Again in his own small apartment, Mr. Edel thought of many things. Of the ancient papyrus which, when decoded, moaned: *"Children are not now as respectful and diligent as they were in the old days."* Of *Henry V.* Of Dr. Fuqua drudging away on pet-food protein determinations and lucky to be doing that. Of his own selfish, miserable, lonely comfort in his castle. Of Foster, the hero-king to be, and of himself, Aristotle to the young Alexander. Had there been a dozen such in his twenty years? There had not. Marie Perrone still sent him her novels, and they were almost popular and very bad. Jim Folwell had gone to Princeton and into the foreign service and that was that. Janice Reeves and Ward Dreiman were married and both teaching at Cornell. What had happened to the hundred thousand others he had taught only God and themselves knew. If they all dropped dead at this instant, tomorrow morning some trucks would not roll for an hour or two, some advertising agencies would come near to missing a few deadlines, some milk would sour and some housewives would bang, perplexed, on the doors of shops that should be open, a few sales would languish unclosed, a few machines would growl for lack of oil. But Foster might land on the moons of Jupiter.

Therefore let him learn, make him learn, how to be great. He would meet his Pistols, Bardolphs, Fluellens, a few Exeters, and without doubt his Cambridges and Scroops: clowns, fuss-budgets, friends and traitors. It could matter to nobody except herself if her agent ripped poor arty Marie Perrone up her back; it might matter a great deal to—he shied at the alternatives—to, let us say, man, if Foster trusted a Pistol to do his work, or passed over a Fluellen for his mannerisms, or failed to know a Scroop when he saw one.

We will arm the young hero-king, he thought comfortably just before sleep claimed him.

Roland Fuqua had been transferred to Toledo by the pet-food company. He wrote to Edel:

Instinct tells me not to queer my luck by talking about it, but anyway—I really believe I'm moving up in the organization. The other day a party from Sales came through the QC labs and one of them, just an ordinary-looking Joe, stopped to talk to me about the test I was running—asked very intelligent questions. You could have knocked me over with a Folin-Wu pipette when they told me who he was afterward: just John McVey himself, Assistant Vice-President in Charge of Sales! Unaccustomed as I am to pipe dreams, it can't be a coincidence that it was me he talked to instead of half a dozen other lab men with seniority; I don't know what he has in mind exactly, maybe some kind of liaison job between QC and Sales, which would put me on Staff level instead of Hourly-Rated. . . .

Mr. Edel felt sick for him. He would have to answer the letter at once; if he put it off he would put it off again and their correspondence would peter out and Fuqua would be betrayed. But what could he tell him—that he *was* pipe-dreaming, that "coincidences" like that happen to everybody a hundred times a day, that Roland Fuqua, Ph.D., would never, at forty-five, move from the quality-control lab to the glittering world of sales?

He stalled for time by stamping and addressing the envelope first, then hung over the typewriter for five minutes of misery. It was Wednesday night; Foster was due for the twelfth and last of his Enrichment sessions. Mr. Edel tried not to cause Fuqua pain by dwelling on the world of teaching he had lost—but *what* else was there to write about?

I'm sure you remember Foster—the fly boy? I've been taking him, on one of those Enrichment things, through Henry V. *This is supposed to win him .001 of a place higher on the graduating-class list and get him into the Academy, and I suppose it will. Things are very simple for Foster, enviably so. He has a titan of engineering for a father who appears to commute between the Minas Gerais power station in Brazil, his consulting service in the city and trouble spots in the I. T. and T. network—maybe I should say commutate. I honestly do not believe that Foster has to lie his way through the personality profiles like the rest of us mortals—*

Now, there was a hell of a thing to put down. He was going to rip the page out and start again, then angrily changed his mind. Fuqua wasn't a cripple; it wasn't Bad Form to mention his folly; it would be merely stupid to pretend that nothing had happened. He finished out the page with a gush of trivia. Sexy little Mrs. Dickman who taught Spanish was very visibly expecting. New dietician in the cafeteria, food cheaper but worse than ever. Rumored retirement of Old Man Thelusson again and one step up for history teachers if true. Best wishes good luck regards to Beth and the youngster, Dave. He whipped the page into folds, slipped it into the envelope and sealed the flap fast, before he could change his mind again. It was time to stop treating Fuqua like a basket case; if convalescence had not begun by now it never would.

His bell rang: Foster was on time, to the minute.

They shook hands rather formally. "Like a cup of coffee, Foster?" Mr. Edel asked.

"No thank you, sir."

"I'll make one for myself, then. Brought your paper? Good. Read it to me."

While he compounded coffee Foster began to read. After much discussion they had settled on "Propaganda and Reality in *Henry V*" as his topic. The boy had read Holinshed where relevant, articles in *The Dictionary of National Biography* and appropriate history texts. Beyond suggesting these, Mr. Edel had left him alone in the actual treatment of his paper. He did not quite know what to expect from Foster beyond careful organization and an absence of gross blunders; he waited with interest.

The paper was a short one—fifteen hundred words, by request. Nevertheless it gave Mr. Edel a few painful shocks. There were two sneers at "deluded groundlings," much reveling in the irony of the fictional Henry's affection for his Welsh captain as against the real Henry who had helped to crush Glendower and extinguish the Welsh as a nation, and fun with the Irishman Macmorris who came loyally from Shakespeare's pen in 1599 while "the general of our gracious empress" was doing his best to extinguish the Irish as a nation. Henry's "*we have now no thoughts in us but France (save those to God)*" was evaluated as "the poet's afterthought." The massacre of the French prisoners at Agincourt, Henry's brutal practical joke with the pretended glove of a French nobleman, his impossibly compressed and eloquent courtship of Katharine, were all somehow made to testify to a cynical Shakespeare manipulating his audience's passions.

The great shock was that Foster approved of all this. "*It was a time of troubles and England was besieged from without and threatened from within. The need of the time was a call to unity, and this Shakespeare provided in good measure. The London mob and the brotherhood of apprentices, always a potential danger to the Peace, no doubt were inspired and pacified for a time by the Shakespearean version of a successful aggressor's early career.*"

Modestly Foster folded his typescript.

It was ground into Mr. Edel that you start by saying whatever words of praise are possible and then go on to criticize. Mechanically he said warm things about the paper's organization, its style, its scholarly apparatus. "But—aren't you taking a rather too utilitarian view of the play? It is propaganda to some extent, but should you stop short with the propaganda function of the play? I'm aware that you're limited by your topic and length, but I wish there had been some recognition of the play's existence as a work of art."

Foster said, smiling, "Well, I'm new at this, Mr. Edel. I didn't know I was supposed to stray. Should I revise it?"

"Oh, no," Mr. Edel said quickly. "I didn't mean to imply that you're unarguably mistaken in anything you said. I don't know why I'm fussing at you about it at all. I suppose you've taken a sort of engineering approach to literature, which is natural enough. Did you ever succeed in engaging your father in the project?"

"I'm afraid not, Mr. Edel. You can imagine."

"He's been away?"

"Why, no." Foster was surprised. But *didn't* his father go away now and then? He thought Foster had said—or *almost* said—

He took the paper from him and leafed through it. "This is quite good enough for a pass, Foster. It'll be read by somebody in the English chairman's office, but that's a formality. Let's say you've completed your Enrichment Option." He stuck out his hand and Foster took it warmly. "That, then, is that. Do you have to run now?"

"With all rods out," Foster said. "I've got to prepare for the Math Team meet, a hundred things. Can I mail that for you?"

It was the letter to Fuqua on his desk. "Why, thanks."

"Thank *you*, Mr. Edel, for the time you've taken with me."

Well worth it, son, Mr. Edel thought after the door closed. There aren't many like you. The paper was a little cold and cynical, but you'll learn. Criticism's heady stuff. Speaking quite objectively, you've done a piece thoroughly consistent with College Freshman English work, and that's what you were supposed to do. If it helps get you into Colorado Springs, I've done my job.

He turned in the paper the next day to the English chairman's office and the assistant chairman read it while he waited, mumbled "Seems quite competent" and entered a "Completed" on Foster's grade card. He let his eyes run over the other grades and whistled. "A beaver," he said.

"All rods out," Mr. Edel smugly corrected him, and went to the door. A freshman girl who knew him, on messenger duty with the principal's office, intercepted him in the corridor. The message: he would please report at once to the principal; Mrs. Giovino would be advised to take such classes as he might be obliged to miss.

"*Classes?*" he asked the girl, unbelievingly.

She knew nothing.

The assistant principal for teaching personnel received him at once, alone in his two-window office. He was a gray man named Sturgis whose pride was getting to the point. "Edel," he asked, "are you sure you're *happy* here?"

Mr. Edel said, recognizing a sheet of typing on Sturgis' desk, "May I ask how you got that letter of mine?"

"Surely. Your young friend Foster turned it in."

"But why? Why?"

"I shall quote: '*I honestly do not believe that Foster has to lie his way through the personality profiles like the rest of us mortals.*' If you believed this, Edel, why did you counsel him to lie? Why did you show him this letter as proof that you lied yourself?"

"Counsel him to lie? I never. I never."

His stammering was guilt; his sweating was guilt. Sturgis pitied him and shook his head. "He kept a little record," Sturgis said. "Ha, a 'log' he called it—he's quite space-minded; did you know?"

"I know. I demand a hearing, goddammit!"

Sturgis was surprised. "Oh, you'll get a hearing, Edel. We always give hearings; you know that."

"I know that. Can I get back to my classes now?"

"Better not. If you're not *happy* here . . ."

Mr. Edel and Foster met that afternoon in the soda shop two blocks from the school. Mr. Edel had been waiting for him, and Foster saw the teacher staring at him from a booth. He excused himself politely from the Math Team crowd around him and joined Mr. Edel.

"I feel I owe you an explanation, sir," Foster said.

"I agree. How could you—why—?"

Foster said apologetically, "They like you to be a little ruthless at the Academy. This will stand out on my record as a sign of moral fiber. No, Mr. Edel, don't try to hit me. It'll make things look that much worse at the hearing. Goodbye, sir."

He rejoined his handsome, quiet crowd at the counter; in a moment they were talking busily about elliptic functions and Fourier series. Mr. Edel slunk from the place knowing that there was only one court of appeal.

3379 Seneca Avenue turned out to be a shocking slum tenement back of a municipal bus garage. The apartment, Mr. Edel thought, after his initial surprise, would be one of those "hideaways"—probably a whole floor run together, equipped with its own heating and air-conditioning, plumbing replaced . . . after all, would Foster Senior give a damn about a fancy address? Not that engineer.

But the Foster apartment, or so said a card tacked to a rust-stiffened bell-pull, was only one of a dozen like it on the cabbage-reeking fifth floor. And the paunchy, unshaven, undershirted man who came to the door and stood reeling in the doorway said: "Yah, I'm Ole Foster. Yah, I got a boy in Nixon High. What the crazy kid do now? He's crazy, that kid. Maybe I get a little drunk sometime, I got a little pension from I hurt my back driving the buses, people don't appreciate, don't realize. You wanna drink? What you say you come for?"

"About your son . . ."

"So I beat him up!" the man yelled, suddenly belligerent. "Ain't I his father? He talks smart to me, I got a right to beat him some, ain't I? People don't appreciate . . ."

Old Foster lost interest and, mumbling, closed the door.

Mr. Edel walked slowly down the stairs, not able to forgive, but feeling at least the beginnings of eventual ease from the knowledge of why he was being destroyed.

DON'T LOOK NOW

HENRY KUTTNER

Henry Kuttner could do anything. Anyhow, he could write any sort of story, from sober and thoughtful examinations like "Private Eye" to wildly funny stories like "Mimsy Were the Borogoves," to mention only two of the yarns nominated for this anthology. "Don't Look Now" stands somewhere in the middle—a fine, horrifying notion carried off with great good humor. This, a difficult trick for anybody, was a specialty of Mr. Kuttner's, and it results in a tone he made peculiarly his own.

The man in the brown suit was looking at himself in the mirror behind the bar. The reflection seemed to interest him even more deeply than the drink between his hands. He was paying only perfunctory attention to Lyman's attempts at conversation. This had been going on for perhaps fifteen minutes before he finally lifted his glass and took a deep swallow.

"Don't look now," Lyman said.

The brown man slid his eyes sidewise toward Lyman, tilted his glass higher, and took another swig. Ice cubes slipped down toward his mouth. He put the glass back on the red-brown wood and signaled for a refill. Finally he took a deep breath and looked at Lyman.

"Don't look at what?" he asked.

"There was one sitting right beside you," Lyman said, blinking rather glazed eyes. "He just went out. You mean you couldn't see him?"

The brown man finished paying for his fresh drink before he answered. "See who?" he asked, with a fine mixture of boredom, distaste and reluctant interest. "Who went out?"

"What have I been telling you for the last ten minutes? Weren't you listening?"

"Certainly I was listening. That is—certainly. You were talking about—bathtubs. Radios. Orson—"

"Not Orson. H. G. Herbert George. With Orson it was just a gag. H. G. *knew*—or suspected. I wonder if it was simply intuition with him? He couldn't have had any proof—but he did stop writing science fiction rather suddenly, didn't he? I'll bet he knew once, though."

"Knew what?"

"About the Martians. All this won't do us a bit of good if you don't listen. It may not anyway. The trick is to jump the gun—with proof. Convincing evidence. Nobody's ever been allowed to produce the evidence before. You *are* a reporter, aren't you?"

Holding his glass, the man in the brown suit nodded reluctantly.

"Then you ought to be taking it all down on a piece of folded paper. I want everybody to know. The whole world. It's important. Terribly important. It explains everything. My life won't be safe unless I can pass along the information and make people believe it."

"Why won't your life be safe?"

"Because of the Martians, you fool. They own the world."

The brown man sighed. "Then they own my newspaper too," he objected, "so I can't print anything they don't like."

"I never thought of that," Lyman said, considering the bottom of his glass, where two ice cubes had fused into a cold, immutable union. "They're not omnipotent, though. I'm sure they're vulnerable, or why have they always kept under cover? They're afraid of being found out. If the world had convincing evidence— Look, people always believe what they read in the newspapers. Couldn't you—"

"Ha," said the brown man with deep significance.

Lyman drummed sadly on the bar and murmured, "There must be some way. Perhaps if I had another drink . . ."

The brown-suited man tasted his Collins, which seemed to stimulate him. "Just what is all this about Martians?" he asked Lyman. "Suppose you start at the beginning and tell me again. Or can't you remember?"

"Of course I can remember. I've got practically total recall. It's something new. Very new. I never could do it before. I can even remember my last conversation with the Martians." Lyman favored the brown man with a glance of triumph.

"When was that?"

"This morning."

"I can even remember conversations I had last week," the brown man said mildly. "So what?"

"You don't understand. They make us forget, you see. They tell us what to do and we forget about the conversation—it's post-hypnotic suggestion, I expect—but we follow their orders just the same. There's the compulsion, though we think we're making our own decisions. Oh, they own the world, all right, but nobody knows it except me."

"And how did you find out?"

"Well, I got my brain scrambled, in a way. I've been fooling around with supersonic detergents, trying to work out something marketable, you know. The gadget went wrong—from some standpoints. High-frequency waves, it was. They went through and through me. Should have been inaudible, but I could hear them, or rather—well, actually I could *see* them. That's what I mean about my brain being scrambled. And after that, I could see and hear the Martians. They've geared themselves so they work efficiently on ordinary brains, and mine isn't ordinary any more. They can't hypnotize me, either. They can command me, but I needn't obey—now. I hope they don't suspect. Maybe they do. Yes, I guess they do."

"How can you tell?"

"The way they look at me."

"How do they look at you?" asked the brown man, as he began to reach for a pencil and then changed his mind. He took a drink instead. "Well? What are they like?"

"I'm not sure. I can see them, all right, but only when they're dressed up."

"Okay, okay," the brown man said patiently. "How do they look, dressed up?"

"Just like anybody, almost. They dress up in—in human skins. Oh, not real ones—imitations. Like the Katzenjammer Kids zipped into crocodile suits. Undressed, I don't know. I've never seen one.

Maybe they're invisible even to me then, or maybe they're just camouflaged. Ants or owls or rats or bats or—'"

"Or anything," the brown man said hastily.

"Thanks. Or anything, of course. But when they're dressed up like humans—like that one who was sitting next to you a while ago, when I told you not to look—"

"That one was invisible, I gather?"

"Most of the time they are, to everybody. But once in a while, for some reason, they—"

"Wait," the brown man objected. "Make sense, will you? They dress up in human skins and then sit around invisible?"

"Only now and then. The human skins are perfectly good imitations. Nobody can tell the difference. It's that third eye that gives them away. When they keep it closed, you'd never guess it was there. When they want to open it, they go invisible—like *that*. Fast. When I see somebody with a third eye, right in the middle of his forehead, I know he's a Martian and invisible, and I pretend not to notice him."

"Uh-huh," the brown man said. "Then for all you know I'm one of your visible Martians."

"Oh, I hope not!" Lyman regarded him anxiously. "Drunk as I am, I don't think so, I've been trailing you all day, making sure. It's a risk I have to take, of course. They'll go to any length—any length at all—to make a man give himself away. I realize that. I can't really trust anybody. But I had to find *someone* to talk to, and I—" He paused. There was a brief silence. "I could be wrong," Lyman said presently. "When the third eye's closed, I can't tell if it's there. Would you mind opening your third eye for me?" He fixed a dim gaze on the brown man's forehead.

"Sorry," the reporter said. "Some other time. Besides, I don't know you. So you want me to splash this across the front page, I gather? Why didn't you go to see the managing editor? My stories have to get past the desk and rewrite."

"I want to give my secret to the world," Lyman said stubbornly. "The question is, how far will I get? You'd expect they'd have killed me the minute I opened my mouth to you—except that I didn't say anything while they were here. I don't believe they take us very seriously, you know. This must have been going on since the dawn of history, and by now they've had time to get careless. They let Fort go pretty far before they cracked down on him. But you notice they were careful never to let Fort get hold of genuine proof that would convince people."

The brown man said something under his breath about a human-interest story in a box. He asked, "What do the Martians do besides hang around bars all dressed up?"

"I'm still working on that," Lyman said. "It isn't easy to understand. They run the world, of course, but why?" He wrinkled his brow and stared appealingly at the brown man. "Why?"

"If they do run it, they've got a lot to explain."

"That's what I mean. From our viewpoint, there's no sense to it. We do things illogically, but only because they tell us to. Everything we do, almost, is pure illogic. Poe's "Imp of the Perverse"—you could give it another name beginning with *M*. Martian, I mean. It's all very well for psychologists to explain why a murderer wants to confess, but it's still an illogical reaction. Unless a Martian commands him to."

"You can't be hypnotized into doing anything that violates your moral sense," the brown man said triumphantly.

Lyman frowned. "Not by another human, but you can by a Martian. I expect they got the upper hand when we didn't have more than ape-brains, and they've kept it ever since. They evolved as we did, and kept a step ahead. Like the sparrow on the eagle's back who hitchhiked till the eagle reached his ceiling, and then took off and broke the altitude record. They conquered the world, but nobody ever knew it. And they've been ruling ever since."

"But—"

"Take houses, for example. Uncomfortable things. Ugly, inconvenient, dirty, everything wrong with them. But when men like Frank Lloyd Wright slip out from under the Martians' thumb long enough to suggest something better, look how the people react. They hate the thought. That's their Martians, giving them orders."

"Look. Why should the Martians care what kind of houses we live in? Tell me that."

Lyman frowned. "I don't like the note of skepticism I detect creeping into this conversation," he announced. "They care, all right. No doubt about it. They *live* in our houses. We don't build for our convenience, we build, under order, for the Martians, the way they want it. They're very much concerned with everything we do. And the more senseless, the more concern. Take wars. Wars don't make sense from any human viewpoint. Nobody really wants wars. But we go right on having them. From the Martian viewpoint, they're useful. They give us a spurt in technology, and they reduce the excess population. And there are lots of other results, too. Colonization, for one thing. But mainly technology. In peacetime, if a guy invents jet propulsion it's too expensive to develop commercially. In wartime, though, it's *got* to be developed. Then the Martians can use it whenever they want. They use us the way they'd use tools or—or limbs. And nobody ever really wins a war—except the Martians."

The man in the brown suit chuckled. "That makes sense," he said. "It must be nice to be a Martian."

"Why not? Up till now, no race ever successfully conquered and ruled another. The underdog could revolt or absorb. If you know you're being ruled, then the ruler's vulnerable. But if the world doesn't know—and it doesn't . . .

"Take radios," Lyman continued, going off at a tangent. "There's no earthly reason why a sane human should listen to a radio. But the Martians make us do it. They like it. Take bathtubs. Nobody contends bathtubs are comfortable—for us. But they're fine for Martians. All the impractical things we keep on using, even though we know they're impractical—"

"Typewriter ribbons," the brown man said, struck by the thought. "But not even a Martian could enjoy changing a typewriter ribbon."

Lyman seemed to find that flippant. He said that he knew all about the Martians except for one thing—their psychology.

"I don't know *why* they act as they do. It looks illogical sometimes, but I feel perfectly sure they've got sound motives for every move they make. Until I get that worked out I'm pretty much at a standstill. Until I get evidence—proof—and help. I've got to stay under cover till then. And I've been doing that. I do what they tell me, so they won't suspect, and I pretend to forget what they tell me to forget."

"Then you've got nothing much to worry about."

Lyman paid no attention. He was off again on a list of his grievances.

"When I hear the water running in the tub and a Martian splashing around, I pretend I don't hear a thing. My bed's too short and I tried last week to order a special length, but the Martian that sleeps there told me not to. He's a runt, like most of them. That is, I think they're runts. I have to deduce, because you never see them undressed. But it goes on like that constantly. By the way, how's your Martian?"

The man in the brown suit set down his glass rather suddenly. "My Martian?"

"Now, listen. I may be just a little bit drunk, but my logic remains unimpaired. I can still put two and two together. Either you know about the Martians or you don't. If you do, there's no point in giving me that 'What, *my* Martian?' routine. I know you have a Martian. Your Martian knows you have a Martian. My Martian knows. The point is, do *you* know? Think hard," Lyman urged solicitously.

"No, I haven't got a Martian," the reporter said, taking a quick drink. The edge of the glass clicked against his teeth.

"Nervous, I see," Lyman remarked. "Of course you *have* got a Martian. I suspect you know it."

"What would I be doing with a Martian?" the brown man asked with dogged dogmatism.

"What would you be doing without one? I imagine it's illegal. If they caught you running around without one they'd probably put you in a pound or something until claimed. Oh, you've got one, all right. So have I. So has he, and he, and he—and the bartender." Lyman enumerated the other barflies with a wavering forefinger.

"Of course they have," the brown man said. "But they'll all go back to Mars tomorrow and then you can see a good doctor. You'd better have another dri—"

He was turning toward the bartender when Lyman, apparently by accident, leaned close to him and whispered urgently, "*Don't look now!*"

The brown man glanced at Lyman's white face reflected in the mirror before them.

"It's all right," he said. "There aren't any Mar—"

Lyman gave him a fierce, quick kick under the edge of the bar. "Shut up! One just came in!"

And then he caught the brown man's gaze and with elaborate unconcern said, "—so naturally, there was nothing for me to do but climb out on the roof after it. Took me ten minutes to get it down the ladder, and just as we reached the bottom it gave one bound, climbed up my face, sprang from the top of my head, and there it was again on the roof, screaming for me to get it down."

"*What?*" the brown man demanded with pardonable curiosity.

"My cat, of course. What did you think? No, never mind, don't answer that." Lyman's face was turned to the brown man's, but from the corners of his eyes he was watching an invisible progress down the length of the bar toward a booth at the very back.

"Now, why did he come in?" he murmured. "I don't like this. Is he anyone you know?"

"Is who—?"

"That Martian. Yours, by any chance? No, I suppose not. Yours was probably the one who went out a while ago. I wonder if he went to make a report and sent this one in? It's possible. It could be. You can talk now, but keep your voice low, and stop squirming. Want him to notice we can see him?"

"*I* can't see him. Don't drag me into this. You and your Martians can fight it out together. You're making me nervous. I've got to go, anyway." But he didn't move to get off the stool. Across Lyman's shoulder he was stealing glances toward the back of the bar, and now and then he looked at Lyman's face.

"Stop watching me," Lyman said. "Stop watching him. Anybody'd think you were a cat."

"Why a cat? Why should anybody— Do I look like a cat?"

"We were talking about cats, weren't we? Cats can see them, quite clearly. Even undressed, I believe. They don't like them."

"Who doesn't like who?"

"Whom. Neither likes the other. Cats can see Martians—sh-h!— but they pretend not to, and that makes the Martians mad. I have a theory that cats ruled the world before Martians came. Never mind. Forget about cats. This may be more serious than you think. I happen to know my Martian's taking tonight off, and I'm pretty sure that was your Martian who went out some time ago.

And have you noticed that nobody else in here has his Martian with him? Do you suppose—" His voice sank. "Do you suppose they could be *waiting for us outside?*"

"Oh, Lord," the brown man said. "In the alley with the cats, I suppose."

"Why don't you stop this yammer about cats and be serious for a moment?" Lyman demanded, and then paused, paled, and reeled slightly on his stool. He hastily took a drink to cover his confusion.

"What's the matter now?" the brown man asked.

"Nothing." Gulp. "Nothing. It was just that—he *looked* at me. With—you know."

"Let me get this straight. I take it the Martian is dressed in—is dressed like a human?"

"Naturally."

"But he's invisible to all eyes but yours?"

"Yes. He doesn't want to be visible just now. Besides—" Lyman paused cunningly. He gave the brown man a furtive glance and then looked quickly down at his drink. "Besides, you know, I rather think you *can* see him—a little, anyway."

The brown man was perfectly silent for about thirty seconds. He sat quite motionless, not even the ice in the drink he held clinking. One might have thought he did not even breathe. Certainly he did not blink.

"What makes you think that?" he asked in a normal voice, after the thirty seconds had run out.

"I—did I say anything? I wasn't listening." Lyman put down his drink abruptly. "I think I'll go now."

"No you won't," the brown man said, closing his fingers around Lyman's wrist. "Not yet you won't. Come back here. Sit down. Now. What was the idea? Where were you going?"

Lyman nodded dumbly toward the back of the bar, indicating either a jukebox or a door marked "Men."

"I don't feel so good. Maybe I've had too much to drink. I guess I'll—"

"You're all right. I don't trust you back there with that—that invisible man of yours. You'll stay right here until he leaves."

"He's going now," Lyman said brightly. His eyes moved with great briskness along the line of an invisible but rapid progress toward the front door. "See, he's gone. Now let me loose, will you?"

The brown man glanced toward the back booth.

"No," he said, "he isn't gone. Sit right where you are."

It was Lyman's turn to remain quite still, in a stricken sort of way, for a perceptible while. The ice in *his* drink, however, clinked audibly. Presently he spoke. His voice was soft, and rather soberer than before.

"You're right. He's still there. You can see him, can't you?"

The brown man said, "Has he got his back to us?"

"You *can* see him, then. Better than I can, maybe. Maybe there are more of them here than I thought. They could be anywhere. They could be sitting beside you anywhere you go, and you wouldn't even guess, until—" He shook his head a little. "They'd want to be *sure*," he said, mostly to himself. "They can give you orders and make you forget, but there must be limits to what they can force you to do. They can't make a man betray himself. They'd have to lead him on—until they were sure."

He lifted his drink and tipped it steeply above his face. The ice ran down the slope and bumped coldly against his lip, but he held it until the last of the pale, bubbling amber had drained into his mouth. He set the glass on the bar and faced the brown man.

"Well?" he said.

The brown man looked up and down the bar.

"It's getting late," he said. "Not many people left. We'll wait."

"Wait for what?"

The brown man looked toward the back booth and looked away again quickly.

"I have something to show you. I don't want anyone else to see."

Lyman surveyed the narrow, smoky room. As he looked the last customer besides themselves at the bar began groping in his pocket, tossed some change on the mahogany and went out slowly.

They sat in silence. The bartender eyed them with stolid disinterest. Presently a couple in the front booth got up and departed, quarreling in undertones.

"Is there anyone left?" the brown man asked in a voice that did not carry down the bar to the man in the apron.

"Only—" Lyman did not finish, but he nodded gently toward the back of the room. "He isn't looking. Let's get this over with. What do you want to show me?"

The brown man took off his wrist watch and pried up the metal case. Two small glossy photograph prints slid out. The brown man separated them with a finger.

"I just want to make sure of something," he said. "First—why did you pick me out? Quite a while ago, you said you'd been trailing me all day, making sure. I haven't forgotten that. And you knew I was a reporter. Suppose you tell me the truth now."

Squirming on his stool, Lyman scowled. "It was the way you looked at things," he murmured. "On the subway this morning— I'd never seen you before in my life, but I kept noticing the way you looked at things, the wrong things, things that weren't there, the way a cat does, and then you'd always look away—I got the idea you could see the Martians, too."

"Go on," the brown man said quietly.

"I followed you. All day. I kept hoping you'd turn out to be— somebody I could talk to. Because if I could *know* that I wasn't the only one who could see them, then I'd know there was still some hope left. It's been worse than solitary confinement. I've been able to see them for three years now. Three years. And I've managed to keep my power a secret even from them. And, some-how, I've managed to keep from killing myself, too."

"Three years?" the brown man said. He shivered.

"There was always a little hope. I knew nobody would believe —not without proof. And how can you get proof? It was only that I—I kept telling myself that maybe you could see them, too, and if you could, maybe there were others—lots of others, enough so we might get together and work out some way of proving to the world . . ."

The brown man's fingers were moving. In silence he pushed a photograph across the mahogany. Lyman picked it up unsteadily.

"Moonlight?" he asked after a moment. It was a landscape under a deep, dark sky with white clouds in it. Trees stood white and lacy against the darkness. The grass was white as if with moonlight, and the shadows blurry.

"No, not moonlight," the brown man said. "Infrared. I'm

strictly an amateur, but lately I've been experimenting with infrared film. And I got some very odd results."

Lyman stared at the film.

"You see, I live near—" The brown man's finger tapped a certain quite common object that appeared in the photograph. "And something funny keeps showing up now and then against it. But only with infrared film. Now, I know chlorophyll reflects so much infrared light that grass and leaves photograph white. The sky comes out black, like this. There are tricks to using this kind of film. Photograph a tree against a cloud, and you can't tell them apart in the print. But you can photograph through a haze and pick out distant objects the ordinary film wouldn't catch. And sometimes, when you focus on something like this"—he tapped the image of the very common object again—"you get a very odd image on the film. Like that. A man with three eyes."

Lyman held the print up to the light. In silence he took the other one from the bar and studied it. When he laid them down he was smiling.

"You know," Lyman said in a conversational whisper, "a professor of astrophysics at one of the more important universities had a very interesting little item in the *Times* the other Sunday. Name of Spitzer, I think. He said that if there were life on Mars, and if Martians had ever visited earth, there'd be no way to prove it. Nobody would believe the few men who saw them. Not, he said, unless the Martians happened to be photographed." Lyman looked at the brown man thoughtfully. "Well," he said, "it's happened. You've photographed them."

The brown man nodded. He took up the prints and returned them to his watch case. "I thought so, too. Only, until tonight I couldn't be sure. I'd never seen one—fully—as you have. It isn't so much a matter of what you call getting your brain scrambled with supersonics as it is of just knowing where to look. But I've been seeing *part* of them all my life, and so has everybody. It's that little suggestion of movement you never catch except just at the edge of your vision, just out of the corner of your eye. Something that's *almost* there—and when you look fully at it, there's nothing. These photographs showed me the way. It's not easy to learn, but it can be done. We're conditioned to look directly at a thing—the particular thing we want to see clearly, whatever it is. Perhaps the Martians gave us that conditioning. When we see a movement at the edge of our range of vision, it's almost irresistible not to look directly at it. So it vanishes."

"Then they can be seen—by anybody?"

"I've learned a lot in a few days," the brown man said. "Since I took those photographs. You have to train yourself. It's like seeing a trick picture—one that's really a composite, after you study it. Camouflage. You just have to learn how. Otherwise we can look at them all our lives and never see them."

"The camera does, though."

"Yes, the camera does. I've wondered why nobody ever caught them this way before. Once you see them on film, they're unmistakable—that third eye."

"Infrared film's comparatively new, isn't it? And then I'll bet you have to catch them against that one particular background— you know—or they won't show on the film. Like trees against clouds. It's tricky. You must have had just the right lighting that day, and exactly the right focus, and the lens stopped down just right. A kind of minor miracle. It might never happen again exactly that way. But— Don't look now."

They were silent. Furtively, they watched the mirror. Their eyes slid along toward the open door of the tavern.

And then there was a long, breathless silence.

"He looked back at us," Lyman said very quietly. "He looked at us . . . that third eye!"

The brown man was motionless again. When he moved, it was to swallow the rest of his drink.

"I don't think that they're suspicious yet," he said. "The trick will be to keep under cover until we can blow this thing wide open. There's got to be some way to do it—some way that will convince people."

"There's proof. The photographs. A competent cameraman ought to be able to figure out just how you caught that Martian on film and duplicate the conditions. It's evidence."

"Evidence can cut both ways," the brown man said. "What I'm hoping is that the Martians don't really like to kill—unless they have to. I'm hoping they won't kill without proof. But—" He tapped his wrist watch.

"There's two of us now, though," Lyman said. "We've got to stick together. Both of us have broken the big rule, *Don't look now.*"

The bartender was at the back, disconnecting the jukebox. The brown man said, "We'd better not be seen together unnecessarily. But if we both come to this bar tomorrow night at nine for a drink—that wouldn't look suspicious, even to them."

"Suppose—" Lyman hesitated. "May I have one of those photographs?"

"Why?"

"If one of us had—an accident, the other one would still have the proof. Enough, maybe, to convince the right people."

The brown man hesitated, nodded shortly, and opened his watch case again. He gave Lyman one of the pictures.

"Hide it," he said. "It's—evidence. I'll see you here tomorrow. Meanwhile, be careful. Remember to play safe."

They shook hands firmly, facing each other in an endless second of final, decisive silence. Then the brown man turned abruptly and walked out of the bar.

Lyman sat there. Between two wrinkles in his forehead there was a stir and a flicker of lashes unfurling. The third eye opened slowly and looked after the brown man.

SEVEN-DAY TERROR

R. A. LAFFERTY

R. A. Lafferty is, comparatively, a new writer. Like most recent arrivals, he spends a good deal of his time in taking new, and very fresh, looks at the sort of thing everybody else has been looking at for years. Some of our most cherished traditions have been reduced to a kind of meaningless and farcical Brownian movement under the hands of this peculiar gentleman.

Judy Merril reprinted this one before I could get to it. I salute, as I am sometimes found doing, her taste, and I admire her speed.

"Is there anything you want to make disappear?" Clarence Willoughby asked his mother.

"A sinkful of dishes is all I can think of. How will you do it?"

"I just built a disappearer. All you do is cut the other end out of a beer can. Then you take two pieces of red cardboard with peepholes in the middle and fit them in the ends. You look through the peepholes and blink. Whatever you look at will disappear."

"Oh."

"But I don't know if I can make them come back. We'd better try it on something else. Dishes cost money."

As always, Myra Willoughby had to admire the wisdom of her nine-year-old son. She would not have had such foresight herself. He always did.

"You can try it on Blanche Manners' cat outside there. Nobody will care if it disappears except Blanche Manners."

"All right."

He put the disappearer to his eye and blinked. The cat disappeared from the sidewalk outside.

His mother was interested. "I wonder how it works. Do you know how it works?"

"Yes. You take a beer can with both ends cut out and put in two pieces of cardboard. Then you blink."

"Never mind. Take it outside and play with it. You hadn't better make anything disappear in here till I think about this."

But when he had gone his mother was oddly disturbed.

"I wonder if I have a precocious child. Why, there's lots of grown people who wouldn't know how to make a disappearer that would work. I wonder if Blanche Manners will miss her cat very much?"

Clarence went down to the Plugged Nickel, a pothouse on the corner.

"Do you have anything you want to make disappear, Nokomis?"

"Only my paunch."

"If I make it disappear it'll leave a hole in you and you'll bleed to death."

"That's right, I would. Why don't you try it on the fireplug outside?"

This in a way was one of the happiest afternoons ever in the neighborhood. The children came from blocks around to play in the flooded streets and gutters, and if some of them drowned (and we don't say that they *did* drown) in the flood (and brother! it was a flood), why, you have to expect things like that. The fire engines (who ever heard of calling fire engines to put out a flood?) were apparatus-deep in the water. The policemen and the ambulance men wandered around wet and bewildered.

"Resuscitator, resuscitator, anybody wanna resuscitator?" chanted Clarissa Willoughby.

"Oh, shut up," said the ambulance attendants.

Nokomis, the barman in the Plugged Nickel, called Clarence aside.

"I don't believe, just for the moment, I'd tell anyone what happened to the fireplug," he said.

"I won't tell if you won't tell," said Clarence.

Officer Comstock was suspicious. "There's only seven possible explanations. One of the seven Willoughby kids did it. I dunno how. It'd take a bulldozer to do it, and then there'd be something left of the plug. But however they did it, one of them did it."

Officer Comstock had a talent for getting near the truth of dark matters. This is why he was walking a beat out here in the boondocks instead of sitting in a chair downtown.

"Clarissa!" said Officer Comstock in a voice like thunder.

"Resuscitator, resuscitator, anybody wanna resuscitator?" chanted Clarissa.

"Do you know what happened to that fireplug?" asked Officer C.

"I have an uncanny suspicion. As yet it is no more than that. When I am better informed I will advise you."

Clarissa was eight years old and much given to uncanny suspicions.

"Clementine, Harold, Corinne, Jimmy, Cyril," he asked the five younger Willoughby chlidren, "do you know what happened to that fireplug?"

"There was a man around yesterday. I bet he took it," said Clementine.

"I don't even remember a fireplug there. I think you're making a lot of fuss about nothing," said Harold.

"City Hall's going to hear about this," said Corinne.

"Pretty dommed sure," said Jimmy, "but I won't tell."

"Cyril!" cried Officer Comstock in a terrible voice. Not a terrifying voice, a terrible voice. He felt terrible now.

"Great green bananas," said Cyril, "I'm only three years old. I don't see how it's even my responsibility."

"Clarence," said Officer Comstock.

Clarence gulped.

"Do you know where that fireplug went?"

Clarence brightened. "No, sir. I don't know where it went."

A bunch of smart alecks from the Water Department came out and shut off the water for a few blocks around and put some kind of cap on in place of the fireplug. "This sure is going to be a funny-sounding report," said one of them.

Officer Comstock walked away discouraged. "Don't bother me, Miss Manners," he said. "I don't know where to look for your cat. I don't even know where to look for a fireplug."

"I have an idea," said Clarissa, "that when you find the cat you will find the fireplug the same place. As yet it is only an idea."

Ozzie Murphy wore a little hat on top of his head. Clarence pointed his weapon and winked. The hat was no longer there, but a little trickle of blood was running down the pate.

"I don't believe I'd play with that any more," said Nokomis.

"Who's playing?" said Clarence. "This is for real."

This was the beginning of the seven-day terror in the heretofore obscure neighborhood. Trees disappeared from the parkings; lampposts were as though they had never been; Wally Waldorf drove home, got out, slammed the door of his car, and there was no car. As George Mullendorf came up the walk to his house his dog, Pete, ran to meet him and took a flying leap to his arms. The dog left the sidewalk, but something happened; the dog was gone and only a bark lingered for a moment in the puzzled air.

But the worst were the fireplugs. The second plug was installed the morning after the disappearance of the first. In eight minutes it was gone and the flood waters returned. Another one was in by twelve o'clock. Within three minutes it had vanished. The next morning fireplug number four was installed.

The water commissioner was there, the city engineer was there, the chief of police was there with a riot squad, the president of the Parent-Teachers Association was there, the president of the university was there, the mayor was there, three gentlemen of the F.B.I., a newsreel photographer, eminent scientists and a crowd of honest citizens.

"Let's see it disappear now," said the city engineer.

"Let's see it disappear now," said the police chief.

"Let's see it disa— It did, didn't it?" said one of the eminent scientists.

And it was gone and everybody was very wet.

"At least I have the picture sequence of the year," said the photographer. But his camera and apparatus disappeared from the midst of them.

"Shut off the water and cap it," said the commissioner. "And don't put in another plug yet. That was the last plug in the warehouse."

"This is too big for me," said the mayor. "I wonder that Tass doesn't have it yet."

"Tass has it," said a little round man. "I am Tass."

"If all of you gentlemen will come into the Plugged Nickel," said Nokomis, "and try one of our new Fire Hydrant Highballs you will all be happier. These are made of good corn whiskey, brown sugar and hydrant water from this very gutter. You can be the first to drink them."

Business was phenomenal at the Plugged Nickel, for it was in front of its very doors that the fireplugs disappeared in floods of gushing water.

"I know a way we can get rich," said Clarissa several days later to her father, Tom Willoughby. "Everybody says they're going to sell their houses for nothing and move out of the neighborhood. Go get a lot of money and buy them all. Then you can sell them again and get rich."

"I wouldn't buy them for a dollar each. Three of them have disappeared already, and all the families but us have their furniture moved out in their front yards. There might be nothing but vacant lots in the morning."

"Good, then buy the vacant lots. And you can be ready when the houses come back."

"Come back? Are the houses going to come back? Do you know anything about this, young lady?"

"I have a suspicion verging on a certainty. As of now I can say no more."

Three eminent scientists were gathered in an untidy suite that looked as though it belonged to a drunken sultan.

"This transcends the metaphysical. It impinges on the quantum continuum. In some ways it obsoletes Boff," said Dr. Velikof Vonk.

"The contingence on the intransigence is the most mystifying aspect," said Arpad Arkabaranan.

"Yes," said Willy McGilly. "Who would have thought that you could do it with a beer can and two pieces of cardboard? When I was a boy I used an oatmeal box and red Crayola."

"I do not always follow you," said Dr. Vonk. "I wish you would speak plainer."

So far no human had been injured or disappeared—except for

a little blood on the pate of Ozzie Murphy, on the lobes of Conchita when her gaudy earrings disappeared from her very ears, a clipped finger or so when a house vanished as the front doorknob was touched, a lost toe when a neighborhood boy kicked at a can and the can was not; probably not more than a pint of blood and three or four ounces of flesh all together.

Now, however, Mr. Buckle the grocery man disappeared before witnesses. This was serious.

Some mean-looking investigators from downtown came out to the Willoughbys'. The meanest-looking one was the mayor. In happier days he had not been a mean man, but the terror had now reigned for seven days.

"There have been ugly rumors," said one of the mean investigators, "that link certain events to this household. Do any of you know anything about them?"

"I started most of them," said Clarissa. "But I didn't consider them ugly. Cryptic, rather. But if you want to get to the bottom of this just ask me a question."

"Did you make those things disappear?" asked the investigator.

"That isn't the question," said Clarissa.

"Do you know where they have gone?" asked the investigator.

"That isn't the question, either," said Clarissa.

"Can you make them come back?"

"Why, of course I can. Anybody can. Can't you?"

"I cannot. If you can, please do so at once."

"I need some stuff. Get me a gold watch and a hammer. Then go down to the drugstore and get me this list of chemicals. And I need a yard of black velvet and a pound of rock candy."

"Shall we?" asked one of the investigators.

"Yes," said the mayor. "It's our only hope. Get her anything she wants."

And it was all assembled.

"Why does she get all the attention?" asked Clarence. "I was the one that made all the things disappear. How does she know how to get them back?"

"I knew it!" cried Clarissa with hate. "I knew he was the one that did it. He read in my diary how to make a disappearer. If I was his mother, I'd whip him for reading his little sister's diary.

That's what happens when things like that fall into irresponsible hands."

She poised the hammer over the gold watch of the mayor on the floor.

"I have to wait a few seconds. This can't be hurried. It'll be only a little while."

The second hand swept around to the point that was preordained for it before the world began. Clarissa suddenly brought down the hammer with all her force on the beautiful gold watch.

"That's all," she said. "Your troubles are over. See, there is Blanche Manners' cat on the sidewalk just where she was seven days ago."

And the cat was back.

"Now let's go down to the Plugged Nickel and watch the fireplug come back."

They had only a few minutes to wait. It came from nowhere and clanged into the street like a sign and a witness.

"Now I predict," said Clarissa, "that every single object will return exactly seven days from the time of its disappearance."

The seven-day terror had ended. The objects began to reappear.

"How," asked the mayor, "did you know they would come back in seven days?"

"Because it was a seven-day disappearer that Clarence made. I also know how to make a nine-day, a thirteen-day, a twenty-seven-day, and an eleven-year disappearer. I was going to make a thirteen-day one, but for that you have to color the ends with the blood from a little boy's heart, and Cyril cried every time I tried to make a good cut."

"You really know how to make all of these?"

"Yes. But I shudder if the knowledge should ever come into unauthorized hands."

"I shudder too, Clarissa. But tell me, why did you want the chemicals?"

"For my chemistry set."

"And the black velvet?"

"For doll dresses."

"And the pound of rock candy?"

"How did you ever get to be mayor of this town if you have

to ask questions like that? What do you think I wanted the rock candy for?"

"One last question," said the mayor. "Why did you smash my gold watch with the hammer?"

"Oh," said Clarissa, "that was for dramatic effect."

COMING ATTRACTION

FRITZ LEIBER

This story, which was one of the five stories most often nominated, does not strike me as a warning, but as a prophecy.

The coupe with the fishhooks welded to the fender shouldered up over the curb like the nose of a nightmare. The girl in its path stood frozen, her face probably stiff with fright under her mask. For once my reflexes weren't shy. I took a fast step toward her, grabbed her elbow, yanked her back. Her black skirt swirled out.

The big coupe shot by, its turbine humming. I glimpsed three faces. Something ripped. I felt the hot exhaust on my ankles as the big coupe swerved back into the street. A thick cloud like a black flower blossomed from its jouncing rear end, while from the fishhooks flew a black shimmering rag.

"Did they get you?" I asked the girl.

She had twisted around to look where the side of her skirt was torn away. She was wearing nylon tights.

"The hooks didn't touch me," she said shakily. "I guess I'm lucky."

I heard voices around us:

"Those kids! What'll they think up next?"

"They're a menace. They ought to be arrested."

Sirens screamed at a rising pitch as two motor police, their rocket-assist jets full on, came whizzing toward us after the coupe. But the black flower had become an inky fog obscuring the whole street. The motor police switched from rocket assists to rocket brakes and swerved to a stop near the smoke cloud.

"Are you English?" the girl asked me. "You have an English accent." Her voice came shudderingly from behind the sleek black satin mask. I fancied her teeth must be chattering. Eyes that were perhaps blue searched my face from behind the black gauze covering the eyeholes of the mask.

I told her she'd guessed right.

She stood close to me. "Will you come to my place tonight?" she asked rapidly. "I can't thank you now. And there's something else you can help me about."

My arm, still lightly circling her waist, felt her body trembling. I was answering the plea in that as much as in her voice when I said, "Certainly."

She gave me an address south of Inferno, an apartment number and a time. She asked me my name and I told her.

"Hey, you!"

I turned obediently to the policeman's shout. He shooed away the small clucking crowd of masked women and barefaced men. Coughing from the smoke that the black coupe had thrown out, he asked for my papers. I handed him the essential ones.

He looked at them and then at me. "British Barter? How long will you be in New York?"

Suppressing the urge to say, "For as short a time as possible." I told him I'd be here for a week or so.

"May need you as a witness," he explained. "Those kids can't use smoke on us. When they do that, we pull them in."

He seemed to think the smoke was the bad thing. "They tried to kill the lady," I pointed out.

He shook his head wisely. "They always pretend they're going to, but actually they just want to snag skirts. I've picked up rippers with as many as fifty skirt snags tacked up in their rooms. Of course, sometimes they come a little too close."

I explained that if I hadn't yanked her out of the way she'd have been hit by more than hooks. But he interrupted. "If she'd thought it was a real murder attempt, she'd have stayed here."

I looked around. It was true. She was gone.

"She was fearfully frightened," I told him.

"Who wouldn't be? Those kids would have scared old Stalin himself."

"I mean frightened of more than 'kids.' They didn't look like kids."

"What did they look like?"

I tried without much success to describe the three faces. A vague impression of viciousness and effeminacy doesn't mean much.

"Well, I could be wrong," he said finally. "Do you know the girl? Where she lives?"

"No," I half lied.

The other policeman hung up his radiophone and ambled toward us, kicking at the tendrils of dissipating smoke. The black cloud no longer hid the dingy façades with their five-year-old radiation flash burns, and I could begin to make out the distant stump of the Empire State Building, thrusting up out of Inferno like a mangled finger.

"They haven't been picked up so far," the approaching policeman grumbled. "Left smoke for five blocks, from what Ryan says."

The first policeman shook his head. "That's bad," he observed solemnly.

I was feeling a bit uneasy and ashamed. An Englishman shouldn't lie, at least not on impulse.

"They sound like nasty customers," the first policeman continued in the same grim tone. "We'll need witnesses. Looks as if you may have to stay in New York longer than you expect."

I got the point. I said, "I forgot to show you all my papers," and handed him a few others, making sure there was a five-dollar bill in among them.

When he handed them back a bit later, his voice was no longer ominous. My feelings of guilt vanished. To cement our relationship, I chatted with the two of them about their job.

"I suppose the masks give you some trouble," I observed. "Over in England we've been reading about your new crop of masked female bandits."

"Those things get exaggerated," the first policeman assured me. "It's the men masking as women that really mix us up. But, brother, when we nab them, we jump on them with both feet."

"And you get so you can spot women almost as well as if they had naked faces," the second policeman volunteered. "You know, hands and all that."

"Especially all that," the first agreed with a chuckle. "Say, is it true that some girls don't mask over in England?"

"A number of them have picked up the fashion," I told him. "Only a few, though—the ones who always adopt the latest style, however extreme."

"They're usually masked in the British newscasts."

"I imagine it's arranged that way out of deference to American taste," I confessed. "Actually, not very many do mask."

The second policeman considered that. "Girls going down the street bare from the neck up." It was not clear whether he viewed the prospect with relish or moral distaste. Likely both.

"A few members keep trying to persuade Parliament to enact a law forbidding all masking," I continued, talking perhaps a bit too much.

The second policeman shook his head. "What an idea. You know, masks are a pretty good thing, brother. Couple of years more and I'm going to make my wife wear hers around the house."

The first policeman shrugged. "If women were to stop wearing masks, in six weeks you wouldn't know the difference. You get used to anything, if enough people do or don't do it."

I agreed, rather regretfully, and left them. I turned north on Broadway (old Tenth Avenue, I believe) and walked rapidly until I was beyond Inferno. Passing such an area of undecontaminated radioactivity always makes a person queasy. I thanked God there weren't any such in England, as yet.

The street was almost empty, though I was accosted by a couple of beggars with faces tunneled by H-bomb scars, whether real or of make-up putty I couldn't tell. A fat woman held out a baby with webbed fingers and toes. I told myself it would have been deformed anyway and that she was only capitalizing on our fear of bomb-induced mutations. Still, I gave her a seven-and-a-half-cent piece. Her mask made me feel I was paying tribute to an African fetish.

"May all your children be blessed with one head and two eyes, sir."

"Thanks," I said, shuddering, and hurried past her.

". . . There's only trash behind the mask, so turn your head, stick to your task: Stay away, stay away—from—the—girls!"

This last was the end of an anti-sex song being sung by some religionists half a block from the circle-and-cross insignia of a femalist temple. They reminded me only faintly of our small tribe of British monastics. Above their heads was a jumble of billboards advertising predigested foods, wrestling instruction, radio handies and the like.

I stared at the hysterical slogans with disagreeable fascination. Since the female face and form have been banned on American signs, the very letters of the advertiser's alphabet have begun to crawl with sex—the fat-bellied, big-breasted capital *B*, the lascivious double *O*. However, I reminded myself, it is chiefly the mask that so strangely accents sex in America.

A British anthropologist has pointed out that, while it took more than five thousand years to shift the chief point of sexual interest from the hips to the breasts, the next transition, to the face, has taken less than fifty years. Comparing the American style with Moslem tradition is not valid; Moslem women are compelled to wear veils, the purpose of which is to make a husband's property private, while American women have only the compulsion of fashion and use masks to create mystery.

Theory aside, the actual origins of the trend are to be found in the antiradiation clothing of World War III, which led to masked wrestling, now a fantastically popular sport, and that in turn led to the current female fashion. Only a wild style at first, masks quickly became as necessary as brassieres and lipsticks had been earlier in the century.

I finally realized that I was not speculating about masks in general, but about what lay behind one in particular. That's the devil of the things; you're never sure whether a girl is heightening loveliness or hiding ugliness. I pictured a cool, pretty face in which fear showed only in widened eyes. Then I remembered her blond hair, rich against the blackness of the satin mask. She'd told me to come at the twenty-second hour—10 P.M.

I climbed to my apartment near the British Consulate; the elevator shaft had been shoved out of plumb by an old blast, a nuisance in these tall New York buildings. Before it occurred to me that I would be going out again, I automatically tore a tab from the film strip under my shirt. I developed it just to be sure. It showed that the total radiation I'd taken that day was still within the safety limit. I'm no phobic about it, as so many people are these days, but there's no point in taking chances.

I flopped down on the daybed and stared at the silent speaker and the dark screen of the video set. As always, they made me think, somewhat bitterly, of the two great nations of the world. Mutilated by each other, yet still strong, they were crippled giants poisoning the planet with their respective dreams of an impossible equality and an impossible success.

I fretfully switched on the speaker. By luck, the newscaster was talking excitedly of the prospects of a bumper wheat crop, sown by planes across a dust bowl moistened by seeded rains. I listened carefully to the rest of the program (it was remarkably clear of Russian telejamming), but there was no further news of interest to me. And, of course, no mention of the moon, though everyone knows that America and Russia are racing to develop their primary bases into fortresses capable of mutual assault and the launching of alphabet bombs toward Earth. I myself knew perfectly well that the British electronic equipment I was helping trade for American wheat was destined for use in spaceships.

I switched off the newscast. It was growing dark, and once again I pictured a tender, frightened face behind a mask. I hadn't had a date since England. It's exceedingly difficult to become acquainted with a girl in America, where as little as a smile often can set one of them yelping for the police—to say nothing of the increasingly puritanical morality and the roving gangs that keep most women indoors after dark. And, naturally, the masks, which are definitely not, as the Soviets claim, a last invention of capitalist degeneracy, but a sign of great psychological insecurity. The Russians have no masks, but they have their own signs of stress.

I went to the window and impatiently watched the darkness gather. I was getting very restless. After a while a ghostly violet cloud appeared to the south. My hair rose. Then I laughed. I had momentarily fancied it a radiation from the crater of the Hellbomb, though I should instantly have known it was only the radio-induced glow in the sky over the amusement and residential area south of Inferno.

Promptly at twenty-two hours I stood before the door of my unknown girl friend's apartment. The electronic say-who-please said just that. I answered clearly, "Wysten Turner," wondering if she'd given my name to the mechanism. She evidently had, for the door opened. I walked into a small empty living room, my heart pounding a bit.

The room was expensively furnished with the latest pneumatic hassocks and sprawlers. There were some midgie books on the table. The one I picked up was the standard hard-boiled detective story in which two female murderers go gunning for each other.

The television was on. A masked girl in green was crooning a love song. Her right hand held something that blurred off into the foreground. I saw the set had a handie, which we haven't in England as yet, and curiously thrust my hand into the handie orifice beside the screen. Contrary to my expectations, it was not like slipping into a pulsing rubber glove, but rather as if the girl on the screen actually held my hand.

A door opened behind me. I jerked out my hand with as guilty a reaction as if I'd been caught peering through a keyhole.

She stood in the bedroom doorway. I think she was trembling. She was wearing a gray fur coat, white-speckled, and a gray velvet evening mask with shirred gray lace around the eyes and mouth. Her fingernails twinkled like silver.

I hadn't occurred to me that she'd expect us to go out.

"I should have told you," she said softly. Her mask veered nervously toward the books and the screen and the room's dark corners. "But I can't possibly talk to you here."

I said doubtfully, "There's a place near the Consulate. . . ."

"I know where we can be together and talk," she said rapidly. "If you don't mind."

As we entered the elevator I said, "I'm afraid I dismissed the cab."

But the cab driver hadn't gone, for some reason of his own. He jumped out and smirkingly held the front door open for us. I told him we preferred to sit in back. He sulkily opened the rear door, slammed it after us, jumped in front and slammed the door behind him.

My companion leaned forward. "Heaven," she said.

The driver switched on the turbine and televisor.

"Why did you ask if I were a British subject?" I said, to start the conversation.

She leaned away from me, tilting her mask close to the window. "See the moon," she said in a quick, dreamy voice.

"But why, really?" I pressed, conscious of an irritation that had nothing to do with her.

"It's edging up into the purple of the sky."

"And what's your name?"

"The purple makes it look yellower."

Just then I became aware of the source of my irritation. It lay in the square of writhing light in the front of the cab beside the driver.

I don't object to ordinary wrestling matches, though they bore me, but I simply detest watching a man wrestle a woman. The fact that the bouts are generally "on the level," with the man greatly outclassed in weight and reach and the masked females young and personable, only makes them seem worse to me.

"Please turn off the screen," I requested the driver.

He shook his head without looking around. "Uh-uh, man," he said. "They've been grooming that babe for weeks for this bout with Little Zirk."

Infuriated, I reached forward, but my companion caught my arm. "Please," she whispered frightenedly, shaking her head.

I settled back, frustrated. She was closer to me now, but silent, and for a few moments I watched the heaves and contortions of the powerful masked girl and her wiry masked opponent on the screen. His frantic scrambling at her reminded me of a male spider.

I jerked around, facing my companion. "Why did those three men want to kill you?" I asked sharply.

The eyeholes of her mask faced the screen. "Because they're jealous of me," she whispered.

"Why are they jealous?"

She still didn't look at me. "Because of him."

"Who?"

She didn't answer.

I put my arm around her shoulders. "Are you afraid to tell me?" I asked. "What *is* the matter?"

She still didn't look my way. She smelled nice.

"See here," I said laughingly, changing my tactics, "you really should tell me something about yourself. I don't even know what you look like."

I half playfully lifted my hand to the band of her neck. She gave it an astonishingly swift slap. I pulled it away in sudden pain. There were four tiny indentations on the back. From one of them a tiny bead of blood welled out as I watched. I looked at her silver fingernails and saw they were actually delicate and pointed metal caps.

"I'm dreadfully sorry," I heard her say, "but you frightened me. I thought for a moment you were going to . . ."

At last she turned to me. Her coat had fallen open. Her evening dress was Cretan Revival, a bodice of lace beneath and supporting the breasts without covering them.

"Don't be angry," she said, putting her arms around my neck. "You were wonderful this afternoon."

The soft gray velvet of her mask, molding itself to her cheek, pressed mine. Through the mask's lace the wet warm tip of her tongue touched my chin.

"I'm not angry," I said. "Just puzzled and anxious to help."

The cab stopped. To either side were black windows bordered by spears of broken glass. The sickly purple light showed a few ragged figures slowly moving toward us.

The driver muttered, "It's the turbine, man. We're grounded." He sat there hunched and motionless. "Wish it had happened somewhere else."

My companion whispered, "Five dollars is the usual amount."

She looked out so shudderingly at the congregating figures that I suppressed my indignation and did as she suggested. The driver took the bill without a word. As he started up, he put his hand out the window and I heard a few coins clink on the pavement.

My companion came back into my arms, but her mask faced the television screen, where the tall girl had just pinned the convulsively kicking Little Zirk.

"I'm so frightened," she breathed.

Heaven turned out to be an equally ruinous neighborhood, but it had a club with an awning and a huge doorman uniformed like a spaceman, but in gaudy colors. In my sensuous daze I rather liked it all. We stepped out of the cab just as a drunken old woman came down the sidewalk, her mask awry. A couple ahead of us turned their heads from the half-revealed face as if from an ugly body at the beach. As we followed them in I heard the doorman say, "Get along, Grandma, and cover yourself."

Inside, everything was dimness and blue glows. She had said we could talk here, but I didn't see how. Besides the inevitable chorus of sneezes and coughs (they say America is fifty per cent allergic these days), there was a band going full blast in the latest robop style, in which an electronic composing machine selects an arbitrary sequence of tones into which the musicians weave their raucous little individualities.

Most of the people were in booths. The band was behind the bar. On a small platform beside them a girl was dancing, stripped to her mask. The little cluster of men at the shadowy far end of the bar weren't looking at her.

We inspected the menu in gold script on the wall and pushed the buttons for breast of chicken, fried shrimps and two Scotches. Moments later, the serving bell tinkled. I opened the gleaming panel and took out our drinks.

The cluster of men at the bar filed off toward the door, but first they stared around the room. My companion had just thrown back her coat. Their look lingered on our booth. I noticed that there were three of them.

The band chased off the dancing girls with growls. I handed my companion a straw and we sipped our drinks.

"You wanted me to help you about something," I said. "Incidentally, I think you're lovely."

She nodded quick thanks, looked around, leaned forward. "Would it be hard for me to get to England?"

"No," I replied, a bit taken aback. "Provided you have an American passport."

"Are they difficult to get?"

"Rather," I said, surprised at her lack of information. "Your country doesn't like its nationals to travel, though it isn't quite as stringent as Russia."

"Could the British Consulate help me get a passport?"

"It's hardly their—"

"Could you?"

I realized we were being inspected. A man and two girls had paused opposite our table. The girls were tall and wolfish-looking, with spangled masks. The man stood jauntily between them like a fox on its hind legs.

My companion didn't glance at them, but she sat back. I noticed that one of the girls had a big yellow bruise on her forearm. After a moment they walked to a booth in the deep shadows.

"Know them?" I asked. She didn't reply. I finished my drink. "I'm not sure you'd like England," I said. "The austerity's altogether different from your American brand of misery."

She leaned forward again. "But I must get away," she whispered.

"Why?" I was getting impatient.

"Because I'm so frightened."

There was chimes. I opened the panel and handed her the fried shrimps. The sauce on my breast of chicken was a delicious steaming compound of almonds, soy and ginger. But something must have been wrong with the radionic oven that had thawed and heated it, for at the first bite I crunched a kernel of ice in the meat. These delicate mechanisms need constant repair and there aren't enough mechanics.

I put down my fork. "What are you really scared of?" I asked her.

For once her mask didn't waver away from my face. As I waited I could feel the fears gathering without her naming them, tiny dark shapes swarming through the curved night outside, converging on the radioactive pest spot of New York, dipping into the margins of the purple. I felt a sudden rush of sympathy, a desire to protect the girl opposite me. The warm feeling added itself to the infatuation engendered in the cab.

"Everything," she said finally.

I nodded and touched her hand.

"I'm afraid of the moon," she began, her voice going dreamy and brittle, as it had in the cab. "You can't look at it and not think of guided bombs."

"It's the same moon over England," I reminded her.

"But it's not England's moon any more. It's ours and Russia's. You're not responsible. Oh, and then," she said with a tilt of her mask, "I'm afraid of the cars and the gangs and the loneliness and Inferno. I'm afraid of the lust that undresses your face. And"—her voice hushed—"I'm afraid of the wrestlers."

"Yes?" I prompted softly after a moment.

Her mask came forward. "Do you know something about the wrestlers?" she asked rapidly. "The ones that wrestle women, I mean. They often lose, you know. And then they have to have a girl to take their frustration out on. A girl who's soft and weak and terribly frightened. They need that, to keep them men. Other men don't want them to have a girl. Other men want them just to fight women and be heroes. But they must have a girl. It's horrible for her."

I squeezed her fingers tighter, as if courage could be transmitted —granting I had any. "I think I can get you to England," I said.

Shadows crawled onto the table and stayed there. I looked up at the three men who had been at the end of the bar. They were the men I had seen in the big coupe. They wore black sweaters and close-fitting black trousers. Their faces were as expressionless as dopers. Two of them stood about me. The other loomed over the girl.

"Drift off, man," I was told. I heard the other inform the girl, "We'll wrestle a fall, sister. What shall it be? Judo, slapsie or kill-who-can?"

I stood up. There are times when an Englishman simply must be maltreated. But just then the foxlike man came gliding in like the star of a ballet. The reaction of the other three startled me. They were acutely embarrassed.

He smiled at them thinly. "You won't win my favor by tricks like this," he said.

"Don't get the wrong idea, Zirk," one of them pleaded.

"I will if it's right," he said. "She told me what you tried to do this afternoon. That won't endear you to me, either. Drift."

They backed off awkwardly. "Let's get out of here," one of them said loudly as they turned. "I know a place where they fight naked with knives."

Little Zirk laughed musically and slipped into the seat beside my companion. She shrank from him, just a little. I pushed my feet back, leaned forward.

"Who's your friend, baby?" he asked, not looking at her.

She passed the question to me with a little gesture. I told him.

"British," he observed. "She's been asking you about getting out of the country? About passports?" He smiled pleasantly. "She likes to start running away. Don't you, baby?" His small hand began to stroke her wrist, the fingers bent a little, the tendons ridged, as if he were about to grab and twist.

"Look here," I said sharply. "I have to be grateful to you for ordering off those bullies, but—"

"Think nothing of it," he told me. "They're no harm except when they're behind steering wheels. A well-trained fourteen-year-old girl could cripple any one of them. Why, even Theda here, if she went in for that sort of thing . . ." He turned to her, shifting his hand from her wrist to her hair. He stroked it, letting the strands slip slowly through his fingers. "You know I lost to-night, baby, don't you?" he said softly.

I stood up. "Come along," I said to her. "Let's leave."

She just sat there. I couldn't even tell if she was trembling. I tried to read a message in her eyes through the mask.

"I'll take you away," I said to her. "I can do it. I really will."

He smiled at me. "She'd like to go with you," he said. "Wouldn't you, baby?"

"Will you or won't you?" I said to her. She still just sat there.

He slowly knotted his fingers in her hair.

"Listen, you little vermin," I snapped at him. "Take your hands off her."

He came up from the seat like a snake. I'm no fighter. I just know that the more scared I am, the harder and straighter I hit. This time I was lucky. But as he crumpled back I felt a slap and four stabs of pain in my cheek. I clapped my hand to it. I could feel the four gashes made by her dagger finger caps, and the warm blood oozing out from them.

She didn't look at me. She was bending over little Zirk and cuddling her mask to his cheek and crooning, "There, there, don't feel bad, you'll be able to hurt me afterward."

There were sounds around us, but they didn't come close. I leaned forward and ripped the mask from her face.

I really don't know why I should have expected her face to be anything else. It was very pale, of course, and there weren't any cosmetics. I suppose there's no point in wearing any under a mask. The eyebrows were untidy and the lips chapped. But as for the general expression, as for the feelings crawling and wriggling across it . . .

Have you ever lifted a rock from damp soil? Have you ever watched the slimy white grubs?

I looked down at her, she up at me. "Yes, you're so frightened, aren't you?" I said sarcastically. "You dread this little nightly drama, don't you? You're scared to death."

And I walked right out into the purple night, still holding my hand to my bleeding cheek. No one stopped me, not even the girl wrestlers. I wished I could tear a tab from under my shirt and test it then and there, and find I'd taken too much radiation, and so be able to ask to cross the Hudson and go down New Jersey, past the lingering radiance of the Narrows Bomb, and so on to Sandy Hook to wait for the rusty ship that would take me back over the seas to England.

POLITICS

MURRAY LEINSTER

This story was written in 1932. In it you'll discover something that works very much like radar, and you'll also note the computer-aimed guns. You will also be involved in a World War II which never happened.

Murray Leinster has been writing sf for quite a long time and has been noted for most of that time for the strong and delightful sense of adventure which his work carries. What has, comparatively, escaped notice is his concern with what man is doing to other men and what man is doing to himself—a concern displayed with enviable passion and control in this story, which has never been reprinted.

I

The War of the Pacific has at least taught one lesson to naval strategists. No naval force can ever be said to be inconsiderable, if officered and manned by a capable and determined personnel.
—*Grahame*, Modern Sea Power (*New York, 1937.*)

Lieutenant MacReady saw the enemy from the *Minnesota*'s fighting top and rejoiced with a bitter rejoicing at the sight. This was in August of 1934, you see, just four days after the Battle of Hungars' Bank, and the *Minnesota*'s whole ship company thirsted for vengeance, both upon the enemy and upon the politicians who had sacrificed the rest of the fleet to win an election. The politicians were safe, but the enemy was here, and the *Minnesota* tore through the water toward them with the speed and fury of an avenging nemesis.

"Enemy in sight, sir," he said crisply into the transmitter strapped to his chest. "Bearing . . ."

"*Reported and ranged,*" said a curt voice in the earphones.

MacReady looked down. The guns of the top forward turret were winding up to extreme range. The top turret was coming around. . . . He felt the shock of the discharge before the blast of sound from the explosion struck him. Three guns, fourteen-inchers, had sent out a ranging salvo. The shells were invisible screaming demons of steel and explosive, hurtling upward now, but they would descend nearly twenty miles away and it was Lieutenant MacReady's task to watch their fall. Or it had been his task before the new range finders were installed while the wreckage of that boiler explosion was being repaired. And it might at any instant be his task again.

He counted the seconds; refocused his glasses; wet his lips. Somehow he knew that the guns were swinging below him. Grim, gray-painted tubes were moving slowly to position. . . . He saw the enemy vessels vaguely. There was what looked like a melee of ships on the horizon's edge. Two huge bulks, one of them listing visibly even at this distance. That would be the *Langley*, an aircraft carrier. The other was the *Saratoga*, also a carrier. Over and about the distant ship tiny motes danced. Aircraft. Army planes from shore, carrying on dogfights in the place of the Navy planes that had shared in the disaster of Hungars' Bank. And there was the *Seattle*, on fire but fighting savagely. He saw the flashes of her guns. The *St. Louis* was with her. They were fighting a rear-guard action to enable the aircraft carriers to get away. Those tiny specks were the destroyers. American destroyers. Half-wrecked and battered but fighting gamely as they limped homeward. . . .

The ranging salvo splashed. Three tremendous waterspouts, rising simultaneously, high above the fighting tops of any ship afloat.

"Right six, up two—" snapped MacReady.

The *Minnesota* burst into flame beneath him. Lieutenant Mac-Ready started at the blast of sound. He was dazed by the mere shock, but he knew that every gun that could be brought to bear ahead had fired in one colossal burst of flame. And before his range correction was completed!

His earphones barked, *"Range that salvo."*

"Y-yes, sir," said Lieutenant MacReady.

He began to count the seconds. The lower forward turret was shifting slightly. Twenty-two, twenty-three . . . The three guns spouted flame and dingy-brown smoke. This was the very latest constant-pressure powder, guaranteed by the ordnance department not to vary more than one thousand pounds to the square inch breech pressure even under service conditions. Fifty-eight, fifty-nine . . .

The *Minnesota* was making twenty-eight knots. Blue water flowed past her with a deceptive smoothness. One of the distant aircraft carriers began to spit tiny flames from its antitorpedo battery. There was a flurry of destroyers—American destroyers meeting an attack. Lieutenant MacReady could see the enemy ships clearly now. Four big ones besides the destroyers. Pocket battleships, ten thousand tons, with more speed, more armor, more hitting power than anything else twice their size afloat. But the *Minnesota* was a forty-thousand-ton ship, the biggest battleship in the world. She was, incidentally, the only first-line ship left to the American Navy after the Battle of Hungars' Bank.

The salvo struck. A monstrous mound of water rose to an incredible height. The stern of an enemy ship showed from behind it. The rest of the enemy vessel was hidden behind the broadside splash. It seemed one single, volcanic eruption of water.

"Right one half," said Lieutenant MacReady into the transmitter before him. "Up . . ."

The mound of water began to fall. The stern of the enemy ship tilted with its descent. It rose upward till the keel showed. It dived slowly . . .

"By God, sir!" said Lieutenant MacReady shrilly. "She's sunk!"

Sixteen-inch shells are good medicine for pocket battleships. MacReady swung his glasses swiftly. There was a ranging salvo of shells still aloft. It was his duty to spot their fall . . .

He saw the splashes. Two of them. One was short. One was an over. The third . . . The stern of the enemy ship grew suddenly hazy.

"Straddled!" barked Lieutenant MacReady.

But the terrific concussion of the ship's whole forward battery tore at his chest. He felt something warm trickling down his chin.

His nose was bleeding. He counted seconds with a strained attention. Another ranging blast below. There was a sudden roaring overhead. Two enemy bombers with a six-fighting-planes escort were racing toward the ship. The Army planes from shore were diving for it. The whole antiaircraft battery of the *Minnesota* barked savagely twice. MacReady heard terrific concussions and the sound of a dogfight going on somewhere up aloft.

I'd be happy, thought MacReady in savage satisfaction, if only some of our politicians were on those ships out there. We're shooting like a streak. We couldn't miss if those damned pol—"

A monster mound of water rose up, obliterating one of the three remaining pocket battleships. MacReady's lips formed the word "*Straddled!,*" but there seemed hardly any need. The mound slowly flattened out, and the sea was clean where it had been. A pocket battleship can stand an amazing lot of pounding, but there simply isn't any armor that will keep out a sixteen-inch shell. And when several of them strike at once the result is deplorable. Seconds later the third pocket battleship was silhouetted by splashes. The whole fabric of the *Minnesota* shuddered beneath MacReady as for the third time every gun that could be brought to bear was fired in one world-filling blast of sound. And seconds later a fourth ranging salvo.

Splashes began to rise about the *Minnesota* herself. But a ten-thousand-ton ship is not a steady firing platform, and though it may carry armament far out of proportion to its size it is really designed for fleet work, with smoke screens, aircraft spotters and other aids to efficiency. The *Minnesota* was a self-contained fighting unit, capable of fighting like a whirlwind, and it was taking the offensive. Which was an advantage in itself. One shell fell fifty yards from the *Minnesota*'s side. The next salvo from the ship that fired it should have done some damage. But then the third broadside struck, and when the sea subsided a pocket battleship was rolling over with a grave dignity, to turn turtle and sink. And seconds later the fourth ranging salvo struck, and as its splashes leaped upward the *Minnesota* roared for the fourth time.

Lieutenant MacReady was dazed and dizzy. He felt the ship changing course beneath him. Three broadsides had struck and three ships were sunk! Of course, the *Minnesota* carried the heaviest metal of any ship afloat, but it wasn't natural! There'd been no time for the spotting of shells and the correction of range. Just a ranging salvo, and as it sent splashes skyward the whole forward battery of the *Minnesota* flamed. No delay. No waiting. Above all, no error! The *Minnesota* fired every gun that could bear. Twenty miles away and a long time later four acres of sea arose mountainously, with scattering splashes outside, and anything afloat in that four acres of sea simply ceased to exist.

It happened again now. The fourth broadside struck, it seemed squarely. When the turmoil of its arrival ceased, the fourth enemy pocket ship was still afloat, but explosions were coming from it with lightninglike rapidity. And suddenly it vomited flame from somewhere amidships, broke jaggedly in half—and the sea was clean.

The *Minnesota* had already changed course. There were only enemy destroyers afloat now, after only four broadsides. The distant American ships drew to one side, fighting savagely as they moved. A torpedo struck home somewhere out there, and a thin sliver of metal which was an American destroyer upended and went down in a clean dive. And the air seemed suddenly full of buzzings as of a myriad mosquitos.

"*Lieutenant MacReady,*" said the curt voice in his headphones. "*You will not be required to spot ranges as long as the new range finders function. You will, however, search for possible subs, and especially for torpedo trails.*"

"Yes, sir," said Lieutenant MacReady exultantly.

He turned to grin at his fellow spotter in the forward fighting top. A ringside seat at the big show! Enemy aircraft were racing for the *Minnesota*, but the Army ships from shore were taking a deadly toll. MacReady glanced back at the distant thin line of the coast. Motes were visible in the sky. More Army planes, coming out from land. Fighting planes all, save one squadron of heavy bombers with a haze of tiny pursuit planes whirling before it for protection.

A pall of blackness arose far away upon the sea. The enemy destroyers were making a smoke screen. The *Seattle* and the *St. Louis* were the targets toward which the lengthening spearhead of blackness reached out. They had been under heavy fire from the pocket ships before the *Minnesota* came out. If the destroyers could sink them and the aircraft carriers, it would amount to victory. Destroyer attacks in daylight against ships like the *Minnesota* are unhealthy, but the lesser and already crippled American ships might be wiped out.

But the *Minnesota* spouted flame from fifty gun muzzles. The antiaircraft guns barked in one monstrous volley. They barked again. There were terrific concussions up aloft, and Lieutenant MacReady saw a huge ball of yellow smoke—T.N.T. smoke—spreading with an enormous velocity in mid-air.

"Got a bomber!" he whispered to himself. He wiped the blood off his face and grinned from ear to ear with sheer excitement.

The broadside landed, fifteen miles away. And it struck not as a concentrated blast of sheer destruction, but as a barrage. Separate splashes rose in glittering similitude of stalagmites on a limestone cavern floor. But each pinnacle, shining in the sun, represented the point of fall of a six-inch shell (they were small and few) or an eight-inch shell (there were more of them) or of mighty sixteen-inch shells themselves. The broadside of the *Minnesota* had deliberately been spread out to cover a huge area thinly. But a destroyer does not need much pounding to be put out of action. The tip of the spearhead of smoke heading for the American destroyers simply ceased to be. And the *Minnesota* flamed again, and again, and again. Six times, at fifteen-second intervals, she belched out coruscating waves of fire. A long time later the broadsides fell.

The antiaircraft batteries barked savagely. Firing like the heavy guns; simultaneous salvos at single targets at single instants. Picking out the enemy bombers and leaving the enemy single-seaters to the Army ships. Over and above the droning of many motors there was now the intermittent sound of colossal explosions. Enemy two-thousand-pound bombs were going off in mid-air as the bombers that carried them were wrecked by screaming hails of metal.

MacReady fixed his glasses upon the distant smoke screen. It was ragged and torn. A single enemy destroyer showed clearly for an instant. It was changing course and streaking for the far horizon. The rest were gone! The forward turret boomed a ranging salvo. MacReady watched feverishly. Army ships coming out from shore in a never-ending stream. Somewhere far aloft— The ranging salvo struck! A quarter mile over! But the forward battery crashed forth for the tenth time in this action. Every gun bearing ahead crashed.

MacReady was bleeding at the nose and ears from the concussions that had battered at him. He was bruised all over. He was deafened and his bloodshot eyes streamed water, but he sat in a stilly glow of satisfaction, wishing only that certain politicians could be upon that panic-stricken destroyer that fled from a hail of death.

He saw the shells land. The fleeing destroyer was emitting a dense cloud of smoke to conceal its trail. But it was lifted a hundred and fifty feet clear as contact-fused shells went off in an inferno of destruction. It was flung above even its own smoke screen. MacReady saw it break in pieces and vanish again behind the smoke.

And then there was only the buzzing of a multitude of motors aloft and all around. The tearing, rasping chatter of machine guns became audible. MacReady gazed upward and saw the Army planes hunt down ruthlessly and relentlessly every enemy plane that was aloft. With bitter satisfaction he watched the flying things go fluttering helplessly downward, or dive as plummets of flame into the sea. His satisfaction was tempered with only a slight regret when the last enemy pilot fought a magnificent lone duel with an Army formation, and entangled two of them in his final, blazing fall.

The *Minnesota* shepherded the other American ships toward the Golden Gate, gleaming and unmarred and belligerent. There were two scout cruisers under her protection, the *Seattle* and the *St. Louis*. The *Seattle* was still on fire, but was getting it under some control. There were two aircraft carriers, one of them listing heavily. There were seven half-wrecked destroyers. That was all. They went limping slowly toward the shore, through waters littered for a space with wave-wetted wings.

They went ahead of the *Minnesota* and entered the harbor. They anchored, watched by silent, stunned, almost panic-stricken crowds which thronged the waterfront and did not cheer at all.

Because this was four days after the Battle of Hungars' Bank. The enemy fleet held the Pacific. The *Minnesota* alone excepted, the whole first line of the American battle fleet was at the bottom of the sea. Save for a few submarines and perhaps half a dozen still-fugitive destroyers—now being hunted down by the victorious enemy—these limping, shattered carcasses of ships constituted the Navy of the United States of America.

And, one day before, the enemy had scornfully broadcast the terms on which it would make peace. Hawaii, Guam, the Philippines and the Panama Canal were the only territorial demands, but an indemnity was insisted on and the enemy also required the surrender of the *Minnesota* and a pledge that the United States would never build more than a minimum number of small, slow cruisers in the future.

Throughout a panic-stricken nation, strong pacifist political pressure was being brought to bear to force Congress to accept those terms.

2

There have been in the past, and there will be in the future, attempts by politicians to dictate naval and military policies for other than naval and military ends. But never again will a civilian official of the United States dare issue a direct order governing naval or military operations! He would be impeached at least. In the present temper of the populace, he would probably be lynched.
—Address to graduating class, U.S. Naval Academy, by the Secretary of the Navy, 1938.

Lieutenant MacReady had been at Annapolis with the commander of the torpedo-boat-destroyer *Wasp*. In those far-off days MacReady had been a lowly plebe, while the destroyer skipper was an upperclassman, but they forgathered on equal terms in MacReady's quarters on the *Minnesota*. MacReady offered libation, and the *Wasp*'s commander raised his arm.

"Here's hell to politicians," he said grimly. "They sank our fleet!"

MacReady made an appropriate gesture, accepting the toast.

"Now shoot it," he commanded. "What happened?"

"If you want to know," said the *Wasp*'s commander bitterly, "they sent the battle fleet out with orders to avoid an action. An election is coming on. Pacifists are strong politically. If we blew the enemy out of the water, they'd denounce us as murderers, vote against the Administration, and change the political complexion of Congress. Therefore the Admiral was told to avoid a fleet action until after elections if he could, and if he couldn't to make sure it wasn't a decisive defeat for the enemy. Isn't that pretty?"

"Damn pretty," said MacReady ironically. "Oh, damn pretty!"

"The enemy fleet was spoiling for a scrap," went on the *Wasp*'s commander more bitterly still. "They've been building pocket battleships, playing with 'em like kids with a new toy. On paper they had more gun power than we did, in more but smaller ships. We had the weight and the punishing power. They thought they could lick us. They came over to force a fleet action. They ignored Hawaii and came on with a supply fleet ten miles long behind 'em. And you can't handle a modern fleet, with destroyer screens and the like, without using wireless! We were picking up their code stuff and trying to decode it. They were doing the same with ours. Both sides were using radio direction finders, of course. They knew where we were, and we knew where they were. But they wanted a fight, and we were ordered to avoid one. It couldn't be avoided!"

" 'Hit first, hit hard, hit often!' " quoted MacReady. "But tell me, old man, *why* did the Admiral split his fleet?"

"Direct, specific orders from Washington!" snapped the *Wasp*'s commander. "We knew the enemy was determined on a fleet action and headed straight for us. The Admiral reported to Washington that a general engagement was absolutely unavoidable and an attempt at anything but a decisive victory was stark madness. He got detailed orders—the plan that sank the fleet! Signed by the President as commander in chief. Politics! Armchair strategy that looked all right on paper, but—my God! The battle fleet was to proceed northwest, with its radio silent. The two aircraft carriers, with escorting destroyers, were to proceed southwest. The carriers were to keep planes aloft, with their wireless outfits going, simulating a battle fleet in movement. The enemy would head for them. At the logical instant they would cut off their wireless and run. And the battle fleet would make a demonstration proving its actual position to be a thousand miles or so from where the enemy thought it was. A trick to gain time. A trick to postpone a battle until after election. That's all! They say the Admiral cried when he read the order."

"Here's hell to politicians," said MacReady morosely. "Why didn't it work?"

"An air photo from forty thousand feet," said the *Wasp*'s commander sardonically, "is of no ordinary use to anybody. It's taken through an infrared filter that fog or clouds can't bother, but the Army doesn't use 'em because they don't give enough detail. But they'll tell the difference between a battle fleet and a pair of aircraft carriers, all right!"

MacReady groaned. The *Wasp*'s skipper went on grimly: "That must have been how they did it. Silenced high-altitude planes and photos taken through eight miles of haze. Anyhow, six hours after the battlefleet headed northwest, the enemy fleet split up, too. They duplicated our maneuver. They sent their supply fleet to meet us, with its wireless going full blast to simulate a battle fleet, and they sent their battle fleet to meet ours, full speed ahead and with its wireless shut off, too. But they didn't leave their carriers behind!"

MacReady groaned again.

"The dirigible *Akron* sighted them," said the destroyer skipper coldly. "They got her in twenty minutes, after she'd sent the alarm back and crashed twelve planes that attacked her. But that was too late. We were eight hundred miles away, with the whole air service! You should have seen those carriers shoot planes into the air! One-two-three they went up! Streaking for the fight! It'd be four hours before the fastest of them got there, but they went! And the damned thing was nearly over when they arrived. Our ships had gone into action with only the ship planes to spot and fight for them. The enemy had four carriers—little ones, but they carried a hell of a lot of planes. Twenty minutes after the opening gun, they'd wiped the skies clean above our fleet. There were only six planes spotting for our whole fleet during the second half hour of the action. With smoke screens in use, you know what that meant! There were only three during the last hour! The enemy laid down smoke screens and potted at our ships from behind 'em. Our destroyers went through the screens and tried to do the spotting the air service should have done. Suicide, but we got two of their pocket ships and one of their superdreadnaughts that way. Meanwhile our boats were going to hell and gone. When the air fleet arrived there was only the old *New York* and the *Michigan* above-water in the first line, and we'd lost two thirds of our destroyers. But they stayed afloat, those two old tubs, taking all the punishment the whole enemy fleet could give 'em, and passing out all they had. Until our planes ran out of gas! It was all over then. They'd flown eight hundred miles to get to the fight. They were nearly out of fuel when they got there. And the enemy expected to gather them in when they made forced landings. Pretty idea, wasn't it?"

Lieutenant MacReady said pungent words.

"They did get three," said the commander of the *Wasp* calmly. "But the rest somehow got blown up or crashed by their pilots before they jumped for the water. It annoyed the enemy. They left the pilots—in the water."

Lieutenant MacReady said more pungent words, much more pungent.

"Meanwhile we on the decoy fleet had been tipped off, Oh, a hell of a time we had! Orders first were to try to join the battle fleet. An hour later the old Admiral knew he couldn't hold out until the air fleet got there, and ordered us to streak for home. The planes couldn't be turned back. They were gone, anyway. He tried to save the carriers and the ships with them. We turned and ran." The destroyer skipper gesticulated bitterly. "Then the destroyers from the supply fleet hit us. We'd sent every plane we had to the fleet action. They'd done nearly the same. So we fought 'em off. For four days we'd been running away from them, fighting night and day, when the *Minnesota* turned up. Those pocket ships only got here this morning. Four days and nights of fighting, Mac! We sank three of their destroyers for every two of us they got, but there were twenty-four of us when we started out, and there were seven of us who came in, and the pocket ships would have finished us if the *Minnesota* hadn't blown hell out of them!"

There was silence. There was no noise anywhere on the *Minnesota* except an unplaceable dim whine which was a dynamo running somewhere. Out the porthole of MacReady's cabin could be seen the dim bulks of the two aircraft carriers that had been brought into port that day. The *Langley* still listed heavily to port, but there were lighters clustered about her side and arc lamps burned brightly. At three separate points, clusters of arc lamps burned vividly on the harbor water.

There was a droning hum overhead. It passed on and out to sea.

"Army planes," the commander of the *Wasp* said heavily. "Doing naval patrol. At least the Army can smother their air force if they try any bombing. But what good'll it do? I haven't got a ship any more. My engines were shot to hell. They're cutting off the bow of the *Wasp* with an underwater torch. They're going to weld it in place of the *Waddy*'s bow, which looks like a full-blown rose. And our stern goes to replace the *Stingray*'s tail. Out of three wrecks they'll make two ships that can steam. It'll take four days, with underwater welding. But what good will it do?"

"It depends," said MacReady without hope, "on our shooting. *And* on politics. You saw our shooting today?"

The *Wasp*'s commander nodded. "I thought of you up there in the fighting top, spotting shells. The air was clear and you could do it—"

"I didn't spot a damned shell," said MacReady. "The new range finders have taken my job away from me and do it ten times as well. We've got fire power now, old horse! And fire control! We've got the new range finders in. Those parallel-beam finders they've been working on for years."

His companion looked puzzled.

"All electrical," explained MacReady. "No observer at all. Two telescopes, one at each end of a baseline, and mounted exactly parallel. Fitted with photoelectric cells instead of eyepieces. You swing the baseline around and they sweep the horizon. And a ship on the horizon changes the amount of light that goes through a narrow slit to the photoelectric cell. It registers the instant the first telescope hits the stern of the ship. A fraction of a second later, because the telescopes are exactly parallel, the ship image registers on the other cell. Both cells register exactly the same changes in current output, but one is a fraction of a second behind the other. Knowing the rate of sweep in seconds or mils of arc, if one photo-electric cell lags behind the other one mil, and you know the base-line, you work out the distance in a hurry. See?"

"Complicated," commented the destroyer skipper distastefully.

"Complicated as hell," agreed MacReady readily. "But, man,

does it work! Those range finders sweep their field ten times per second, ranging each way. We range the enemy ship twenty times per second and get electric impulses to read off. But, better than that, we range our own shell splashes and the target together, with the same instrument, at the same time! See the point?"

"M-m-m-m. That looks good!"

"It's even better!" insisted MacReady. "We get electric impulses, instantaneous, instead of observer's figures. The impulses go to an integrator that calculates the range and declination. That feeds into a computer that works up the firing data—barometer, wind, humidity, and so on—and that goes to a relay that lays the gun! All working at the same time! The gun's laid on the target from the first second or two. Constant ranging gives speed and course of the target. The computer dopes 'em out, shifts the gun to where the target will be when the shells land, and we fire a salvo. And then the splashes get ranged by the same outfit in relation to the target! Errors in the firing data and powder lot—even wear on the gun gears—are automatically corrected! Then we let go a broadside. It blows hell out of the target! Gun for gun and ship for ship, the *Minnesota*'s the top fighting machine in the world! And half our superiority comes from those finders. Why, man, our antiaircraft finders range a plane, compute its course and speed in three dimensions, lay twenty guns on its most probable position at the time of shell burst, and fire the guns, all in two fifths of a second! They can do everything but play 'Home Sweet Home' on a piccolo!"

"Then," said the commander of the *Wasp*, "why in hell weren't the other ships fitted with them?"

"Dear heart," protested MacReady in fine irony, "haven't you ever heard of politics? We have a few men with guts in Washington. We have also a large number of elderly maiden ladies with pants on. The range finders were in production. They were shipped here to be fitted. War broke out. There was a wave of popular sentiment against the rude and brutal practice of defending one's country against anybody else. The fleet was ordered to sea at once, because if it didn't get to sea the pacifists might manage to forbid its sailing! With the old range finders and air spotting we were on equal terms with the enemy. We could fight, anyhow! But even after the fleet had sailed the political pacifists managed to get those orders issued that you wot of, which sank our fleet. Politics, you see! It's sweet and pretty! And the *Minnesota* has the range finders installed simply because one of our boilers blew up. It killed sixteen men. We had to be left in port, and while we were getting the mess cleaned up and repaired the skipper put in the new finders. That's why we're damned near a match for the whole enemy navy!"

"And what good does it do?" asked the commander of the *Wasp* bitterly. "You're making 'em a present. The peace terms call for the surrender of the *Minnesota*, and these damned politicians are going to accept 'em!"

Lieutenant MacReady leaned forward confidentially.

"Old boy," he said under his breath, "the Secretary of the Navy is *not* an elderly maiden lady with pants on. There has never yet been an American warship surrendered without a fight. Our skipper has told him we can have some destroyers ready to fight again in six days, and asked permission to commit suicide in his own ship. The Army's going to help, by fighting off enemy planes if an action takes place within a hundred miles of shore. So if the enemy wants the *Minnesota* he'll have to take her! The Secretary thinks he can hold off surrender, in Washington, for those six days. If he can't, we go out before, without the destroyers, and smash our wireless so we can't be ordered to come back. And it will be suicide, and highly immoral, to fight against a gallant enemy who has sunk our ships and left our plane pilots to drown because they blew up their ships rather than hand them over, but—well, it'll be better than the other thing, won't it?"

"You're damn right!" said the commander of the *Wasp* hungrily. "I can shovel coal, or wash mess dishes, or—or—"

"I think," said Lieutenant MacReady magnanimously, "that it can be arranged. The Secretary of the Navy will be fired. The pacifists will write in the school history books that we were murderers. But maybe, if we work it right, the politicians won't object. Because we'll be sunk. I know *I'd* hate to be a politician and have a Navy man look me in the eye!"

The commander of the *Wasp* stood up.

"I'm going back to slave-drive my men," he said feverishly. "We've got to get those destroyers ready. Only time for one more. Here's hell to politicians!"

3

A politician is a man who believes that the greatest catastrophe that can possibly befall his country is the election of somebody else to the office he wants. —Leinster, Politics (*New York, 1931*).

The *Minnesota* lay at anchor in San Francisco Harbor. The sun shone down placidly upon the scene. There were flags flying everywhere. Some of them were "peace flags" and they flew brightly. Some were American flags; they were at half-mast. The city was still and dead. Newspapers came out at frequent intervals with huge hundred-and-twenty-point headlines and very nearly identical contents. Two destroyers had made port in Alaska. They had refueled and gone to sea again. One destroyer, battered and in a sinking condition, had made the port of Vancouver, B.C., and was unable to put out again. She was interned. It was rumored that American submarines had located the enemy fleet with radio direction finders and had submerged in its path. Motors silent and men still as death, they had allowed the screen of destroyers and light craft to pass overhead. They had risen among the capital ships of the enemy navy. They had sunk three ships before they were destroyed. The enemy command denied the rumor. There was no other war news. Peace news was oratory in print, accounts of meetings and resolutions and other activities of the persons opposed to war even in self-defense.

In San Francisco the only signs of life or energy were displayed in two places only. One was the Navy Yard, where men worked frantically against time with electric-welding and oxyacetylene apparatus, doing work that required months of time and elaborate equipment in days instead and with makeshift materials. The *Langley* was having a patch made for the torpedo blast in her side. It was being welded in one piece on shore. It would be sunk alongside and welded in place by Ellsworth underwater torches in the hands of divers. The *Wasp* was a fragment of herself, her bow and stern cut away and only her shell-torn middle section beached in shallow water to rust away. Every one of the returned vessels was aswarm with men. Their own crews were laboring like madmen to get them in shape to steam. They did not hope to attain to real battle efficiency. They only hoped to patch them up so they could share in the last foray of the fighting forces of the United States Navy. If they could steam, and if they could fire a gun, the crews of these ships would mutiny if forbidden a place at the suicide of the fleet.

The other spot where activity was in order was the headquarters of those organizations which opposed the prosecution of war against even a declared enemy. Speakers bustled in and out. Banners flew and gaudy placards smote the eye. Orators moved to strategic points to explain to half-stunned crowds that war was evil in itself and that the disaster of Hungars' Bank was the direct act of Providence, disapproving of America. Suitably edited portions of Scripture were available for distribution. And constantly through that activity for the service of abstract good ran the threat of political action, and an insistence upon the power of little mean men at the polls to undo the actions of bigger men who were deaf to the clamor of fanatics.

The orators ranged everywhere. Marine sentries stopped them at the Navy Yard gates, firmly refusing entry even to deputations of sad-eyed, hysterically righteous women intent upon pleading with the sailors not to murder the sons of other women, regardless of the fact that those sons of other women had not hesitated to sink the American battle fleet. It was uncomfortable anywhere to be in a military or naval uniform, because of the reproaches of convinced opponents of war. Pacifism had become respectable within the past four years, and its proponents took full advantage of the immunity accorded to respectable men. An enthusiastic orator even had himself rowed alongside the *Minnesota* and began a moving speech addressed to the sailors, advocating mutiny and the consistent violation of all the articles of war, and was lured below the slop chute by a sergeant of marines. It was pure accident, of course, that the ship's garbage was discharged at just that time, but an indignant protest was immediately telegraphed to the Secretary of the Navy and all other Cabinet officers.

That was in San Francisco. In Washington there were parades in favor of peace. The President, being by American custom not only a government executive but also the leader of a political party, was forced for the sake of his party's chances in the coming elections to devote four hours in one day to the hearing of spokesmen for different groups of antiwar delegates from antiwar societies throughout the nation. The War and Navy departments were picketed by determined, passionately sincere advocates of peace at any price. Senators and members of the House of Representatives were besieged by opponents of carnage.

In London, the American ambassador was dryly informed that the British Government, though in sympathy with the present embarrassments of the American Government, would delay for the present the taking up of the unquestionably just claims of British subjects against the states which while in the Confederacy had sold bonds in England and later repudiated them. The American ambassador took the hint and cabled desperately that if the United States announced its renunciation of self-defense its standing before the world would be forever gone. In Germany there was laughter and ironically bitter comments in the journals. In France there was alarm and indignation at the threatened disappearance of an ally through what its official press termed national suicide. In Central and South America there was pure panic. Republics which heretofore had maintained a chip-on-the-shoulder attitude toward the United States now made frantic representations that the Monroe Doctrine would be without force behind it. They begged, they implored, they pleaded with the United States not to adopt a course which would ultimately involve their ruin with its own.

But in the United States foreign opinion had no weight. Pacifism was an issue which would decide an election. It would determine whether Tweedledum should stay in office or be thrown out for Tweedledee. It was a matter of politics, and therefore much more important than national prestige or national security or the national honor itself to all the Tweedledums in office and all the Tweedledees without.

The Secretary of the Navy was fighting for time, with the Secretary for War ably seconding him. These two men, at least, would lose their political status with the triumph of a no-defense attitude in the coming elections. Their place was to be taken —so the righteous had it—by a Secretary for Peace. And they fought tooth and nail, by argument and persuasion and browbeating and cajoling, to stem the panic of Congressmen in terror of political oblivion. But on the fourth day the Secretary of the

Navy wired to San Francisco in code: *"Peace proposals considered in Congress tomorrow. Will probably be accepted the day after. I take responsibility of ordering you to use your own judgment in operations against the enemy."*

The Secretary of the Navy would have committed political suicide when the order became known. But he would be able to look at himself in a mirror without shrinking. The captain of the *Minnesota* read the telegram with a grim and weary smile. He tossed it across his desk.

"We'll go out in the morning. The only question is, is that crazy MacReady right? And how many destroyers will we have?"

"Two, sir, plus the scout cruisers and the aircraft carriers. And the planes that went out to try MacReady's idea are due back at any moment, sir."

The message from the Secretary of the Navy neither interrupted nor intensified the feverish labor going on upon the battered ships that had limped into port four days before. An interruption would have slowed things up. An intensification would have been impossible. Repairs were being made with a reckless disregard for mere deficiencies in materials or means. One marvelous assemblage of plates and machinery had parts of six separate vessels in it. Another was repaired from four, one of them a troop transport stolen from the Army while somebody painstakingly looked the other way. Depth-bomb sowers were being equipped for a new purpose, and a strictly improvised munitions plant was unloading Army shells of one type and reloading their contents into naval shells of another sort entirely, which lacked full charges.

And Lieutenant MacReady was rapidly attaining to a state approaching heaven. A flight of Navy planes had gone out to sea, far beyond the view of pacifists and politicians. They had laid down a smoke screen of the thickest and heaviest sort, and made certain tests. Then they laid down a second and made other tests. And they went roaring back to shore with Lieutenant MacReady filled with a stilly rapture.

He found the commander of the *Wasp* in his quarters, picking threads out of one sleeve of his uniform coat.

"Pulling off some gold braid," he said ruefully to MacReady.

"Mac, there's no room for me on this damned ship. So I'm pulling some gold braid off. I'll look like a petty officer without it, and I'm stowing away till the action begins."

"Hold on," said MacReady unsteadily. "I'm sort of dizzy with success. But you've a right to share in it. You gave me the idea first. I'll go to the skipper and ask."

"What idea? What in hell?"

"You talked about the enemy using an infrared filter to photograph the battle fleet through eight miles of haze. It made me think. Have you ever seen the sun through a smoke screen?"

"Of course! It's red."

"Quite true," said MacReady. "The blue rays are filtered out by a smoke screen or by dust. Only reds remain. The sun gets redder as the smoke screen gets thicker, because only the very longest of visible rays get through. The question came up, did infrared rays get stopped at all?"

"Mac!"

"The photoelectric cells in our range finders," said MacReady with a strange precision, "are sensitive to infrared. We went out to sea with a baby range finder. We put on camera filters that shut off everything but the infrared rays. The range finder worked perfectly well. Then we laid down a smoke screen. The finder still worked. Then we laid down another one, thick and wide and deep. And the finder still worked. We're going to fight the last fight of the *Minnesota* that way. We'll be independent of aircraft for spotting, even if we're deep in the middle of a smoke screen ourselves. And so I'll see if I've got a pull with the skipper."

A long time later he came back. His eyes were glowing.

"You'll sit up in the fighting top with me, old horse. We go into action at dawn."

The commander of the *Wasp* started up. "Praise God! You're sure?"

"At the present," said MacReady evenly, "the enemy fleet is bombarding Seattle. The word came through five minutes ago. It's steaming past on the way south. Every ship, as it passes, flings a few broadsides into the town. The present estimate is that half the civilian population is wiped out—and the fleet is still passing. The enemy intention is evidently to hasten our acceptance of their peace terms."

The *Wasp*'s commander clenched his fists and swore helplessly. "We'll sail in time to meet them just after dawn," said Mac-Ready calmly. "The *Minnesota* and what destroyers we've patched up, against the battle fleet that sank our own. Old horse, we ought to have a gaudy suicide. And so—" he poured libation— "here's hell to politicians!"

4

Strategy was defined by General Forrest, C.S.A., as "getting the mostest men there the firstest." Fire superiority may be similarly explained as getting the most shells to the target first. And fire superiority is the lesson to be learned from the Battle of the California Coast.—Grahame, Modern Sea Power.

The dawn came quietly over the hills to eastward. In a vast silence the darkness thinned and the stars paled, and little winking shore lights faded to obscurity as the sky turned gray, and nearly white, and then took on its normal blueness with only a small pinkish glow above the sun itself.

The *Minnesota* was headed north. Ahead of her there were five destroyers in line, with a scout cruiser at either end. The monster aircraft carriers trailed behind her, their decks white with land planes. More tiny destroyers darted here and there about them. In the rear, again, two fleet submarines plowed along at twenty knots. They had come into harbor with their crews bleary-eyed from exhaustion just three hours before the *Minnesota* sailed. And they were going out again, refueled and with their torpedo racks refilled, with half their crews sleeping the twitching slumber of exhaustion in their bunks. Fresh men would navigate them until the action began. Then the exhausted men would rise and share in it. It was their right, and they had demanded it.

The rim of the sun peered over the eastern horizon. Vividly scarlet, it was not the dull-red ball that presages a sultry morning. It came slowly and heavily up over the edge of the world and like some monstrous balloon broke awkwardly free and swam upward into the sky. The sea became abruptly a cerulean blue, and the waves glittered and flashed in the sunshine.

Lieutenant MacReady, up in the *Minnesota*'s fighting top, turned to the former skipper of the *Wasp*. He pointed to a trailing wake of gulls, fluttering tirelessly after the ship.

"I've watched those things for hours, in my time," he observed. "They'll see something today. Thank God we've got clear weather! Old horse, we've got a fine day to die in!"

The skipper of the *Wasp* was searching the sky ahead through binoculars.

"The enemy," he said briefly. "See?"

He pointed. An infinitesimal speck against the pale-blue sky was hovering too steadily to be a gull. Lieutenant MacReady spoke crisply into the transmitter strapped to his chest. There was a sudden flurry over on one of the aircraft carriers. Half a dozen planes shot upward, climbing steeply. They passed nearly over the *Minnesota*. The two in the fighting top could see the helmeted, goggled head of the last pilot as he went streaking in the wake of the rest.

"Never had much use for the Army," said MacReady absently, with his eyes searching the skyline ahead, "but they're turning out pretty good eggs. They do like a scrap, anyhow."

The tiny fleet moved steadily onward. The sun shone upon the vessels, and they were gleaming and defiant in its early rays. But the *Minnesota* alone was unblemished. Patches showed clearly on the rest. A sailor was absorbedly engaged in painting something on the *Stingray*. He was trying to cover up a rust spot that had appeared almost overnight on an unpainted weld.

Silence and stillness. Far overhead, the fighting planes from the carrier were mere specks, as tiny as the ship they had gone up to destroy. That enemy observation-plane turned tail and fled. The American planes raced after it. They went beyond the horizon and disappeared.

The clamor of a gong sounded below. Lieutenant MacReady turned to his companion and grinned. "Mess! But they'll send something up for us."

The fleet went on. Fifteen minutes. Half an hour. An hour. The sea was clean before them. Then tiny pinpoints appeared on the horizon.

"Enemy destroyers," said MacReady. He spoke into his strapped-on transmitter and looked down at the guns. They remained motionless. The *Minnesota* went on steadily, ignoring the distant tiny ships, awaiting enemies worthy of her steel. Her destroyer escort kept formation. The attitude of the American fleet was that of scorn.

More pinpoints. More destroyers. They drew closer, but not too close. They spread about, keeping to a thirty-thousand-yard range. They hemmed in the horizon ahead and to westward. Heavier ships appeared—scout cruisers. The sea seemed speckled with enemy craft. Light ships closed in the horizon behind the *Minnesota*.

"That's so they can mop up if we try to run for it," said Mac-Ready. "Ready for torpedo attacks at the end of the action. Lord! There're a bunch of them!"

There were a bunch of them. Three fourths of the destroyer force that had come across the Pacific. As many as the American battle fleet had taken into the Battle of Hungars' Bank. They turned the horizon on three sides of the *Minnesota* into something fancifully resembling a picket fence.

Enemy pocket battleships came into view, steaming at full speed to be in at the death. They deployed in line ahead, cutting off the *Minnesota* from the open sea. But they did not fire a gun. Now little specks began to appear in the air above the enemy fleet, and still there was no offensive movement. Then the six full-sized battleships of the enemy came grandly over the edge of the world. They moved for an apparently predetermined position.

"This isn't to be a battle," said MacReady. "They're figuring it as an execution—a beautiful example of fire superiority and fire control. Considering the psychology of our gallant foes, I imagine they'll try to blow us out of the water with a simultaneous broadside from every ship in the fleet. It would be neat, and probably effective. Or do you suppose they think we came out to surrender?"

The ten destroyers with the *Minnesota* suddenly belched forth black smoke from their funnels and shot ahead. Weaving back and forth, darting here and there, they began to make an impenetrable smoke screen between the *Minnesota* and her enemies. MacReady flung back his head to look at the land. Yes! A long black thread-like line was lengthening from the shore. Army planes. Five miles from the *Minnesota* that line bifurcated—split in two.

"God bless 'em!" said MacReady comfortably." They're just on time! They'll give the destroyers a busy morning. Every bomber the Army owns is in that line! We've got air superiority in this action!"

The *Minnesota* was in the center of perhaps a square mile of open sea, with a growing wall of blackness about her. But from the fighting top MacReady could see over it.

He watched the enemy ships building up a precise, ceremonial formation for the destruction of the *Minnesota*. MacReady's eyes gleamed suddenly. The top forward turret swung in place and its guns wound up to nearly maximum elevation.

"They do love ceremony, the enemy," he said gently. "They're arranging themselves for our destruction as if it were a review. If I were the Old Man, I'd not bother about ranging salvos after the first spotting. We've got them all ranged, anyhow, and with one salvo for wind and barometer and so on, I'd fire broadsides only."

The *Minnesota*'s top turret guns flashed ear-splittingly—the first ranging salvo. The destroyers were weaving madly about, extending and thickening the smoke screen about her. It would have blinded any other ship in the world and made her utterly dependent upon aircraft observation. But spotting is exacting work, and the Army observers wouldn't be efficient in spotting for the Navy anyhow. The enemy evidently counted upon it. The smoke screen was wide and thick. Here and there it billowed upward enough to obscure the horizon. But a long time later MacReady saw three splashes rising mountainously near one of the pocket battleships of the enemy. He opened his mouth automatically to telephone a correction, but before he could speak the *Minnesota* let loose. And this time she was broadside on to her target. Not only her forward battery, but fore and aft, with all her main and secondary battery, she flung a hurtling hell of steel and flame toward the enemy. The recoil made her whole vast fabric shudder. Fifteen seconds later she flamed again. Fifteen seconds; the air split asunder with the same concussion. Fifteen seconds . . . With unvarying, mathematical precision, she let go twelve broadsides in three minutes. It was impossible to discover that her gun muzzles shifted.

She came about in a long sweep. MacReady and the skipper of the *Wasp* ignored their bleeding noses and the bruises of sheer concussion. They swept the horizon, quivering like hounds on the scent.

"One—two—three!" MacReady counted in an awed voice. "Three of them sunk, by God! Thank God for heavy metal! And another one's out of action, or I'm a Swede! *Ah-h-h-h!*"

An apparently uninjured speck, against the very edge of the world, tore itself apart with a sudden vehemence. There was a flash and a monstrous ball of dense black smoke. Then there was another gap in the ceremonial formation which was to execute the *Minnesota*. Either it had forgotten that the American ship was the most powerful war vessel in the world or it had counted upon no more than human accuracy in its shellfire. But there was no human factor-of-error in the gun-laying on the *Minnesota* now. She was a machine, and the most deadly fighting machine on earth.

Flashes appeared along that distant line of ships. The *Minnesota* dived into the smoke screen all about. A destroyer darted aside to give it room. The smoke screen had been laid in long spreading trails of blackness. From aloft it would look like a rather untidily executed maze. MacReady caught a glimpse of the foredeck of the *Langley*—its afterdeck was blotted out by a hill of densest black—and plane after plane after plane was taking off with the regularity and precision of bullets going out of a machine gun. He saw a spreading fan of planes rising from another spot—the other carrier. Then the *Minnesota* vanished from beneath him as it went swiftly into darkness. A long distance away he saw the other fighting top above a sea of black. Black billows rolled lazily about the horizon. He saw a ship on fire, in the enemy line. That was the work of one of the fleet subs. The enemy did not know of their existence or escape. They took a heavy toll between them, and one of them blew itself to atoms beneath the pocket battleship that rammed it. Which was not healthy for the pocket battleship.

MacReady heard his companion shouting. He was chattering excitedly into the telephone transmitter strapped to his chest. A concussion wave struck him. The ship was firing again. The gas blasts from the guns blew the smoke screen crazily about. One; fifteen seconds—two; fifteen seconds—three . . . Six broadsides the *Minnesota* fired from the thickest of its own smoke screen.

Hell broke loose a half mile astern. A six-inch shell screamed between the fighting tops of the *Minnesota*. That was a stray. The storm of fire from the capital ships of the enemy fleet was pouring into the ocean where the *Minnesota* might have been, but wasn't. They couldn't see her. Her smoke screen hid her before they had fired ranging salvos. And range readings by even trained observers are not much good without trial salvos and spottings. The *Minnesota* had started the action on her own terms, which, with air superiority on her side, were much better than the enemy had intended.

Two minutes of silence save for the screaming of enemy shells searching for the ship. The smoke screen was lengthening and spreading. The *Minnesota* had four square miles of blackness in which to hide, but it was blackness only to the enemy. MacReady caught a glimpse of a monstrous dogfight going on aloft. Enemy aircraft could not spot the *Minnesota* from above their own ships. So intricately woven was her protecting screen that a position nearly vertically above her was essential. The enemy aircraft were trying to get it. The Army ships were keeping them from it. The solitary American battleship was using tactics which not only were entirely new, they were tactics which were impossible to a ship without control of the air, without eyes to penetrate the screen and prevent collision with her tiny consorts, and without utterly perfect spotting for her shells.

Enemy shells shrieked all about. An eight-incher landed somewhere and burst with a sickening detonation. The whole sea seemed to be boiling. Shell splashes leaped upward above the smoke screen, glittering in the sunlight. They were visible to the enemy, but not especially helpful without a sight of their target. There was a flickering ball of madly fighting planes a mile and a half to the right. Something huge and winged burst out of it and raced toward the *Minnesota*'s fighting tops, with a dozen Army single-seaters pouring lead at it and two enemy combat planes dying magnificently in the attempt to protect it.

The big ship's antiaircraft battery crashed venomously. There was a colossal, an incredible explosion. The huge winged thing vanished in an expanding ball of flame. Two combat ships shriveled and fell with it. Another reeled and a wing came off, and it began to descend, whirling crazily like a maple leaf. The rest of them turned and went madly back toward the ball of roaring, crackling fighting things.

The *Minnesota* shuddered again. And again. And again. Broadsides of every gun that would bear fired from abysmal blackness into the bright sunshine. Storms of screaming metal, flying shrieking through space, to fall twenty miles away. From the tail of his eye MacReady saw a magnificent duel of two fighting planes ended in the fraction of a second as the trajectory of some ship's broadside passed through the area of their combat. They were annihilated. But MacReady could not see it all. He was battered at and pounded by waves of sheer concussion. He heard a voice beside him, thinly, and it was the commander of the *Wasp*, but MacReady could not make out what he was saying and did not try. Then he caught a glimpse of the enemy fleet as the rolling billows of the smoke screen lowered for an instant.

The noise did not lessen for an instant, and it was like the din of all hell let loose. But MacReady did not hear it, because something huge over in the enemy lines was pointing its bow skyward and going down slowly by the stern. A monstrous mound of water rose above it as a broadside struck. The mound subsided, and that monstrous ship was only a third of a ship above-water. It was going down and down . . . A pocket battleship was on fire. A broadside struck one of the enemy's big ships. Fifteen seconds later, another. Fifteen seconds later still, a third. Fifteen seconds later still, a fourth. . . .

"Fire power!" cried MacReady exultantly amid the tumult of ten thousand explosions. "We've got it! The heaviest broadside in the world! Infrared screens. Beam range finders that spot our own shells with the targets they strike! Powder that varies less than a thousand pounds' pressure at the breech! Six ships we've sunk, old horse! Six ships! And we're barely scratched! Why doesn't the enemy use his destroyers? Their big ships are no good! If they want to finish us, why don't they bring on their destroyers?"

As if to answer him, he saw. The *Minnesota* ran into an area where its smoke screen had partly settled down and spread out. It was still not in view of the enemy capital ships. Only the fighting tops and a quarter of the masts were clear. But the smoke screen ended a half mile away and the line of enemy destroyers were in full charge. Full speed ahead, bones in their teeth, straining every nerve for the velocity needed to make a success of their suicidal dash for the *Minnesota.* Twenty of them in a magnificent squadron plunging for the target of their fleet.

One of them rose and buckled as a thousand-pound bomb exploded in the sea in contact with its hull. The Army bombers were at work. A second lost its tail and came to a halt, spitting smoke and stream and bitterly despairing streams of antiaircraft shells. A third ran into an aerial bomb and started a dive that ended on the bottom. The *Minnesota*'s antitorpedo battery exploded thunderously. Again. Again. Again. . . . Six terrific volleys. Six destroyers died. The bombers got to work again on what were left. The smoke screen heaved slowly upward and blotted out the view.

There were twenty square miles of smoke screen for the *Minnesota* to play in now, and the Army held the air against the most desperate assaults of an enemy now in actually a desperate position. The American battleship was the most powerful battleship on earth—even on paper. She could range her shots and spot them through a smoke screen that made her invisible to the enemy. The Army had held the air above her from the first. Now it was fighting for the air above the enemy. American air bombs sank one enemy aircraft carrier. A pocket battleship's steering gear was wrecked by a bombing squadron who went on about their other business and left a flight of torpedo planes to finish her off. The enemy fleet was in exactly the position into which, with the assistance of American politicians, it had maneuvered the American battle fleet off Hungars' Bank. The *Minnesota* had control of the air and fought not only behind but in a smoke screen. The enemy ships were necessarily firing nearly at random, despite their enormous numerical superiority, while the *Minnesota* fired broadside after broadside with an uncanny accuracy. And its broadside was the heaviest afloat. In this action, because of the unhuman accuracy of its range-finder spotting, it secured a larger percentage of hits than any other vessel had ever made, in action or out of it.

"All they've got left," panted the commander of the *Wasp,* "is subs!" He was hoarse, though he could never remember speaking a word before, and much less shouting. "They've tried everything else. They'll try their subs now!"

MacReady's nose and ears were bleeding from concussion. His eyes were bloodshot and watering from the same cause. He was gory and horrible to look at, but he grinned exultantly.

"The wind's blowing the smoke screen southward at fourteen knots. We're moving with it. There's no sub on earth can travel fourteen knots submerged, and you can bet your other collar, old horse, that no sub's going to get to us on the surface!"

A faint howl came up from below. It sounded even above the tumult of explosions all about and the uproar of aircraft aloft. There was no fighting above the *Minnesota* now. The fighting was taking place above the enemy fleet. The howl came up again, thin and reedy but triumphant. MacReady recognized it. It was a simultaneous roar of pure delight from the officers and men of the *Minnesota*. And MacReady's earphones gave him the cause of it an instant later:

"*The enemy has formed a smoke screen for his own protection from our fire!*"

And Lieutenant MacReady and the commander of the now tri-sected *Wasp* arose and danced clumsily about the fighting top of the *Minnesota* and shrieked themselves hoarse from pure joy.

Because, of course, if the *Minnesota*'s range finders could range and spot shells through a smoke screen to direct her fire out of it, they could also work through two to direct her fire into another. And the enemy's control of the air was gone forever, so his only possible hope would be to destroy the accuracy of the *Minnesota*'s fire. It was incredible. It was impossible. But it was true.

So the action of the ninth of August, 1934, more commonly known as the Battle of the California Coast, was completed with two blankets of blackness floating upon the sea. The *Minnesota* remained deep in one mass of impenetrable darkness, and her guns boomed and boomed and boomed, sending shells screaming to the targets futilely hiding in the heart of another darkness or with even greater futility trying to flee.

The action had started at half past six in the morning. At three in the afternoon—it was seven o'clock by Washington time—an official order reached the *Minnesota* by wireless and in the official naval code. There had been a stormy, a tumultuous session in Congress. The bombardment of Seattle had had the effect the enemy anticipated. Instead of two days of debate, a conclusion was reached in one. A resolution had been passed accepting the preliminary peace terms of the enemy. The President of the United States was commanded to issue the orders meeting the enemy's requirements for an armistice.

As commander in chief of the military and naval forces of the United States, he issued the historic order:

To the Senior Officer Commanding American Vessels of War in the Pacific Ocean.
Immediately on receipt of this order you will surrender all vessels under your command to the officer in command of the enemy battle fleet off our coasts.

And the captain of the *Minnesota* radioed his even more historic reply:

To the President of the United States.
There is no longer an enemy battle fleet off our coasts. We have destroyed it.

As a matter of politics, the Battle of the California Coast had the extraordinary result of making pacifism no longer respectable. In any case it immediately ceased to be a political issue, because America instantly backslid into patriotism. Our politicians, in the remaining three days before election, vied with each other in patriotic fervor. Where before they had competed for the noblest expressions of resignation to the will of Providence, now they struggled to outdo each other in the ingenuity of the demands they proposed we should make upon the enemy as the price of peace. And they were voted for on that basis.

But at any rate, until America forgets, the Army and the Navy are not toys for politicians any longer.

MEMENTO HOMO

WALTER M. MILLER, JR.

*The work of Walter M. Miller, Jr., is beginning to re-
ceive from fans the sort of respect which it has for some
years received from authors and editors. His earnest
poetry has made itself felt in one novel (the best-selling*
A Canticle for Leibowitz) *and two volumes of short
stories. Here is a fine example of his shorter work, not
included in either of his collections.*

. . . quia pulvis es et in pulverem reverteris.

Old Donegal was dying. They had all known it was coming, and
they watched it come—his haggard wife, his daughter, and now
his grandson, home on emergency leave from the pre-astronautics
academy. Old Donegal knew it, too, and had known it from the
beginning, when he had begun to lose control of his legs and was
forced to walk with a cane. But most of the time he pretended to
let them keep the secret they shared with the doctors—that the
operations had all been failures, and that the cancer that fed at his
spine would gnaw its way brainward until the paralysis engulfed
vital organs, and then Old Donegal would cease to be. It would
be cruel to let them know that he knew.

Once, weeks ago, he had joked about the approaching shadows.
"Buy the plot back where people won't walk over it, Martha," he
said. "Get it way back under the cedars—next to the fence. There
aren't many graves back there yet. I want to be alone."

"Don't *talk* that way, Donny!" his wife had choked. "You're
not dying."

His eyes twinkled maliciously. "Listen, Martha, I want to be buried face down. I want to be buried with my back to space, understand? Don't let them lay me out like a lily."

"Donny, *please!*"

"They oughta face a man the way he's headed," Donegal grunted. "I been up—*way* up. Now I'm going straight down."

Martha had fled from the room in tears. He had never done it again, except to the interns and nurses, who, while they insisted that he was going to get well, didn't mind joking with him about it.

Martha can bear my death, he thought, can bear preknowledge of it. But she couldn't bear thinking that he might take it calmly. If he accepted death gracefully, it would be like deliberately leaving her, and Old Donegal had decided to help her believe whatever would be comforting to her in such a troublesome moment.

"When'll they let me out of this bed again?" he complained.

"Be patient, Donny," she sighed. "It won't be long. You'll be up and around before you know it."

"Back on the moon run, maybe?" he offered. "Listen, Martha, I been planetbound too long. I'm not too old for the moon run, am I? Sixty-three's not so old."

That had been carrying things too far. She knew he was hoaxing, and dabbed at her eyes again. The dead must humor the mourners, he thought, and the sick must comfort the visitors. It was always so.

But it was harder, now that the end was near. His eyes were hazy, and his thoughts unclear. He could move his arms a little, clumsily, but feeling was gone from them. The rest of his body was lost to him. Sometimes he seemed to feel his stomach and his hips, but the sensation was mostly an illusion offered by higher nervous centers, like the "ghost arm" that an amputee continues to feel. The wires were down, and he was cut off from himself.

He lay wheezing on the hospital bed, in his own room, in his own rented flat. Gaunt and unshaven, gray as winter twilight, he lay staring at the white net curtains that billowed gently in the breeze from the open window. There was no sound in the room but the sound of breathing and the loud ticking of an alarm clock. Occasionally he heard a chair scraping on the stone terrace next door, and the low mutter of voices, sometimes laughter, as the servants of the Keith mansion arranged the terrace for late-afternoon guests.

With considerable effort he rolled his head toward Martha, who sat beside the bed, pinch-faced and weary.

"You ought to get some sleep," he said.

"I slept yesterday. Don't talk, Donny. It tires you."

"You ought to get more sleep. You never sleep enough. Are you afraid I'll get up and run away if you go to sleep for a while?"

She managed a brittle smile. "There'll be plenty of time for sleep when . . . when you're well again." The brittle smile fled and she swallowed hard, like swallowing a fishbone. He glanced down, and noticed that she was squeezing his hand spasmodically.

There wasn't much left of the hand, he thought. Bones and ugly tight-stretched hide spotted with brown. Bulging knuckles with yellow cigarette stains. My hand. He tried to tighten it, tried to squeeze Martha's thin one in return. He watched it open and contract a little, but it was like operating a remote-control mechanism. Goodbye, hand, you're leaving me the way my legs did, he told it. I'll see you again in hell. How hammy can you get, Old Donegal? You maudlin ass.

"Requiescat," he muttered over the hand, and let it lie in peace.

Perhaps she heard him. "Donny," she whispered, leaning closer, "won't you let me call the priest now? Please."

He rattled a sigh and rolled his head toward the window again. "Are the Keiths having a party today?" he asked. "Sounds like they're moving chairs out on the terrace."

"Please, Donny, the priest?"

He let his head roll aside and closed his eyes, as if asleep. The bed shook slightly as she quickly caught at his wrist to feel for a pulse.

"If I'm not dying, I don't need a priest," he said sleepily.

"That's not right," she scolded softly. "You know that's not right, Donny. You know better."

Maybe I'm being too rough on her? he wondered. He hadn't minded getting baptized her way, and married her way, and occasionally priest-handled the way she wanted him to when he was home from a space run; but when it came to dying, Old Donegal wanted to do it his own way.

He opened his eyes at the sound of a bench being dragged across the stone terrace. "Martha, what kind of a party are the Keiths having today?"

"I wouldn't know," she said stiffly. "You'd think they'd have a little more respect. You'd think they'd put it off a few days."

"Until—?"

"Until you feel better."

"I feel fine, Martha. I like parties. I'm glad they're having one. Pour me a drink, will you? I can't reach the bottle any more."

"It's empty."

"No it isn't, Martha, it's still a quarter full. I know. I've been watching it."

"You shouldn't have it, Donny. Please don't."

"But this is a party, Martha. Besides, the doctor says I can have whatever I want. Whatever I want, you hear? That means I'm getting well, doesn't it?"

"Sure, Donny, sure. Getting well."

"The whiskey, Martha. Just a finger in a tumbler, no more. I want to feel like it's a party."

Her throat was rigid as she poured it. She helped him get the tumbler to his mouth. The liquor seared his throat, and he gagged a little as the fumes clogged his nose. Good whiskey, the best— but he couldn't take it any more. He eyed the green stamp on the neck of the bottle on the bed table and grinned. He hadn't had whiskey like that since his space days. Couldn't afford it now, not on a blastman's pension.

He remembered how he and Caid used to smuggle a couple of fifths aboard for the moon run. If they caught you it meant suspension, but there was no harm in it, not for the blast-room men who had nothing much to do from the time the ship acquired enough velocity for the long, long coaster ride until they started the rockets again for lunar landing. You could drink a fifth, jettison the bottle through the trash lock, and sober up before you were needed again. It was the only way to pass the time in the cramped cubicle, unless you ruined your eyes trying to read by the glow lamps. Old Donegal chuckled. If he and Caid had stayed on the run, Earth would have a ring by now, like Saturn—a ring of Old Granddad bottles.

"You said it, Donny-boy," said the misty man by the billowing curtains. "Who else knows the Gegenschein is broken glass?"

Donegal laughed. Then he wondered what the man was doing there. The man was lounging against the window, and his un-zipped space rig draped about him in an old familiar way. Loose plug-in connections and hose ends dangled about his lean body. He was freckled and grinning.

"Caid," Old Donegal breathed softly.

"What did you say, Donny?" Martha answered.

Old Donegal blinked hard and shook his head. Something let go with a soggy snap, and the misty man was gone. I'd better take it easy on the whiskey, he thought. You got to wait, Donegal, old lush, until Nora and Ken get here. You can't get drunk until they're gone, or you might get them mixed up with memories like Caid's.

Car doors slammed in the street below. Martha glanced toward the window.

"Think it's them? I wish they'd get here. I wish they'd hurry."

Martha arose and tiptoed to the window. She peered down to-ward the sidewalk, put on a sharp frown. He heard a distant mutter of voices and occasional laughter, with group footsteps milling about on the sidewalk. Martha murmured her disapproval and closed the window.

"Leave it open," he said.

"But the Keiths' guests are starting to come. There'll be such a racket." She looked at him hopefully, the way she did when she prompted his manners before company came.

Maybe it wasn't decent to listen in on a party when you were dying, he thought. But that wasn't the reason. Donegal, your chamber pressure's dropping off. Your brains are in your butt end, where a spacer's brains belong, but your butt end died last month. She wants the window closed for her own sake, not yours.

"Leave it closed," he grunted. "But open it again before the moon run blasts off. I want to listen."

She smiled and nodded, glancing at the clock. "It'll be an hour and a half yet. I'll watch the time."

"I hate that clock. I wish you'd throw it out. It's loud."

"It's your medicine clock, Donny." She came back to sit down at his bedside again. She sat in silence. The clock filled the room with its clicking pulse.

"What time are they coming?" he asked.

"Nora and Ken? They'll be here soon. Don't fret."

"Why should I fret?" He chuckled. "That boy—he'll be a good spacer, won't he, Martha?"

Martha said nothing, fanned at a fly that crawled across his pillow. The fly buzzed up in an angry spiral and alighted on the ceiling. Donegal watched it for a time. The fly had natural-born space legs. I know your tricks, he told it with a smile, and I learned to walk on the bottomside of things before you were a maggot. You stand there with your magnasoles hanging to the hull, and the rest of you's in free fall. You jerk a sole lose, and your knee flies up to your belly, and reaction spins you half around and near throws your other hip out of joint if you don't jam the foot down fast and jerk up the other. It's worse'n trying to run through knee-deep mud with snowshoes, and a man'll go nuts trying to keep his arms and legs from taking off in odd directions. I know your tricks, fly. But the fly was born with his magnasoles, and he trotted across the ceiling like Donegal never could.

"That boy Ken—he ought to make a damn good space engineer," wheezed the old man.

Her silence was long, and he rolled his head toward her again. Her lips tight, she stared down at the palm of his hand, unfolded his bony fingers, felt the cracked calluses that still welted the shrunken skin, calluses worn there by the linings of space gauntlets and the handles of fuel valves, and the rungs of get-about ladders during free fall.

"I don't know if I should tell you," she said.

"Tell me what, Martha?"

She looked up slowly, scrutinizing his face. "Ken's changed his mind, Nora says. Ken doesn't like the academy. She says he wants to go to medical school."

Old Donegal thought it over, nodded absently. "That's fine. Space medics get good pay." He watched her carefully.

She lowered her eyes, rubbed at his calluses again. She shook her head slowly. "He doesn't want to go to space."

The clock clicked loudly in the closed room.

"I thought I ought to tell you, so you won't say anything to him about it," she added.

Old Donegal looked grayer than before. After a long silence, he rolled his head away and looked toward the limp curtains.

"Open the window, Martha," he said.

Her tongue clucked faintly as she started to protest, but she said nothing. After frozen seconds, she sighed and went to open it. The curtains billowed, and a babble of conversation blew in from the terrace of the Keith mansion. With the sound came the occasional brassy discord of a musician tuning his instrument. She clutched the window sash as if she wished to slam it closed again.

"Well! Music!" grunted Old Donegal. "That's good. This is some shebang. Good whiskey and good music and you." He chuckled, but it choked off into a fit of coughing.

"Donny, about Ken—"

"No matter, Martha," he said hastily. "Space medic's pay is good."

"But, Donny—" She turned from the window, stared at him briefly, then said, "Sure, Donny, sure," and came back to sit down by his bed.

He smiled at her affectionately. She was a man's woman, was Martha—always had been, still was. He had married her the year he had gone to space—a lissome, wistful, old-fashioned lass, with big violet eyes and gentle hands and gentle thoughts—and she had never complained about the long and lonely weeks between blast-off and glide-down, when most spacers' wives listened to the psychiatrists and soap operas and soon developed the symptoms that were expected of them, either because the symptoms were chic or because they felt they should do something to earn the pity that was extended to them. "It's not so bad," Martha had assured him. "The house keeps me busy till Nora's home from school, and then there's a flock around till dinner. Nights are a little empty, but if there's a moon I can always go out on the porch and look at it and know where you are. And Nora gets out the telescope you built her, and we make a game of it. 'Seeing if Daddy's still at the office' she calls it."

"Those were the days," he muttered.

"What, Donny?"

"Do you remember that Steve Farran song?"

She paused, frowning thoughtfully. There were a lot of Steve Farran songs, but after a moment she picked the right one and sang it softly . . .

> "O moon whereo'er the clouds fly,
> Beyond the willow tree,
> There is a ramblin' space guy
> I wish you'd save for me.
> Mare Tranquilitatis,
> O dark and tranquil sea,
> Until he drops from heaven,
> Rest him there with thee . . ."

Her voice cracked, and she laughed. Old Donegal chuckled weakly.

"Fried mush," he said. "That one made the cats wilt their ears and wail at the moon. I feel real crazy," he added. "Hand me the king kong, fluffmuff."

"Keep cool, Daddy-O, you've had enough." Martha reddened and patted his arm, looking pleased. Neither of them had talked that way, even in the old days, but the outdated slang brought back memories—school parties, dances at the Rocketport Club, the early years of the war when Donegal had jockeyed an R-43 fighter in the close-space assaults against the Soviet satellite project. The memories were good.

A brassy blare of modern "slide" arose suddenly from the Keith terrace as the small orchestra launched into its first number. Martha caught an angry breath and started toward the window.

"Leave it," he said. "It's a party. Whiskey, Martha. Please—just a small one."

She gave him a hurtful glance.

"Whiskey. Then you can call the priest."

"Donny, it's not right. You know it's not right—to bargain for such as that."

"All right. Whiskey. Forget the priest."

She poured it for him, and helped him get it down, and then went out to make the phone call. Old Donegal lay shuddering over the whiskey taste and savoring the burn in his throat. Jesus, but it was good.

You old bastard, he thought, you got no right to enjoy life

when nine tenths of you is dead already, and the rest is foggy as a thermal dust-rise on the lunar *mare* at hell-dawn. But it wasn't a bad way to die. It ate your consciousness away from the feet up; it gnawed away the present, but it let you keep the past, until everything faded and blended. Maybe that's what eternity is, he thought—one man's subjective past, all wrapped up and packaged for shipment, a single space-time entity, a one-man microcosm of memories, when nothing else remains.

"If I've got a soul, I made it myself," he told the gray nun at the foot of his bed.

The nun held out a pie pan, rattled a few coins in it. "Contribute to the Radiation Victims' Relief?" the nun purred softly.

"I know you," he said. "You're my conscience. You hang around the officers' mess, and when we get back from a sortie you make us pay for the damage we did. But that was forty years ago."

The nun smiled, and her luminous eyes were on him softly. "Mother of God!" he breathed, and reached for the whiskey. His arm obeyed. The last drink had done him good. He had to watch his hand to see where it was going, and squeezed the neck until his fingers whitened so that he knew that he had it, but he got it off the table and onto his chest, and he got the cork out with his teeth. He had a long pull at the bottle, and it made his eyes water and his hands grow weak. But he got it back to the table without spilling a bit, and he was proud of himself.

The room was spinning like the cabin of a gyro-gravved ship. By the time he wrestled it to a standstill, the nun was gone. The blare of music from the Keith terrace was louder, and laughing voices blended with it. Chairs scraping and glasses rattling. A fine party, Keith, I'm glad you picked today. This shebang would be the younger Keith's affair. Ronald Tonwyler Keith III, scion of Orbital Engineering and Construction Company—builders of the moonshuttle ships that made the run from the satellite station to Luna and back.

It's good to have such important neighbors, he thought. He wished he had been able to meet them while he was still up and about. But the Keiths' place was walled in, and when a Keith came out he charged out in a limousine with a chauffeur at the wheel, and the iron gate closed again. The Keiths built the wall when the surrounding neighborhood began to grow shabby with age. It had once been the best of neighborhoods, but that was before Old Donegal lived in it. Now it consisted of sooty old houses and rented flats, and the Keith place was really not a part of it any more. Nevertheless, it was really something when a pensioned blastman could say, "I live out close to the Keiths—you know, the *Ronald* Keiths." At least, that's what Martha always told him.

The music was so loud that he never heard the doorbell ring, but when a lull came he heard Nora's voice downstairs and listened hopefully for Ken's. But when they came up, the boy was not with them.

"Hello, skinny-britches," he greeted his daughter.

Nora grinned and came over to kiss him. Her hair dangled about his face, and he noticed that it was blacker than usual, with the gray streaks gone from it again.

"You smell good," he said.

"You don't, Pops. You smell like a sot. Naughty!"

"Where's Ken?"

She moistened her lips nervously and looked away. "He couldn't come. He had to take a driver's lesson. He really couldn't help it. If he didn't go, he'd lose his turn, and then he wouldn't finish before he goes back to the academy." She looked at him apologetically.

"It's all right, Nora."

"If he missed it, he wouldn't get his copter license until summer."

"It's okay. Copters! Hell, the boy should be in jets by now!"

Several breaths passed in silence. She gazed absently toward the window and shook her head. "No jets, Pop. Not for Ken."

He glowered at her. "Listen! How'll he get into space? He's got to get his jet licenses first. Can't get in rockets without 'em."

Nora shot a quick glance at her mother. Martha rolled her eyes as if sighing patiently. Nora went to the window to stare down toward the Keith terrace. She tucked a cigarette between scarlet lips, lit it, blew nervous smoke against the pane.

"Mom, can't you call them and have that racket stopped?"

"Donny says he likes it."

Nora's eyes flitted over the scene below. "Female butterflies and puppy-dogs in sport jackets. And the cadets." She snorted. "Cadets! Imagine Ron Keith the Third ever going to space. The old man buys his way into the academy, and they throw a brawl as if Ronny passed the Compets."

"Maybe he did," growled Old Donegal.

"Hah!"

"They live in a different world, I guess," Martha sighed.

"If it weren't for men like Pops, they'd never've made their fortune."

"I like the music, I tell you," grumbled the old man.

"I'm half a mind to go over there and tell them off," Nora murmured.

"Let them alone. Just so they'll stop the racket for blast-away."

"Look at them! Polite little pattern-cuts, all alike. They take pre-space because it's the thing to do. Then they quit before the payoff comes."

"How do you know they'll quit?"

"That party—I bet it cost six months' pay, spacer's pay," she went on, ignoring him. "And what do real spacers get? Oley gets killed, and Pop's pension wouldn't feed the Keiths' cat."

"You don't understand, girl."

"I lost Oley. I understand enough."

He watched her silently for a moment, then closed his eyes. It was no good trying to explain, no good trying to tell her the dough didn't mean a damn thing. She'd been a spacer's wife, and that was bad enough, but now she was a spacer's widow. And Oley? Oley's tomb revolved around the sun in an eccentric orbit that spun in close to Mercury, then reached out into the asteroid belt, once every 725 days. When it came within rocket radius of Earth, it whizzed past at close to fifteen miles a second.

You don't rescue a ship like that, skinny-britches, my darling daughter. Nor do you salvage it after the crew stops screaming for help. If you use enough fuel to catch it, you won't get back. You just leave such a ship there forever, like an asteroid, and it's a damn shame about the men trapped aboard. Heroes all, no doubt— but the smallness of the widow's monthly check failed to confirm the heroism, and Nora was bitter about the price of Oley's memory, perhaps.

Ouch! Old Donegal, you know she's not like that. It's just that she can't understand about space. You ought to make her understand.

But did he really understand, himself? You ride hot in a roaring blast room, hands tense on the mixer controls and the pumps, eyes glued to instruments, body sucked down in a four-gravity thrust, and wait for the command to choke it off. Then you float free and weightless in a long nightmare as the beast coasts moonward, a flung javelin.

The "romance" of space—drivel written in the old days. When you're not blasting, you float in a cramped hotbox, crawl through dirty mazes of greasy pipe and cable to tighten a lug, scratch your arms and bark your shins, get sick and choked up because no gravity helps your gullet get the food down. Liquid is worse, but you gag your whiskey down because you have to.

Stars? You see stars by squinting through a viewing lens, and it's like a photo transparency, and if you aren't careful you'll get an eyeful of Old Blinder and back off with a punch-drunk retina.

Adventure? Unless the skipper calls for course correction, you float around in the blast cubicle with damn little to do between blast-away and moon-down, except sweat out the omniscient accident statistics. If the beast blows up or gets gutted in space, a statistic had your name on it, that's all, and there's no fighting back. You stay outwardly sane because you're a hog for punishment; if you weren't, you'd never get past the psychologists.

"Did you like horror movies when you were a kid?" asked the psych. And you'd damn well better answer yes, if you want to go to space.

Tell her, old man, you're her pop. Tell her why it's worth it, if you know. You jail yourself in a coffin-size cubicle, and a crazy beast thunders berserk for uncontrollable seconds, and then you soar in ominous silence for the long long hours. Grow sweaty, filthy, sick, miserable, idle—somewhere out in Big Empty, where man's got no business except the trouble he always makes for himself wherever he goes. Tell her why it's worth it, for pay less than a good bricklayer's. Tell her why Oley would do it again.

"It's a sucker's run, Nora," he said. "You go looking for kicks, but the only kicks you get to keep is what Oley got. God knows why—but it's worth it."

Nora said nothing. He opened his eyes slowly. Nora was gone. Had she been there at all?

He blinked around at the fuzzy room and dissolved the shifting shadows that sometimes emerged as old friendly faces, grinning at him. He found Martha.

"You went to sleep," said Martha. "She had to go. Kennie called. He'll be over later, if you're not too tired."

"I'm not tired. I'm all head. There's nothing much to get tired."

"I love you, Old Donegal."

"Hold my hand again."

"I'm holding it, old man."

"Then hold me where I can feel it."

She slid a thin arm under his neck and bent over his face to kiss him. She was crying a little, and he was glad she could do it now without fleeing the room.

"Can I talk about dying now?" he wondered aloud.

She pinched her lips together and shook her head.

"I lie to myself, Martha. You know how much I lie to myself?"

She nodded slowly and stroked his gray temples.

"I lie to myself about Ken, and about dying. If Ken turned spacer, I wouldn't die—that's what I told myself. You know?"

She shook her head. "Don't talk, Donny, please."

"A man makes his own soul, Martha."

"That's not true. You shouldn't say things like that."

"A man makes his own soul, but it dies with him, unless he can pour it into his kids and his grandchildren before he goes. I lied to myself. Ken's a yellow-belly. Nora made him one, and the boots won't fit."

"Don't, Donny. You'll excite yourself again."

"I was going to give him the boots—the overboots with magnasoles. But they won't fit him. They won't ever fit him. He's a lily-livered lapdog, and he whines. Bring me my boots, woman."

"Donny!"

"The boots, they're in my locker in the attic. I want them."

"What on earth!"

"Bring me my goddam space boots and put them on my feet. I'm going to wear them."

"You can't; the priest's coming."

"Well, get them anyway. What time is it? You didn't let me sleep through the moon-run blast, did you?"

She shook her head. "It's half an hour yet. I'll get the boots if you promise not to make me put them on you."

"I want them on."

"You can't, until Father Paul's finished."

"Do I have to get my feet buttered?"

She sighed. "I wish you wouldn't say things like that. I wish you wouldn't, Donny. It's sacrilege, you know it is."

"All right—'anointed'," he corrected wearily.

"Yes, you do."

"The boots, woman, the boots."

She went to get them. While she was gone, the doorbell rang, and he heard her quick footsteps on the stairs, and then Father Paul's voice asking about the patient. Old Donegal groaned inwardly. After the priest, the doctor would come, at the usual time, to see if he were dead yet. The doctor had let him come home from the hospital to die, and the doctor was getting impatient. Why don't they let me alone? he growled. Why don't they let me handle it in my own way, and stop making a fuss over it? I can die and do a good job of it without a lot of outside interference, and I wish they'd quit picking at me with syringes and sacraments and enemas. All he wanted was a chance to listen to the orchestra on the Keith terrace, to drink the rest of his whiskey, and to hear the beast blast away for the satellite on the first lap of the run to Luna.

It's going to be my last day, he thought. My eyes are going fuzzy, and I can't breathe right, and the throbbing's hurting my head. Whether he lived through the night wouldn't matter, because delirium was coming over him, and then there would be the coma, and the symbolic fight to keep him pumping and panting. I'd rather die tonight and get it over with, he thought, but they probably won't let me go.

He heard their voices coming up the stairs:

"Nora tried to get them to stop it, Father, but she couldn't get in to see anybody but the butler. He told her he'd tell Mrs. Keith, but nothing happened. It's just as loud as before."

"Well, as long as Donny doesn't mind . . ."

"He just says that. You know how he is."

"What're they celebrating, Martha?"

"Young Ronald's leaving—for pre-space training. It's a going-away affair."

They paused in the doorway. The small priest smiled in at Donegal and nodded. He set his black bag on the floor inside, winked solemnly at the patient.

"I'll leave you two alone," said Martha. She closed the door, and her footsteps wandered off down the hall.

Donegal and the young priest eyed each other warily.

"You look like hell, Donegal," the padre offered jovially. "Feeling nasty?"

"Skip the small talk. Let's get this routine over with."

The priest humphed thoughtfully, sauntered across to the bed, gazed down at the old man disinterestedly. "What's the matter? Don't want the 'routine'? Rather play it tough?"

"What's the difference?" he growled. "Hurry up and get out. I want to hear the beast blast off."

"You won't be able to," said the priest, glancing at the window, now closed again. "That's quite a racket next door."

"They'd better stop for it. They'd better quiet down for it. They'll have to turn it off for five minutes or so."

"Maybe they won't."

It was a new idea, and it frightened him. He liked the music, and the party's gaiety, the nearness of youth and good times—but it hadn't occurred to him that it wouldn't stop so he could hear the beast.

"Don't get upset, Donegal. You know what a blast-off sounds like."

"But it's the last one. The last time. I want to hear."

"How do you know it's the last time?"

"Hell, don't I know when I'm kicking off?"

"Maybe, maybe not. It's hardly your decision."

"It's not, eh?" Old Donegal fumed. "Well, bigawd, you'd think it wasn't. You'd think it was Martha's and yours and that damfool medic's. You'd think I got no say-so. Who's doing it, anyway?"

"I would guess," Father Paul grunted sourly, "that Providence might appreciate His fair share of the credit."

Old Donegal made a surly noise and hunched his head back into the pillow to glower.

"You want me?" the priest asked. "Or is this just a case of wifely conscience?"

"What's the difference? Give me the business and scram."

"No soap. Do you want the sacrament, or are you just being kind to your wife? If it's for Martha, I'll go *now*."

Old Donegal glared at him for a time, then wilted. The priest brought his bag to the bedside.

"Bless me, Father, for I have sinned."

"Bless you, son."

"I accuse myself . . ."

Tension, anger, helplessness—they had piled up on him, and now he was feeling the aftereffects. Vertigo, nausea, and the black confetti—a bad spell. The whiskey—if he could only reach the whiskey. Then he remembered he was receiving a sacrament and struggled to get on with it. Tell him, old man, tell him of your various rottennesses and vile transgressions, if you can remember some. A sin is whatever you're sorry for, maybe. But, Old Donegal, you're sorry for the wrong things, and this young Jesuitical gadget wouldn't like listening to it. I'm sorry I didn't get it instead of Oley, and I'm sorry I fought in the war, and I'm sorry I can't get out of this bed and take a belt to my daughter's backside for making a puny whelp out of Ken, and I'm sorry I gave Martha such a rough time all these years—and wound up dying in a cheap flat, instead of giving her things like the Keiths had. I wish I had been a sharpster, contractor, or thief . . . instead of a common laboring spacer, whose species lost its glamor after the war.

Listen, old man, you made your soul yourself, and it's yours. This young dispenser of oils, Substances and mysteries wishes only to help you scrape off the rough edges and gouge out the bad spots. He will not steal it, nor distort it with his supernatural chisels, nor make fun of it. He can take nothing away, but only cauterize and neutralize, he says, so why not let him try? Tell him the rotten messes.

"Are you finished, my son?"

Old Donegal nodded wearily, and said what he was asked to say, and heard the soft mutter of Latin that washed him inside and behind his ghostly ears—". . . *ego te absolvo in Nomine Patris* . . ."—and he accepted the rest of it lying quietly in the candlelight and the red glow of the sunset through the window, while the priest anointed him and gave him Bread, and read the words of the soul in greeting its Spouse: "I was asleep, but my heart waked; it is the voice of my beloved calling: come to me, my love, my dove, my undefiled . . ." and from beyond the closed window came the sarcastic wail of a clarinet painting hot slides against a rhythmic background.

It wasn't so bad, Old Donegal thought when the priest was done. He felt like a schoolboy in a starched shirt on Sunday morning, and it wasn't a bad feeling, though it left him weak.

The priest opened the window for him again and repacked his bag. "Ten minutes till blast-off," he said. "I'll see what I can do about the racket next door."

When he was gone Martha came back in, and he looked at her face and was glad. She was smiling when she kissed him, and she looked less tired.

"Is it all right for me to die now?" he grunted.

"Donny, don't start that again."

"Where's the boots? You promised to bring them."

"They're in the hall. Donny, you don't want them."

"I want them, and I want a drink of whiskey, and I want to hear them fire the beast." He said it slow and hard, and he left no room for argument.

When she had got the huge boots over his shrunken feet, the magnasoles clanged against the iron bedframe and clung there, and she rolled him up so that he could look at them, and Old Donegal chuckled inside. He felt warm and clean and pleasantly dizzy.

"The whiskey, Martha, and for God's sake make them stop the noise till after the firing. Please!"

She went to the window and looked out for a long time. Then she came back and poured him an insignificant drink.

"Well?"

"I don't know," she said. "I saw Father Paul on the terrace, talking to somebody."

"Is it time?"

She glanced at the clock, looked at him doubtfully and nodded. "Nearly time."

The orchestra finished a number, but the babble of laughing voices continued. Old Donegal sagged. "They won't do it. They're the Keiths, Martha. Why should I ruin their party?"

She turned to stare at him, slowly shook her head. He heard

someone shouting, but then a trumpet started softly, introducing a new number. Martha sucked in a hurt breath, pressed her hands together and hurried from the room.

"It's too late," he said after her.

Her footsteps stopped on the stairs. The trumpet was alone. Donegal listened, and there was no babble of voices, and the rest of the orchestra was silent. Only the trumpet sang—and it puzzled him, hearing the same slow bugle notes of the call played at the lowering of the colors.

The trumpet stopped suddenly. Then he knew it had been for him.

A brief hush—then thunder came from the blast station two miles to the west. First the low reverberation, rattling the windows, then the rising growl as the sleek beast knifed skyward on a column of blue-white hell. It grew and grew until it drowned the distant traffic sounds and dominated the silence outside.

Quit crying, you old fool, you maudlin ass . . .

"My boots," he whispered, "my boots . . . please . . ."

"You've got them on, Donny."

He sank quietly then. He closed his eyes and let his heart go up with the beast, and he sank into the gravity padding of the blast room, and Caid was with him, and Oley. And when Ronald Keith III instructed the orchestra to play "Blast-Room Man," after the beast's rumble had waned, Old Donegal was on his last moon run, and he was grinning. He'd had a good day.

Martha went to the window to stare out at the thin black trail that curled starward above the blast station through the twilight sky. Guests on the terrace were watching it, too.

The doorbell rang. That would be Ken, too late. She closed the window against the chill breeze and went back to the bed. The boots, the heavy, clumsy boots—they clung to the bedframe, with his feet half out of them. She took them off gently and set them out of company's sight. Then she went to answer the door.

THE BRIGHT ILLUSION

C. L. MOORE

C. L. Moore (Mrs. Henry Kuttner) is the only author nominated each of whose stories was nominated more than once. Both "Vintage Season" and "No Woman Born" have been republished several times and are almost as available as they ought to be.

"The Bright Illusion," a rather earlier story, was published in 1934 and has never been reprinted. I can't understand this state of affairs, but I am extremely happy to remedy it.

Through the blinding shimmer of sun upon sand, Dixon squinted painfully at the curious mirage ahead. He was reeling with thirst and heat and weariness, and about him the desert heaved in long, blurred waves, but through the haze of his own weakness, and through the sun haze upon the desert, he peered anxiously at the thing and could not make it out.

Nothing he had ever seen or heard of could cause such a mirage as this. It was a great oval of yellow light, bulging up convexly from the earth like some translucent golden egg half buried in the sand. And over its surface there seemed to be an immense busyness, as if it was covered with tiny, shimmering things that moved constantly. He had never seen anything remotely resembling it before.

As he toiled through the sand toward the bright illusion, he became aware of darker specks around it haphazardly, specks that as he approached took on the aspect of men grotesquely sprawled in attitudes of death. He could not make it out. Of course it was a mirage, yet it did not recede as he advanced, and the details of those sprawled bodies became clearer and clearer, and the great translucent oval loomed up against the sky mystifyingly.

He thought he must be dreaming, or perhaps a little unbalanced by heat and thirst. He had been struggling through this burning sand under this burning sun for a long while now, and there were times when the rush of illusion swallowed him up, and he could hear water splashing and fountains tinkling in the empty desert about him. This must be a hallucination, then, for it could scarcely be a mirage. He was almost upon it, and it had so real a look—those bodies, sprawling—

He stumbled over the first, for somehow his muscles did not co-ordinate very well now. It was the sun-withered body of an old man in the Legion uniform, his kepi fallen forward over his face. The next was that of an Arab in a tangle of dirty white garments, and beyond him was the almost-fresh corpse of a boy in khaki shorts and sun helmet.

Dixon wondered duly what had happened to them and why the bodies were in such varying stages of decomposition. He lifted a dragging head and peered at the great egg-shaped thing bulging up from the sand. It reminded him of a huge bubble of golden water, save that bubbles were round, and—

Belatedly, caution returned to him. These dead men must have met their deaths somehow through the presence of the great egg. He had better advance more cautiously or— And then the pull seized him. He had come too near. Something inexorable and slow was dragging him forward—or was it that the great bubble was advancing toward him?

Sky and sand reeled. And the distance between him and the great egg-shaped thing lessened and lessened and—and somehow he found himself flat against a great golden translucency that shivered against him with the strangest motion, as if it was alive and hungry for—

He felt that he should be afraid, yet somehow he was not aware of fear at all. The golden light was closing over him and around him with a queer, engulfing motion. He shut his eyes and relaxed utterly in the impassive grip of the thing.

Dixon was lying motionless in the midst of a golden radiance that seemed crystal clear, yet so obstructed his vision that he could see only a few yards away, and the desert landscape outside was as unreal as a dream. The most delicious sensation of rest and well-being was surging through him in slow waves that succeeded one another like ripples on a shore, each leaving an increasing residue of serenity and luxurious comfort. Thirst and hunger and weariness had vanished in a breath. He knew no fear or anxiety. In a trancelike calm he lay there, feeling the waves flow through him unbroken, staring up into the lucid golden light without wonder or surprise.

How long he lay there he never knew. In the perfect peace of the glow enfolding him, he was very dimly aware that the all-penetrating waves were washing through him in a way which queerly suggested searching. They permeated every atom of him, flooding his brain with light and calmness.

In his tranced quiet he knew, without actually realizing, that memory in lightning flashes was reeling through his mind. Abstract memories of things he had learned in college and in afterlife. Snatches of literature, fragments of sciences. Mathematical problems solved in breathtaking speed and supplanted by chemical formulas that melted into the bits of psychology remembered from schooldays. Impassively he lay there, scarcely realizing the flashing reviews that passed through his light-flooded brain.

And then the tempo of the ripples that went over him began to change. His mind awoke by degrees from its pleasant coma, though his body still lay relaxed. And now the wavelets in the queerest way were beating upon his brain tantalizingly. Little fragments of thoughts not his own blew through his mind and faded.

He struggled to grasp them. He clutched at the vanishing tags, striving to weld them together, feeling obscurely that if he could retain each small flutter as it wavered through his mind, if he could put them together and fuse them in a unit, he might understand.

Very slowly he succeeded. Very slowly the waves as they flowed through him began to surrender their meanings to his clutching mind: meanings that solidified and amplified with each succeeding wave, building themselves up slowly as ripple after ripple washed serenely through the straining brain that was learning so painfully to comprehend their significance.

By degrees Dixon realized that some intelligence was striving to communicate with him. The knowledge did not come in words or even word forms introduced into his brain. But it came, slowly and inexorably, building up and up as wave after measured wave flowed through him and vanished, leaving a residue of knowledge to be increased by the next.

And the vast, the almost divine, impersonality of it staggered him. This being—intelligence, presence—was so utterly abstract a thing that even in the knowledge it imparted to him there was no hint of personality or consciousness of individual being. There could have been no "I" in its supervocabulary of thought ripples. Divinely serene, divinely abstract, it allowed knowledge to flow through the brain of the man suspended in its heart. And by measured degrees that knowledge built itself up in his mind.

He had been chosen. For a long while this being had been waiting here, trapping the men who came near enough, sending its light waves in floods through their minds to illuminate their thoughts and their capacity for knowledge, probing their intelligences. All those others lying outside had been found wanting. The being had discarded them and waited, in its serene passivity, until the right man came by.

This much flowed through his brain. Then there was a hiatus, to permit him to absorb the knowledge, to understand. After a while the wavelets began to beat through him again in their measured slowness. He became aware of vast, dim voids, blank stretches empty of space or time or any of the myriad dimensions. He knew that through these, while long periods elapsed which yet had no relation to the time he understood, the great light-bubble had traveled from some origin unthinkably far away, on a quest. He realized that it had at last emerged from those gray, formless voids into the interstellar space of his own universe; that it had made its way here, driven by a vast purpose he could not grasp, and had come to rest upon the desert sands, to lie in wait.

Again there was a gap in the thought waves, and again Dixon lay still, assimilating that stunning knowledge. And yet, somehow, he was not greatly surprised or in the remotest way skeptical. He waited.

Presently the flow began again. There was, in another part of space, a world which this being desired—or no, not desired; there was nothing so human or personal a thing as desire about it. A world which it meant to have; a very alien world, he gathered, from the sort he knew. Peopled by alien creatures and built in other dimensions than those which formed his own universe.

These people worshiped a powerful god. And it was this worship—this godhood—which the being that enfolded him meant to possess. It tried to give him a glimpse of why, but the thought waves which flowed through his brain were incomprehensible and remote—not knowledge, but a jumble of unrelated impressions, without coherence. After a few vain attempts to instill the reason for its purpose into his mind, the being apparently dismissed the point as unnecessary and went on.

This god which it meant to dispossess was very powerful; so powerful that of itself the being could do nothing to overthrow it, could not even pass the barriers set up to guard the strange world. It had need of an intelligent, animate creature from a world different enough in structure so that the god's peculiar powers would have no effect upon him.

Gradually the measured beats made it clear to Dixon that he was the chosen envoy. He was to be transported there, armed in potent ways, sent out into the new world to overthrow the god's domain and make way for his sponsor to take possession.

There was a long hiatus after that. Dixon lay quiet, rather stunned by the magnitude of the thing. The being which engulfed him must have sensed the growing rebellion in his mind, for after a while the beats began again. And Dixon knew that the proposition was not a compulsory one. But—the knowledge flowed casually through him—though he was free to be released and set back upon his journey if he refused the plan, he would inevitably die soon, die very unpleasantly.

There was no water within any possible reach, and a band of veiled Tuaregs was scouring the desert nearby in search of that Arab who lay in a huddle of dirty white robes outside the egg-shaped bubble. If he did not die of thirst before they caught him, he would die in a manner infinitely more undesirable at their hands. But, of course, if he so desired, he was free to go.

Dixon digested this information thoughtfully, hesitating, though he knew he had no choice. His blind stumbling through the desert could have no other end than slow death, as he had been aware even before he came upon the great bubble. And if there were Tuaregs near— Even in the bodily trance that cradled him he shuddered. He had seen victims of Tuareg tortures, miraculously alive after days and days of— He turned his mind from that. No; he had no choice.

And gradually a little spark of excitement began to burn in him. What an adventure! And though death might lie at the end of it, there was at least a hope for life, and he knew he had not even that if he refused. Consent was forming in his mind, but, even before it crystallized, the being must have known, for about him the lucid radiance suddenly began to cloud and change. Milkiness flooded through it and through his body and his brain. Oblivion swallowed him up.

When realization returned to Dixon it came slowly. Layer by layer the oblivion melted from his mind. He had a vague impression of vast spaces traversed and barriers surmounted, and somehow he sensed an indefinable difference in the space that surrounded the bubble, though it was indefinite how he knew it. A little beat quivered through him, and another, clearing away the fogs of his consciousness. Then knowledge began to pulse again through him in measured flow.

They had crossed gulfs greater than he could comprehend. They were suspended now above the world of their destination. He was to look briefly upon it, for even through the protecting walls of the light-bubble the thing that he would see was so alien to him that in his present form he could not bear to gaze upon it long.

Then the light about Dixon cleared to translucence, and somehow he was looking out and down upon a scene that stunned his eyes with its violence. He had an instant's impression of a land that shrieked and raved with maniacal color beyond any conception of color as he knew it. He turned his eyes wincingly away and stared down at the scene immediately below. And though in point of actual space it must have been very far away, he could see everything quite clearly and with a wider radius of vision than he was accustomed to. It was as if in one glance he encompassed the whole circle of the horizon.

The world below was one vast city that reeled away in terrace below crazy terrace out to a skyline that shimmered with white dazzle. And the colors that blazed and howled and agonized over the insane angles of the place turned him sick and dizzy. They were incredible angles and impossible colors, the tints and the tilts of madness—wild, staggering lines and arcs and jagged peaks, crazy inclines broken by ridges of eruptive color, zigzag bridges, buildings that leaned out in gravity-defying angles.

All these incredible terraces mounted up and up in diminishing arcs to the topmost tier of all. This was small and smooth, though over its pavement the insane colors sprawled blotchily. And in the very center a mighty column rose, blacker than any darkness he had ever seen before. On its height burned a pale flame.

But the inhabitants! Dixon could see them quite clearly despite the distance. They were sinuous and serpentine, and their motions were blurs of swiftness, poems of infinite grace. They were not men—they had never been men in any stage of their evolution. And if the colors of the buildings were agony to his eyes, the living, unstable hues that writhed and crawled over the beings below were so frightful that his gaze rebelled. For this reason he never knew just how they were shaped.

There was one standing just below the great black pillar whereon burned the flame, and of this he had the clearest view. It was boneless and writhing, livid with creeping color. Its single great eye, lucid and expressionless, stared from an unfeatured, mouthless face, half scarlet and half purple, between which two shades a wedge of nameless green broadened as he looked away.

He had seen this much before the pellucid crystal began to cloud about him once more and the slow knowledge began its beat through his brain. He must look no longer, or something disastrous might happen to his benumbed senses. He understood by now that it was not in his own form that he was to go out into the crazy land. He was sure, even without that seeping knowledge, that his own body could never endure the colors of the place, nor could his own material feet tread the dizzy angles. Many of the streets and bridges were too steep for human feet to walk.

And he was understanding, as the slow waves flowed on, how different these people were from his own kind. Not only in appearance; their very substance was different from flesh and blood, the atoms arranged in different patterns. They obtained nourishment in an incomprehensible way from some source he could not understand. Their emotions and habits and purposes were alien to all his experience, and among them even the sexes were not those he knew. They were more numerous than mankind's two, and their functions were entirely different. Reproduction here was based on an utterly alien principle.

When the pause came in the waves of knowledge, Dixon was a little dizzy with the complete strangeness of this place and with wonder how he would be enabled to enter it. He lay still, wondering, until the flow began again.

Then the knowledge of the way he was to be introduced into the strange god's domain began to surge in deliberate beats through his brain. It seemed simple, yet the magnitude of it was staggering. A sort of veil of illusion was to be dropped between him and these alien beings. To them, his form would seem one of their own. Through the veil his speech would be filtered and changed into their indescribable mode of communication. And to him they would have the appearance of humanity, their speech would be understandable, their curious emotions translated into familiarity.

Even their multiple sexes would be resolved arbitrarily into two. For though this being could not approach any nearer the strange god whose flame burned upon the pillar, it seemed to have immense power even from this distance in the crazy world below.

The slow-beating waves made him aware that during his sojourn in the strange place he would be guided and in a measure protected, and that this knowledge would still flow through his brain. All this was possible, he understood, because of his own complete difference from anything in this world—such a difference that he would not cause even a ripple upon the surface of the god's consciousness until the time came for his overthrow.

Then again the cloudiness began to clear, until Dixon was looking out through crystal walls upon that reeling city below. For an instant it shuddered with mad colors before his aching eyes. And then over the whole crazy panorama the queerest blurring came. He looked down upon a changing world wherein the wild colors faded and ran together and the staggering angles of that mighty vista below were obscured in structural changes whose purpose he began to understand.

Before his eyes a splendid and stately city was taking shape. Out of the ruin of eye-wrenching color rose tier beyond tier of white pillars and translucent domes. Roofs of alabaster formed themselves under a sky whose pallor was deepening into blue.

When he tore his eyes away from that magnificent vista, terrace dropping away below terrace, crowned with domes and spires and columns wreathed in green, far out to the distant horizon, he saw that over the crowded streets with their swarms of multicolored horrors a stranger change was falling. Out of the mingling indistinctnesses of those colors without name, the semblance of humanity grew. People of noble stature and stately bearing, robed in garments of shining steel, took form before his eyes.

In less time than it takes to tell, a metropolis of familiar aspect stretched invitingly under his gaze. That nightmare of colors was gone as a nightmare goes, leaving no faintest trace behind. Yet he knew as he looked down that in reality nothing was changed. The writhing people still flashed with infinite speed and grace through tiptilted streets of gravity-defying angles. He blinked and looked again, but the illusion held steady—a stupendous city, smiling under a blue, familiar sky.

Slowly through his consciousness beat the realization that, once down there in the metamorphosed world, he must search out the temple of the god, find its vulnerable spot, provide as it were a window, so that through his eyes the being which had brought him here could see its enemy's weakness and instruct Dixon further. And it was impressed upon him, too, that all possible speed must be made, for though there was little danger that the god would realize the inimical presence, yet his very safeguard was his greatest danger. Dixon was so alien to the ultimate particles of his being that, though this protected him from the god, it made his maintenance in the strange world very difficult. It was a strain even upon the vast powers of the light-bubble being to keep that veil of illusion stretched protectingly between him and this world, the very sight and touch of which would send him mad if he was exposed to it long unguarded.

There was a little pause after this, and Dixon lay still, awed by the unthinkable difference between his own structure of mind and body and that of the strange place and people below. Then with breathtaking abruptness, darkness dropped over him. One instant he lay serenely cradled in golden radiance, the next he was dropping through blackness with a queer, high scream in his ears as if he fell through some resisting atmosphere which was not air. Physically he was protected, but he could hear the thin sound of it in varying intensities.

And then without warning the darkness broke, and he found his feet upon solid ground without any hint of jar. He was simply standing upon a marble pavement under a clear blue sky and looking out over a breath-stopping vista of world-city, dropping away in terrace below shining terrace to a distant skyline, out and away in broadening tiers. Light shimmered dazzlingly upon faraway steel figures moving through the streets below, away and away until they were no more than tiny pinpricks of shimmer on the horizon's edge. From each broad circular terrace a marble ramp led down to the next beneath, and over these the steel-bright people were swarming in busy hordes.

And Dixon knew, even as he stared with caught breath at the magnificence of it, that in reality he stood at the apex of a city of madness that reeled away below him in tier after crazy tier, a nightmare of meaningless angles and raving color, through whose streets things writhing and dreadful and acrawl with living hues were flashing with movements of blurring speed. All this splendor was a veil across his eyes. What unknowable activities were really taking place below? On what nameless errands were these busy crowds bound? Then a little sound at his side turned him from the dizzy thoughts tormenting his brain, and he flashed an abrupt glance sidewise, alert for danger. Then he caught his breath and stared.

She was slim as a sword blade in her steel robe, standing under the mighty tower of the black pillar, and she was lovelier than a dream. Her hair swung in black page-boy curls to her shoulders, and from under the darkness of it eyes as blue as steel met his unwaveringly. She was all bright metal to his first glance, steel-molded curves of her under the armored robe, steel lights upon her burnished hair, steel-bright eyes shining. All steel and brightness—but Dixon saw that her mouth was soft and colored like hot embers. And for an instant he wanted to burst into crazy song. It was an inexplicable feeling that he had never known before, a heady delight in being alive. But even through the exultation, he knew that he looked upon an illusion. He knew that she was a faceless, crawling thing, without sex, without any remotest kinship to anything he knew. And yet this illusion was very lovely and—

She was looking up at him with startled eyes, and now she spoke, a little breathlessly, in a sweet, tinkling voice. "You—you have come? Oh, whence have you come?" And he thought that she was striving hard not to believe something which she wanted with all her soul to think true.

There was no answer he could give. He glanced around helplessly at the blue, empty sky, at the great pillar rising behind her, at the pale flame burning so steadily upon its summit. That blaze held him for an instant, and in the instant he stood with eyes uplifted the girl must have thought she had her answer, for she caught her breath in a gasp that was half a sob, and in one swift motion she fell to her knees before him, a miracle of sliding grace in that close gown of steel, so that the light rippled all down her sweet, slim body and lay bluely on the wings of her hair that swung forward as she bent her head.

"I knew it! I knew!" she breathed. "I knew my god would send you! Oh, praise great IL, who has sent me such an envoy!"

Dixon looked down upon the bent black head, his eyes troubled. If she believed him a messenger from the god, it would simplify his task enormously. And yet . . . He had entertained no scruples about displacing the god of a maniacal world peopled with writhing monstrosities, but this was different, somehow. This girl . . .

"I am the high priestess of our god," she murmured, as if in answer to his half-formed query. "I have served IL with all my heart for many cycles now, but only he knows how I have prayed for the coming of an envoy among us. Such honor is enough to—to—" The sweet voice choked suddenly on a sob, as if the answer to her prayer was too much for her to endure unmoved.

Dixon bent and took her chin in his hand, lifting her face to his. The steel-bright eyes were dazzling with diffused tears. The red mouth trembled. She was looking up at him with awe and worship upon her face, and suddenly he knew that he wanted no worship from her. He resented that look of respect and awe. He wanted—well, he wanted her to see a man, not a divine messenger. He wanted to—

Then the queerest madness came over him, deliciously—and he

acted. He stooped swiftly and set his lips over the trembling red lips of the girl, and for an instant the whole strange world reeled and swam in a heady pleasure like nothing he had ever known before.

When he straightened and stood looking down upon her, she met his eyes with purest bewilderment in hers, one hand hovering at her lips and incomprehension radiant in every line of her. Her blue gaze was traveling over him from head to foot in swift, puzzled glances.

And then realization swept back upon him tremendously. To her he wore the writhing shape that was hers in reality. That troubled blue gaze was the gaze of a single pale eye which traveled over the crawling limbs of a monster. He was not even sure that, to her, kneeling denoted homage and wondered in what alien way she was actually expressing her awe.

It was an uncanny feeling which was to haunt him through all his hours here—the knowledge that what he looked upon was unreal, the wonder as to what was actually taking place behind the mask of humanity which only he could see. That kiss—how had it seemed to her? What nameless gesture had he seemed to perform before her eyes—her eye? For he had kissed a monstrosity that had no mouth. Remembering the glimpse he had caught of a one-eyed, featureless face crawling with alive colors, he shuddered and turned back to the kneeling girl as if for reassurance.

Dixon was aware of a curious emptiness within him because of this beauty which was only an illusion—had never been, would never be. He was looking straight into her steel-blue eyes now, and she was smiling very tremulously and with that puzzled look still upon her face. He could see the little shimmering tumult her heart made under the dazzle of her robe. And she was not even female! He narrowed his eyes and strove to pierce the mirage for a moment; to convince himself that here knelt a colored horror of sinuosity and sexlessness. And everything within him cried out protestingly. She was human—she was lovely—she was everything desirable and sweet. And she did not even exist save as a crawling horror upon whom in her normal guise he could never dare to look.

Then, as if to refute that, she flashed up at him a small, uncertain smile which made her so unmistakably human and sweet that he disbelieved everything but her own reality, and she said, "What —what was the meaning of that, O divine envoy?"

He frowned. "You are to call me Dixon," he said. "And that was—well, just a form of greeting."

"The way they greet one another in great IL's domain—in Paradise? Then . . ." She rose in one swift motion. Before he realized what was happening she had risen upon her sandaled toes and her warm mouth was brushing his. "Then I return your greeting, O Dixon."

Involuntarily his arms closed around her. Her body was firm and soft and warm in his clasp—the body of a living human girl, a mirage more real than reality. And again he wondered what nameless rites she was actually performing behind the illusory veil which masked her real, writhing self. And because she felt so pleasant in his arms he released her abruptly and stepped back, knowing the first quickening of uneasiness. Good heaven, could it be possible for a man to fall in love with a hallucination?

She looked up at him serenely, evidently feeling that she had mastered a difficult point of divine etiquette.

"How pleasant a thing is this new way of greeting!" she murmured, half to herself. "And now, O Dixon, you have but to command me in all things. What would you in IL's world-city?"

Dixon debated swiftly with himself. After all, lovely though she seemed, she was—and he must bear this in mind constantly, lest something dangerous befall—she was a sinuous, faceless thing, a creeping horror with the tints of an incredible spectrum. She was no more than this, and he must find his way, by her help, into the god IL's temple and let the light-being look through his eyes so that he might find IL's vulnerable spot. After that—well, he must do as he was commanded. IL would be overthrown, his own sponsor would usurp the godship, and that would be all. As for these beings which peopled the world, no doubt the change of gods would be a startling thing, but there was no help for it. He had but to perform his own part and then go.

"O Dixon!" the sweet, light voice of the girl broke in upon his thoughts. "O Dixon, would you see how IL's temple is kept by his worshipers? Would you see how devoutly his world adores him?"

"Yes," said Dixon thankfully. "You may lead me to IL's temple."

She genuflected again, a poem of grace in that steel gown along which the light slid in long lines as she moved, and the dark hair swung forward about her face. Then she turned and crossed the terrace toward a ramp which led down into the city. They went down the slope of it—what eye-tormenting angles of spanning actually led downward he could not even guess—and emerged upon a broad street lined with pillared buildings. There were throngs of steel-robed people here who parted in devout rows as the priestess came down the ramp.

She paused at the head of the street and lifted her arms, and Dixon heard her voice ringing clearly over the crowd. "Great IL has answered our prayers at last," she cried. "He has sent us an envoy from his own divinity. Here is the messenger from our god!"

A murmur went over the crowd—a murmur of awe and rejoicing. And then they knelt in long, sinuous rows as if a wind had blown across a field of sword blades. And with incredible swiftness the whisper ran back along the street, from mouth to mouth. He imagined it rippling out and out, down and down, from terrace to terrace, until it reached the ultimate limits of the whole tiered world.

They stepped down among the kneeling throngs, walking a lane of steel worshipers, and by the time they had reached the end of the street Dixon could see flecks of light far away below hurrying upward as the news spread. Up through the pillared streets and the green terraces they came swarming, men and women in robes of linked metal, with intent, awe-struck faces upturned. Dixon moved on with a long stride, a divine messenger from a god marching in triumph through a city without ends or boundaries, for as far as he could see the steel flecks that were people flashed up through the buildings below. And their multitudes were breathtaking. The whole vast city swarmed with living steel as wave after wave of armored people rolled upward toward the heights. His brain reeled with the numbers of them.

Over the bowed heads of the throngs as they advanced, Dixon glanced curiously at the buildings which lined the streets, casting about for some clue to the sort of life those people led. He found nothing. The marble pillars and walls rose as blankly as stage sets along the streets. A mask had been set for him over the realities of the place, but it was not a living mask. There were no shops, no markets, no residences. Rows of noncommittal pillars faced him blankly, betraying no secrets. Apparently the light-being had been unable to do more than mask the strangeness of this world. It could not infuse into it the spirit of a daily life so utterly alien as man's.

They went on through the dead-faced streets, down another ramp, and always the people dropped to their knees, perfectly the illusion of humanity. What, he wondered, were they actually doing? In what weird, incredible way were they really expressing their devotion? It was, of course, better not to know.

Dixon watched the girl before him walking proudly and lightly through the homage-stricken throngs, her dark head high, the steel robe rippling over the loveliness of her body as she moved. Presently she paused for him, smiling over her shoulder in a way that made his heart quicken, and turned in under the great arch of a doorway.

It was not a particularly imposing structure; no more than a marble-columned building with a huge dark portal. But, once inside, Dixon stopped in stunned astonishment at the vastness spread out before him.

It must have occupied the whole interior of all the terraces above—a mighty dome about which the buildings and streets overhead were the merest shell. In the dimness he could not descry the limits of it, but he saw that the whole vast temple was built in the shape of a great dome. For temple it must be. He knew that instinctively. There was the shadow of divinity in it, somehow—a vast calm. And for an instant, as he stared about the great place, he forgot even the presence of the girl at his side.

In the very center of the wide, dark floor lay a pool of pale radiance which somehow gave the impression that it seethed and boiled, though its surface lay untroubled under the lofty dome of the roof. And above the pool the ceiling was shaped like a burning lens to gather and concentrate the radiance arising from it. This centered at the apex of the roof in a dazzle of light at which he could not look directly. He realized that the center of this burning brilliance must be just under the pillar which crowned the topmost terrace—the pillar upon which burned the flame of IL.

Beyond the column of light rising from the pool, Dixon saw

dimly in the gloom of the great temple the glimmer of steel robes. There was an arch in the far wall, so distant he could scarcely make it out, and in this doorway a small steel figure stood. As he watched, the sonorous boom of a gong rang through the dimness. The air trembled with sound, and through the shaking twilight the figure stepped out resolutely, crossing the floor with even, unhurried strides. He could not tell at that distance if it was man or woman, but it approached the radiant pool with, somehow, a sort of restrained eagerness that he was at a loss to understand. It reached the brink and did not pause. The haze of light rising from the pool swallowed it without a flicker. And the great dome was empty again save for themselves.

Dixon turned, awe-struck, to the girl, questions hovering on his mouth. Just in time he remembered his role and rephrased the query: "And how do you interpret this, priestess?"

She smiled up at him bewilderingly. It irritated him that his heart made that odd little leap whenever she smiled so, and he missed the first of her answer in watching the way her lips moved to frame the words she spoke.

". . . continually, at every beat of the signal," she was saying, "so that there is never an interval through all time when one of us has not completed his cycles and is ready to return into the flame." The gong sounded above her light voice. "See? Here comes another. And for countless ages it has been so, for our numbers are great enough so that the stream of voluntary sacrifices need never falter. So we nourish IL's flame and keep it burning."

Dixon said nothing. His eyes were upon her, but the bright illusion was swimming curiously in a mist that was closing down over him, and he was becoming aware of a strange pulsing of his own blood, as if—yes, as if familiar waves of knowledge were beginning their beat through his receptive brain. For a timeless interval he stood rigid, receiving that intelligence, feeling all he had seen and heard draining out of him into the vast reservoir of knowledge which was the light-being, feeling the voiceless commands of it flowing in. Ripple after ripple of the incoming tide rose in his brain. And gradually, in measured beats, he learned that this pool was the source of the pale flame burning upon the pillar, but that it was not essentially a part of it. The god IL drew his power from the dissolving lives of those people who sacrificed themselves—and this was the only way to destroy them, for they could not die otherwise—but IL was not present in the pool. IL was the flame on the column, no more, feeding upon the reflection from below. And if the rising light could be cut off temporarily IL's power would fail at its source. The invader could make an entrance and fight it out with him.

And now for an instant all the thought flow ceased; then in sharply clear ripples of intense emphasis came the syllables of a word. It was a word without meaning to Dixon, a word whose very sounds were unlike those of any language that man speaks. But he knew that he must speak it, and that the cadences of the sound would somehow open the way for the light-being to enter. With the impression of that word upon him the ripples ceased. A profound quiet reigned in his mind.

Out of that quiet the great domed temple slowly took form about him again. He heard the gong notes trembling through the air and saw another steel-robed figure pacing toward the pool. He turned his head and looked down into the high priestess' face at his shoulder. He had only to speak the word now and accomplish IL's overthrow—and then leave. Leave her—never see her again, except perhaps in dreams.

Her eyes met his with a little kindling under the blueness of them, and her mouth trembled into a smile as she met his gaze. She had the look of one eager and taut and waiting, and there was perfect faith in her eyes. And in that instant he knew he could not betray it.

"No," he murmured aloud. "No, my dear; I can't—I simply can't do it!"

Her brows drew together in exquisite bewilderment. "Do what?" she asked in a light whisper, to match his own lowered tone. "Do what?" But somehow the answer seemed not to interest her, for she did not pause for a reply. She had met his eyes and was staring up in a sort of dazed surprise, her blue gaze plunging into his with rigid intensity. And slowly she began to speak, in a tiny, breathless murmur. "I think . . . I think I see, O Dixon, the strangest things . . . in your eyes. Dreadful things and shapes without meaning . . . and something like a veil between us. . . . Dixon . . . nothing is clear . . . and yet—and yet, Dixon, my own face is looking back at me out of your eyes."

He caught his breath suddenly in a painful gasp, and in one involuntary motion he had her in his arms. She clung to him blindly. He could feel the trembling that shivered through her steel-sheathed body, and her heart's pounding shook them both.

"I am afraid, Dixon—I am afraid!" she wailed softly. "What is it that frightens me so, Dixon?"

He did not answer. There was no answer. But he hugged her close and felt the sweet firmness of her body against his and knew helplessly that he loved the illusion that was herself and would always love it.

Dixon was frightened, too; frightened at the depth of the emotion that shook him, for he was remembering the clinging of her soft mouth to his, and how beautifully her body curved under the embrace of her metal robe, and that the loveliness which filled his arms and his heart was no more than an illusion to mask something so grotesque that he could never bear to look upon it unmasked. Lovely body, lovely face, sweet, warm mouth upon his—was this all? Could love rise from no more than a scrap of beautifully shaped flesh? Could any man love more than that with such intensity as shook him now?

He loosed her from one arm and set his finger under her chin, lifting her face to his. Her eyes met his own, blue and puzzled and afraid, and shining with something very splendid which all but blotted out her bewilderment and her terror.

"I love you," he murmured. "I don't care—I love you."

"Love?" she echoed in her light whisper. "Love?" And he saw in her eyes that the word had no meaning for her.

The room reeled about him for an instant. Somehow he had never thought of that. Knowing as he did of the immense gulf between them and the strangeness of the emotions which swayed these creatures of such alien race, yet it had not occurred to him that anywhere throughout the cosmos where living beings dwelt there could be a species to which love had no meaning. Was she, then, incapable of feeling it? Good heaven, was he doomed to love an empty body, soulless, the mirage masking a sexless being who could not return any emotion he knew?

He looked down and saw the diffused radiance behind her eyes, shining and very tender, and the bewilderment upon her face, and he thought, somehow, that he was hovering on the very brink of something vaster than anything he had ever known before—an idea too splendid to be grasped. Yet when he looked down into her eyes he thought he understood—almost—

Suddenly all about him the world trembled. It was as if the whole vast place were the reflection in a pool, and a ripple had passed blurringly over the surface. Then everything righted itself. But he understood. He had been here too long. The veil between him and this alien world was wearing thin.

"No—I *can't* go!" he groaned and gripped the girl closer in his arms.

He must have spoken aloud, for he felt her stir against him and heard her anxious voice. "Go? O Dixon, Dixon—take me with you! Don't leave me, Dixon!"

Some fantastic hope flowered suddenly within him. "Why not?" he demanded. "Why not? Tell me!" And he shook her a little in his urgency.

"I don't know," she faltered. "I only know that—that—O Dixon, that I shall be so lonely when you have gone. Take me—please take me!"

"Why?" he demanded inexorably. For he thought now that he was hovering very near the understanding of the vast and splendid thing which had almost dawned upon him before the world shook.

"Because I . . . because . . . I don't understand it, Dixon, I can't tell you why—I haven't the words. But since you came I—is it that I have been waiting for you always? For I never knew until you came how lonely I had been. And I cannot let you go without me. O Dixon, is this what you call love?"

There was pain in her voice and in her veiled eyes. And the thought came to him that love was like an infectious germ, spreading pain wherever it rooted itself. Had he brought it to her—infected her too with the hopeless passion he knew? For it was wildly hopeless. In a moment or so he must leave this alien place forever, and no power existent could maintain very long the illusory veil through which they knew love.

Could his own new love for her endure the sight of her real self? And what would happen to this strange flowering of an emotion nameless and unknown to her—her love for him? Could it bear the look of his human shape, unmasked? And yet, he asked himself desperately, could a love as deep and sincere as the love he bore her be so transient a thing that he could not endure the sight of her in another guise? Could—

Again that queer flickering flashed over the world. Dixon felt the ground underfoot tilt dangerously, and for a moment insane colors stabbed at his eyes and the whole room reeled and staggered. Then it was still again. He had scarcely noticed. He swung her around to face him, gripping her shoulders and staring down compellingly into her eyes.

"Listen!" he said rapidly, for he knew his time was limited now, perhaps to seconds. "Listen! Have you any idea what you are asking?"

"Only to go with you," she said. "To be with you, wherever you are. And if you are indeed IL's messenger—perhaps a part of his godhead—then shall I enter the flame and give myself to IL? In that way can I join you and be one with you?"

He shook his head. "I am not from IL. I have been sent to destroy him. I'm a man from a world so different from yours that you could never bear to look upon me in my real form. You see me as an illusion, just as I see you. And I must go back to my own world now—alone."

Her eyes were dizzy with trying to understand.

"You are—not from IL? Not as you seem? Another world? Oh, but take me with you! I must go—I must!"

"But, my dearest, I can't. Don't you understand? You couldn't live an instant in my world—nor I much longer in yours."

"Then I will die," she said calmly. "I will enter the flame and wait for you in death. I will wait forever."

"My darling, not even that." He said it gently. "Not even in death can we be together. For when you die you go back to IL, and I go—I go—back to another god, perhaps. I don't know. But not to IL."

She stood, blank-eyed, in his grasp, trying to force her mind into the incredible belief. When she spoke, the words came slowly, as if her thoughts were speaking aloud.

"I don't understand," she said. "But I know . . . you speak the truth. If I die by the flame—in the only way there is for me to die —we are parted forever. I can't! I won't! I will not let you go! Listen to me—" and her voice dropped to a soft whisper—"you say you came to destroy IL? Why?"

"As the envoy of another god, who would take his place."

"I have given my whole life to the worship of IL," she murmured to herself, very gently. And then, in a stronger voice: "But destroy him, Dixon! There may be a chance that way—there is none now. Oh, I may be a traitor—worse than a traitor. There is no word to describe one who betrays his god into destruction, no word terrible enough. But I would do it—yes, gladly, now. Destroy him, and let me seek another death somewhere, somehow—let me die as you die. Perhaps your god can release me into your sort of death, and I can wait for you there until you come. Oh, Dixon, please!"

The idea was a staggering one, but for a wild moment Dixon knew hope again. Might it not be that—that—

Quite suddenly he understood. He looked down on the loveliness of her with unseeing eyes. In these past few moments of insanity, learning that she loved him, too, enough that she begged death of him if in that way they might be united, in these few moments he came to realize that the flesh meant nothing. It was not her body he loved. And a great relief flooded him, to be sure of that—sure that it was not merely infatuation, or desire for the loveliness which did not exist save as a mirage before his eyes. No, it was love, truly and completely, despite the shape she wore, despite the nameless sex that was hers. Love for herself—the essential self, however deeply buried beneath whatever terrible guise. And though her very substance was alien to him, and though no creature in all her ancestry had ever known love before, she loved him. Nothing else mattered.

And then without warning the great dome before him wavered and contorted into impossible angles, like the reflections in a flawed mirror. And Dixon felt the firm curved body in his arms melting fluidly into a different form and texture. It squirmed . . .

He stood at the entrance to a mighty room that staggered with frantic color, reeled with eye-stunning angles and incredible planes. And in his arms— He looked down. He clasped a creature at which he could not bear to look directly, a thing whose wild-looped limbs and sinuous body rippled and crawled with the moving tints of madness. It was slippery and horrible to the touch, and from the midst of a shifting, featureless face a great lucid eye stared up at him with desperate horror, as if it was looking upon something so frightful that the very sight was enough to unseat its reason.

Dixon closed his eyes after that one revolting glimpse, but he had seen in the eye upturned to him enough of dawning comprehension to be sure that it was she whom he held. And he thought that despite the utter strangeness of that one staring eye there was somewhere in the clarity of it, and the steadfastness, a glimmer of the innermost spark which was the being he loved—that spark which had looked from the blue gaze he had seen in its human shape. With that inner spark of life she was the same.

He tightened his grip upon her—or it—though his flesh crept at the contact and he knew that the feel was as revolting to it as to himself, and looked out over that shallow, color-stained head upon the vast room before him. His eyes throbbed savagely from those fierce colors never meant for human eyes to see. And though the creature in his arms hung acquiescent, he knew the effort it must cost to preserve that calm.

A lump rose in his throat as he realized the significance of that—such utter faith in him, though he wore a shape terrible enough to bring the fear of madness into that great lucid eye when it rested upon him. But he knew he could not stand there long and retain his own sanity. Already the colors were raving almost audibly through his brain, and the ground heaved underfoot, and he was sure that neither of them could endure much more of this. So he gripped the dreadful thing which housed the being he loved, and almost of itself he felt that incredibly alien word rip itself from his lips.

It was not a word to be set down in any written characters. Its sound to his ears was vague and indeterminate, like a whisper heard over too great distances to have any form. But the moment it left his lips he felt a vast, imponderable shifting in the substance of the temple. And, like a shutter's closing, the room went black. Dixon gave one involuntary sob of relief as the maniacal colors ceased their assault upon his brain, and he felt the dreadful thing in his arms go rigid in the utter blackness. For a moment everything was still as death.

And then through the dark around them a tiny shiver ran, the least little stir of motion, the thinnest thread of sound. It pierced Dixon's very eardrums and shuddered thrillingly along his nerves.

And with incredible swiftness that tiny stirring and that infinitesimal sound grew and swelled and ballooned into a maelstrom of rushing tumult, louder and louder, shriller and shriller. Around them in the blackness swooped and stormed the sounds of a mightier conflict than any living man could ever have heard before—a battle of gods, invisible in the blackness of utter void.

That stunning uproar mounted and intensified until he thought his head would burst with the infinite sound of it, and forces beyond comprehension stormed through the air. The floor seemed to dissolve under him, and space whirled in the dark so that he was conscious of neither up nor down. The air raved and shrieked. Blind and deafened and stunned by the magnitude of the conflict, Dixon hugged his dreadful burden and waited.

How long it went on he never knew. He was trying to think as the turmoil raged around his head, trying to guess what would come next; if the light-being in its victory could unite them in any way, in life or in death. He could think of that quite calmly now, death and union. For life without her, he knew unquestioningly, would be a sort of living death, alone and waiting. Living was where she was, and if she were dead, then life lay only in death for him. His head reeled with the wild wonderings and with the noise of battle raving about them both. For eternities, it seemed to him, the whole universe was a maelstrom, insanity shrieked in his ears, and all the powers of darkness swooped and screamed through the void about him. But, after an endless while, very gradually he began to realize that the tumult was abating. The roaring in his ears faded slowly; the wild forces storming through the dark diminished. By infinite degree the uproar died away. Presently again the stillness of death descended through the blackness upon the two who waited.

There was a long interval of silence, nerve-racking, ear-tormenting. And then, at long last, out of that darkness and silence spoke a voice, vast and bodiless and serene. And it was not the voice of the light-being. It spoke audibly in Dixon's brain, not in words, but in some nameless speech which used instead of syllables some series of thought forms that were intelligible to him.

"My chosen priestess," said the voice passionlessly, "so you would have had me destroyed?"

Dixon felt the convulsive start of the creature in his arms and realized dimly that the same wordless speech, then, was intelligible to them both. He realized that only vaguely, with one corner of his mind, for he was stunned and overwhelmed with the realization that it must be the god IL speaking—that his own sponsor had been overcome.

"And you, Dixon," the voice went on evenly, "sent by my enemy to open the way. You are a very alien creature, Dixon. Only by the power I wrested from that being which assaulted me can I perceive you at all, and your mind is a chaos to me. What spell have you cast over my chosen priestess, so that she no longer obeys me?"

"Have you never heard of love?" demanded Dixon aloud.

The query faded into the thick darkness without an echo, and a profound stillness followed in its wake. He stood in the blind dark and utter silence, clutching his love, waiting. Out of that quiet the god-voice came at last:

"Love"—in a musing murmur. "Love—no! there is no such thing in all my universe. What is it?"

Dixon stood helpless, mutely trying to frame an answer. For who can define love? He groped for the thought forms, and very stumblingly he tried to explain, knowing as he did so that it was as much for the benefit of her he held in his arms as for the god, because, although she loved, she could not know the meaning of love, or what it meant to him. When he had ceased, the silence fell again heavily.

At last IL said, "So—the reigning principle of your own system and dimension. I understand that much. But there is no such thing here. Why should it concern you? Love is a thing between the two sexes of your own race. This priestess of mine is of another sex than those you understand. There can be no such thing as this love between you."

"Yet I saw her first in the form of a woman," said Dixon. "And I love her."

"You love the image."

"At first it may be that I did. But now—no; there's much more of it than that. We may be alien to the very atoms. Our minds may be alien, and all our thoughts, and even our souls. But, after all, alien though we are, that alienage is of superficial things. Stripped down to the barest elemental beginning, we have one kinship—we share life. We are individually alive, animate, free-willed. Somewhere at the very core of our beings is the one vital spark of life, which in the last analysis is *self*, and with that one spark we love each other."

The deepest silence fell again when he had ended—a silence of the innermost brain.

Out of it at last IL said, "And you, my priestess? What do you say? Do you love him?"

Dixon felt the shape in his arms shudder uncontrollably. She—he could not think of her as "it"—stood in the very presence of her god, heard him address her in the black blindness of his presence, and the awe and terror of it was almost enough to shake her brain. But after a moment she answered in a small, faltering murmur, the very ghost of a reply, and in some curious mode of speech which was neither vocal nor entirely thought transfer. "I—I do not know that word, O mighty IL. I know only that there is no living for me outside his presence. I would have betrayed your godhead to free me, so that I might die in his way of death, and meet him again beyond—if there can be any beyond for us. I would do all this again without any hesitation if the choice was given me. If this is what you call love—yes; I love him."

"He is," said IL, "a creature of another race and world and dimension. You have seen his real form, and you know."

"I do not understand that," said the priestess in a surer voice. "I know nothing except that I cannot—will not live without him. It is not his body I . . . love, nor do I know what it is which commands me so. I know only that I do love him."

"And I you," said Dixon. It was a very strange sensation to be addressing her thus, from brain to brain. "The sight of you was dreadful to me, and I know how I must have looked to you. But the shock of that sight has taught me something. I know now. The shape you wear and the shape you seemed to wear before I saw you in reality are both illusions, both no more than garments which clothe that . . . that living, vital entity which is yourself—the real you. And your body does not matter to me now, for I know that it is no more than a mirage."

"Yes," she murmured. "Yes, I understand. You are right. The

bodies do not matter now. It goes so much deeper than that."

"And what," broke in the voice of IL, "is your solution of this problem?"

It was Dixon who broke the silence that fell in mute answer to the query. "There can be no such thing as union for us anywhere in life. In death, perhaps—but I do not know. Do you?"

"No," said IL surprisingly.

"You—you do not? You—a god?"

"No. I have taken these beings who worship me back into the flame. The energy which was theirs in life supports me—but something escapes. I do not know what. Something too intangible even for me to guess at. No—I am a god, and I do not know what comes after death."

Dixon pondered that for a long while. There was an implication in it somewhere which gave him hope, but his brain was so dazed he could not grasp it. At last the light broke, and he said joyfully, "Then—why, then you cannot keep us apart! We can die and be free."

"Yes. I have no hold over you. Even if I would wreak vengeance upon you for your part in my betrayal, I could not. For death will release you into—I do not know what. But it will be release."

Dixon swallowed hard. Half-doubts and hesitations crowded his mind, but he heard his own voice saying steadily, "Will you do that for us—release us?"

In the silence as he waited for an answer he was trying to realize that he stood on the threshold of death; trying to understand, his mind probing ahead eagerly for the answer which might lie beyond. And in the timeless moment he waited he was very sure, for whatever lay ahead could not be extinction and surely not separation. This was the beginning; surely it could not end so soon, unfulfilled, all the questions unanswered.

No; this love which linked them, two beings so alien, could not flicker out with their lives. It was too great—too splendid, far too strong. He was no longer uncertain, no longer afraid, and hope began to torment him exquisitely. What lay beyond? What vast existences? What starry adventures, together? Almost impatiently he poised on the brink of death.

Through this IL's voice spoke with a vast, passionless calm. "Die, then," said IL.

For an instant the darkness lay unbroken about them. Then a little flicker ran indescribably through it. The air shook for a breathless moment.

And IL was alone.

AND NOW THE NEWS

THEODORE STURGEON

*I suppose "And Now the News" is the oddest story in
this collection. This is perfectly natural: its author has
apparently made a specialty of arriving from new directions with peculiar, even unique, treasures. I am not at
all sure, as a matter of fact, that this story is sf at all. I
would like to hope it is, but it seems uncomfortably
plausible.*

*A great many of Mr. Sturgeon's stories were nomi-
nated for inclusion here. Check the Honor Roll for
availability and hunt them up. They're worth the search.*

The man's name was MacLyle, which by looking at you can tell
wasn't his real name, but let's say this is fiction, shall we? MacLyle
had a good job in, well, a soap concern. He worked hard and made
good money and got married to a girl called Esther. He bought a
house in the suburbs, and after it was paid for he rented it to some
people and bought a home a little farther out and a second car and
a freezer and a power mower and a book on landscaping and settled down to the worthy task of giving his kids all the things he
never had.

He had habits and he had hobbies, like everybody else and (like
everybody else) his were a little different from anybody's. The
one that annoyed his wife the most, until she got used to it, was
the news habit, or maybe hobby. MacLyle read a morning paper
on the eight-fourteen and an evening paper on the six-ten, and the
local paper his suburb used for its lost dogs and auction sales took
up forty after-dinner minutes. And when he read a paper he read
it, he didn't mess with it. He read page one first and page two next,
and so on all the way through. He didn't care too much for books,
but he respected them in a mystical sort of way, and he used to say

a newspaper was a kind of book, and so would raise particular hell if a section was missing or in upside down, or if the pages were out of line. He also heard the news on the radio. There were three stations in town with hourly broadcasts, one on the hour, and he was usually able to catch them all. During these five-minute periods he would look you right in the eye while you talked to him and you'd swear he was listening to you, but he wasn't. This was a particular trial to his wife, but only for five years or so. Then she stopped trying to be heard while the radio talked about floods and murders and scandal and suicide. Five more years and she went back to talking right through the broadcasts, but by the time people are married ten years things like that don't matter; they talk in code anyway, and nine tenths of their speech can be picked up anytime like ticker tape. He also caught the seven-thirty news on Channel 2 and the seven-forty-five news on Channel 4 on television.

Now, it might be imagined from all this that MacLyle was a crotchety character with fixed habits and a neurotic neatness, but this was far from the case. MacLyle was basically a reasonable guy who loved his wife and children and liked his work and pretty much enjoyed being alive. He laughed easily and talked well and paid his bills. He justified his preoccupation with the news in a number of ways. He would quote Donne: ". . . *any man's death diminishes me, because I am involved in mankind . . . ,*" which is pretty solid stuff and hard to argue down. He would point out that he made his trains and his trains made him punctual, but that because of them he saw the same faces at the same time day after endless day, before, during, and after he rode those trains, so that his immediate world was pretty circumscribed, and only a constant awareness of what was happening all over the earth kept him conscious of the fact that he lived in a bigger place than a thin straight universe with his house at one end, his office at the other, and a railway track in between.

It's hard to say just when MacLyle started to go to pieces, or even why, though it obviously had something to do with all that news he exposed himself to. He began to react, very slightly at first; that is, you could tell he was listening. He'd *shh!* you, and if you tried to finish what you were saying he'd run and stick his head in the speaker grille. His wife and kids learned to shut up when the news came on, five minutes before the hour until five after (with MacLyle switching stations) and every hour on the half hour, and from seven-thirty to eight for the TV, and during the forty minutes it took him to read the local paper. He was not so obvious about it when he read his paper, because all he did was freeze over the pages like a catatonic, gripping the top corners until the sheets shivered, knotting his jaw and breathing from his nostrils with a strangled whistle.

Naturally all this was a weight on his wife Esther, who tried her best to reason with him. At first he answered her, saying mildly that a man has to keep in touch, you know; but very quickly he stopped responding altogether, giving her the treatment a practiced suburbanite gets so expert in, as when someone mentions a lawn mower just too damn early on Sunday morning. You don't say yes and you don't say no, you don't even grunt, and you don't move your head or even your eyebrows. After a while your interlocutor goes away. Pretty soon you don't hear these ill-timed annoyances any more than you appear to.

It needs to be said again here that MacLyle was, outside of his pecularity, a friendly and easygoing character. He liked people and invited them and visited them, and he was one of those adults who can really listen to a first-grade child's interminable adventures and really care. He never forgot things like the slow leak in the spare tire or antifreeze or anniversaries, and he always got the storm windows up in time, but he didn't rub anyone's nose in his reliability. The first thing in his whole life he didn't take as a matter of course was this news thing that started so small and grew so quickly.

So after a few weeks of it his wife took the bull by the horns and spent the afternoon hamstringing every receiver in the house. There were three radios and two TV sets, and she didn't understand the first thing about them, but she had a good head and she went to work with a will and the can-opening limb of a pocketknife. From each receiver she removed one tube, and, one at a time, so as not to get them mixed up, she carried them into the kitchen and meticulously banged their bases against the edge of the sink, being careful to crack no glass and bend no pins, until she could see the guts of the tube rolling around loose inside. Then she replaced them and got the back panels on the sets again.

MacLyle came home and put the car away and kissed her and turned on the living-room radio and then went to hang up his hat. When he returned the radio should have been warmed up, but it wasn't. He twisted the knobs a while and bumped it and rocked it back and forth a little, grunting, and then noticed the time. He began to feel a little frantic and raced back to the kitchen and turned on the little ivory radio on the shelf. It warmed up quickly and cheerfully and gave him a clear sixty-cycle hum, but that was all. He behaved badly from then on, roaring out the information that the sets didn't work, either of them, as if that wasn't pretty evident by that time, and flew upstairs to the boys' room, waking them explosively. He turned on their radio and got another sixty-cycle note, this time with a shattering microphonic when he rapped the case, which he did four times, whereupon the set went dead altogether.

Esther had planned the thing up to this point, but no further, which was the way her mind worked. She figured she could handle it, but she figured wrong. MacLyle came downstairs like a pallbearer, and he was silent and shaken until seven-thirty, time for the news on TV. The living-room set wouldn't peep, so up he went to the boys' room again, waking them just as they were nodding off again, and this time the little guy started to cry. Mac-Lyle didn't care. When he found out there was no picture on the set, he almost started to cry, too, but then he heard the sound come in. A TV set has an awful lot of tubes in it and Esther didn't know audio from video. MacLyle sat down in front of the dark screen and listened to the news. *"Everything seemed to be under control in the riot-ridden border country in India,"* said the TV set. Crowd noises and a background of Beethoven's "Turkish March." *"And then . . ."* Cut music. Crowd noise up: *gabble-wurra* and a scream. Announcer over: *"Six hours later, this was the scene."* Dead silence, going on so long that MacLyle reached out and thumped the TV set with the heel of his hand. Then, slow swell, Ketelbey's "In a Monastery Garden." *"On a more cheerful note, here are the six finalists in the Miss Continuum contest."* Background music, "Blue Room," interminably, interrupted only once, when the announcer said through a childish chuckle, *"And she meant it!"* MacLyle pounded himself on the temples. The little guy continued to sob. Esther stood at the foot of the stairs wringing her hands. It went on for thirty minutes like this. All MacLyle said when he came downstairs was that he wanted the paper—that would be the local one. So Esther faced the great unknown and told him frankly she hadn't ordered it and wouldn't again, which of course led to full and righteous confession of her activities of the afternoon.

Only a woman married better than fourteen years can know a man well enough to handle him so badly. She was aware that she was wrong, but that was quite overridden by the fact that she was logical. It would not be logical to continue her patience, so patience was at an end. That which offendeth thee, cast it out, yea, even thine eye and thy right hand. She realized too late that the news was so inextricably part of her husband that in casting it out she cast him out, too. And out he went, while whitely she listened to the rumble of the garage door, the car door speaking its sharp syllables, clear as *"Exit"* in a playscript; the keen of a starter, the mourn of a motor. She said she was glad and went into the kitchen and tipped the useless ivory radio off the shelf and retired, weeping.

And yet, because true life offers few clean cuts, she saw him once more. At seven minutes to three in the morning she became aware of faint music from somewhere; unaccountably it frightened her, and she tiptoed about the house looking for it. It wasn't in the house, so she pulled on MacLyle's trench coat and crept down the steps into the garage. And there, just outside in the driveway, where steel beams couldn't interfere with radio reception, the car stood where it had been all along, and MacLyle was in the driver's seat dozing over the wheel. The music came from the car radio. She drew the coat tighter around her and went to the car and opened the door and spoke his name. At just that moment the radio said *"And now the news . . . ,"* and MacLyle sat bolt upright and *shh'd* furiously. She fell back and stood a moment in a strange transition from unconditional surrender to total defeat. Then he shut the car door and bent forward, his hand on the volume control, and she went back into the house.

After the news report was over and he had recovered himself from the stab wounds of a juvenile delinquent, the grinding agonies of a derailed train, the terrors of the near-crash of a C-119, and the fascination of a Cabinet officer, charter member of the

We Don't Trust Nobody Club, saying in exactly these words that there's a little bit of good in the worst of us and a little bit of bad in the best of us, all of which he felt keenly, he started the car (by rolling it down the drive, because the battery was almost dead) and drove as slowly as possible into town.

At an all-night garage he had the car washed and greased while he waited, after which the Automat was open and he sat in it for three hours drinking coffee, holding his jaw set until his back teeth ached, and making occasional, almost inaudible noises in the back of his throat. At nine he pulled himself together. He spent the entire day with his astonished attorney, going through all his assets, selling, converting, establishing, until when he was finished he had a modest packet of cash and his wife would have an adequate income until the children went to college, at which time the house would be sold, the tenants in the older house evicted, and Esther would be free to move to the smaller home with the price of the larger one added to the basic capital. The lawyer might have entertained fears for MacLyle except for the fact that he was jovial and loquacious throughout, behaving like a happy man—a rare form of insanity, but acceptable. It was hard work, but they did it in a day, after which MacLyle wrung the lawyer's hand and thanked him profusely and checked into a hotel.

When he awoke the following morning he sprang out of bed, feeling years younger, opened the door, scooped up the morning paper and glanced at the headlines.

He couldn't read them.

He grunted in surprise, closed the door gently, and sat on the bed with the paper in his lap. His hands moved restlessly on it, smoothing and smoothing until the palms were shadowed and the type hazed. The shouting symbols marched across the page like a parade of strangers in some unrecognized lodge uniform, origins unknown, destination unknown, and the occasion for marching only to be guessed at. He traced the letters with his little finger, he measured the length of a word between his index finger and thumb and lifted them up to hold them before his wondering eyes. Suddenly he got up and crossed to the desk, where signs and placards and printed notes were trapped like a butterfly collection under glass—the breakfast menu, something about valet service, something about checking out. He remembered them all and had an idea of their significance—but he couldn't read them. In the drawer was stationery, with a picture of the building and no other buildings around it, which just wasn't so, and an inscription which might have been in Cyrillic for all he knew. Telegram blanks, a bus schedule, a blotter, all bearing hieroglyphs and runes as far as he was concerned. A phone book full of strangers' names in strange symbols.

He requested of himself that he recite the alphabet. "A," he said clearly, and "Eh?" because it didn't sound right and he couldn't imagine what would. He made a small foolish grin and shook his head slightly and rapidly, but grin or no, he felt frightened. He felt glad, or relieved—most happy, anyway, but still a little frightened.

He called the desk and told them to get his bill ready, and dressed and went downstairs. He gave the doorman his parking check and waited while they brought the car round. He got in and turned the radio on and started to drive west.

He drove for some days, in a state of perpetual, cold, and (for all that) happy fright—roller-coaster fright, horror-movie fright—rememering the significance of a stop sign without being able to read the word STOP across it, taking caution from the shape of a railroad-crossing notice. Restaurants look like restaurants, gas stations like gas stations; if Washington's picture denotes a dollar and Lincoln's five, one doesn't need to read them. MacLyle made out just fine. He drove until he was well into one of those square states with all the mountains and cruised until he recognized the section where, years before he was married, he had spent a hunting vacation. Avoiding the lodge he had used, he took back roads until, sure enough, he came to that deserted cabin in which he had sheltered one night, standing yet, rotting a bit but only around the edges. He wandered in and out of it for a long time, memorizing details because he could not make a list, and then got back into his car and drove to the nearest town, not very near and not very much of a town. At the general store he bought shingles and flour and nails and paint—all sorts of paint, in little cans, as well as big containers of house paint—and canned goods and tools. He ordered a knock-down windmill and a generator, eighty pounds of modeling clay, two loaf pans and a mixing bowl, and a war-surplus jungle hammock. He paid cash and promised to be back in two weeks for the things the store didn't stock, and wired (because it could be done over the phone) his lawyer to arrange for the pre-determined eighty dollars a month which was all he cared to take for himself from his assets. Before he left he stood in wonder be-fore a monstrous piece of musical plumbing called an ophicleide which stood, dusty and majestic, in a corner. (While it might be easier on the reader to make this a French horn or a sousaphone—which would answer narrative purposes quite as well—we're done telling lies here. MacLyle's real name is concealed, his home town cloaked, and his occupation disguised, and dammit, it really was a twelve-keyed, 1824, fifty-inch, obsolete brass ophicleide.) The storekeeper explained how his great-grandfather had brought it over from the old country and nobody had played it for two gen-erations except an itinerant tuba player who had turned pale green on the first three notes and put it down as if it was full of percussion caps. MacLyle asked how it sounded and the man told him terrible. Two weeks later MacLyle was back to pick up the rest of his stuff, nodding and smiling and saying not a word. He still couldn't read, and now he couldn't speak. Even more, he had lost the power to understand speech. He had paid for the pur-chases with a hundred-dollar bill and a wistful expression, and then another hundred-dollar bill, and the storekeeper, thinking he had turned deaf and dumb, cheated him roundly but at the same time felt so sorry for him that he gave him the ophicleide. MacLyle loaded up his car happily and left. And that's the first part of the story about MacLyle's being in a bad way.

MacLyle's wife Esther found herself in a peculiar position. Friends and neighbors offhandedly asked her questions to which she did not know the answers, and the only person who had any information at all, MacLyle's attorney, was under bond not to tell her anything. She had not, in the full and legal sense, been de-serted, since she and the children were provided for. She missed MacLyle, but in a specialized way; she missed the old reliable Mac-Lyle, and he had, in effect, left her long before that perplexing night when he had driven away. She wanted the old MacLyle back again, not this untrolleyed stranger with the grim and spastic pre-occupation with the news. Of the many unpleasant facets of this stranger's personality, one glowed brightest, and that was that he was the sort of man who would walk out the way he did and stay away as long as he had. Ergo, he was that undesirable person just as long as he stayed away, and tracking him down would, if it returned him against his will, return to her only a person who was not the person she missed.

Yet she was dissatisfied with herself, for all that she was the injured party and had wounds less painful than the pangs of conscience. She had always prided herself on being a good wife and had done many things in the past which were counter to her reason and her desires, purely because they were consistent with being a good wife. So as time went on she gravitated away from the "What shall I do?" area into the "What ought a good wife to do?" spectrum and, after a great deal of careful thought, went to see a psychiatrist.

He was a fairly intelligent psychiatrist, which is to say he caught on to the obvious a little faster than most people. For example, he became aware in only four minutes of conversation that MacLyle's wife Esther had not come to him on her own behalf, and, further, decided to hear her out completely before resolving to treat her. When she had quite finished and he had dug out enough corroborative detail to get the picture, he went into a long silence and cogitated. He matched the broad pattern of MacLyle's case with his reading and his experience, recognized the challenge, the clinical worth of the case, the probable value of the heirloom-diamond pendant worn by his visitor. He placed his finger tips together, lowered his fine young head, gazed through his eyebrows at MacLyle's wife Esther, and took up the gauntlet. At the prospects of getting her husband back safe and sane, she thanked him quietly and left the office with mixed emotions. The fairly intelligent psychiatrist drew a deep breath and began making arrangements with another head-shrinker to take over his other patients, both of them, while he was away, because he figured to be away quite a while.

It was appallingly easy for him to trace MacLyle. He did not go near the lawyer. The solid foundation of all skip tracers and bureaus of missing persons, in their *modus operandi*, is the piece of applied psychology which dictates that a man might change his name and his address, but he will seldom—can seldom—change the things he does, particularly the things he does to amuse himself.

The ski addict doesn't skip to Florida, though he might make Banff instead of a habitual Mont Tremblant. A philatelist is not likely to mount butterflies. Hence when the psychiatrist found among MacLyle's papers some snapshots and brochures, dating from college days, of the towering Rockies, of bears feeding by the roadside, and especially of season after season's souvenirs of a particular resort to which he had never brought his wife and which he had not visited since he married her, it was worth a feeler, which went out in the form of a request to that state's police for information on a man of such-and-such a description driving so-and-so with out-of-state plates, plus a request that the man not be detained or warned, but only that he, the fairly intelligent psychiatrist, be notified. He threw out other lines, too, but this is the one that hooked the fish. It was a matter of weeks before a state patrol car happened by MacLyle's favorite general store; after that it was a matter of minutes before the information was in the hands of the psychiatrist. He said nothing to MacLyle's wife Esther except goodbye for a while, and this bill is payable now, and then took off, bearing with him a bag of tricks.

He rented a car at the airport nearest MacLyle's hideout and drove a long, thirsty, climbing way until he came to the general store. There he interviewed the proprietor, learning some eighteen hundred items about how bad business could get, how hot it was, how much rain hadn't fallen and how much was needed, the tragedy of being blamed for high markups when anyone with the brains God gave a goose ought to know it cost plenty to ship things out here, especially in the small quantities necessitated by business being so bad and all; and betwixt and between he learned eight or ten items about MacLyle—the exact location of his cabin, the fact that he seemed to have turned into a deaf-mute who was also unable to read, and that he must be crazy because who but a crazy man would want eighty-four different half-pint cans of house paint or, for that matter, live out here when he didn't have to?

The psychiatrist got loose after a while and drove off, and the country got higher and dustier and more lost every mile, until he began to pray that nothing would go wrong with the car, and, sure enough, ten minutes later something did. Any car that made a noise like the one he began to hear was strictly a shot-rod, and he pulled over to the side to worry about it. He turned off the motor and the noise went right on, and he began to realize that the sound was not in the car or even near it, but came from somewhere uphill. There was a mile and a half more of the hill to go, and he drove it in increasing amazement, because that sound got louder and more impossible all the time. It was sort of like music, but like no music currently heard on this or any other planet. It was a solo voice, brass, with muscles. The upper notes, of which there seemed to be about two octaves, were wild and unmusical, the middle was rough, but the low tones were like the speech of these mountains themselves, big up to the sky, hot, and more natural than anything ought to be, basic as a bear's fang. Yet all the notes were perfect, their intervals were perfect—this awful noise was tuned like an electronic organ. The psychiatrist had a good ear, though for a while he wondered how long he'd have any ears at all, and he realized all these things about the sound, as well as the fact that it was rendering one of the more primitive fingering studies from Czerny, Book One, the droning little horror that goes: *do mi fa sol la sol fa mi, re fa sol la ti la sol fa, mi sol la . . .* , inchworming up the scale and then descending hand over hand.

He saw blue sky almost under his front tires and wrenched the wheel hard over, and found himself in the grassy yard of a made-over prospector's cabin; but that he didn't notice right away, because sitting in front of it was what he described to himself, startled as he was out of his professional detachment, as the craziest-looking man he had ever seen.

He was sitting under a parched, wind-warped Engelmann spruce. He was barefoot up to the armpits. He wore the top half of a skivvy shirt and a hat the shape of one of those conical Boy Scout tents when one of the Boy Scouts has left the pole home. And he was playing, or anyway practicing, the ophicleide, and on his shoulders was a little moss of spruce needles, a small shower of which descended from the tree every time he hit on or under the low B flat. Only a mouse trapped inside a tuba during band practice can know precisely what's it's like to stand that close to an operating ophicleide.

It was MacLyle, all right, looming well fed and filled out. When he saw the psychiatrist's car he went right on playing, but, catching the psychiatrist's eye, he winked, smiled with the small corner of lip which showed from behind the large cup of the mouthpiece, and twiddled three fingers of his right hand, all he could manage of a wave without stopping. And he didn't stop, either, until he had scaled the particular octave he was working on and let himself down the other side. Then he put the ophicleide down carefully and let it lean against the spruce tree, and got up. The psychiatrist had become aware, as the last stupendous notes rolled away down the mountain, of his extreme isolation with this offbeat patient, of the unconcealed health and vigor of the man, and of the presence of the precipice over which he had almost driven his car a moment before, and had rolled up his window and buttoned the door lock and was feeling grateful for them. But the warm good humor and genuine welcome on MacLyle's sunburned face drove away fright and even caution, and almost before he knew what he was doing the psychiatrist had the door open and was stooping up out of the car, thinking, *Merry* is a disused word, but that's what he is, by God, a merry man. He called him by name, but MacLyle either didn't hear him or didn't care; he just put out a big warm hand and the psychiatrist took it. He could feel hard flat calluses in MacLyle's hand, and the controlled strength an elephant uses to lift a bespangled child in its trunk; he smiled at the image, because after all MacLyle was not a particularly large man, there was just that feeling about him. And once the smile found itself there it wouldn't go away.

He told MacLyle that he was a writer trying to soak up some of this magnificent country and had just been driving wherever the turn of the road led him, and here he was; but before he was half through he became conscious of MacLyle's eyes, which were in some indescribable way very much on him but not at all on anything he said; it was precisely as if he had stood there and hummed a tune. MacLyle seemed to be willing to listen to the sound until it was finished, and even to enjoy it, but that enjoyment was going to be all he got out of it. The psychiatrist finished anyway, and MacLyle waited a moment as if to see if there would be any more, and when there wasn't he gave out more of that luminous smile and cocked his head toward the cabin. MacLyle led the way, with his visitor bringing up the rear with some platitudes about nice place you got here. As they entered, he suddenly barked at that unresponsive back, "Can't you hear me?" and MacLyle, without turning, only waved him on.

They walked into such a clutter and clabber of colors that the psychiatrist stopped dead, blinking. One wall had been removed and replaced with glass panes; it overlooked the precipice and put the little building afloat on haze. All the walls were hung with plain white chenille bedspreads, and the floor was white, and there seemed to be much more light indoors here than outside. Opposite the large window was an oversized easel made of peeled poles, notched and lashed together with baling wire, and on it was a huge canvas, most nonobjective, in the purest and most uncompromising colors. Part of it was unquestionably this room, or at least its air of colored confusion here and all infinity yonder. The ophicleide was in the picture, painstakingly reproduced, looking like the hopper of some giant infernal machine, and in the foreground some flowers; but the central figure repulsed him—more, it repulsed everything which surrounded it. It did not look exactly like anything familiar and, in a disturbed way, he was happy about that.

Stacked on the floor on each side of the easel were other paintings, some daubs, some full of ruled lines and overlapping planes, but all in this achingly pure color. He realized what was being done with the dozens of colors of house paint in little cans which had so intrigued the storekeeper.

In odd places around the room were clay sculptures, most mounted on pedestals made of sections of tree trunks large enough to stand firmly on their sawed ends. Some of the pedestals were peeled, some painted, and in some the bark texture or the bulges or clefts in the wood had been carried right up into the model, and in others clay had been knived or pressed into the bark all the way down to the floor. Some of the clay was painted, some not, some ought to have been. There were free forms and gollywogs, a marsupial woman and a guitar with legs, and some, but not an overweening number, of the symbolisms which preoccupy even fairly intelligent psychiatrists. Nowhere was there any furniture per se. There were shelves at all levels and of varying lengths, bearing nail kegs, bolts of cloth, canned goods, tools and cooking utensils. There was a sort of table, but it was mostly a workbench, with a vise at one end and, at the other, half finished, a crude but exceedingly ingenious foot-powered potter's wheel.

He wondered where MacLyle slept, so he asked him, and again MacLyle reacted as if the words were not words but a series of pleasant sounds, cocking his head and waiting to see if there would be any more. So the psychiatrist resorted to sign language, making a pillow of his two hands, laying his head on it, closing his eyes. He opened them to see MacLyle nodding eagerly, then going to the white-draped wall. From behind the chenille he brought a hammock, one end of which was fastened to the wall. The other end he carried to the big window and hung on a hook screwed to a heavy stud between the panes. To lie in that hammock would be to swing between heaven and earth like Mahomet's tomb, with all that sky and scenery virtually surrounding the sleeper. His admiration for this idea ceased as MacLyle began making urgent indications for him to get into the hammock. He backed off warily, expostulating, trying to convey to MacLyle that he only wondered, he just wanted to know—no, *no*, he wasn't tired, dammit; but MacLyle became so insistent that he picked the psychiatrist up like a child sulking at bedtime and carried him to the hammock. Any impulse to kick or quarrel was quenched by the nature of this and all other hammocks to be intolerant of shifting burdens, and by the proximity of the large window, which he now saw was built leaning outward, enabling one to look out of the hammock straight down a minimum of four hundred and eighty feet. So all right, he concluded, if you say so. I'm sleepy.

So for the next two hours he lay in the hammock watching MacLyle putter about the place, thinking more or less professional thoughts.

He doesn't or can't speak (he diagnosed): aphasia, motor. He doesn't or can't understand speech: aphasia, sensory. He won't or can't read and write: alexia. And what else?

He looked at all that art—if it *was* art, and any that was, was art by accident—and the gadgetry: the chuntering windmill outside, the sashweight door closer. He let his eyes follow a length of clothesline dangling unobtrusively down the leaning center post to which his hammock was fastened, and the pulley and fittings from which it hung, and its extension clear across the ceiling to the back wall, and understood finally that it would, when pulled, open two long, narrow horizontal hatches for through ventilation. A small door behind the chenille led to what he correctly surmised was a primitive powder room, built to overhang the precipice, the most perfect no-plumbing solution for that convenience he had ever seen.

He watched MacLyle putter. That was the only word for it, and his actions were the best example of puttering he had ever seen. MacLyle lifted, shifted, and put things down, backed off to judge, returned to lay an approving hand on the thing he had moved. Net effect, nothing tangible—yet one could not say there was no effect, because of the intense satisfaction the man radiated. For minutes he would stand, head cocked, smiling slightly, regarding the half-finished potter's wheel, then explode into activity, sawing, planing, drilling. He would add the finished piece to the cranks and connecting rods already completed, pat it as if it were an obedient child, and walk away, leaving the rest of the job for some other time. With a wood rasp he carefully removed the nose from one of his dried clay figures and meticulously put on a new one. Always there was this absorption in his own products and processes, and the air of total reward in everything. And there was time, there seemed to be time enough for everything, and always would be.

Here is a man, thought the fairly intelligent psychiatrist, in retreat, but in a retreat the like of which my science has not yet described. For observe: he has reacted toward the primitive in terms of supplying himself with his needs with his own hands and by his own ingenuity, and yet there is nothing primitive in those needs themselves. He works constantly to achieve the comforts which his history has conditioned him to in the past—electric lights, cross-ventilation, trouble-free waste disposal. He exhibits a profound humility in the low rates he pays himself for his labor: he is building a potter's wheel apparently in order to make his own cooking vessels, and, since wood is cheap and clay free, his vessel can cost him less than engine-turned aluminum only by a very low evaluation of his own efforts.

His skills are less than his energy (mused the psychiatrist). His carpentry, like his painting and sculpture, shows considerable intelligence, but only moderate training; he can construct but not beautify, draw but not draft, and reach the artistically pleasing only by not erasing the random shake, the accidental cut; so that real creation in his work is, like any random effect, rare and unpredictable. Therefore his reward is in the area of satisfaction—about as wide a generalization as one can make.

What satisfaction? Not in possessions themselves, for this man could have bought better for less. Not in excellence in itself, for he obviously could be satisfied with less than perfection. Freedom, perhaps, from routine, from dominations of work? Hardly, because for all that complexity of this cluttered cottage, it had its order and its system; the presence of an alarm clock conveyed a good deal in this area. He wasn't dominated by regularity—he used it. And his satisfaction? Why, it must lie in this closed circle, himself to himself, and in the very fact of noncommunication!

Retreat . . . retreat. Retreat to savagery and you don't engineer your cross-ventilation or adjust a five-hundred-foot gravity flush for your john. Retreat into infancy and you don't design and build a potter's wheel. Retreat from people and you don't greet a stranger like—

Wait.

Maybe a stranger who had something to communicate, or some way of communication, wouldn't be so welcome. An unsettling thought, that. Running the risk of doing something MacLyle didn't like would be, possibly, a little more unselfish than the challenge warranted.

MacLyle began to cook.

Watching him, the psychiatrist reflected suddenly that this withdrawn and wordless individual was a happy one, in his own matrix; further, he had fulfilled all his obligations and responsibilities and was bothering no one.

It was intolerable.

It was intolerable because it was a violation of the prime directive of psychiatry—at least, of that school of psychiatry which he professed, and he was not going to confuse himself by considerations of other, less-tried theories—*It is the function of psychiatry to adjust the aberrate to society, and to restore or increase his usefulness to it.* To yield, to rationalize this man's behavior as balance, would be to fly in the face of science itself; for this particular psychiatry finds its most successful approaches in the scientific method, and it is unprofitable to debate whether or not it is or is not a science. To its practitioner it is, and that's that; it has to be. Operationally speaking, what has been found true, even statistically, must be Truth, and all other things, even Possible, kept the hell out of the toolbox. No known Truth allowed a social entity to secede this way, and, for one, this fairly intelligent psychiatrist was not going to give this—this *suicide* his blessing.

He must, then, find a way to communicate with MacLyle, and when he had found it he must communicate to him the error of his ways. Without getting thrown over the cliff.

He became aware that MacLyle was looking at him, twinkling. He smiled back before he knew what he was doing, and obeyed MacLyle's beckoning gesture. He eased himself out of the hammock and went to the workbench, where a steaming stew was set out in earthenware bowls. The bowls stood on large plates and were surrounded by a band of carefully sliced tomatoes. He tasted them. They were obviously vine-ripened and had been speckled with a dark-green paste which, after studious attention to its aftertaste, he identified as fresh basil mashed with fresh garlic and salt. The effect was symphonic.

He followed suit when MacLyle picked up his own bowl, and they went outside and squatted under the old Engelmann spruce to eat. It was a quiet and pleasant occasion, and during it the psychiatrist had plenty of opportunity to size up his man and plan his campaign. Hs was quite sure now how to proceed, and all he needed was opportunity, which presented itself when MacLyle rose, stretched, smiled, and went indoors. The psychiatrist followed him to the door and saw him crawl into the hammock and fall almost instantly asleep.

The psychiatrist went to his car and got out his bag of tricks. And so it was that late in the afternoon, when MacLyle emerged stretching and yawning from his nap, he found his visitor under the spruce tree, hefting the ophicleide and twiddling its keys in a perplexed and investigatory fashion. MacLyle strode over to him and lifted the ophicleide away with a pleasant I'll-show-you smile, got the monstrous contraption into position, and ran his tongue around the inside of the mouthpiece, large as a demitasse. He had barely time to pucker up his lips at the strange taste there before his irises rolled up completely out of sight and he collapsed like a grounded parachute. The psychiatrist was able only to snatch

away the ophicleide in time to keep the mouthpiece from knock-
ing out MacLyle's front teeth.

He set the ophicleide carefully against the tree and straightened
MacLyle's limbs. He concentrated for a moment on the pulse, and
turned the head to one side so saliva would not drain down the
flaccid throat, and then went back to his bag of tricks. He came
back and knelt, and MacLyle did not even twitch at the bite of
the hypodermics: a careful blend of the nonsoporific tranquilizers
Frenquel, chlorpromazine and Reserpine, and a judicious dose of
scopolamine, a hypnotic.

The psychiatrist got water and carefully sponged out the man's
mouth, not caring to wait out another collapse the next time he
swallowed. Then there was nothing to do but wait, and plan.

Exactly on schedule, according to the psychiatrist's wrist watch,
MacLyle groaned and coughed weakly. The psychiatrist immediately and in a firm quiet voice told him not to move. Also
not to think. He stayed out of the immediate range of MacLyle's
unfocused eyes and explained that MacLyle must trust him, because he was there to help, and not to worry about feeling
mixed-up or disoriented. "You don't know where you are or how
you got here," he informed MacLyle. He also told MacLyle, who
was past forty, that he was thirty-seven years old, but he knew
what he was doing.

MacLyle just lay there obediently and thought these things over
and waited for more information. He didn't know where he was
or how he had got here. He did know that he must trust this voice,
the owner of which was here to help him; that he was thirty-seven
years old; and his name. In these things he lay and marinated. The
drugs kept him conscious, docile, submissive and without guile.
The psychiatrist observed and exulted: oh you azacyclonol, he
chanted silently to himself, you pretty piperidyl, handsome hydro-
chloride, subtle Serpasil . . . Confidently he left MacLyle and
went into the cabin, where, after due search, he found some decent clothes and some socks and shoes, and brought them out and
wrapped the supine patient in them. He helped MacLyle across
the clearing and into his car, humming as he did so, for there is
none so happy as an expert faced with excellence in his specialty.
MacLyle sank back into the cushions and gave one wondering
glance at the cabin and at the blare of late light from the bell of

the ophicleide; but the psychiatrist told him firmly that these things had nothing to do with him, nothing at all, and MacLyle smiled relievedly and fell to watching the scenery go by, passive as a Pekingese. As they passed the general store MacLyle stirred, but said nothing about it. Instead he asked the psychiatrist if the Ardsmere station was open yet, whereupon the psychiatrist could barely answer him for the impulse to purr like a cat: the Ardsmere station, two stops before MacLyle's suburban town, had burned down and been rebuilt almost six years ago; so now he knew for sure that MacLyle was living in a time preceding his difficulties—a time during which, of course, MacLyle had been able to talk. He crooned his appreciation for chlorpromazine (which had helped MacLyle be tranquil) and he made up a silent song, "O Doll o' Mine, Scopolamine"—which had made him so very suggestible. But all of this the psychiatrist kept to himself, and he answered gravely that yes, they had the Ardsmere station operating again. And did he have anything else on his mind?

MacLyle considered this carefully, but since all the immediate questions were answered—unswervingly he *knew* he was safe in the hands of this man, whoever he was, he knew (he thought) his correct age and that he was expected to feel disoriented, and he was also under a command not to think—he placidly shook his head and went back to watching the road unroll under their wheels. "Fallen Rock Zone," he murmured as they passed a sign. The psychiatrist drove happily down the mountain and across the flats, back to the city where he had hired the car. He left it at the railroad station ("Rail Crossing Road," murmured MacLyle) and made reservations for a compartment on the train, aircraft being too open and public for his purposes and far too fast for the hourly rate he suddenly decided to apply.

They had time for a silent and companionable dinner before train time, and then at last they were aboard, solid ground beneath, a destination ahead, and the track joints applauding.

The psychiatrist turned off all but one reading lamp and leaned forward. MacLyle's eyes dilated readily to the dimmer light, and the psychiatrist leaned back comfortably and asked him how he felt. He felt fine and said so. The psychiatrist asked him how old he was and MacLyle told him thirty-seven, but he sounded doubtful.

Knowing that the scopolamine was wearing off but the other drugs, the tranquilizers, would hang on for a bit, the psychiatrist drew a deep breath and removed the suggestion; he told MacLyle the truth about his age and brought him up to the here and now. MacLyle just looked puzzled for a few minutes and then his features settled into an expression that can only be described as not unhappy. "Porter," was all he said, gazing at the push button on the partition with its little metal sign, and he announced that he could read now.

The psychiatrist nodded sagely and offered no comment, being quite willing to let a patient stew in his own juice as long as he produced essence.

MacLyle abruptly demanded to know why he had lost the powers of speech and reading. The psychiatrist raised his eyebrows a little and his shoulders a good deal and smiled one of those you-tell-me smiles, and then got up and suggested they sleep on it. He got the porter in to fix the beds and as an afterthought told the man to come back with the evening papers. Nothing can orient a cultural expatriate better than the evening papers. The man did. MacLyle paid no attention to this, one way or the other. He just climbed into the psychiatrist's spare pajamas thoughtfully and they went to bed.

The psychiatrist didn't know if MacLyle had awakened him on purpose or whether the train's slowing down for a watering stop had done it, or both; anyway, he awoke about three in the morning to find MacLyle standing beside his bunk looking at him fixedly. He closed his eyes and screwed them tight and opened them again, and MacLyle was still there, and now he noticed that Mac-Lyle's reading lamp was lit and the papers were scattered all over the floor.

MacLyle said, "You're some kind of a doctor," in a flat voice.

The psychiatrist admitted it.

MacLyle said, "Well, this ought to make some sense to you. I was skiing out here years ago when I was a college kid. Accident, fellow I was with broke his leg. Compound. Made him comfortable as I could and went for help. Came back, he'd slid down the mountain, thrashing around, I guess. Crevasse, down in the bottom; took two days to find him, three days to get him out. Frostbite. Gangrene."

The psychiatrist tried to look as if he were following this.

MacLyle said, "The one thing I always remember, him pulling back the bandages all the time to look at his leg. Knew it was gone, couldn't keep himself from watching the stuff spread around and upward. Didn't like to; *had* to. Tried to stop him, finally had to help him or he'd hurt himself. Every ten, fifteen minutes all the way down to the lodge, fifteen hours, looking under the bandages."

The psychiatrist tried to think of something to say and couldn't, so he looked wise and waited.

MacLyle said, "That Donne, that John Donne I used to spout, I always believed that."

The psychiatrist began to misquote the thing about send not to ask for whom the bell . . .

"Yeah, that, but especially '*any man's death diminishes me, because I am involved in mankind.*' I believed that," MacLyle repeated. "I believed more than that. Not only death. Damn foolishness diminishes me because I am involved. People all the time pushing people around diminishes me. Everybody hungry for a fast buck diminishes me." He picked up a sheet of newspaper and let it slip away; it flapped off to the corner of the compartment like a huge grave-moth. "I was getting diminished to death and I had to watch it happening to me like that kid with the gangrene, so that's why." The train, crawling now, lurched suddenly and yielded. MacLyle's eyes flicked to the window, where neon beer signs and a traffic light were reluctantly being framed. MacLyle leaned close to the psychiatrist. "I just had to get uninvolved with mankind before I got diminished altogether, everything mankind did was my fault. So I did and now here I am involved again." MacLyle abruptly went to the door. "And for that, thanks."

From a dusty throat the psychiatrist asked him what he was going to do.

"Do?" asked MacLyle cheerfully. "Why, I'm going out there and diminish mankind right back." He was out in the corridor with the door closed before the psychiatrist so much as sat up. He banged it open again and leaned in. He said in the sanest of all possible voices, "Now, mind you, doctor, this is only one man's opinion," and was gone. He killed four people before they got him.

THE CUSTODIAN

WILLIAM TENN

*William Tenn has written, as far as I know, stories of
three kinds. Many of them are funny, even farcical (and
good farce is a very rare thing in sf, or, indeed, anywhere else). Some of them are thoughtful, quiet, intense
explorations of an idea, a tendency, or a human being.
A few of them, unfortunately, are standard reworkings
of standard sf themes. These last received no nominations in this poll. A great many of Mr. Tenn's fine
stories also received no nominations. Among the nominated stories, though, "The Custodian" stands out.*

*For one thing, it has never been reprinted in an an-
thology. For another, it is a blend of the first and second
types mentioned. It is, regardless of what you may believe after the first reading, a serious and even, possibly,
important exploration. It is also, in its own way, an extremely funny story. I don't know why it's funny, or
even how the humor is managed. I wish I did know.*

*If you haven't read this one before, and possibly you
haven't, you can find it again in Mr. Tenn's collection
Of All Possible Worlds. You can also find a great many
other good stories there and in other collections by this
many-sided and astonishingly bearded gnome.*

May 9, 2190—Well, I did it! It was close, but fortunately I have a
very suspicious nature. My triumph, my fulfillment, was almost
stolen from me, but I was too clever for them. As a result, I am
happy to note in this, my will and testament, I now begin my last
year of life.

No, let me be accurate. This last year of my life, the year that I
will spend in an open tomb, really began at noon today. Then, in

the second sub-basement of the Museum of Modern Astronautics, I charged a dial for the third successive time and got a completely negative response. That meant that I, Fiyatil, was the only human being alive on Earth. What a struggle I have had to achieve that distinction!

Well, it's all over now, I'm fairly certain. Just to be on the safe side, I'll come down and check the anthropometer every day or so for the next week, but I don't think there's a chance in the universe that I'll get a positive reading. I've had my last, absolutely my final and ultimate battle with the forces of righteousness—and I've won. Left in secure, undisputed possession of my coffin, there's nothing for me to do now but enjoy myself. And that shouldn't be too hard. After all, I've been planning the pleasures for years!

Still, as I tugged off my suit of berrillit blue and climbed upstairs into the sunlight, I couldn't help thinking of the others. Gruzeman, Prejaut, and possibly even Mo-Diki—they'd have been here with me now if only they'd had a shade less academic fervor, a touch more of intelligent realism.

Too bad, in a way. And yet it makes my vigil more solemn, more glorious. As I sat down on the marble bench between Rozinski's heroic statues of the Spaceman and Spacewoman, I shrugged and dismissed the memories of Gruzeman, Prejaut, and Mo-Diki.

They had failed. I hadn't.

I leaned back, relaxing for the first time in more than a month. My eyes swept over the immense bronze figures towering above me, two pieces of sculpture yearning agonizingly for the stars, and I burst into a chuckle. The absolute incongruity of my hiding place hit me for the first time—imagine, the Museum of Modern Astronautics! Multiplied by the incredible nervous tension, the knuckle-biting fear of the past five days, the chuckle bounced up and down in my throat and became a giggle, then a splutter, and finally a reverberating, chest-heaving laugh that I couldn't stop. It brought all the deer out of the museum park to stand in front of the marble bench where Fiyatil, the last man on Earth, choked and coughed and wheezed and cackled at his senile accomplishment.

I don't know how long the fit might have held me, but a cloud, merely in the course of its regular duties as a summer cloud, happened to slide in front of the sun. That did it. I stopped laughing, as if a connection had been cut, and glanced upward.

The cloud went on, and the sunlight poured down as warmly as ever, but I shivered a bit.

Two pregnant young does came a little closer and stood watching as I massaged my neck. Laughter had given it a crick.

"Well, my dears," I said, tossing them a quotation from one of my favorite religions, "it would seem that in the midst of life we are at last truly in death."

They munched at me impassively.

May 11, 2190—I have spent the last two days putting myself and my supplies in order and making plans for the immediate future. Spending a lifetime in sober preparation for the duties of custodianship is one thing. Finding suddenly that you have become *the* custodian, the last of your sect as well as your race, and yet, peculiarly, the fulfillment of them both—that is quite another thing. I find myself burning with an insane pride. And a moment later I turn cold with the incredible, the majestic responsibility that I face.

Food will be no problem. In the commissary of this one institution there are enough packaged meals to keep a man like myself well fed for ten years, let alone twelve months. And wherever I go on the planet, from the Museum of Buddhist Antiquities in Tibet to the Panorama of Political History in Sebastopol, I will find a similar plenty.

Of course, packaged meals are packaged meals: somebody else's idea of what my menu should be. Now that the last Affirmer has gone, taking with him his confounded austerity, there is no longer any need for me to be a hypocrite. I can at last indulge my taste for luxury and bathe my tongue in gustatory baubles. Unfortunately I grew to manhood under Affirmer domination, and the hypocrisies I learned to practice in sixty cringing years have merged with the essential substance of my character. I doubt, therefore, that I will be preparing any meals of fresh food from the ancient recipes.

And then, too, meals of fresh food would involve the death of creatures that are currently alive and enjoying themselves. This seems a bit silly under the circumstances. . . .

Nor did I need to put any of the automatic laundries into operation. Yet I have. Why clean my clothes, I asked myself, when I can discard a tunic the moment it becomes slightly soiled and step into a newly manufactured garment, still stiff in memory of the machine matrix whence it came? Habit told me why I couldn't. Custodian concepts make it impossible for me to do what an Affirmer in my position would find easiest: shrug out of the tunic on a clear patch of ground and leave it lying behind me like a huge, brightly colored dropping. On the other hand, much Affirmer teaching that my conscious mind has been steadfastly rejecting for decades, I find to my great annoyance, has seeped into the unconscious osmotically. The idea of deliberately destroying anything as functional, if relatively unaesthetic, as a dirty Tunic, Male, Warm-Season, Affirmer Ship-Classification Number 2352558.3, appalls me—even against my will.

Over and over again I tell myself that Affirmer Ship-Classification Numbers now mean nothing to me. Less than nothing. They are as meaningless as cargo symbols on the Ark to the stevedores who loaded it, the day after Noah sailed.

Yet I step into a one-seater flyball for a relaxing tour of the museum grounds, and something in my mind says, Number 58184.72. I close my teeth upon a forkful of well-seasoned Luncheon Protein Component and note that I am chewing Ship-Classification Numbers 15762.94 through 15763.01. I even remind myself that it is a category to be brought aboard among the last, and only when the shipboard representative of the Ministry of Survival and Preservation has surrendered his command to the shipboard representative of the Ministry of the Journey.

Not a single Affirmer walks the earth at the moment. Together with their confounded multiplicity of government bureaus—including the one in which all people professing Custodianism had to be registered, the Ministry of Antiquities and Useless Relics—they are now scattered among a hundred or so planetary systems in the galaxy. But all this seems to matter not a bit to my idiotically retentive mind, which goes on quoting texts memorized decades ago for Survival Placement Examinations long since superseded and forgotten by those in authority.

They are so efficient, the Affirmers, so horribly, successfully efficient. As a youngster, I confided to my unfortunately loquacious comrade, Ru-Sat, that I had begun creative painting on canvas in my leisure hours. Immediately my parents, in collaboration with my recreational adviser, had me volunteered into the local Children's Extra Work for Extra Survival Group, where I was assigned to painting numbers and symbols on packing cases. "Not pleasure but persistence, persistence, persistence will preserve the race of man," I had to repeat from the Affirmer catechism before I was allowed to sit down to any meal from that time on.

Later, of course, I was old enough to register as a conscientious Custodian. "Please," my father choked at me when I told him, "don't come around any more. Don't bother us. I'm speaking for the entire family, Fiyatil, including your uncles on your mother's side. You've decided to become a dead man: that's your business now. Just forget you ever had parents and relatives—and let us forget we had a son."

This meant I could free myself from Survival chores by undertaking twice as much work with the microfilm teams that traveled from museum to museum and archaeological site to skyscraper city. But still there were the periodic Survival Placement Exams, which everyone agreed didn't apply to Custodians but insisted we take as a gesture of good will to the society which was allowing us to follow our consciences. Exams which necessitated putting aside a volume entitled *Religious Design and Decoration in Temples of the Upper Nile* for the dreary, dingy, well-thumbed *Ship-Classification Manual and Uniform-Cargo-Stowage Guide*. I had given up the hope of being an artist myself, but those ugly little decimals took up time that I wished to spend contemplating the work of men who had lived in less fanatic and less frenzied centuries.

They still do! So powerful is habit that, now that I have no questions on dehydration to answer ever again, I still find myself doing the logarithmic work necessary to find out where a substance is packed once its water is removed. It is horribly frustrating to be mired after all in an educational system from which I turned completely away!

Of course, the studies I am involved in at the moment probably don't help very much. Yet it is very important for me to pick up enough information from the elementary educatories in this museum, for example, to insure my not having to worry about the possibility of a flyball breakdown over a jungle area. I'm no technician, no trouble shooter. I have to learn instead how to choose equipment in good working order and how to start operating it without doing any damage to delicate components.

This technological involvement irritates me. Outside, the abandoned art of seventy thousand years beckons—and here I sit, memorizing dull facts about the power plants of worker robots, scrutinizing blueprints of the flyballs' antigrav screws, and acting for all the world like an Affirmer captain trying to win a commendation from the Ministry of the Journey before he blasts off.

Yet it is precisely this attitude that is responsible for my being here now, instead of sitting disconsolately aboard the Affirmer scout ship with Mo-Diki, Gruzeman and Prejaut. While they exulted in their freedom and charged about the planet like creaky old colts, I made for the Museum of Modern Astronautics and learned how to operate and read an anthropometer and how to activate the berrillit blue. I hated to waste the time, but I couldn't forget how significant to an Affirmer, especially a modern one, is the concept of the sacredness of human life. They had betrayed us once; they were bound to come back to make certain that the betrayal left no loose ends in the form of Custodians enjoying fulfillment. I was right then, and I know I am right now—but I get so bored with the merely useful.

Speaking of the anthropometer, I had a nasty shock two hours ago. The alarm went off—and stopped. I scurried downstairs to it, shaking out the berrillit-blue suit as I ran and hoping desperately that I wouldn't blow myself up in the course of using it a second time. By the time I got to the machine, it had stopped caterwauling. I charged the all-directional dial over ten times and got no response. Therefore, according to the anthropometer manual, nothing human was moving about anywhere in the entire solar system. I had keyed the machine to myself electroencephalographically so that I wouldn't set off the alarm. Yet the alarm *had* gone off, indisputably recording the presence of humanity other than myself, however temporary its existence had been. It was very puzzling.

My conclusion is that some atmospheric disturbance or faulty connection inside the anthropometer set the machine off. Or possibly, in my great joy over being left behind a few days ago, I carelessly damaged the apparatus. I heard the Affirmer scout ship radio the news of the capture of my colleagues to a mother vessel waiting beyond Pluto; I *know* I'm the sole survivor on Earth. Besides, if it had been skulking Affirmers who set the alarm off, their own anthropometer would have detected me at the same time, since I had been walking about unprotected by the insulating effect of berrillit blue. The museum would have been surrounded by flyball crews and I'd have been caught almost immediately.

No, I cannot believe I have anything more to fear from Affirmers. They have satisfied themselves with their last-moment return of two days ago, I am positive. Their doctrine would forbid any further returns, since they would be risking their own lives. After all, there are only 363 days left—at most—before the sun goes nova.

May 15, 2190—I am deeply disturbed. In fact, I am frightened. And worst of it is, I do not know of what. All I can do now is wait.

Yesterday I left the Museum of Modern Astronautics for a preliminary tour of the world. I planned to spend two or three weeks hopping about in my flyball before I made any decision about where I would stay for the bulk of my year.

My first error was the choice of a first destination. Italy. It is very possible that if my little problem had not come up I would have spent eleven months there before going on with my preliminary survey. The Mediterranean is a dangerous and sticky body of water to anyone who had decided that, his own talents being inadequate or aborted, he may most fittingly spend his life cherishing the masterpieces presented to humanity by other, much more fortunate individuals.

I went to Ferrara first, since the marshy, reclaimed plain outside the city was a major Affirmer launching site. I lingered a little while at one of my favorite buildings, the Palazzo dei Diamanti, shaking my head as helplessly as ever at the heavy building stones of which it is constructed and which are cut and faceted like so many enormous jewels. To my mind, the city itself is a jewel, now somewhat dulled, that sparkled madly in the days of the Este court. One little city, one tiny, arrogant court—I would so happily have traded them for the two billion steadfastly boorish Affirmers.

Over sixty years of almost unchallenged political control, and did an entire planetful of them produce a single competitor for a Tasso or an Ariosto? And then I realized that at least one native Ferraran would have felt at ease in the world that has just departed from me, its last romantic. I remembered that Savonarola had been born in Ferrara. . . .

The plain outside Ferrara also reminded me of the dour Dominican. The launching field, stretching away for quite a few flat miles, was strewn with enough possessions discarded at the last moment to make a truly towering Bonfire of Vanities.

But what pathetic vanities! Here, a slide rule that some ship's commander had ordered thrown out before take-off because the last inspection had revealed it to be in excess of what the *Ship-Classification Manual* listed as the maximum number of slide rules necessary for a vessel of that size. There, a mimeographed collection of tally sheets that had been dropped out of the closing air lock after every last item had been checked off as per regulations —one check *before* the item by the Ministry of Survival and Preservation, and one check *after* the item by the Ministry of the Journey. Soiled clothing, somewhat worn implements, empty fuel and food drums lay about on the moist ground. Highly functional articles all, that had somehow come in the course of time to sin against function—and had fallen swiftly from use. And, surprisingly, an occasional doll, not looking very much like a doll, to be sure, but not looking like anything that had an objective purpose either. Staring about me at the squalid debris dotted so rarely with sentiment, I wondered how many parents had writhed with shame when, despite their carefully repeated admonitions and advance warnings, the last search had discovered something in the recesses of a juvenile tunic that could only be called an old toy—or, worse yet, a keepsake.

I remembered what my recreational adviser had said on that subject, long years ago: "It's not that we believe that children shouldn't have toys, Fiyatil; we just don't want them to become attached to any particular toy. Our race is going to leave this planet that's been its home from the beginning. We'll be able to take with us only such creatures and objects as are usable to make other creatures and objects which we'll need for sustenance wherever we come down. And because we can't carry more than so much weight in each ship, we'll have to select from among the usable objects those which are essential.

"We won't take anything along because it's pretty, or because a lot of people swear by it, or because a lot of people *think* they need it. We'll take it along only because nothing else will do an important job so well. That's why I come to your home every month or so to inspect your room, to make certain that your bureau drawers contain only new things, that you're not falling into dangerous habits of sentimentality that can lead only to Custodianism. You've got far too nice a set of folks to turn into *that* kind of person."

Nonetheless, I chuckled to myself, I had turned into that kind of person. Old Tobletej had been right: the first step on the road to ruin had been bureau drawers crammed with odds and ends of memory. The twig on which had sat the first butterfly I'd ever caught, the net with which I'd caught him, and the first butterfly himself. The wad of paper that a certain twelve-year-old lady had thrown at me. A tattered copy of a real printed book—no facsimile broadcast, this, but something that had once known the kiss of type instead of the hot breath of electrons. The small wooden model of Captain Karma's starship, *Man's Hope*, which an old space hand at Lunar Line launching field had given me along with much misinformation. . . .

Those paunchy bureau drawers! How my parents and teachers had tried to teach me neatness and a hatred of possessions! And here was I, now grown into man's estate, smug over my possession of a quantity of artistic masterpieces the like of which no Holy Roman Emperor, no Grand Khan, would have dared to dream about.

I chuckled once more and started looking for the launching-site robots. They were scattered about, almost invisible in the unimportant garbage of the spaceship field. After loading the ship, they had simply wandered about until they had run down. I activated them once more and set them to cleaning the field. This is something I will do in every one of the two hundred or so launching sites on Earth, and this is the chief reason I have been studying robotics. I want Earth to look as pretty as possible when she dies. I never could be an Affirmer, I am afraid; I form strong attachments.

Feeling as I did, I just couldn't continue on my trip without taking the quickest, the most cursory glance at Florence. Naturally. But, as I should have expected, I got drunk on oils and marbles and metalwork. Florence was empty of Florentines, but the glorious galleries were still there. I walked across the fine Ponte Vecchio, the only one of the famous Arno bridges to have escaped destruction in the Second World War. I came to Giotto's campanile and the baptistery doors by Ghiberti and I began to feel despair, desperation. I ran to the Church of Santa Croce to see Giotto's frescoes and the Convent of St. Mark's for Fra Angelico. What good was one year, what could I see of even a single city like this in a bare twelve months? I could view, I could gallop by, but what would I have time to *see?* I was in the Boboli gardens trying frantically to decide whether to look up Michelangelo's "David," which I'd seen once before, or some Donatello which I hadn't, when the alarms went off.

Both of them.

The day before I'd left, I'd put together a small anthropometer that had originally been developed for locating lost colonists in the Venusian swamps. It was based on an entirely different design than the big machine that I'd found in the Hall of Gadgets. Since the circuits were unlike, and they had been planned for use in entirely different atmospheres, I believed they would serve as excellent checks on each other. I'd set the alarms to the frequency of my flyball communicator and had left the museum fairly confident that the only thing that could make both anthropometers go off would be the presence of a man other than myself.

I flew back to the museum, feeling very confused. Both pieces of equipment had responded the same way. The alarm had gone off, indicating the sudden materialization of man on the planet. Then, when the stimulus had disappeared, both alarms had stopped. No matter how many times I charged the directional dials on each anthropometer, there was not the faintest suspicion of mankind within their extreme range, which is a little under one half of a light-year.

The initial confusion had given way to a strong feeling of discomfort. Something is very wrong here on Earth, something other than the sun's getting ready to explode in a year. Possibly I have the nontechnician's blind faith in a piece of apparatus which I don't fully understand, but I don't believe that the anthropometers should be acting this way unless something really abnormal is occurring.

It has pleased me to look upon this planet as an oceangoing ship about to sink, and myself as the gallant captain determined to go down with her. Abruptly, I feel as if the ship were beginning to act like a whale.

I know what I must do. I'll move a supply of food down to the Hall of Gadgets and sleep right under the anthropometers. The alarm usually lasts for a minute or two. I can leap to my feet, charge the all-direction dials and get enough of a reading right then to know exactly where the stimulus is coming from. Then I will pop into my flyball and investigate. It's really very simple.

Only, I don't *like* it.

May 17, 2190—I feel thoroughly ashamed of myself, as only an old man who has been seeing ghosts in the graveyard should be ashamed. That, in fact, is the only excuse I can make of myself. I have, I suppose, been thinking too much about death recently. The coming extinction of Earth and the solar system; my death, which is inevitably involved with it; the death by the million of creatures of uncounted species, the death of proud old cities that man has reared and occupied for centuries . . . Well, perhaps the association with ghosties and beasties and other strange phenomena is understandable. But I *was* getting frightened.

When the alarms went off again this morning, I got a directional reading. My destination was the Appalachian Mountain region in eastern North America.

The moment I got out of the flyball and took in the pale-azure fog covering the cave mouth in front of me, I began to understand —and feel ashamed. Through the fog, which thinned in one place and thickened in others as I watched, I could see several bodies lying on the floor of the cave. Obviously, one of them had to be alive for the anthropometer to have reacted as soon as a patch of berrillit blue got meager enough to make the presence of a human mind detectable. I walked round to the back of the cave and found no exit.

I went back to the museum in the flyball and returned with the necessary equipment. I deactivated the berrillit blue fog at the entrance and walked inside cautiously.

The interior of the cave, which had evidently been furnished as a domestic and comfortable hideout, was completely wrecked. Somebody had managed to get an activator as well as a quantity of berrillit blue which had not been given any particular shape and which, therefore, was about as stable as hydrogen and oxygen—if it is permissible to use a metaphor from chemistry to illustrate negative-force-field concepts. The berrillit blue had been activated as a sort of curtain across the mouth of the cave and had blown up immediately. But, since the activator was still operating and the entrance was fairly narrow, it continued to function as a curtain of insulating negative force, a curtain which had holes in it through which one could occasionally "peek" by means of the anthropometer at the people imprisoned inside.

There were three bodies near the entrance, two male and one female, rather youthful-looking. From the quantity and type of statuary on the walls of the cave, it was easy to deduce that these people had belonged to one of the numerous religious Custodian groups, probably the Fire in the Heavens cult. When, in the last week of the exodus, the Affirmers had denounced the Crohiik Agreement and stated that the Affirmation of Life required that even those who didn't Affirm had to be protected against themselves, these people had evidently taken to the mountains. Evading the subsequent highly effective search, they had managed to stay hidden until the last great vessel left. Then, suspecting as I had that at least one scout ship would return for a final roundup, they had investigated the properties of the anthropometer and found out about the only insulator, berrillit blue. Unfortunately, they had not found out enough.

Deep in the rear of the cave, a body twisted brokenly to meet me. It was a young woman. My first reaction was absolute astonishment at the fact that she was still alive. The explosion seemed to have smashed her thoroughly below the waist. She had crawled from the cave mouth to the interior, where the group had stored most of their food and water. As I teetered, momentarily undecided whether to leave her and get medication and blood plasma from a hospital in the region or to risk moving her immediately, she rolled over on her back.

She had been covering a year-old infant with her body, evidently uncertain when the berrillit might blow again. And somehow, in spite of what must have been tremendous agony, she had been feeding the child.

I bent down and examined the baby. He was quite dirty and covered with his mother's blood, but otherwise unharmed. I picked him up and, in answer to the question in the woman's eyes, I nodded.

"He'll be all right," I said.

She started what may have been a nod in reply and stopped halfway through to die. I examined her carefully and, I will admit, a shade frantically. There was no pulse—no heartbeat.

I took the child back to the museum and constructed a sort of playpen for him out of empty telescope sections. Then I went back to the cave with three robots and had the people buried. I admit the gesture was superfluous, but it wasn't only a matter of neatness. However fundamental our differences, we were all of Custodian persuasion, generally speaking. It somehow made me feel as if I were snapping my fingers in the face of the entire smug Affirmation to respect Fire in Heavens eccentricities in this fashion.

After the robots had completed their work, I placed a piece of the religious statuary (it was remarkably badly done, by the way) at the head of each grave and even said a short prayer, or rather a sermon. I developed the thought that I had suggested approximately a week earlier to some deer—to wit, that in the midst of life we are in death. I did not joke about it, however, but spoke seriously on the subject for several minutes. The robots who were my audience seemed even less excited by the intelligence than the deer had been.

May 21, 2190—I am annoyed. I am very, very annoyed, and my great problem at the moment is that I lack an object on which to expend my annoyance.

The child has been an incredible amount of trouble.

I took him to the largest medical museum in the Northern Hemisphere and had him thoroughly examined by the best pediatric diagnostic machinery. He seems to be in excellent health, which is fortunate for both of us. And his dietary requirements, while not the same as mine, are fairly simple. I got a full tape on the kind of food he needs and, after a few readjustments in the commissary of the Museum of Modern Astronautics, I have arranged for this food to be prepared and delivered to him daily. Unfortunately, he does not seem to regard this arrangement, which took up an inordinate amount of my time, as wholly satisfactory.

For one thing, he will not accept food from the regulation robot nursemaid which I have activated for him. This, I suspect, is because of his parents' odd beliefs: he probably has never encountered mechanical affection before. He will eat only when I feed him.

That situation alone is intolerable, but I have found it almost impossible to leave him guarded by the robot nursemaid. Though he does little more than crawl, he manages to do this at a surprisingly fast pace and is always disappearing into dark corridors of the museum. Then an alarm is flashed to me and I have to break off my examination of the gigantic palace of the Dalai Lama, the Potala, and come scudding back from Lhasa halfway across the world to the museum. Even then it would take us hours to find him—and by "us" I mean every robot at my disposal—if I were not able to resort to the anthropometer. This admirable gadget points out his hiding place very swiftly; and so, pulling him out of the firing chamber of the Space Howitzer in the Hall of Weapons, I return him to his playpen. Then, if I dare, and if it is not time for him to be fed, I may return—briefly—to the Tibetan plateau.

I am at present engaged in constructing a sort of enormous cage for him, with automatic heating and toilet facilities and devices that will screen out undesirable animals, insects, and reptiles. Though this is taking up far too much of my time, it will be an excellent investment, I believe.

I don't know quite what to do about the feeding problem. The only solution I can find in any of the literature on the subject that offers promise is the one about letting him go hungry if he refuses food from normal sources. After a brief experiment, however, in which he seemed cheerfully resigned to starvation, I was forced to give in. I now handle every one of his meals.

The trouble is that I don't know whom to blame. Since I have been a Custodian from early manhood, I failed to see the need to reproduce. I have never been interested even slightly in children. I know very little about them and care less.

I have always felt that my attitude was admirably summed up by Socrates' comments in the *Symposium:*

Who, upon reflecting on Homer and Hesiod and other such great poets, would not rather have their children than ordinary human ones? Who would not like to emulate them in the creation of children such as theirs, which have preserved their memory and given them everlasting glory? . . . Many are the temples which have been raised in their honor for the sake of such children as they have had, which were never raised in honor of anyone for the sake of his mortal children.

Unfortunately, we are the only two humans alive on Earth, this child and I. We are going to our doom together; we ride the same round tumbril. And the treasures of the world, which were wholly mine less than a week ago, now belong at least partially to him. I wish we could discuss the matters at issue, not only to arrive at more equitable arrangements, but also for the sheer pleasure of the discussion. I have come to the conclusion that I began this journal out of unconscious terror when I discovered, after the Affirmers left, that I was completely alone.

I find myself getting very wistful for conversation, for ideas other than my own, for opinions against which mine might be measured. Yet according to the literature on the subject, while this child may begin talking on any day now, we will be immersed in catastrophe long before he learns to argue with me. I find that sad, however inevitable.

How I wander! The fact is that once again I am being prevented from studying art as I would like. I am an old man and should have no responsibilities; I have all but laid down my life for the privilege of this study. It is extremely vexing.

And conversation. I can just imagine the kind of conversation I might be having with an Affirmer at the moment, were one to have been stranded here with me. What dullness, what single-minded biological idiocy! What crass refusal to look at, let alone admit, the beauty his species has been seventy millennia in the making! The most he might have learned if he is European, say, is a bit about the accepted artists of his culture. What would he know of Chinese paintings, for example, or cave art? Would he be able to understand that in each there were primitive periods followed by eras of lusty development, followed in turn by a consolidation of artistic gains and an increase in formalization, the whole to be rounded off by a decadent, inner-groping epoch which led almost invariably into another primitive and lusty period? That these have occurred again and again in the major cultures, so that even the towering genius of a Michelangelo, a Shakespeare, a Beethoven will likely be repeated—in somewhat different terms—in another complete cycle? That there was a Michelangelo, a Shakespeare, and a Beethoven in each of several different flower periods in ancient Egyptian art?

How could an Affirmer understand such concepts when he lacks the basic information necessary to understanding? When their ships departed from the moribund solar system laden only with artifacts immediately usable? When they refused to let their offspring keep childhood treasures for fear of developing sentimentality, so that when they came to colonize Procyon XII there would be no tears for either the world that had died or the puppy that had been left behind?

And yet history plays such incredible jokes on man. They who ran away from their museums, who kept nothing but a cold microfilm record of what lay in their investment houses of culture, will learn that man's sentimentality is not to be frustrated. The bleak, efficient ships that brought them to these alien worlds will become museums of the past as they oxydize out of existence on the strange sands. Their cruelly functional lines will become the inspiration for temples and the cause of alcoholic tears.

What in the world is happening to me? How I run on! After all, I merely wanted to explain why I was annoyed.

May 29, 2190—I have made several decisions. I don't know if I shall be able to implement the most important of them, but I will try. In order, however, to give myself what I most need at the moment, time, I shall write much less in this journal, if I write any more at all. I will try very hard to be brief.

To begin with the least important decision: I have named the child Leonardo. Why I chose to name him after a man who, for all his talents—in fact, *because* of his talents—I regard as the most spectacular failure in the history of art, I do not know. But Leonardo was a well-rounded man, something which the Affirmers are not—and something which I am beginning to admit I am not.

By the way, the child recognizes his name. He is not yet able to pronounce it, but it is positively miraculous the way he recognizes it. And he makes a sound which is very like mine. In fact, I might say——

Let me go on.

I have decided to attempt an escape from Earth—with Leonardo. My reasons are many and complex, and I'm not certain that I understand them all, but one thing I do know: I have felt responsibility for a life other than my own and can no longer evade it. This is not a tardy emergence into Affirmer doctrine, but in a very real sense my own ideas come to judgment. Since I believe in the reality of beauty, especially beauty made with the mind and hands of man, I can follow no other course.

I am an old man and shall achieve little with the rest of my life. Leonardo is an infant: he represents raw potential; he might become anything—a song beyond Shakespeare's, a thought above Newton, above Einstein, or an evil beyond Gilles de Retz, a horror past Hitler. But the potential should be realized. I think that under my tutelage it is less likely to be evil, and that there *I* have a potential to be realized. In any case, even if Leonardo represents a zero personally, he may *carry* the germ plasm of a Buddha, of a Euripides, of a Freud. And *that* potential must be realized. . . .

There is a ship. Its name is *Man's Hope* and it was the first ship to reach the stars, almost a century ago when it had just been discovered that our sun would explode and become a nova in a little less than a hundred years. It was the ship that discovered for man the heart-quickening fact that other stars have planets and that many of those planets are habitable to him.

It was a long time ago that Captain Karma brought his starship back down on the soil of Earth with the news that escape was possible. That was long before I was born, long before humanity divided unequally into Custodian and Affirmer and long, long before either group were the unwinking fanatics they had become five years ago.

The ship is in the Museum of Modern Astronautics. I know it

has been kept in good condition. I also know that twenty years ago, before the Affirmers had developed the position that absolutely nothing might be taken physically from a museum, the ship was equipped with the latest Léugio Drive. The motive was that, if it were needed on Exodus Day, it might make the trip to a star in months instead of the years it had required originally.

The only thing that I do not know is whether I, Fiyatil, the Custodian of Custodians and art critic extraordinary, can learn to run it in the time that Leonardo and I have left. But as one of my favorite comic characters remarked about the possibility of a man chopping his own head off: a man can *try*. . . .

There is something else on my mind, even more exciting in a way, but this comes first. I find myself looking at the sun a good deal these days, and very searching, too! Very!

November 11, 2190—I can do it. With the help of two robots which I will modify for the purpose, I can do it. Leonardo and I could leave immediately. But I have my other project to complete.

And this is my other project: I am going to use all the empty space in the ship. It was built originally for different motors and a very large crew, and I am going to use that space as a bureau drawer. Into that bureau drawer I will stuff the keepsakes of humanity, the treasures of its childhood and adolescence—at least, as many as I can get in.

For weeks I have been collecting treasures from all over the world. Incredible pottery, breathtaking friezes, glorious statuary, and oil paintings almost beyond counting litter the corridors of the museum. Brueghel is piled on Bosch, Bosch on Dürer. I am going to bring a little of everything to that star toward which I point my ship, a little to show what the real things were like. I am including things like the holograph manuscripts of Jane Austen's *Pride and Prejudice*, Beethoven's Ninth Symphony, Gogol's *Dead Souls*, Mark Twain's *Huckleberry Finn*, and holographs of Dickens' letters and Lincoln's speeches. There are many others, but I cannot take everything. Within responsible limits, I must please myself.

Therefore, I am not taking anything from the Sistine Chapel ceiling. I have carved out two bits of the "Last Judgment" instead. They are my favorites: the soul that suddenly realizes that it is condemned, and the flayed skin on which Michelangelo painted his own portrait. The only trouble is that fresco weighs so much! Weight, weight, weight—it is almost all I think about now. Even Leonardo follows me about and says, "Weight, weight, weight!" He pronounces nothing else so well.

Still, what should I take of Picasso? A handful of oils, yes, but I must take the "Guernica." And there is more weight.

I have some wonderful Russian copper utensils and some Ming bronze bowls. I have a lime spatula from eastern New Guinea made of oiled wood that has a delightfully carved handle (it was used in chewing betel nut and lime). I have a wonderful alabaster figure of a cow from ancient Sumer. I have an incredible silver Buddha from northern India. I have some Dahoman brass figures of a grace to shame Egypt and Greece. I have a carved-ivory container from Benin, West Africa, showing a thoroughly fifteenth-century-European Christ on the Cross. I have the Venus of Willendorf, Austria, the figure that was carved in the Aurignacian epoch of the Paleolithic and which is part of the artistic tradition of the Venus art of prehistoric mankind.

I have miniatures by Hilliard and Holbein, satiric prints by Hogarth, a beautiful Kangra painting of the eighteenth century on paper that shows astonishingly little Mughal influence, Japanese prints by Takamaru and Hiroshige—and where may I stop? How may I choose?

I have pages from the Book of Kells, which is an illuminated hand-executed manuscript of almost unmatched beauty; and I have pages from the Gutenberg Bible, put together in the infancy of printing, which has illuminated pages to give the *effect* of a hand-copied manuscript, because the printers didn't want their invention discovered. I have a tughra of Suleiman the Magnificent, a calligraphic emblem that formed headings for his imperial edicts; and I have a Hebrew Scroll of the Law whose calligraphy outshines the jewels which encrust the poles on which it is wound.

I have Coptic textiles of the sixth century and Alençon lace of the sixteenth. I have a magnificent red krater vase from one of Athens' maritime colonies and a wooden figurehead of a minister from a New England frigate. I have a Rubens nude and "Odalisque" by Matisse.

In architecture I am taking the Chinese *Compendium of Archi-*

tecture, which I think has never been equaled as a text, and a model of a Le Corbusier house built by him. I would love to take one building, the Taj Mahal, but I *am* taking the pearl that the Mogul gave to her for whom he built the ineffable tomb. It is a reddish pearl, shaped like a pear and about three and a half inches long; shortly after it was buried with her, it turned up in the possession of an emperor of China who set it on gold leaves and surrounded it with jade and emeralds. At the turn of the nineteenth century it was sold somewhere in the Near East for a tiny, ridiculous sum and ended in the Louvre.

And a tool: a small stone fist ax, the first thing known to have been made by human creatures.

All this I have collected near the ship. But I've sorted none of it. And, I suddenly remember, I have collected as yet no furniture, no decorated weapons, no etched glass . . .

I must hurry, hurry!

November 2190—Shortly after I finished the last entry, I glanced upward. There were green specks on the sun, and strange orange streamers seemed to plume out to all points of the compass. Evidently there was not to be a year. These were the symptoms of death that the astronomers had predicted.

So there was an end to my collecting—and my sorting was done in less than a day. The one thing I suddenly found I had to do, when it became obvious that my sections of Michelangelo would be too heavy, was to go to the Sistine Chapel ceiling after all. This time I cut out a relatively tiny thing—the finger of the Creation as it stabs life into Adam. And I decided to take da Vinci's "La Gioconda," even though his "Beatrice d'Este" is more to my taste: the Mona Lisa's smile belongs to the world.

All posters are represented by one Toulouse-Lautrec. I dropped the "Guernica"; Picasso is represented instead by an oil from his blue period and a single striking ceramic plate. I dropped Harold Paris' "The Eternal Judgment" because of its bulk; all I have of his now is the print *Buchenwald No. 2*, *"Where Are We Going?"* And somehow or other, in my last-minute haste, I seemed to have selected a large number of Safavid bottles from Iran of the sixteenth and seventeenth centuries. Let future historians and psychologists puzzle out the reason for my choices; they are now irrevocable.

We are proceeding toward Alpha Centauri and should arrive in five months. How will we and all our treasures be received, I wonder? I suddenly feel insanely cheerful. I don't think it has anything to do with my rather belated realization that I, who have so little talent and have failed so miserably in the arts, will achieve a place in the history of art like no other man—a kind of aesthetic Noah. No, it is the fact that I am carrying both the future and the past to a rendezvous where they still have a chance to come to terms.

A moment ago Leonardo bounced a ball against the visiplate, and, looking at it, I observed that old Sol was expanding apoplectically. As I remarked to him then, "I find, to my astonishment, that in the midst of death I am—at last, at last!—truly in life."

THE NEW ACCELERATOR

H. G. WELLS

The notion behind "The New Accelerator" is no longer novel. The breezy reality given to it, however, is an original patent of the author.

As always, Mr. Wells seems to be prophesying in a number of directions at once; the final lines of the story bring to memory instantly all of the discussions regarding scientific irresponsibility to which we have all grown so used these last twenty years.

Mr. Wells, of course, needs no introduction. If not the founder, he remains the first great popularizer of modern sf, and an author, by the way, whose mass of work outside this field deserves and will almost certainly get revival.

Certainly, if ever a man found a guinea when he was looking for a pin it is my good friend Professor Gibberne. I have heard before of investigators over-shooting the mark, but never quite to the extent that he has done. He has really, this time at any rate, without any touch of exaggeration in the phrase, found something to revolutionise human life. And that when he was simply seeking an all-round nervous stimulant to bring languid people up to the stresses of these pushful days. I have tasted the stuff now several times, and I cannot do better than describe the effect the thing had on me. That there are astonishing experiences in store for all in search of new sensations will become apparent enough.

Professor Gibberne, as many people know, is my neighbour in Folkestone. Unless my memory plays me a trick, his portrait at various ages has already appeared in *The Strand Magazine*—I think late in 1899; but I am unable to look it up because I have lent that volume to some one who has never sent it back. The reader may, perhaps, recall the high forehead and the singularly long black eyebrows that give such a Mephistophelian touch to his face. He occupies one of those pleasant detached houses in the mixed style that makes the western end of the Upper Sandgate Road so interesting. His is the one with the Flemish gables and the Moorish portico, and it is in the room with the mullioned bay window that he works when he is down here, and in which of an evening we have so often smoked and talked together. He is a mighty jester, but, besides, he likes to talk to me about his work; he is one of those men who find a help and stimulus in talking, and so I have been able to follow the conception of the New Accelerator right up from a very early stage. Of course, the greater portion of his experimental work is not done in Folkestone, but in Gower Street, in the fine new laboratory next to the hospital that he has been the first to use.

As everyone knows, or at least as all intelligent people know, the special department in which Gibberne has gained so great and deserved a reputation among physiologists is the action of drugs upon the nervous system. Upon soporifics, sedatives, and anæsthetics he is, I am told, unequalled. He is also a chemist of considerable eminence, and I suppose in the subtle and complex jungle of riddles that centres about the ganglion cell and the axis fibre there are little cleared places of his making, glades of illumination, that, until he sees fit to publish his results, are inaccessible to every other living man. And in the last few years he has been particularly assiduous upon this question of nervous stimulants, and already, before the discovery of the New Accelerator, very successful with them. Medical science has to thank him for at least three distinct and absolutely safe invigorators of unrivalled value to practising men. In cases of exhaustion the preparation known as Gibberne's B Syrup has, I suppose, saved more lives already than any lifeboat round the coast.

"But none of these things begin to satisfy me yet," he told me nearly a year ago. "Either they increase the central energy without affecting the nerves or they simply increase the available energy by lowering the nervous conductivity; and all of them are unequal and local in their operation. One wakes up the heart and viscera and leaves the brain stupefied, one gets at the brain champagne fashion and does nothing good for the solar plexus, and what I want—and what, if it's an earthly possibility, I mean to have—is a stimulant that stimulates all round, that wakes you up for a time from the crown of your head to the tip of your great toe, and makes you go two—or even three to everybody else's one. Eh? That's the thing I'm after."

"It would tire a man," I said.

"Not a doubt of it. And you'd eat double or treble—and all that. But just think what the thing would mean. Imagine yourself with a little phial like this"—he held up a bottle of green glass and marked his points with it—"and in this precious phial is the power to think twice as fast, move twice as quickly, do twice as much work in a given time as you could otherwise do."

"But is such a thing possible?"

"I believe so. If it isn't, I've wasted my time for a year. These various preparations of the hypophosphites, for example, seem to show that something of the sort . . . Even if it was only one and a half times as fast it would do."

"It *would* do," I said.

"If you were a statesman in a corner, for example, time rushing up against you, something urgent to be done, eh?"

"He could dose his private secretary," I said.

"And gain—double time. And think if *you*, for example, wanted to finish a book."

"Usually," I said, "I wish I'd never begun 'em."

"Or a doctor, driven to death, wants to sit down and think out a case. Or a barrister—or a man cramming for an examination."

"Worth a guinea a drop," said I, "and more—to men like that."

"And in a duel again," said Gibberne, "where it all depends on your quickness in pulling the trigger."

"Or in fencing," I echoed.

"You see," said Gibberne, "if I get it as an all-round thing it will really do you no harm at all—except perhaps to an infinitesimal degree it brings you nearer old age. You will just have lived twice to other people's once."

"I suppose," I meditated, "in a duel—it would be fair?"

"That's a question for the seconds," said Gibberne.

I harked back further. "And you really think such a thing *is* possible?" I said.

"As possible," said Gibberne, and glanced at something that

went throbbing by the window, "as a motor-bus. As a matter of fact—"

He paused and smiled at me deeply, and tapped slowly on the edge of his desk with the green phial. "I think I know the stuff. . . . Already I've got something coming." The nervous smile upon his face betrayed the gravity of his revelation. He rarely talked of his actual experimental work unless things were very near the end. "And it may be, it may be—I shouldn't be surprised —it may even do the thing at a greater rate than twice."

"It will be rather a big thing," I hazarded.

"It will be, I think, rather a big thing."

But I don't think he quite knew what a big thing it was to be, for all that.

I remember we had several subsequent talks about the stuff. "The New Accelerator" he called it, and his tone about it grew more confident on each occasion. Sometimes he talked nervously of unexpected physiological results its use might have, and then he would get a bit unhappy; at others he was frankly mercenary, and we debated long and anxiously how the preparation might be turned to commercial account. "It's a good thing," said Gibberne, "a tremendous thing. I know I'm giving the world something, and I think it only reasonable we should expect the world to pay. The dignity of science is all very well, but I think somehow I must have the monopoly of the stuff for, say, ten years. I don't see why *all* the fun in life should go to the dealers in ham."

My own interest in the coming drug certainly did not wane in the time. I have always had a queer twist towards metaphysics in my mind. I have always been given to paradoxes about space and time, and it seemed to me that Gibberne was really preparing no less than the absolute acceleration of life. Suppose a man repeatedly dosed with such a preparation: he would live an active and record life indeed, but he would be an adult at eleven, middle-aged at twenty-five, and by thirty well on the road to senile decay. It seemed to me that so far Gibberne was only going to do for anyone who took his drug exactly what Nature has done for the Jews and Orientals, who are men in their teens and aged by fifty, and quicker in thought and act than we are all the time. The marvel of drugs has always been great to my mind; you can madden a man, calm a man, make him incredibly strong and alert or a helpless log, quicken this passion and allay that, all by means of drugs, and here was a new miracle to be added to this strange armoury of phials the doctors use! But Gibberne was far too eager upon his technical points to enter very keenly into my aspect of the question.

It was the seventh or eighth of August when he told me the distillation that would decide his failure or success for a time was going forward as we talked, and it was on the tenth that he told me the thing was done and the New Accelerator a tangible reality in the world. I met him as I was going up the Sandgate Hill towards Folkestone—I think I was going to get my hair cut; and he came hurrying down to meet me—I suppose he was coming to my house to tell me at once of his success. I remember that his eyes were unusually bright and his face flushed, and I noted even then the swift alacrity of his step.

"It's done," he cried, and gripped my hand, speaking very fast; "it's more than done. Come up to my house and see."

"Really?"

"Really!" he shouted. "Incredibly! Come up and see."

"And it does—twice?"

"It does more, much more. It scares me. Come up and see the stuff. Taste it! Try it! It's the most amazing stuff on earth." He gripped my arm and, walking at such a pace that he forced me into a trot, went shouting with me up the hill. A whole charabancful of people turned and stared at us in unison after the manner of people in charabancs. It was one of those hot, clear days that Folkestone sees so much of, every colour incredibly bright and every outline hard. There was a breeze, of course, but not so much breeze as sufficed under these conditions to keep me cool and dry. I panted for mercy.

"I'm not walking fast, am I?" cried Gibberne, and slackened his pace to a quick march.

"You've been taking some of this stuff," I puffed.

"No," he said. "At the utmost a drop of water that stood in a beaker from which I had washed out the last traces of the stuff. I took some last night, you know. But that is ancient history now."

"And it goes twice?" I said, nearing his doorway in a grateful perspiration.

"It goes a thousand times, many thousand times!" cried Gibberne, with a dramatic gesture, flinging open his Early English carved-oak gate.

"Phew!" said I, and followed him to the door.

"I don't know how many times it goes," he said, with his latch-key in his hand.

"And you—"

"It throws all sorts of light on nervous physiology, it kicks the theory of vision into a perfectly new shape! . . . Heaven knows how many thousand times. We'll try all that after— The thing is to try the stuff now."

"Try the stuff?" I said, as we went along the passage.

"Rather," said Gibberne, turning on me in his study. "There it is in that little green phial there! Unless you happen to be afraid?"

I am a careful man by nature, and only theoretically adventurous. I *was* afraid. But on the other hand there is pride.

"Well," I haggled. "You say you've tried it?"

"I've tried it," he said, "and I don't look hurt by it, do I? I don't even look livery and I *feel*—"

I sat down. "Give me the potion," I said. "If the worst comes to the worst it will save having my hair cut, and that I think is one of the most hateful duties of a civilised man. How do you take the mixture?"

"With water," said Gibberne, whacking down a carafe.

He stood up in front of his desk and regarded me in his easy chair; his manner was suddenly affected by a touch of the Harley Street specialist. "It's rum stuff, you know," he said.

I made a gesture with my hand.

"I must warn you in the first place as soon as you've got it down to shut your eyes, and open them very cautiously in a minute or so's time. One still sees. The sense of vision is a question of length of vibration, and not of multitude of impacts; but there's a kind of shock to the retina, a nasty giddy confusion just at the time if the eyes are open. Keep 'em shut."

"Shut," I said. "Good!"

"And the next thing is, keep still. Don't begin to whack about. You may fetch something a nasty rap if you do. Remember you will be going several thousand times faster than you ever did before, heart, lungs, muscles, brain—everything—and you will hit hard without knowing it. You won't know it, you know. You'll feel just as you do now. Only everything in the world will seem to be going ever so many thousand times slower than it ever went before. That's what makes it so deuced queer."

"Lor'," I said. "And you mean—"

"You'll see," said he, and took up a measure. He glanced at the material on his desk. "Glasses," he said, "water. All here. Mustn't take too much for the first attempt."

The little phial glucked out its precious contents. "Don't forget what I told you," he said, turning the contents of the measure into a glass in the manner of an Italian waiter measuring whiskey. "Sit with the eyes tightly shut and in absolute stillness for two minutes," he said. "Then you will hear me speak."

He added an inch or so of water to the dose in each glass.

"By-the-bye," he said, "don't put your glass down. Keep it in your hand and rest your hand on your knee. Yes—so. And now—"

He raised his glass.

"The New Accelerator," I said.

"The New Accelerator," he answered, and we touched glasses and drank, and instantly I closed my eyes.

You know that blank non-existence into which one drops when one has taken "gas." For an indefinite interval it was like that. Then I heard Gibberne telling me to wake up, and I stirred and opened my eyes. There he stood as he had been standing, glass still in hand. It was empty, that was all the difference.

"Well?" said I.

"Nothing out of the way?"

"Nothing. A slight feeling of exhilaration, perhaps. Nothing more."

"Sounds?"

"Things are still," I said. "By Jove! yes! They *are* still. Except the sort of faint *pat, patter*, like rain falling on different things. What is it?"

"Analysed sounds," I think he said, but I am not sure. He glanced at the window. "Have you ever seen a curtain before a window fixed in that way before?"

I followed his eyes, and there was the end of the curtain, frozen, as it were, corner high, in the act of flapping briskly in the breeze.

"No," said I; that's odd."

"And here," he said, and opened the hand that held the glass.

Naturally I winced, expecting the glass to smash. But, so far from smashing, it did not even seem to stir; it hung in mid-air—motionless. "Roughly speaking," said Gibberne, "an object in these latitudes falls sixteen feet in the first second. This glass is falling sixteen feet in a second now. Only, you see, it hasn't been falling yet for the hundredth part of a second. That gives you some idea of the pace of my Accelerator." And he waved his hand round and round, over and under the slowly sinking glass. Finally he took it by the bottom, pulled it down and placed it very carefully on the table. "Eh?" he said to me, and laughed.

"That seems all right," I said, and began very gingerly to raise myself from my chair. I felt perfectly well, very light and comfortable, and quite confident in my mind. I was going fast all over. My heart, for example, was beating a thousand times a second, but that caused me no discomfort at all. I looked out of the window. An immovable cyclist, head down and with a frozen puff of dust behind his driving-wheel, scorched to overtake a galloping charabanc that did not stir. I gaped in amazement at this incredible spectacle. "Gibberne," I cried, "how long will this confounded stuff last?"

"Heaven knows!" he answered. "Last time I took it I went to bed and slept it off. I tell you, I was frightened. It must have lasted some minutes, I think—it seemed like hours. But after a bit it slows down rather suddenly, I believe."

I was proud to observe that I did not feel frightened—I suppose because there were two of us. "Why shouldn't we go out?" I asked.

"Why not?"

"They'll see us."

"Not they. Goodness, no! Why, we shall be going a thousand times faster than the quickest conjuring trick that was ever done. Come along! Which way shall we go? Window, or door?"

And out by the window we went.

Assuredly of all the strange experiences that I have ever had, or imagined, or read of other people having or imagining, that little raid I made with Gibberne on the Folkestone Leas, under the influence of the New Accelerator, was the strangest and maddest of all. We went out by his gate into the road, and there we made a minute examination of the statuesque passing traffic. The tops of the wheels and some of the legs of the horses of this charabanc, the end of the whip-lash and the lower jaw of the conductor—who was just beginning to yawn—were perceptibly in motion, but all the rest of the lumbering conveyance seemed still. And quite noiseless except for a faint rattling that came from one man's throat! And as parts of this frozen edifice there were a driver, you know, and a conductor, and eleven people! The effect as we walked about the thing began by being madly queer and ended by being—disagreeable. There they were, people like ourselves and yet not like ourselves, frozen in careless attitudes, caught in mid-gesture. A girl and a man smiled at one another, a leering smile that threatened to last for evermore; a woman in a floppy capeline rested her arm on the rail and stared at Gibberne's house with the unwinking stare of eternity; a man stroked his moustache like a figure of wax, and another stretched a tiresome stiff hand with extended fingers towards his loosened hat. We stared at them, we laughed at them, we made faces at them, and then a sort of disgust of them came upon us, and we turned away and walked round in front of the cyclist towards the Leas.

"Goodness!" cried Gibberne, suddenly; "look there!"

He pointed, and there at the tip of his finger and sliding down the air with wings flapping slowly and at the speed of an exceptionally languid snail—was a bee.

And so we came out upon the Leas. There the thing seemed madder than ever. The band was playing in the upper stand, though all the sound it made for us was a low-pitched, wheezy rattle, a sort of prolonged last sigh that passed at times into a sound like the slow, muffled ticking of some monstrous clock. Frozen people stood erect; strange, silent, self-conscious-looking dummies hung unstably in mid-stride, promenading upon the grass. I passed close to a poodle dog suspended in the act of leaping, and watched the slow movement of his legs as he sank to earth.

"Lord, look *here!*" cried Gibberne, and we halted for a moment before a magnificent person in white faint-striped flannels, white shoes, and a Panama hat, who turned back to wink at two gaily dressed ladies he had passed. A wink, studied with such leisurely deliberation as we could afford, is an unattractive thing. It loses any quality of alert gaiety, and one remarks that the winking eye does not completely close, that under its drooping lid appears the lower edge of an eyeball and a line of white.

"Heaven give me memory," said I, "and I will never wink again."

"Or smile," said Gibberne, with his eye on the lady's answering teeth.

"It's infernally hot, somehow," said I. "Let's go slower."

"Oh, come along!' said Gibberne.

We picked our way among the bath-chairs in the path. Many of the people sitting in the chairs seemed almost natural in their passive poses, but the contorted scarlet of the bandsmen was not a restful thing to see. A purple-faced gentleman was frozen in the midst of a violent struggle to refold his newspaper against the wind; there were many evidences that all these people in their sluggish way were exposed to a considerable breeze, a breeze that had no existence so far as our sensations went. We came out and walked a little way from the crowd, and turned and regarded it. To see all that multitude changed to a picture, smitten rigid, as it were, into the semblance of realistic wax, was impossibly wonderful. It was absurd, of course; but it filled me with an irrational, an exultant sense of superior advantage. Consider the wonder of it! All that I had said and thought and done since the stuff had begun to work in my veins had happened, so far as those people, so far as the world in general went, in the twinkling of an eye.

"The New Accelerator—" I began, but Gibberne interrupted me.

"There's that infernal old woman!" he said.

"What old woman?"

"Lives next door to me," said Gibberne. "Has a lapdog that yaps. Gods! The temptation is strong!"

There is something very boyish and impulsive about Gibberne at times. Before I could expostulate with him he had dashed forward, snatched the unfortunate animal out of visible existence, and was running violently with it towards the cliff of the Leas. It was most extraordinary. The little brute, you know, didn't bark or wriggle or make the slightest sign of vitality. It kept quite stiffly in the attitude of somnolent repose, and Gibberne held it by the neck. It was like running about with a dog of wood.

"Gibberne," I cried, "put it down!" Then I said something else.

"If you run like that, Gibberne," I cried, "you'll set your clothes on fire. Your linen trousers are going brown as it is!"

He clapped his hand on his thigh and stood hesitating on the verge.

"Gibberne," I cried, coming up, "put it down. This heat is too much! It's our running so! Two or three miles a second! Friction of the air!"

"What?" he said, glancing at the dog.

"Friction of the air," I shouted. "Friction of the air. Going too fast. Like meteorites and things. Too hot. And, Gibberne! Gibberne! I'm all over pricking and a sort of perspiration. You can see people stirring slightly. I believe the stuff's working off! Put that dog down."

"Eh?" he said.

"It's working off," I repeated. "We're too hot and the stuff's working off! I'm wet through."

He stared at me. Then at the band, the wheezy rattle of whose performance was certainly going faster. Then with a tremendous sweep of the arm he hurled the dog away from him and it went spinning upward, still inanimate, and hung at last over the grouped parasols of a knot of chattering people. Gibberne was gripping my elbow. "By Jove!" he cried. "I believe it is! A sort of hot pricking and—yes. That man's moving his pocket-handkerchief! Perceptibly. We must get out of this sharp."

But we could not get out of it sharply enough. Luckily perhaps! For we might have run, and if we had run we should, I believe, have burst into flames. Almost certainly we should have burst into flames! You know, we had neither of us thought of that. . . . But before we could even begin to run the action of the drug had ceased. It was the business of a minute fraction of a second. The effect of the New Accelerator passed like the drawing of a curtain, vanished in the movement of a hand. I heard Gibberne's voice in infinite alarm. "Sit down," he said, and flop, down upon the turf at the edge of the Leas I sat—scorching as I sat. There is a patch of burnt grass there still where I sat down. The whole stagnation seemed to wake up as I did so, the disarticulated vibration of the band rushed together into a blast of music, the promenaders put their feet down and walked their ways, the papers and flags began flapping, smiles passed into words, the winker finished his wink and went on his way complacently, and all the seated people moved and spoke.

The whole world had come alive again, was going as fast as we were, or rather we were going no faster than the rest of the world. It was like slowing down as one comes into a railway station. Everything seemed to spin round for a second or two, I had the most transient feeling of nausea, and that was all. And the little dog which had seemed to hang for a moment when the force of Gibberne's arm was expended fell with a swift acceleration clean through a lady's parasol!

That was the saving of us. Unless it was for one corpulent old gentleman in a bath-chair, who certainly did start at the sight of us and afterwards regarded us at intervals with a darkly suspicious eye, and finally, I believe, said something to his nurse about us, I doubt if a solitary person remarked our sudden appearance among them. Plop! We must have appeared abruptly. We ceased to smoulder almost at once, though the turf beneath me was uncomfortably hot. The attention of everyone—including even the Amusements Association band, which on this occasion, for the only time in its history, got out of tune—was arrested by the amazing fact, and the still more amazing yapping and uproar caused by the fact, that a respectable, over-fed lapdog sleeping quietly to the east of the bandstand should suddenly fall through the parasol of a lady on the west—in a slightly singed condition due to the extreme velocity of its movements through the air. In these absurd days, too, when we are all trying to be as psychic and silly and superstitious as possible! People got up and trod on other people, chairs were overturned, the Leas policeman ran. How the matter settled itself I do not know—we were much too anxious to disentangle ourselves from the affair and get out of range of the eye of the old gentleman in the bath-chair to make minute inquiries. As soon as we were sufficiently cool and sufficiently recovered from our giddiness and nausea and confusion of mind to do so we stood up and, skirting the crowd, directed our steps back along the road below the Metropole towards Gibberne's house. But amidst the din I heard very distinctly the gentleman who had been sitting beside the lady of the ruptured sunshade using quite unjustifiable threats and language to one of those chair-attendants who have "Inspector" written on their caps. "If you didn't throw the dog," he said, "who *did?*"

The sudden return of movement and familiar noises, and our natural anxiety about ourselves (our clothes were still dreadfully hot, and the fronts of the thighs of Gibberne's white trousers were scorched a drabbish brown), prevented the minute observations I should have liked to make on all these things. Indeed, I really made no observations of any scientific value on that return. The bee, of course, had gone. I looked for that cyclist, but he was already out of sight as we came into the Upper Sandgate Road, or hidden from us by traffic; the charabanc, however, with its people now all alive and stirring, was clattering along at a spanking pace almost abreast of the nearer church.

We noted, however, that the window-sill on which we had stepped in getting out of the house was slightly singed, and that the impressions of our feet on the gravel of the path were unusually deep.

So it was I had my first experience of the New Accelerator. Practically we had been running about and saying and doing all sorts of things in the space of a second or so of time. We had lived half an hour while the band had played, perhaps, two bars. But the effect it had upon us was that the whole world had stopped for our convenient inspection. Considering all things, and particularly considering our rashness in venturing out of the house, the experience might certainly have been much more disagreeable than it was. It showed, no doubt, that Gibberne has still much to learn before his preparation is a manageable convenience, but its practicability it certainly demonstrated beyond all cavil.

Since that adventure he has been steadily bringing its use under control, and I have several times, and without the slightest bad result, taken measured doses under his direction; though I must confess I have not yet ventured abroad again under its influence. I may mention, for example, that this story has been written at one sitting and without interruption, except for the nibbling of some chocolate, by its means. I began at six-twenty-five, and my watch is now very nearly at the minute past the half-hour. The convenience of securing a long, uninterrupted spell of work in the midst of a day full of engagements cannot be exaggerated. Gibberne is now working at the quantitative handling of his preparation, with especial reference to its distinctive effects upon different types of constitution. He then hopes to find a Retarder with which to dilute its present rather excessive potency. The Retarder will, of course, have the reverse effect to the Accelerator; used alone it should enable the patient to spread a few seconds over many hours of ordinary time, and so to maintain an apathetic inaction, a glacierlike absence of alacrity, amidst the most animated or irritating surroundings. The two things together must necessarily work an entire revolution in civilised existence. It is the beginning of our escape from that Time Garment of which Carlyle speaks. While this Accelerator will enable us to concentrate ourselves with tremendous impact upon any moment or occasion that demands our utmost sense and vigour, the Retarder will enable us to pass in passive tranquillity through infinite hardship and tedium. Perhaps I am a little optimistic about the Retarder, which has indeed still to be discovered, but about the Accelerator there is no possible sort of doubt whatever. Its appearance upon the market in a convenient, controllable, and assimilable form is a matter of the next few months. It will be obtainable of all chemists and druggists, in small green bottles, at a high but, considering its extraordinary qualities, by no means excessive price. Gibberne's Nervous Accelerator it will be called, and he hopes to be able to supply it in three strengths: one in two hundred, one in nine hundred, and one in two thousand, distinguished by yellow, pink, and white labels respectively.

No doubt its use renders a great number of very extraordinary things possible; for, of course, the most remarkable and, possibly, even criminal proceedings may be effected with impunity by thus dodging, as it were, into the interstices of time. Like all potent preparations it will be liable to abuse. We have, however, discussed this aspect of the question very thoroughly, and we have decided that this is purely a matter of medical jurisprudence and altogether outside our province. We shall manufacture and sell the Accelerator, and, as for the consequences—we shall see.

THE HONOR ROLL

I know perfectly well that the listings which follow are not complete. I've made them as complete as possible, and I hope they'll enable you to know something about the history of the stories in the Honor Roll, and to hunt up and find the ones which I've not been able to include and which you haven't already read.

The Honor Roll comes in three sections. First is a listing of those stories which received the most nominations, as well as a separate listing for nominations of a given author. (This proved necessary to give anything like a true picture of the choices; as you'll note—to provide one example—eleven people agreed that Theodore Sturgeon should be in this list, but only two of those eleven agreed on the same story.) Second is the full Honor Roll, containing such information about original publication, anthology and collection reprints, etc., as I've been able to unearth. (Any additions will be gratefully received.) And third is a bibliography of all anthologies and authors' collections mentioned.

Once again: my regret at being unable to include more than one volume's worth of stories is greater than I can say. I can give you no better advice than—having read this selection—to go out and hunt up all the others. I did, and I'm grateful to have had the chance.

L.M.J.

TOP-VOTED STORIES

4 VOTES EACH
  Nightfall, by Isaac Asimov
  The Cold Equations, by Tom Godwin
  Coming Attraction, by Fritz Leiber
  Vintage Season, by C. L. Moore
  A Martian Odyssey, by Stanley G. Weinbaum

3 VOTES EACH
  The Enormous Radio, by John Cheever
  Helen O'Loy, by Lester del Rey
  Requiem, by Robert A. Heinlein

The Mindworm, by C. M. Kornbluth
The Twonky, by Henry Kuttner
Vengeance for Nikolai, by Walter M. Miller, Jr.
No Woman Born, by C. L. Moore

2 VOTES EACH

Poor Little Warrior, by Brian Aldiss
The Quest for St. Aquin, by Anthony Boucher
The Veldt, by Ray Bradbury
Who Goes There?, by John W. Campbell, Jr.
The Nine Billion Names of God, by Arthur C. Clarke
By His Bootstraps, by Robert A. Heinlein
Lifeline, by Robert A. Heinlein
They, by Robert A. Heinlein
As Easy as ABC, by Rudyard Kipling
The Country of the Kind, by Damon Knight
The Marching Morons, by C. M. Kornbluth
Don't Look Now, by Henry Kuttner
Mimsy Were the Borogoves, by Henry Kuttner
The Night He Cried, by Fritz Leiber
The Colour out of Space, by H. P. Lovecraft
Casey Agonistes, by Richard McKenna
A Canticle for Leibowitz, by Walter M. Miller, Jr.
The Bright Illusion, by C. L. Moore
He Walked Around the Horses, by H. Beam Piper
E for Effort, by T. L. Sherred
A Saucer of Loneliness, by Theodore Sturgeon
Generation of Noah, by William Tenn

TOP-VOTED AUTHORS

Votes
Received

14	Robert A. Heinlein
11	Fritz Leiber, Theodore Sturgeon
9	Henry Kuttner, C. L. Moore
8	C. M. Kornbluth
7	Walter M. Miller, Jr.
6	Isaac Asimov, William Tenn
4	Brian Aldiss, Ray Bradbury, Avram Davidson, Lester del Rey, Tom Godwin, Damon Knight, Stanley G. Weinbaum
3	John Cheever, George P. Elliott, Judith Merril, H. G. Wells

2   Poul Anderson, Alfred Bester, James Blish, Anthony Boucher, Arthur C. Clarke, Rudyard Kipling, Katherine Maclean, Richard Matheson, Richard McKenna, Robert Sheckley, Clifford B. Simak, A. E. Van Vogt, Jack Williamson

BIBLIOGRAPHY
of editions referred to in the Honor Roll

I. ANTHOLOGIES
  (*Editor's name follows book title.*)

A. D. 2500, Angus Wilson. London: Heinemann, 1955.
Adventures in Time and Space, Raymond J. Healy and J. Francis McComas.
  New York: Random House, 1946.
Aspects of Science Fiction, G. D. Doherty. London: Murray, 1959.
Assignment in Tomorrow, Frederik Pohl. New York: Hanover House, 1954.
Astounding Science Fiction Anthology, The, John W. Campbell, Jr. New
  York: Simon and Schuster, 1952.

Beachheads in Space, August Derleth. New York: Pellegrini & Cudahy, 1954.
Best from Fantasy & Science Fiction, The, Series 2, Anthony Boucher and
  J. Francis McComas. Boston: Little, Brown, 1953.
——————, Series 4 and 5, Anthony Boucher. Garden City, N.Y.: Doubleday,
  1955, 1956. New York: Ace, 1960, 1961.
——————, Series 6 and 8, Anthony Boucher. Doubleday, 1957, 1959.
——————, Series 9 and 10, Robert P. Mills. Doubleday, 1960, 1961.
——————, Series 12, Avram Davidson. Doubleday, 1963.
Best from Startling Stories, The, Samuel S. Mines. New York: Holt, 1953.
Best of Science Fiction, The, Groff Conklin. New York: Crown, 1946.
*Best Science Fiction Stories of 1949, The,** Everett F. Bleiler and T. E. Dikty.
  New York: Fell, 1949.
Best Science Fiction Stories of 1950, The, Bleiler and Dikty. Fell, 1950.
Best Science Fiction Stories of 1951, The, Bleiler and Dikty. New York:
  Fell, 1951; Bantam, 1955.
Best Science Fiction Stories of 1952, The, Bleiler and Dikty. Fell, 1952;
  Bantam, 1955.
Best Science Fiction Stories of 1953, The, Bleiler and Dikty. Fell, 1953.
Best Science Fiction Stories of 1954, The, Bleiler and Dikty. Fell, 1954.
Best Science Fiction Stories and Novels of 1955, The, T. E. Dikty. New
  York, Fell, 1955; Fawcett, 1957.
Best Science Fiction Stories and Novels of 1956, The, Dikty. Fell, 1956;
  Fawcett, 1958.
Best Science Fiction Stories and Novels, No. 9 (1958), Dikty. Chicago:
  Advent, 1958.

* *Abbreviated in the Honor Roll as* BEST SF STORIES '49.

Best SF: Science Fiction Stories, Vols. 1-5, Edmund Crispin. London: Faber and Faber, 1955, 1956, 1958, 1961, 1963.

Beyond Human Ken, Judith Merril. New York: Random House, 1952; Pennant, 1954.

Beyond the Barriers of Space and Time, Judith Merril. New York: Random House, 1954.

Beyond the End of Time, Frederik Pohl. Garden City, N. Y.: Doubleday, 1952.

Beyond the Stars and Other Stories. Published by Jubilee, Australia.

Beyond Time and Space, August Derleth. New York: Pellegrini & Cudahy, 1950; Berkley, 1958.

Big Book of Science Fiction, The, Groff Conklin. New York: Crown, 1950; Berkley, 1957.

Century of Great Short Science Fiction Novels, A, Damon Knight. New York: Delacorte, 1964; Dell, 1965.

Century of Science Fiction, A, Damon Knight. New York: Simon and Schuster, 1962.

Children of Wonder, William Tenn. New York: Simon and Schuster, 1953. Garden City, N.Y.: Permabook, 1954.

Coming of the Robots, The, Sam Moskowitz. New York: Collier, 1963.

Contact, Noel Keyes. New York: Paperback Library, 1963.

Crossroads in Time, Groff Conklin. Garden City, N.Y.: Permabook, 1953.

Dark Side, The, Damon Knight. Garden City, N.Y.: Doubleday, 1965.

Decade of Fantasy and Science Fiction, A, Robert P. Mills. Garden City, N.Y.: Doubleday, 1960.

Earth in Peril, The, Donald A. Wollheim. New York: Ace, 1957.

Fantasia Mathematica, Clifton Fadiman. New York: Simon and Schuster, 1958.

Fifty Short Science Fiction Tales, Isaac Asimov and Groff Conklin. New York: Collier, 1963.

First Flight, Damon Knight. New York: Lancer, 1963.

Five Galaxy Short Novels, H. L. Gold. Garden City, N.Y.: Doubleday, 1958.

Frontiers of Space, Everett F. Bleiler and T. E. Dikty. New York: Bantam, 1955.

Galaxy of Ghouls, Judith Merril. New York: Lion, 1955.

Galaxy Reader of Science Fiction (1st and 2nd), H. L. Gold. New York: Crown, 1952, 1954.

——— (3rd and 5th), H. L. Gold. Garden City, N.Y: Doubleday.

Get Out of My Sky, Leo Margulies. New York: Fawcett, 1960.

Giant Anthology of Science Fiction, Leo Margulies and Oscar J. Friend. New York: Merlin, 1954.

Girl with the Hungry Eyes and Other Stories, The. New York: Avon Books, Inc.

Great Science Fiction Stories, Smith. New York: Fawcett.
Great Stories of Science Fiction, Murray Leinster. New York: Random House, 1951.
Great Stories of Space Travel, Groff Conklin. New York: Tempo, 1963.

Hugo Winners, The, Isaac Asimov. Garden City, N.Y.: Doubleday, 1962.
Human?, Judith Merril. New York: Lion, 1954.
Human and Other Beings, Allen de Graeff. New York: Collier, 1963.

Imagination Unlimited, Everett F. Bleiler and T. E. Dikty. New York: Farrar, Straus & Young, 1952.
Introducing Science Fiction, Brian Aldiss.
Invaders of Earth, Groff Conklin. New York: Vanguard, 1952.
Invasion of the Robots, The, Roger T. Elwood. New York: Belmont Books, 1965.
Invisible Men, Basil Davenport. New York: Ballantine, 1960.

Journey to Infinity, Martin Greenberg. New York: Gnome, 1951.
Journeys in Science Fiction, Richard L. Loughlin and Lillian M. Popp. New York: Globe, 1961.

Mathematical Magpie, The, Clifton Fadiman. New York: Simon and Schuster, 1962.
Men on the Moon, Donald A. Wollheim. New York: Ace, 1958.
My Best Science Fiction Story, Leo Margulies and Oscar J. Friend. New York: Merlin, 1949; Pocket Books, 1954.

New Tales of Space and Time, Raymond Healy. New York: Holt.
No Limits, Joseph W. Ferman. New York: Ballantine, 1965.

Omnibus of Science Fiction, Groff Conklin. New York: Crown, 1952; Berkley, 1956.
Other Worlds, Phil Stong. New York: Wilfred Funk, 1941. Garden City, N.Y.: Garden City Books, 1942.
Outer Reaches, The, August Derleth. New York: Pellegrini & Cudahy, 1951; Berkley, 1958.

Penguin Science Fiction, Brian Aldiss. London: Penguin, 1961.
Pocket Book of Science Fiction, The, Donald A. Wollheim. New York: Pocket Books, 1943.
Post Reader of Fantasy and Science Fiction, The. Garden City, N.Y.: Doubleday, 1964. New York: Popular Library, 1965.
Prize Science Fiction, Donald A. Wollheim. New York: McBride, 1953.

Robot and the Man, The, Martin Greenberg. New York: Gnome, 1953.

Science Fiction Carnival, Fredric Brown and Mack Reynolds. Chicago: Shasta, 1957. New York: Bantam, 1957.

Science Fiction Galaxy, Groff Conklin. Garden City, N.Y.: Garden City Books, 1950.

Science Fiction Terror Tales, Groff Conklin. New York: Gnome, 1955.

17 x Infinity, Groff Conklin. New York: Dell, 1963.

Shadow of Tomorrow, Frederik Pohl. Garden City, N.Y.: Doubleday, 1953.

Shape of Things, The, Damon Knight. New York: Popular Library, 1965.

Shot in the Dark, Judith Merril. New York: Bantam, 1950.

Six Great Short Novels of Science Fiction, Groff Conklin. New York: Dell, 1954.

Space Pioneers, André Norton. Cleveland: World, 1954.

Spectrum, Vols. 1–4, Kingsley Amis and Robert Conquest. London: Gollancz, 1961–1964. American editions of Vols. 1–3, titled *Spectrum I, Spectrum II* and *Spectrum III,* published in New York by Berkley, 1963, 1964, 1965.

Star of Stars, Frederik Pohl. Garden City, N.Y.: Doubleday, 1960.

Star Science Fiction Stories, Nos. 1 and 2, Frederik Pohl. New York: Ballantine Books, Inc.

Stories for Tomorrow, William Sloane. New York: Funk & Wagnalls, 1954.

Strange Ports of Call, August Derleth. New York: Pellegrini & Cudahy, 1948.

Tales of Science Fiction, Ball.

Terror in the Modern Vein, Donald A. Wollheim. New York: Hanover House, 1955.

Timeless Stories for Today and Tomorrow, Ray Bradbury. New York: Bantam, 1952.

Tomorrow the Stars, Robert A. Heinlein. Garden City, N.Y.: Doubleday, 1952. New York: New American Library, 1953.

Tomorrow x 4, Leo Margulies. Greenwich, Conn.: Fawcett, 1964.

Treasury of Great Science Fiction, Anthony Boucher. Garden City, N.Y.: Doubleday, 1959.

Treasury of Science Fiction, Groff Conklin. New York: Doubleday, 1958.

Treasury of Science Fiction Classics, Harold W. Kuebler. Garden City, N.Y.: Doubleday, 1955.

Uberwindung von Raum und Zeit, Gotthard Günther. Karl Rausch, publisher, 1952.

World of Wonder, Fletcher Pratt. New York: Twayne, 1952.

World's Best Science Fiction, 1965, The, David A. Wollheim and Terry Carr. New York: Ace, 1965.

Worlds of Science Fiction, The, Robert P. Mills. New York: Dial, 1963; Paperback Library, 1965.

Writing Fiction, R. V. Cassill. New York: Pocket Books, 1963.

Year's Best Science Fiction, The, Annuals 6–8, Judith Merril. New York: Simon and Schuster, 1961–1963; Dell, 1962–1964.

Year's Greatest SF, The, Annuals 1956–1959, Judith Merril. New York: Gnome, 1956–1959; Dell, 1956–1959.
Yet More Penguin Science Fiction, Brian Aldiss. London, Penguin.

II. AUTHORS' COLLECTIONS

Asimov, Isaac, *Earth Is Room Enough.* New York: Doubleday, 1957.
————, *I, Robot.* New York: Doubleday, 1950. Reprint edition, New York: New American Library, 1956.
Ballard, J. G., *Billenium.* New York: Berkley Publishing Corp., 1962.
————, *The Voices of Time.* New York: Berkley Publishing Corp., 1962.
Bester, Alfred, *Starburst.* New York: New American Library, 1958.
Blish, James, *Galactic Cluster.* New York: New American Library, 1959.
Bradbury, Ray, *Fahrenheit 451.* New York: Ballantine Books, Inc.
————, *The Illustrated Man.* Garden City: Doubleday, 1951. Reprint edition, New York: Bantam Books, 1952.
————, *R is For Rocket.* Garden City: Doubleday, 1962. Reprint edition, New York: Bantam Books, 1965.
Brown, Fredric, *Honeymoon in Hell.* New York: Bantam Books, 1958.
Campbell, John W., Jr., *Who Goes There?* Chicago: Shasta Publishers. Reprint edition titled *The Thing,* Chicago: Shasta Publishers.
Cheever, John, *The Enormous Radio & Other Stories.* New York: Funk and Wagnalls, 1953. Reprint edition, New York: Harper & Row, 1965.
Christopher, John, *The 22nd Century.* New York: Lancer Books.
Cogswell, Theodore, *The Wall Around the World.* New York: Lancer Books.
Elliott, George P., *Among the Dangs.*
Forster, E. M., *The Eternal Moment & Other Stories.*
Heard, H. F., *The Great Fog & Other Weird Tales.*
Heinlein, Robert A., *The Man Who Sold the Moon.* Chicago: Shasta Publishers, 1950.
————, *The Menace from the Earth.* New York: Gnome Press, 1959. Reprint edition, New York: New American Library, 1962.
————, *Revolt in 2100.* Chicago: Shasta Publishers, 1953. Reprint edition, New York: New American Library.
————, *The Unpleasant Profession of Jonathan Hoag.* New York: Gnome Press, 1959. Reprint edition titled *6xH,* New York: Pyramid Books, 1961.
Jameson, Malcolm, *Bullard of the Space Patrol.*
Kipling, Rudyard, *A Diversity of Creatures.*
Kornbluth, C. M., *The Marching Morons.* New York: Ballantine Books, 1959.
Leiber, Fritz, *A Pail of Air.* New York: Ballantine Books, 1964.
Lovecraft, H. P., *The Colour Out of Space & Others.* Sauk City, Wisconsin: Arkham House. Reprinted edition titled *The Dunwich Horror & Others,* New York: Lancer Books.

Maloney, Russell, *It's Still Maloney.*

Matheson, Richard, *Born of Man & Woman.* Chamberlain Press, 1954. Reprint edition titled *Third from the Sun,* New York: Bantam Books, 1955.

Merril, Judith, *Out of Bounds.* New York: Pyramid Publications, 1960.

Nasvadba, Josef, *Vampires, Ltd.*

Sheckley, Robert, *Pilgrimage to Earth.* New York: Bantam Books, 1957.

———, *Untouched by Human Hands.* New York: Ballantine Books, 1954.

Shiras, Wilmar H., *Children of the Atom.*

Smith, Cordwainer, *You Will Never Be the Same.* Evanston, Illinois: Regency Books, 1963.

Sturgeon, Theodore, *Caviar.* New York: Ballantine Books.

———, *E Pluribus Unicorn.* New York: Abelard Press, 1953. Reprint edition, New York: Ballantine Books, 1956.

———, *A Way Home.*

Tenn, William, *Of All Possible Worlds.* New York, Ballantine Books, 1955.

Vonnegut, Kurt, *Canary in a Cat House.* Greenwich, Conn.: Fawcett Publications, 1961.

Weinbaum, Stanley G., *A Martian Odyssey and Others.* New York: Lancer Books, 1962.

White, E. B., *The Second Tree from the Corner.* New York: Harper & Bros., 1954. Reprint edition, New York: Perennial Library, 1965.

Wilhelm, Kate, *The Mile-Long Spaceship.* New York: Berkley Publishing Corp., 1963.

III. ORIGINAL SOURCES

AUTHOR & STORY	1ST MAGAZINE APPEARANCE	BOOK APPEARANCES*
ABERNATHY, ROBERT		
Single Combat	If, May '63	
ALDISS, BRIAN		
Hothouse	F&SF,† Feb. '61	
Poor Little Warrior	F&SF, Apr. '58	BEST FROM F&SF (8)
		PENGUIN SF
Shards	F&SF, Apr. '62	
ANDERSON, POUL		
Call Me Joe	ASF,‡ Apr. '57	BEST SF STORIES & NOVELS ('58)
		CENTURY OF SF
		SPECTRUM (3)
Sister Planet	Satellite SF, May '59	GET OUT OF MY SKY
ASIMOV, ISAAC		
Dreaming Is a Private Thing	F&SF, Dec. '55	YEAR'S GREATEST SF ('56)
		EARTH IS ROOM ENOUGH
Liar!	Aston. Stories, May '41	HUMAN?
		I, ROBOT
Nightfall	ASF, Sept. '41	ADVEN. IN TIME AND SPACE
		ASF ANTHOL.
		PENGUIN SF
		GREAT SF STORIES
		ÜBERWINDUNG VON RAUM UND ZEIT
BALLARD, J. G.		
Prima Belladonna	Science Fantasy (20)	YEAR'S GREATEST SF ('57)
		BILENNIUM
The Voices of Time	New Worlds 99	SPECTRUM (3)
		VOICES OF TIME

---

* *Anthologies are in roman capitals, authors' collections in italic capitals. See Bibliography for full book titles.*
† Fantasy & Science Fiction.
‡ Astounding Science Fiction.

AUTHOR & STORY	1st MAGAZINE APPEARANCE	BOOK APPEARANCES
BANKS, RAYMOND E.		
Rabbits to the Moon	F&SF, July '59	DECADE OF F&SF
BATES, HARRY		
Alas, All Thinking	ASF, June '35	OTHER WORLDS IMAGINATION UNLTD.
BEAUMONT, CHARLES		
The Vanishing American	F&SF, Aug. '55	BEST FROM F&SF (5) INVISIBLE MEN
BENÉT, STEPHEN VINCENT		
By the Waters of Babylon (*orig. title* Place of the Gods)	Sat. Eve. Post, July 31, '37	POCKET BOOK OF SF
BESTER, ALFRED		
5,271,009 (*also titled* The Starcomber)	F&SF, Mar. '54	ASSNMT. IN TOMORROW *STARBURST*
Of Time and Third Avenue	F&SF, Oct. '51	BEST SF STORIES '52 CENT. OF SF *STARBURST*
BIXBY, JEROME		
It's a Good Life		STAR SF STORIES (2)* BEST SF (4) INTRODUCTION TO SF STAR OF STARS
BLISH, JAMES		
A Case of Conscience	If, July '53	BEST SF (1)
Tomb Tapper	ASF, July '56	*GALACTIC CLUSTER*
BLOCH, ROBERT		
Day Broke	Star SF Mag., Jan. '58	STAR OF STARS
BOUCHER, ANTHONY		
The Quest for St. Aquin		NEW TALES OF SPACE AND TIME* BEST SF (5) WORLDS OF SF
BRADBURY, RAY		
The Dragon	Playboy, '55	*R IS FOR ROCKET*
Fahrenheit 451 (*orig. title* The Fireman)	Galaxy, Feb. '51	*FAHRENHEIT 451*
The Veldt (*orig. title* The World Children Made)	Sat. Eve. Post, Sept. 23, '50	BEYOND THE BARRIERS OF SPACE AND TIME *ILLUSTRATED MAN*
BROWN, FREDRIC		

---

* *Book in which story appeared originally.*

AUTHOR & STORY	1st MAGAZINE APPEARANCE	BOOK APPEARANCES
Honeymoon in Hell	Galaxy, Nov. '50	1st GALAXY READER OF SF *HONEYMOON IN HELL*
BUDRYS, A. J. *(under name* PAUL JANVIER)		
Silent Brother	ASF, Feb. '56	YEAR'S GREATEST SF ('57)
CAMPBELL, JOHN W., JR. *(under name* DON A. STUART)		
Twilight	ASF, Nov. '34	*WHO GOES THERE?* (*also titled* THE THING)
Who Goes There?	ASF, Aug. '38	ADVEN. IN TIME & SPACE *ÜBERWINDUNG . . .* *WHO GOES THERE?* (*also titled* THE THING)
CARR, TERRY		
Hop Friend	F&SF, Nov. '62	BEST FROM F&SF (12)
CHEEVER, JOHN		
The Enormous Radio	New Yorker, May 17, '47	TIMELESS STORIES *ENORMOUS RADIO & OTHER STORIES*
CHRISTOPHER, JOHN		
The New Wine	Standard Mags., '53	BEST SF (1) *22ND CENTURY*
CLARKE, ARTHUR C.		
The Nine Billion Names of God		STAR SF (1)* STORIES FOR TOMORROW BEST SF (2) ASPECTS OF SF MATH. MAGPIE
CLIFTON, MARK		
What Have I Done?	ASF, May '52	BEYOND HUMAN KEN
COGSWELL, THEODORE		
The Wall Around the World	Beyond, Sept. '53	BEYOND BARRIERS OF SP. & T. *WALL AROUND THE WORLD*
DAVIDSON, AVRAM		
The Certificate	F&SF, Mar. '59	DECADE OF F&SF
The Golem	F&SF, Mar. '55	BEST FROM F&SF (5) YEAR'S GREATEST SF (56)
Now Let Us Sleep	Venture, Sept. '57	YEAR'S GREATEST SF '58 NO LIMITS

* *Book in which story appeared originally.*

AUTHOR & STORY	1st MAGAZINE APPEARANCE	BOOK APPEARANCES
The Sources of the Nile	F&SF, Jan. '61	WORLDS OF SF TOMORROW X 4
DEL REY, LESTER		
Helen O'Loy	ASF, Dec. '38	BEYOND HUMAN KEN ASSNMT. IN TOMORROW COMING OF THE ROBOTS
Nerves	ASF, Dec. '42	ADVEN. IN T. & SP.
DICK, PHILIP K.		
The Golden Man	If, Apr. '54	BEYOND BARRIERS OF SP. & T.
DICKSON, GORDON R.		
Black Charlie	Galaxy, Apr. '54	5TH GALAXY READER
ELLIOTT, GEORGE P.		
Among the Dangs	Esquire, June '62	YEAR'S BEST SF (7) AMONG THE DANGS
The Nracp	Hudson Review, Fall '49	HUMAN & OTHER BEINGS AMONG THE DANGS
Sandra	Epoch, Fall '53	TREAS. OF GREAT SF WRITING FICTION
FARMER, PHILIP JOSÉ		
The Lovers	Startling Stories	
FAST, HOWARD		
The Large Ant	Fantastic Universe, Feb. '60	YEAR'S BEST SF (6) CONTACT SPECTRUM (4)
FORSTER, E. M.		
The Machine Stops		SF GALAXY TREAS. OF SF CLASSICS 17 X INFINITY ETERNAL MOMENT AND OTHER STORIES
FYFE, H. B.		
Moonwalk	Space SF, Nov. '52	SPACE PIONEERS MEN ON THE MOON
GALLUN, RAYMOND Z.		
Derelict	ASF, Oct. '35	COMING OF THE ROBOTS
GODWIN, TOM		
The Cold Equations	ASF, Aug. '54	BEST SF STORIES & NOVELS '55 BEST SF (3) BEYOND THE STARS ASPECTS OF SF

AUTHOR & STORY	1st MAGAZINE APPEARANCE	BOOK APPEARANCES
GOULART, RON		
Letters to the Editor	F&SF, Apr. '52	BEST FROM F&SF (2)
GUNN, JAMES E.		
Wherever You May Be	Galaxy, May '53	5 GALAXY SHORT NOVELS
HAMILTON, EDMOND		
What's It Like Out There?	Startling, Dec. '52	BEST FROM STARTLING STORIES
		CENT. OF SF
HARNESS, CHARLES L.		
The New Reality	Thrilling Wonder Stories, Dec. '50	BEST SF STORIES '51 SHAPE OF THINGS
HAWKINS, WILLARD		
The Dwindling Sphere	ASF, Mar. '40	
HEARD, H. F.		
The Great Fog		TREAS. OF SF
		GREAT FOG & OTHER WEIRD TALES
HEINLEIN, ROBERT A.		
All You Zombies	F&SF, Mar. '59	WORLDS OF SF
		UNPLEASANT PROFESSION OF JONATHAN HOAG (6 X H)
And He Built A Crooked House	ASF, Feb. '41	POCKET BOOK OF SF
		FANTASIA MATHEMATICA
		UNPLEASANT PROFESSION OF JONATHAN HOAG (6 X H)
Blowups Happen	ASF, Sept. '40	BEST OF SF
		ASF ANTHOL.
		BEST SF (2)
(under name ANSON MACDONALD)		
By His Bootstraps	ASF, Oct. '41	ADVEN. IN T. & SP.
		GIANT ANTHOL. OF SF (as HEINLEIN)
		SPECTRUM (1) (as HEINLEIN)
		MENACE FROM EARTH
Coventry	ASF, July '40	REVISED IN 6 GREAT SHORT NOVELS OF SF
		REVOLT IN 2100
Lifeline	ASF, Aug. '39	FIRST FLIGHT
		TALES OF SF

AUTHOR & STORY	1st MAGAZINE APPEARANCE	BOOK APPEARANCES
		MAN WHO SOLD THE MOON (*hardcover edition only*)
Requiem	ASF, June '40	ADVEN. IN T. & SP.
		MAN WHO SOLD THE MOON
(*as* MacDonald)		
Solution Unsatisfactory	ASF, May '41	BEST OF SF
They	Unknown, Apr. '41	WORLD OF WONDER
		SF TERROR TALES
		TERROR IN MODERN VEIN
		DARK SIDE
		UNPLEASANT PROFESSION OF JONATHAN HOAG (*6 X H*)
HENNEBERG, CHARLES		
The Blind Pilot	F&SF, June '60	BEST FROM F&SF (9)
JAMESON, MALCOLM		
Admiral's Inspection	ASF, Apr. '40	*BULLARD OF THE SPACE PATROL*
KELLEAM, JOSEPH E.		
The Eagles Gather	ASF, Apr. '42	CROSSROADS IN TIME
KELLY, FRANK J.		
Star Ship Invincible	ASF, June '35	
KEYES, DANIEL		
Flowers for Algernon	F&SF, Apr. '59	BEST FROM F&SF (9)
		YEAR'S BEST SF (5)
		BEST SF (4)
		HUGO WINNERS
KIPLING, RUDYARD		
As Easy as ABC	London Mag., Apr. '12	SF GALAXY
		17 X INFINITY
		DIVERSITY OF CREATURES
KNIGHT, DAMON		
Cabin Boy	Galaxy, Sept. '51	1ST GALAXY READER
		GREAT STORIES OF SPACE TRAVEL
The Country of the Kind	F&SF, Feb. '56	YEAR'S GREATEST SF ('56)
		YET MORE PENGUIN SF
What Rough Beast	F&SF, Feb. '59	BEST FROM F&SF (9)
KORNBLUTH, C. M.		
The Little Black Bag	ASF, July '50	BEYOND THE END OF TIME
The Marching Morons	Galaxy, Apr. '51	BEST SF STORIES '52
		STORIES FOR TOMORROW
		SPECTRUM (4)
		MARCHING MORONS

AUTHOR & STORY	1st MAGAZINE APPEARANCE	BOOK APPEARANCES
The Mindworm	Worlds Beyond, Dec. '50	BEST SF STORIES '51
The Silly Season	F&SF, Fall '50	TOMORROW THE STARS EARTH IN PERIL
Theory of Rocketry	F&SF, July '58	BEST FROM F&SF (8)
KUTTNER, HENRY		
Deadlock	ASF, Aug. '42	ROBOT & THE MAN
Don't Look Now	Startling, Mar. '48	MY BEST SF STORY SHAPE OF THINGS
(as LEWIS PADGETT)		
Mimsy Were the Boro-goves	ASF, Feb. '43	TREAS. OF SF ÜBERWINDUNG . . .
(as Padgett)		
Private Eye	ASF, Jan. '49	
(as Padgett)		
The Twonky	ASF, Sept. '42	ADVEN. IN T. & SP.
LAFFERTY, R. A.		
Seven Day Terror	If, Mar. '62	YEAR'S BEST SF (8)
LEIBER, FRITZ		
A Bad Day for Sales	Galaxy, Jul. '53	SHADOW OF TOMORROW 2ND GALAXY READER BEST SF STORIES 50 SHORT SF TALES
The Big Holiday	F&SF, Jan. '53	BEST SF STORIES '54
Coming Attraction	Galaxy, Nov. '50	BEST SF STORIES '51 1ST GALAXY READER PAIL OF AIR
A Deskful of Girls	F&SF, Apr. '58	BEST FROM F&SF (8)
The Last Letter	Galaxy, Jun. '58	5TH GALAXY READER
The Night He Cried		STAR SF (1)* GALAXY OF GHOULS
Smoke Ghost	Unknown, Oct. '41	HUMAN?
LEINSTER, MURRAY		
Politics	Amazing, Jun. '32	
LONG, FRANK BELKNAP		
Long, Long Ago	Capt. Future, Fall '41	
LOVECRAFT, H. P.		
The Colour Out of Space	Amazing, Sept. '27	OMNIBUS OF SF *DUNWICH HORROR &*

* Book in which story appeared originally.

AUTHOR & STORY	1st MAGAZINE APPEARANCE	BOOK APPEARANCES
		OTHERS *(COLOUR OUT OF SPACE & OTHERS)*
MacFARLANE, WALLACE		
To Watch the Watchers	ASF, Jun. '49	
MacLEAN, KATHERINE		
Incommunicado	ASF, Jun. '50	6 GREAT SHORT NOVELS OF SF
Unhuman Sacrifice	ASF, Nov. '58	SPECTRUM (1) CENT. OF SF
MALONEY, RUSSELL		
Inflexible Logic	New Yorker, Feb. 3, '40	TIMELESS STORIES FANT. MATH. *IT'S STILL MALONEY*
MALPASS, E. L.		
When Grandfather Flew to the Moon	London Observer, Jan. 2, '55 *(under title* The Return of the Moon Man*)*	A.D. 2500 YEAR'S BEST SF (5) *(under listed title)* TALES OF SF
MATHESON, RICHARD		
Born of Man and Woman	F&SF, Summer '50	BEST SF STORIES '50 CHILDREN OF WONDER *BORN OF MAN & WOMAN (3RD FROM THE SUN)*
Lover When You're Near Me	Galaxy, May '52	BEST SF STORIES '53 2ND GALAXY READER *BORN OF MAN & WOMAN (3RD FROM THE SUN)*
McKENNA, RICHARD		
Casey Agonistes	F&SF, Sept. '58	BEST FROM F&SF (9) YEAR'S GREATEST SF ('59)
MERRIL, JUDITH		
Project Nursemaid	F&SF, Oct. '55	6 GREAT SHORT NOVELS OF SF
That Only a Mother	ASF, Jun. '48	WORLDS OF WONDER CHILDREN OF WONDER FIRST FLIGHT *OUT OF BOUNDS*
Whoever You Are	Startling, Dec. '52	*OUT OF BOUNDS*
MERRIT, A.		
The People of the Pit	Amazing, Mar. '27	

AUTHOR & STORY	1st MAGAZINE APPEARANCE	BOOK APPEARANCES
MILLER, P. SCHUYLER		
The Cave	ASF, Jan. '43	CROSSROADS IN TIME
MILLER, R. DEWITT		
The Master Shall Not Die	ASF, Mar. '38	
MILLER, WALTER M., JR.		
The Big Hunger	ASF, Oct. '52	PRIZE SF
A Canticle for Leibowitz	F&SF, Apr. '55	BEST FROM F&SF (4) BEST SF STORIES & NOVELS '56
Death of a Spaceman (Memento Homo)	Amazing, Mar. '54	
Vengeance for Nikolai	Venture, Mar. '57	NO LIMITS
MOORE, C. L.		
The Bright Illusion	ASF, Oct. '34	
No Woman Born	ASF, Dec. '44	TREAS. OF SF GREAT STORIES OF SF BEST SF (1) TOMORROW X 4
(as LAWRENCE O'DONNELL)		
Vintage Season	ASF, Sept. '46	TREAS. OF SF SPECTRUM (2)
MOORE, WARD		
Second Trip to Mars	Sat. Eve. Post, Aug. 28, '54	POST READER OF F&SF
NASVADBA, JOSEF		
Vampires, Ltd.		WORLD'S BEST SF '65 VAMPIRES, LTD.
PANGBORN, EDGAR		
Angel's Egg	Galaxy, Jun. '51	INVADERS OF EARTH BEST SF (2) CENT. OF SF
PIPER, H. BEAM		
He Walked Around the Horses	ASF, Apr. '48	WORLDS OF WONDER BEST SF (3)
RICHARDSON, R. S.		
(as PHILIP LATHAM)		
The XI Effect	ASF, Jan. '50	IMAGINATION UNLTD. BEST SF (1)
ROCKLYNNE, ROSS		
Jackdaw	ASF, Aug. '42	BEST OF SF
RUSSELL, ERIC FRANK		
Metamorphosite	ASF, Dec. '46	JOURNEY TO INFINITY

BIBLIOGRAPHY / 347

AUTHOR & STORY	1st MAGAZINE APPEARANCE	BOOK APPEARANCES
		BEACHHEADS IN SPACE
SCHMITZ, JAMES H.		
The Witches of Karres	ASF, Dec. '49	ASF ANTHOL.
SHECKLEY, ROBERT		
Pilgrimage to Earth	Playboy, Sept. '56 (*under title* "Love, Inc.")	SPECTRUM (1) *PILGRIMAGE TO EARTH*
Specialist	Galaxy, Mar. '53	2ND GALAXY READER CONTACT *UNTOUCHED BY HUMAN HANDS*
SHERRED, T. L.		
E for Effort	ASF, May '47	BIG BOOK OF SF ASF ANTHOL. CENT. OF GREAT SHORT SF NOVELS
SHIRAS, WILMAR H.		
In Hiding	ASF, Nov. '48	BEST SF STORIES '49 GREAT STORIES OF SF CHILDREN OF WONDER GREAT SF STORIES
SIMAK, CLIFFORD D.		
Tools	ASF, Jul. '42	TREAS. OF SF
SMITH, CLARK ASHTON		
The Vaults of Yoh-Vombis	Avon Fantasy Reader (1)	
SMITH, CORDWAINER		
The Game of Rat and Dragon	Galaxy, Oct. '55	BEST SF STORIES & NOVELS '56 BEST SF (3) 3RD GALAXY READER *YOU WILL NEVER BE THE SAME*
SMITH, EVELYN E.		
Not Fit for Children	Galaxy, May '53	2ND GALAXY READER
STRIBLING, T. S.		
Green Splotches	Adventure Mag., Jun. 3, '20	POCKET BOOK OF SF
STURGEON, THEODORE		
And Now the News	F&SF, Dec. '56	BEST FROM F&SF (6)
Baby Is Three	Galaxy, Oct. '52	CHILDREN OF WONDER *MAGABOOK* (3)
Killdozer!	ASF, Nov. '44	BEST OF SF SPECTRUM (3)

AUTHOR & STORY	1st MAGAZINE APPEARANCE	BOOK APPEARANCES
The Man Who Lost the Sea	F&SF, Oct. '59	BEST FROM F&SF (9) YEAR'S BEST SF (5)
Microcosmic God	ASF, Apr. '41	POCKET BOOK OF SF CAVIAR
A Saucer of Loneliness	Galaxy, Feb. '53	2ND GALAXY READER WORLDS OF SF E PLURIBUS UNICORN
The Sex Opposite	Fantastic, Oct. '52	E PLURIBUS UNICORN
The Sky Was Full of Ships	Thrilling Wonder, Jun. '47	SHOT IN THE DARK SHAPE OF THINGS
Thunder and Roses	ASF, Nov. '47	STRANGE PORTS OF CALL MY BEST SF STORY ASF ANTHOL. WAY HOME
(as E. HUNTER WALDO)		
The Ultimate Egoist	Unknown, Feb. '41	HUMAN? (as STURGEON)
ᴾENN, WILLIAM		
Brooklyn Project	Planet Stories, Fall, '48	SHOT IN THE DARK 17 X INFINITY
The Custodian	If, Nov. '53	OF ALL POSSIBLE WORLDS
Generation of Noah	Suspense, Spring '51	BEST SF STORIES '52 FRONTIERS OF SPACE OF ALL POSSIBLE WORLDS (British edition only)
The House Dutiful	ASF, Apr. '48	BEYOND HUMAN KEN
Venus and the Seven Sexes		GIRL WITH HUNGRY EYES & OTHERS* SF CARNIVAL
ᴾEVIS, WALTER		
Far From Home	F&SF, Dec. '58	BEST FROM F&SF (9)
ᴛHOMAS, THEODORE L.		
The Far Look	ASF, Aug. '56	YEAR'S GREATEST SF ('56)
ᵛAN VOGT, A. E.		
Co-operate or Else!	ASF, Apr. '42	OUTER REACHES
Dormant	Startling, Nov. '48	BEST FROM STARTLING STORIES BEST SF (1) SHAPE OF THINGS

* Book in which story appeared originally.

* Book in which story appeared originally.